A SCI-FI GAMER FRIENDS-TO-LOVERS MÉNAGE ROMANCE

SUMMONING THEIR ELEMENTALIST

BOOK THREE
LOOKING FOR GROUP

SHANNON PEMRICK

Summoning Their Elementalist
Looking For Group | Book Three

Copyright © 2019 Shannon Pemrick
www.shannonpemrick.com

Cover Design by Covers by Combs

ISBN 978-1-950128-04-4 (paperback)
ISBN 978-1-950128-15-0 (hardcover)
ISBN 978-1-950128-03-7 (ebook)

For my player number two.

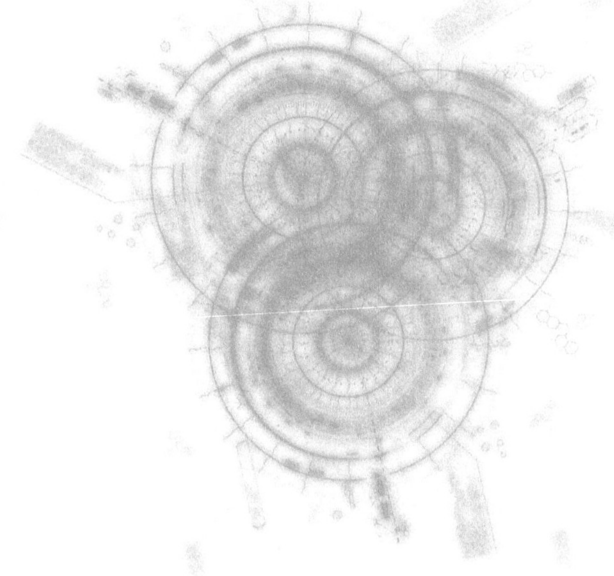

BOOKS BY SHANNON PEMRICK

LOOKING FOR GROUP
Spellbinding His Ranger
Protecting His Priestess
Summoning Their Elementalist
Binding Their Elementalist

VALKYRIES RISING
Valkyrie Destiny
Valkyrie Lost
Valkyrie Renewed
Valkyrie Restored
Valkyrie Confused
Valkyrie Condemned

EXPERIMENTAL HEART
Destiny
Pieces
Secrets
Exposed
Surrendered
Reborn

ORACLE'S PATH
Prophecy of Convergence
Prophecy of Unbroken Oaths

Prophecy Tested
Prophecy Chosen

See all books and learn more at
www.shannonpemrick.com

As Shira pressed the button on the refrigerator, water splashed into the glass, cool against her palm. Pain pulsed and crept along her abdomen and side. Shira pressed her other hand against the area where skin met acrylic, the source of the pain, though she knew it wouldn't help.

Once the glass was full, she grabbed two pills off the kitchen counter and popped them into her mouth. These painkillers would help, but she was in for a long day today.

Her eyes swept over the weekly pill case she'd forgotten to put away, today's box empty and tomorrow's filled with more than anyone should have to worry about. *Sometimes I wonder why I bother...*

She left the spacious kitchen, walking through the small foyer to the open living room. Snake, her black German Shepherd, padded after her, her ever-faithful shadow. Shira sat down on the plush couch and picked

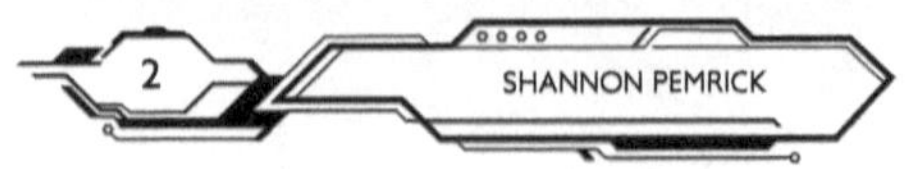

up the tablet she'd set down earlier on the coffee table. Snake hopped up with her and laid his head on her lap.

The screen scrolled as Shira viewed the application displayed. Early afternoon sun filtered in through the nearby bay window, and the TV played an old anime for background noise. She tucked a red strand of hair behind her ear with a fair hand. Her eyes skimmed the most important information, but ultimately nothing stuck out and she swiped it off her screen so she could get to the next application.

Her parents ran one of the largest fashion design studios in the world. That meant everyone wanted their designs to be selected, even if they didn't have a remote shot. And with her parents out of the country on a business trip, that left her in charge of fielding applications in their absence.

Sure, they could do this remotely, but Shira didn't mind helping them out. It allowed her parents to focus on something worthwhile and she got to work with the added benefit of being from the comfort of her own home.

Beats looking like the useless bum with nothing left going for—

Shira shook the though from her mind. Wasn't good to go down that dark rabbit hole.

Snake stretched and yawned before laying his head back down in her lap, looking up at her with his big brown eyes. She patted her faithful companion with a cybernetic limb, bright lights flickering behind the clear fiberglass structure, pistons and other moving components working hard to ensure the device worked properly. The false nerves sent signals to the neuro-mod in her head. Even after several months of testing, she was still trying to get used to the sensation.

After her accident five, almost six years ago, resulting in her losing nearly half of her body, it was to be expected. Since limb regeneration wasn't feasible yet, and obtaining a donated part beyond basic organ transplants for experimental surgeries wasn't easy, she'd all but given up hope technology would even get to this point. It didn't help other problems in her life, but it was something.

Snake went on high alert, sitting up on the couch and staring at the front door. He chuffed; Shira's brow rose.

"Shira," a deep, semi-robotic voice said from the infrastructure of her house. "Mercedes is here."

That explains it. She and her best friend had agreed to have lunch together today, but between all the work Shira had to do and some of the pain she was in today, they agreed to have lunch at her place. "Thanks, Orion."

There was a knock on the door and Snake barked, bolting from the couch to the door. Shira chuckled as he barked a few more times before spinning in circles. He knew exactly who was here.

"Snake," Shira said.

Her companion came to a halt, ears pricked, and stared at her.

"Öffnen," she said in German.

Snake reacted to the command and pulled on the door handle. The door swung open and on the other side stood Mercedes, a tall and slender woman with sun-kissed skin and gorgeous golden hair that flowed past her shoulders. A beaded necklace hung around her neck.

Snake started up his excited spin again. Mercedes' blue eyes crinkled in the corners as she laughed and then praised and fed him attention. Shira's companion ate it all up. *Such a ladies' man.*

Once finished, Mercedes held up the paper bag. "Got lunch."

"Where did you end up going?" Shira asked.

"To the sandwich shop down the street. Figured an easy meal would be best for today."

Shira agreed. Mercedes shut the front door and waltzed through the foyer into the living room. She plopped down on the couch next to Shira and pulled out the wrapped sandwiches and soups, as well as bags of chips. They divvied up the food and dug in.

"How's the workload?" Mercedes asked.

Shira shrugged and stirred her soup. "Constant. Not as bad as the last time they went away, but I'm only three days in, so we'll see what happens by the end of the week."

Mercedes bit into a chip, her eyes glinting. "No distractions from your boyfriends?"

Shira rolled her eyes. *Great, this again.* "Don't start. Jasper and Zach are not my boyfriends, and never will be."

"It's no secret to anyone they're interested in you. They're among the rare few out there who don't care that you have cybernetics. You should capitalize on the fact that *two* men like that are vying for your attention."

Cybernetics had an unfortunate stigma. While life-saving, or just life-improving, society had succumbed to treating those with cybernetics as inhuman. The treatment was so horrible at times, many of those with them struggled to not believe it themselves. It's what had cost Shira her modeling career. *And my one hope for a—*

She shook the negative thoughts of the past from her

head. "I don't date, and I don't hook up with guildmates." *Besides, they're together. I know better than to touch that.* "I'd like to drop this topic. You know I don't like it."

"Oh, you know I have to tease you every now and then." Mercedes grinned. "I mean, you used to get on me about Takashi all the time."

Shira chuckled. "Yeah, and who hooked up with him in the end? I don't hear you complaining, ever. You're all too happy to be with him, especially now that's he's moved in with you."

"Which means there's still hope for you." Mercedes winked. "C'mon, just admit it, you like them, too."

Shira shook her head and refused to continue the topic. A smile that screamed "I won" spread across her friend's face. But she hadn't. Shira didn't see them that way. She bit into her sandwich. *At least, that's what I keep telling myself.*

Those two made it far more difficult to keep at a distance than she liked. Sure, they may be fascinated with her now, but once they found out just how messed up she was, and how much she still needed Snake, even with the cybernetics and the time that'd passed since the accident, they'd back off. *Everyone always does…*

Mercedes scooped some of her soup. "I'm surprised you aren't in a PvP match with them right now."

PvP, Player vs. Player, was a game mode type in the virtual reality game Lusara Fates. Shira was introduced to the game thanks to Narissa, her cybernetics doctor and friend, when her other client and friend—*and now boyfriend as of seven days ago*—Ajax, had gotten her addicted to it. He'd revolutionized the gaming experience, creating an immersive session where one hooked themselves up through special tech chairs and were sucked in via the mind. Even though there were some consoles and handhelds still hanging on in 2107, it was the pretty much the only way to play games. And it's how Shira met Jasper and Zach.

Shira held up her tablet. "I do have to work."

"But this is them." Mercedes winked. "As much as they need to focus on twos matches, they'd rather do threes with you."

"They know this is something important I have to handle," Shira said. "And they have a tournament to prepare for."

It wasn't uncommon for people to find work in Lusara Fates, beyond actually working for Lion Rage on the game, like their friend Darius did. Takashi had an entire business built around their in-game economics that seamlessly meshed with real life. And Jasper and Zach had found work on the competitive PvP side of the game.

"The two of them are currently blowing up her phone," Orion said. "I've just muted Shira's notifications so she can accomplish her tasks."

Mercedes snickered and Shira sighed. Her AI assistant was supposed to be on her side and keep that a secret. "I thought I taught you about loyalty."

"Oh, you did. Snitches get stitches," he said. "But I am an advanced computer program. I can't get stitches."

Mercedes rolled over on the couch laughing. Shira grumbled, "Watch it, or I'll reprogram you."

"But, that would require you to spend hundreds of hours to reteach important tasks you require of me," he said. "Are you sure you want to do that?"

Her face scrunched. He had her there. That'd be a pain. And, all in all, even with all his annoying quirks, she liked her assistant the way he was.

"You now have three new messages from them," Orion said. "And you have one from Narissa."

Shira shook her head while Mercedes continued to laugh. She snatched her phone and took a look at Narissa's message first. She figured it'd be less of a headache to deal with. She was wrong.

I want to talk to you about the contract.

Shira knew it. Ever since Narissa forwarded a modeling contract to her for some new venture with Narissa's company, and she said *no*, Narissa would text her every now and then to express her desire for Shira to reconsider.

*It'll be good for you. And I promise it'll
help with the stigma around those with
cybernetics.*

Shira wished Narissa would drop this. She wasn't going to get back into that. She had her moment before the accident; it was gone now. And wishful thinking wasn't part of Shira's dictionary. She was too jaded for fairytales.

She jumped over to Jasper and Zach's messages. Scrolling through them, they were all pretty much the same. Either asking if she wanted to join for some matches, why she wasn't on yet, or why she wasn't responding. The most recent ones told her Serenity would be home soon, so if she wanted to get into

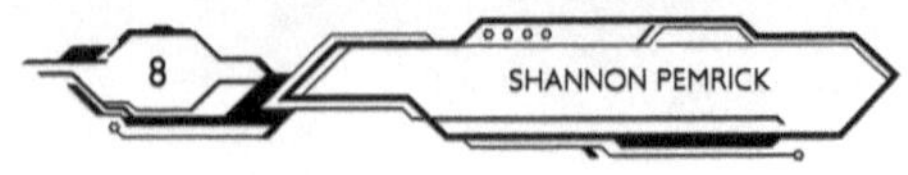

matches with them, it'd have to be now or after Serenity went down for bed.

Shira typed out a message.

> *You two are ridiculous. I told you both this*
> *morning I had more applications and work*
> *to deal with.*

Jasper replied back first.

> *Yeah, but it's late. You should be done*
> *by now, right?*

She shook her head and glanced at the time before responding.

> *It's barely noon here, dingbat.*

> *Well it's three here and Serenity is going*
> *to be done with her afterschool program*
> *in an hour.*

She'd known them for several years now, and yet Jasper still couldn't wrap his head around the time difference between the East coast and the West coast.

Zach jumped in.

> *We're just bored. We'd like to do some*
> *threes matches to break up our day.*
> *You're always the best cure. You make*
> *the day fun.*

Shira pushed away the heat rising in her. One of them always knew just what to say to make her feel a little more special than she was. But she wouldn't give in to it. Shira typed back.

The two of you need to be ready for the first qualifier tournament this weekend. So twos matches are all you should be doing.

The two of them had scored a sponsorship from Ajax and his gaming company, GameTech, allowing them to qualify for one of the Lusara Fates competitions held during Gamer Nine in Los Angeles in November. It was the largest gaming convention around these days—and the longest. While most were only three days long, Gamer Nine ran for five.

But even with a sponsorship, the pair needed to rank high enough in the qualifier tournaments, held during the last weekend in September and the first three weekends in October, in order to participate during Gamer Nine for the large-sum prize and various opportunities for notoriety.

Jasper sent the next message.

If you'd finally agree to join us, we could skip to threes for the tournament instead. There's still time.

Shira glowered at her phone, now just plain old annoyed. These two refused to let go of that stupid notion. It didn't matter how often she said "no," they continued to pester and insist she join an official paid team with them.

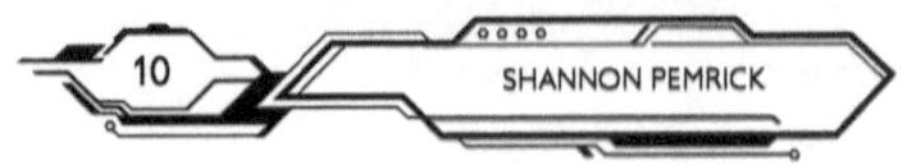

Mercedes rested her chin on Shira's shoulder. "You know you want to tell them yes."

Shira swatted her away. "Don't read my texts, Miss Nosey."

"I'm only looking out for you." Mercedes chuckled. "And we both know these two may just be more stubborn than you."

Her friend might not be wrong there, but Shira had something stronger than stubbornness—crippling issues. "It's just not going to happen."

"So many of us from the guild are going to Gamer Nine. We want you to be able to go, too, even if it's not to participate in PvP matches."

Shira's lips pressed together and her eyes fell to her lap. "I'm sorry. I just… I… can't go to that type of building. Not after…"

Mercedes frowned. "I know it's scary, Shira, but you have to reclaim your life one of these days."

Shira's shoulders tightened, dark memories of the past threatening to surface. She knew that's all they were, memories. There wasn't a day that didn't go by that she didn't struggle with something, and she chose to run away rather than face it. "You know I've tried, Cede, I really have. But…"

She sighed. It took Shira five years just to get comfortable seeing Narissa in her office. The first three, she'd have a panic attack just thinking about going there, let alone the mental stress she endured by going.

Shira still had to close her eyes when she went through downtown Los Angeles, so as to not look at the tall buildings. When she could, she tried to avoid the location altogether.

She shook her head. "I can't go to a place that's so similar to the one where the accident happened."

"So it's just going to the event?" Mercedes put her sandwich down. "If we agreed to do a few things outside the building, you'd go? You'd meet the two of them if they asked?"

Shira pressed her lips together. This was one question she wasn't sure how to answer. A part of her said yes, that'd be no problem, as long as they went somewhere with smaller buildings. But another side reminded her how she reacted when she video chatted with them a few months ago for the first time. That'd been so hard for her to do, and she hadn't done it since.

"Serenity's birthday is also falling around that weekend. You know they're going to bring her, and she's going to want to see you."

Shira frowned. Mercedes would pull that. Everyone knew at this point she had a soft spot for Jasper's daughter. But even the little girl couldn't quell the fear pricking at the back of her mind.

"My apologies for interrupting, Miss Mercedes," a robotic voice said from Mercedes' phone on the coffee table. "But the shop is calling."

Mercedes groaned. "Great, they probably need me to come back early so I can fix another mistake of theirs. Thanks for letting me know, Tasha."

She answered the phone and walked away. Shira went back to eating and looking over the application on her tablet. But her mind wandered back to what Mercedes was asking. Was it really only the building that scared her?

Shira realized she never responded to Zach.

No, I'm not going to do it, so stop asking.

Jasper responded.

Wow, killer hang time.

Sorry, Mercedes is here having lunch with me.

*Tell her I'll give her something cool if
she helps us convince you.*

Shira's brow rose as she typed back.

Something "cool?" Really?

Mercedes returned. "I'm going to have to leave. They really can't do anything without me there to babysit them."

Shira chuckled and held up her phone. "Before you do…"

Her friend read the messages and laughed, pulling up the Lusara Fates game mobile chat app and sending them a message, talking aloud as she went. "I've already tried to help you out, but she's too stubborn for her own good. And come up with a better bribe than something 'cool.'"

The pair laughed when he sent back a frowning-face emoji. Shira then received a picture text. She nearly fell off the couch in a fit of laughter at the sight of the men's in-game elf models pleading with her. The tall, muscular elf with long black hair, clad in dark leather armor—that was Jasper—stuck out his bottom lip with his head tilted up and wide-eyed into a puppy pout, and Zach—also tall, muscular, and dark-haired, a stark contrast to his real self, clad in plate armor—clasped his hands together, he too with big puppy-dog eyes.

Mercedes sputtered on her own laughter. "They're picking up tips from Serenity."

"Too bad it only works for children."

Her friend rocked her head back and forth. "I don't know. The men I know are pretty weak to that as well."

Mercedes' phone rang again and she groaned. "Tasha, tell them I'm on my way and to stop pestering me."

"I will do that."

Shira helped Mercedes clean up her meal and walked her to the door. Snake padded along with them. "Catch you again soon?"

Mercedes nodded. "Of course. Maybe next time you'll be up for going out, and Takashi will have some free time to join us, too."

She liked that idea.

"And, Shira"—Mercedes pulled her into a tight hug—"Consider what I'm saying, okay? You have to fight your demons one of these days. And if two guys want you, don't take it for granted. It's hard enough finding one. You know that. We've gone through similar problems with boyfriends and dates."

Shira's eyes cut away to the ground. "It's not that simple; you know that, Cede."

"I never said it was. But that doesn't mean you should give up. You got me to see that. Now it's your turn." Her friend pulled away and headed for her fancy, antique 2011 white Bugatti Veyron. "I'll catch you later!"

Shira waved and headed back into the house, her

mind heavy with thoughts. Jasper and Zach were happy together. They'd been together since Jasper lost his wife unexpectedly. And then there was the factor of Serenity. She was so young, and had already grown quite attached to Shira with the limited contact they'd had over voice chats. Shira didn't want to hurt her if things went south. *Because no matter how optimistic I try to be, it will go that way.* She knew she'd either ruin her friendship with the two men, or destroy the happy life they had. And that wasn't right.

It doesn't matter, I don't hook up with guildmates. She made that rule after she made the mistake of hooking up with a past guildmate. She'd made it clear to him it wouldn't go beyond VR, and it was purely a physical relationship, but he didn't listen. When the time came for him to start inquiring about making their "relationship" a real thing, he didn't handle it well when she said no. The situation had caused too many problems with the guild—to the point that he was expelled—and then he tried to run their name through the dirt for revenge. As well as she knew these two, and how they'd probably not do that, Shira refused to take the risk.

Shira sat down on the couch and swiped the application on her tablet, jumping right into the next one.

"Shira," Orion said. "Your *not*-boyfriends have sent you another few messages. I believe they're just messing with you at this point, as I told them they'd killed you from all the laughing they'd caused you to do, but that only stalled them for a few moments."

Shira chuckled. That sounded like them. They could be pests at times, but they really did respect the work she did for her parents. "Just relay the same canned response until I get these applications done. They're not the only ones who can play that game."

"Alright, I'll tell them your relationship with beer and work is complicated, so they may have a chance later."

Shira laughed. Not the exact response she'd asked for, but it was too good not to okay. Jasper and Zach would get a kick out of the response.

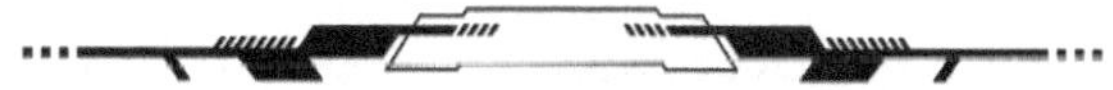

Jasper drummed his fingers on the table he and Zach sat at in the guild hall's bar. Serenity had gone down for bed easily tonight, and Shira said she'd team up with them, but she still hadn't shown up. He understood she had a lot of work to do, and he respected that a great deal, but she had a habit of pushing herself too much. He wanted her to take some time for herself and have fun. *And if she'd finally let Zach and me in, we could show her just how fun we can be.*

He sighed. That desire was looking more and more like a pipe dream with every day she continued to force her distance from them.

Zach nudged him in the arm, his plate armor clanking. "Calm down. She's not the type to bail."

"I know. But she's been acting wicked weird today."

"She's been busy."

Jasper shook his head. "It's not just that."

He couldn't place it. It was how she worded her messages. He and Zach had known her long enough that he could now pick up when something was off about her, even in a text form. Something else was up.

"You think she and Mercedes were talking about some things that got her out of sorts?" Zach asked.

Shira didn't like to let it be known how easily certain things bothered her. She tried to be strong and confident in front of everyone. But Jasper and Zach had seen the dark side of their own lives. They knew someone running when they saw it. And Shira might as well have a big sign with flashing lights.

Jasper worked his jaw. "Not sure." He sighed. "I don't know. Maybe I'm overthinking this. I just… wish she'd be willing to talk to us more about things like this."

Zach leaned in and grabbed his hand. "We'll get her to open up. We just need to find the right angle."

But what more can we do? There was only so far they could push before they crossed a line and lost her.

The sound of jangling half-plate armor and a woman's heavy breathing caught their attention. They turned to see a short, buxom woman running up to them, her dark brown hair bouncing around her shoulders. *Finally.*

Zach smiled at Shira. "You made it."

She stopped in front of them and took a deep breath. "Yeah, sorry about that. Something came up."

Red flags waved in Jasper's mind. He was right. Something was wrong. "You okay?"

She nodded. "Don't worry. Nothing I can't handle."

Jasper and Zach glanced at each other. They didn't buy it for a second.

Shira looked between them. "What?"

Jasper shrugged and stood up. "Nothing. Let's go kick some ass."

They grouped up and queued for a threes brawl match, Zach picking DPS for this round—damage per second—with his warrior class instead of his usual tank selection. Shira chose to heal with her elementalist instead of DPS, and Jasper of course had only one choice, with his rogue as a DPS-only class. Zach and he had other classes to use for tournaments in case their opponents' competitions required some strategic changes, but they did best with their rogue-and-warrior combo. And Shira, all her class picks complimented them regardless of their choices.

The game teleported them into a PvP lobby with another team of three. They were up against a sorcerer, a priest, and a berserker. Not a bad combo, but priests weren't as good as elementalists in the healing aspect for PvP. And while the berserker would be an issue, the sorcerer would be their weakest link.

The ten-second map-selection timer began. A little fun the developers put in for the PvP teams that enjoyed a quick round of trash.

The other team started immediately, whistling at Shira like you would to call a dog. Jasper's lip curled. He hated this kind of behavior. While only a small minority of players, it happened enough to put women off from playing. *Except women like Shira.*

Shira leaned closer to their opponents, her hand up to her ear. "I think I hear your master calling, boys. You might want to run now with your tail between your legs before you're punished."

Jasper and Zach snickered, but the other team also found something funny. The sorcerer grinned at Shira. "We'll show you just who the master here is, babe."

Her eyes darkened at the mention of the pet name. *Oh boy.* In chat, she mumbled, "Target."

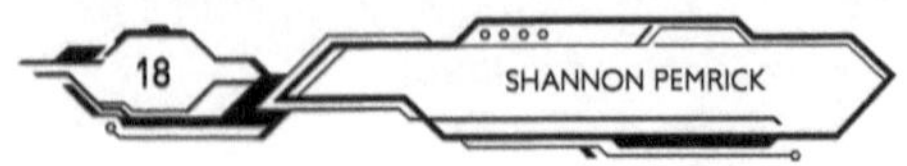

Well, they had their orders. Jasper figured it best to give her a hand now. "Don't look now, Zach, but I think these three kids think they're man enough to tame our fire."

Zach chuckled. "I'll bring the popcorn."

"Get fucked." The berserker spat at them.

"Sorry, but if you were hoping to be the one to help me with that, you'll have to wait your turn." Jasper pointed to Zach. "He's got me booked up all night."

The timer hit two seconds. This was where teams would get off one last insult before forced into the start positions of the map. Shira was the quickest.

She stuck her middle finger in her mouth, sliding it out painfully slowly in a way that sent a need down to Jasper's groin, and then presented her extended, wet middle finger to their opponents before walking away.

The other team was left speechless, while Jasper and Zach roared with laughter. Once they calmed themselves, they ran to catch up with her.

"You should use that gesture more, Shira," Zach said. "The looks on their faces were priceless."

Shira grinned. "I do quite enjoy it. It's fun seeing the brains shut off."

"We all know, the moment they saw you that had already happened. No doubt they're thinking they can get your contact if they impress ya enough," Jasper said, though he loathed to admit it. The idea of her hooking up with someone, while ignoring his and Zach's advances, irritated him to no end.

Shira's nose scrunched. He loved it when she did that; it was such an adorable look. He assumed it'd be even more so on the real her. He and Zach had only seen her face twice, one being a still image he'd saved to his phone after she'd sent it to try and prove some stupid point that she wasn't desirable with all her cybernetics, which hadn't gone the way she'd expected in the end.

"I'm going to pass," Shira said. "I'm not interested in polishing any dirks." Her eyes cut to Jasper, jumped to Zach, and then glanced away. "I'm more of a broadsword kind of gal."

Jasper rested his hands on the hilts of the daggers strapped to his hips, rendered speechless. She did not just say that to him and then non-verbally praise Zach. Zach folded over with laughter and Jasper placed his hand on his chest. "Ow! You're not supposed to throw shade at your teammate."

Shira shrugged, her expression smug. "Besides, I saw the profile of one of them. He's fifteen, and I'm not looking for that type of 'get into jail free card.' That's not my type of monopoly play."

Jasper lost it. She was on her game tonight, and it was amazing. Even if one of those insults had hit his ego.

The timer hit zero and a map was selected, forcing them to compose themselves. An ancient temple courtyard was randomly selected, and the area around them changed. Another timer started, this one a countdown for the match to start.

Jasper activated his stealth ability. He was still visible to his teammates, but the opponents couldn't see him. Zach drew his impractically large sword with its odd-shaped blade and carved magical runes. *Fantasy games. Gotta love it.* Glancing at Shira, who was glancing appreciatively at Zach's weapon, playing off her earlier comment, Jasper's eyes scanned her impractical, revealing half-plate getup. One thing he definitely wouldn't

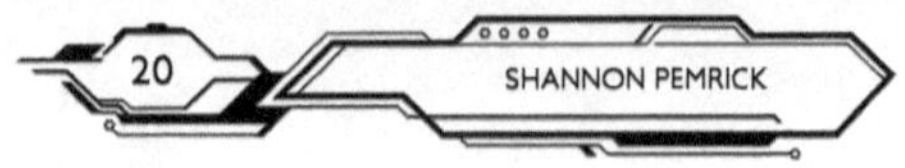

complain about with these games. *Though, that one-sided look to Zach needs improvement.*

He poked them both in the ass with the tips of his daggers before sneaking off to get into a good assassination position. Shira grumbled out an insult, making him grin. "Rogue, babe."

She scoffed, muttering about calling being called babe, and readied herself. Zach took up position a few feet in front of her. He may have gone DPS instead of tank for the extra damage output, but she'd be a prime target as a healer. They'd need to be cautious with their opponent's tactics.

The time hit zero and the match began.

CHAPTER 2

Zach deflected an incoming blow from his warrior opponent and countered with a swing of his own. He met his mark, but the opposing druid healed his teammate just as fast. *Dammit, he's not out of mana yet?*

Shira roared in frustration. "Stunned again!"

Zach bashed his opponent before dashing to her rescue. The other team's rogue slashed at her avatar in her frozen state. They'd done so well at their last match. This time, though, not so much.

The warrior Zach faced got in a lucky swing during his retreat; Zach cringed, but continued on. The nerve simulations for the VR systems were top-notch. You felt like you were really getting beaten on. Though, of course, for safety reason, the pain was suppressed to healthy levels, and even more so for PvP matches.

Zach activated his dash ability and slammed into the rogue, pushing him back. The stun chance from the attack hadn't triggered, but Jasper was ready and came up from behind, slashing the rogue several times, one eliciting a bleed effect. Outnumbered, the rogue disengaged and vanished. Zach and Jasper nodded and Jasper vanished as well, while Zach re-engaged with the warrior from before. The druid kept his opponent's health up, but Shira's stunned state wore off when Zach needed it, and his health shot up. She also let loose a multi-target lightning strike, hitting both the warrior and the druid. A slowing effect took hold on the druid, allowing Zach to activate several abilities and reduce the opposing warrior's health by a sizable amount.

Once the druid recovered, they were back to where they'd started, but at least the assault had reduced the guy's mana pool, a required resource his class relied on to cast his spells. Shira's class also relied on this, forcing her to be strategic with her spell use, and Zach and Jasper to be careful not to mess up.

Shira screamed in frustration again. Zach looked back to find her paralyzed, the rogue going to town on her again. Jasper came up and unleashed a flurry of blows, but it wasn't until Zach jumped in that their opponent backed off. That didn't help Shira, though. Her health had been reduced to less than half. *Stuns are unreal.*

"Fuck rogues!" Shira shouted.

Jasper came up beside her and winked. "Well, if you're offering, this one won't say no."

Zach chuckled and Shira rolled her eyes. "Get back to fighting."

"Do we get a reward if we listen?" Zach couldn't stop himself from jumping in. Her reactions were fun.

"Yeah, I won't kick your asses."

He snorted, amused. *Typical response from her.*

The opposing team converged on them, their target being Shira. Zach cursed when he realized which paralyzing effect the rogue had managed to use. It was their best attack, a thirty-second stun. If they didn't keep her safe, she'd be done for and they'd lose.

And this team wasn't giving them time to breathe. The warrior rushed in immediately and unleashed a deadly assault. Jasper and Zach tried to stop her, but she wasn't relenting from their blows. The druid healer kept her health level, and then the rogue joined in.

Shira's stun suddenly broke, sooner than he expected, and she tried her best to heal herself up, but it was already too late. She fell to ground, her health reduced to zero.

A timer appeared—ten seconds to make a difference—but without a healer, and the opposing team's still doing well on mana, they were done for this match.

The match ended, and Shira's life restored to full. She got up off the ground just as their stage changed back and they were standing outside the guild hall, Shira grumbling to herself. "Man, I really thought that item proc would come in time. Oh well."

At least she took the loss well. Zach's eyes darted to Jasper. *Him, on the other hand…*

Jasper's balled-up fists shook, his eyes narrowed and his lip curled as he stared at the ground. "Where did we go so wrong?"

Shira pursed her lips. "Why do you get so worked up when we lose? It's not that big of a deal."

"It is a big deal!" he snapped.

Shira recoiled, her eyes wide. Zach took a step forward. "That was out of line, Jasper."

She didn't know why losing upset him. Even if she did, taking his anger out on her wasn't right. And it certainly wouldn't encourage her to want to be around them.

Jasper's arms fell limp at his side, his shoulders slouching. He didn't look at either of them. "Yeah, you're right. Sorry."

The three looked up when they heard someone approaching. She was a curvaceous elf-avatar woman of tan complexion. Her deep blue eyes pinned on Jasper and then cut to Zach. Her red painted lips curved into a frown when her eyes fell on Shira. *Great, what does she want?*

Jasper crossed his arms. "What do you want, Stacey?"

Stacey pouted, as if they wouldn't see her young-appearing avatar and see the forty-something woman behind it. "Why must you act like this every time we see each other?"

"Because you only come looking for us to have a field day bitchin' about one thing or anothah." Jasper's eyes narrowed. "So what do you want?"

Stacey huffed. *Why must she act like this?* She always tried to pretend she was younger than she was. It was creepy. "I came to check on the two of you because I noticed you weren't in matches." Her eyes narrowed at Shira. "Now I know why."

Here we go. "We've been in matches all day," Zach said.

"Earlier, yes. But not recently." Stacey rested her hands on her hips, as if her disapproving posture would help her. "Need I remind you there's a tournament Saturday, and you promised the company you'd be making it through the qualifiers for Gamer Nine, after you went ahead and found an outside sponsor *before* running your plans by me, your manager, and subsequently the company?"

Manager was a loose term. Rather than working with them to make them a stronger team, she barked asinine orders, awkwardly and not-so-subtly attempted to flirt, and bothered them with hang-out request during off hours. It was why they tried to avoid her at all costs, since requests with the company to replace her had failed.

"Are you going deaf or something?" Jasper asked. "We just told you we've been in matches all day. We just got out of one!"

Stacey's eyes narrowed. "Yes, out of a threes match. But last I checked, you're a twos team with the company, and that's what you signed up to participate in for the tournament. But instead of getting ready, you're goofing off with your *friend*."

A muscle in Zach's neck twitched. At least she used the word friend for Shira this time. She'd used far less professional words in the past, which did get forwarded to the company in their formal complaints. Zach didn't understand what their manager's deal was with Shira.

Shira grunted. "This *friend* is helping with their prep."

Stacey's gaze snapped to Shira. "Excuse you?"

"Threes matches may not be what they signed up for, but it exercises tactical thinking, improvised team coordination. And it changes the mental thought process, reducing the repetitive mind-stress singular long-period play styles endure." Shira held her head high. "So, *Miss Manager*, you'd be wise to back the fuck off."

Fuck, that attitude is hot. Zach wasn't sure if what she said was true or made up, but he didn't really care. It sounded legit enough to him, and he liked this confident

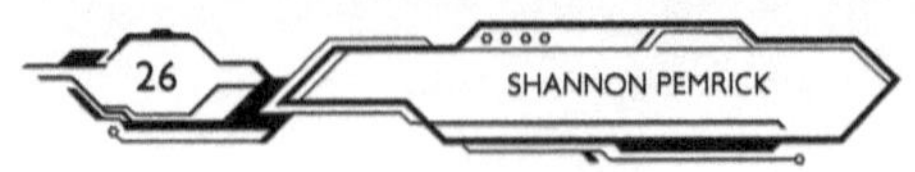

side of her. It drew him in like no other woman had, cementing the surprising change he felt toward her over the years.

Stacey almost snarled. "How dare you speak to me like that."

"Well, if you'd take the hint, I wouldn't have to." Shira had such a smug look on her face. "They're going to be ready for this qualifier, and they're going to win. And it won't be because you nag like an old hag."

The utter shock and offense that crossed Stacey's face sent Zach and Jasper into a fit of laughter. *That was a good insult,* he had to admit.

Stacey went red in the face. "Get back to practicing, or you'll be seeing me make a report to the company."

Shira sneered. "I'll be sure to have a counter report ready."

Their manager spun on her heels and stalked off. Jasper fell over, and Zach struggled to find it in him to breathe. He really hoped they weren't waking Serenity up. Of all the things the body did when hooked up to the VR gaming chairs, laugher wasn't always contained just within the simulation.

"Okay, okay, you two can calm down now," Shira said. "It wasn't *that* funny."

When they continued, she rolled her eyes. "Maybe I *should* make you two go back to twos."

That sobered them up. Jasper pleaded with his eyes. "Please don't."

Shira crossed her arms. "As much as I loathe to agree with her, your manager is right—you do need to keep practicing together, and with more comps than just warrior and rogue."

"But you told her you were helping with threes." He wagged his finger at her. "Don't tell me thatcha lied. We've gone over this. I can't let you be a bad influence on our daughtah."

Shira rolled her eyes. "You both are a worse influence than me. And I didn't completely lie. There are benefits to switching up between team sizes and play styles. You should do standard arena matches, but also get some other play types in, just to keep your minds fresh."

"But if we go back to twos, she'll have won," Zach put forth. "You don't want that, do you?"

Shira's head flew back. "Oh my god, you two are ridiculous. At this rate, you should just log off and go to bed." She nodded. "Actually, that's a good idea for you both. Sleep is just as important as getting your play time in, and it's late where you are."

Jasper jabbed his chest with his thumb. "We Bostonians are night owls. We don't need sleep for a while."

Shira snorted. "Yeah, but your little owlet needs to be up at the crack of dawn for her flight lessons."

Zach snickered. "She's not wrong."

Jasper narrowed his eyes. "You're supposed to be helping me here."

Zach held out a hand to Shira. "I can't fight logic."

"No, but Jasper is going to try and bash through it." Shira mumbled. "You'd think he was a berserker and not a rogue."

Jasper grinned and Zach held his breath. He knew that look. *Let's see how far this gets him.*

Jasper slipped his arm around her waist, and pulled her close, speaking low. "I could show you just what kind of rogue I am."

Shira scoffed, her cheeks tinting a shade, and then pushed him away. "No thanks."

Jasper pouted, making her laugh. "That won't help, either."

Zach shook his head. He tried, that was for sure. He did get a small reaction, which meant their antics did have an effect on her, but she was adamant about resisting their charms.

Shira clapped her hands together. "Besides, I need to hop off."

Zach's brow rose. That was out of the blue. "Why?"

"I need to do something."

Why so vague? She was acting odd again. During their first match, he noticed she wasn't herself. And the second match, it was like she wasn't there for most of the fight, and not because of those rogue stuns. It was as if she wasn't connected to the game entirely.

Jasper frowned. Zach could tell he was also trying to understand what was up, but instead of pressing, he scratched the back of his head. "Okay. I guess we'll catch you tomorrow, yeah?"

She smiled and nodded. "After I get more applications sorted."

Shira logged off before Jasper could complain about that. He grumbled to himself and Zach laughed. "You know, people do need to make money, and not all of them do so through the game."

"She makes money in the game."

"Yeah, but not like us."

Jasper's nose scrunched. "She could if she'd just take us up on our offah."

"True, but I think we're missing something important. Besides, that's the least of our worries."

Jasper nodded. "You noticed it, too."

"Yeah. She wasn't in it today like she normally is. I've been running it through, and I'm wondering if she's having a pain-flare day."

Jasper's eyes widened. "Shit, you think so?"

He nodded. "Even with applications stacking up, she's always up for some PvP. And how she played in those two matches, that was wicked sloppy for her. That last match, I think she was only half-connected to the game."

Shira didn't talk much about her accident. At all, really. And she didn't discuss with them anything to do with her cybernetics or how she was feeling in regards to her health. For the first couple of years, Jasper and Zach assumed her health was good after she'd gotten the medical attention she needed. But they later overheard her and Mercedes talking about residual pain and mental health concerns related to their accidents. That's when they realized how much Shira was trying to fight through on her own.

They'd tried to get her to open up, but it was a slow process. One thing they did know was that Shira had pain flares at least once a month, if not more, and, based on her actions, they guessed she fought all day with it.

That meant PvP should be off-limits to her. With the mind experiencing simulated pain through the game, it wouldn't mix well with any physical pain she was already enduring.

Jasper swallowed. "What if you're right? What if she logged off because it was getting worse?"

Zach was figuring the same. It'd explain the sudden need to exit.

Jasper's shoulders sagged. "Why won't she talk to us about it? What else do we have to do to get her to trust us?"

Zach's lips pressed into a thin line. "I don't think it's a matter of trust."

Jasper's brow rose. "What do you mean?"

"Let's log off and talk. We don't need Stacey breathing down our necks."

Jasper agreed and they logged out of the game. Once the chair with curved screens released Zach from the neurological hookups, he glanced around the room to adjust to the dim light. Old tournament and game posters covered the walls, along with shelves holding up past trophies he and Jasper had won. A couple of gaming sculptures and Funko Pop figures stood amongst the trophies, and on another wall they had some of their old game consoles, like a PlayStation 4 and Nintendo GameCube.

Jasper climbed out of his chair next to Zach's, the low light illuminating his partner's many tattoos, and sat down at a table they'd set up in their room for them to discuss work business in the room and keep it separate from home life—a difficult task when you worked out of your home. Zach pulled up his seat next to Jasper.

Jasper's green eyes met Zach's. "So, what did you mean?"

"I think she's driven by fear." Zach had been thinking about this for some time. It was the only thing he could come up with. "Whatever her accident was, it's had all kinds of ramifications. She lost her modeling career. She told us she can't get a date to save her life, which is absolutely ridiculous—"

Jasper grunted. "Tell me about it."

"—She's struggled to get through after everything that's happened to her, and she's done it on her own. We both know she stopped talking to a professional." She said so herself when they'd asked once. "She used some lame excuse as to why, but it's all related to how she's acting now."

"So, she's afraid to let us in because we'll know more than she wants us to?" Jasper shook her head. "That doesn't make sense."

"To her it does. If I had to guess, she wants to spare us from knowing. She's rationalizing her actions as a good thing, because she cares, and doesn't want us mixed up with what's going on with her. Even if that means not knowing when she's dealing with a health crisis."

Jasper rubbed his face. "So, should we give up on this plan?"

"Do you want to?"

Jasper stared at him for a moment. "No. Of course I don't." He paused. "Do you?"

Zach's brow spiked. "Why counter my question?"

Jasper gave him a long, hard look. "Because we both know you were hesitant about this idear in the first place. And if you're not comfortable with pursing her togethah, then we'll stop." He reached out and wrapped his hand around the back of Zach's neck, pulling him in for a strong, breath-stealing kiss. His blood simmered under his skin, desire rippling through him and threatening to halt their conversation at hand. "I'm not doing anything that'll lose you."

It was true, Zach was unsure. Ever since meeting Jasper, he knew he was the man he wanted. But knowing

Jasper wasn't interested in men, he stayed a faithful friend, even though it hurt. After they came together when Sara died, it took Zach a while to accept that Jasper truly did care. So when Jasper started to show interest in Shira, Zach worried he'd lose his partner to her.

Until he allowed himself to really get to know Shira, too.

She was the only woman to entice him the way she did. *Not even Amy made me feel this way.* He couldn't explain it. And as unsure as he was about this working out, he and Jasper had discussed the serious idea of including her in their relationship several times at great length.

"I mean it when I say I want to do this," Zach finally said. "I want us to keep trying. We both understand that her accident was horrific. Otherwise she wouldn't have so many cybernetics. I think we need to find a different approach, though, because we're not getting anywhere with what we've already tried."

Jasper tapped his fingers on the table. "Do you have anything in mind? Because I don't."

Zach wasn't sure, either. Shira didn't make things easy for them, that's for sure. "Maybe we should stop trying to get her to make the threes team a thing."

Jasper's brow ticked up. "I don't see how that's supposed to help, but I'm listening."

"We like the competitive nature of PvP. And she enjoys PvP, but it's clear she doesn't want to make a career out of it." Zach drummed his fingers on the table. "But she held her own against Stacey quite well, and even had me convinced of her reasons to be joining us for threes. We don't have a coach. We never needed one, since we'd decided not to do a standard five-member team."

Realization dawned on Jasper. "You think she'd go for that?"

Zach shrugged. "I don't know, but it's worth a shot."

"Okay. So that's one idea. What else do we have to work with?"

Silence fell over them as they thought this over. But nothing came to Zach. And thinking with no return was starting to give him a headache.

"Well, if the idears aren't coming"—Jasper leaned in again—"Then let's take Shira's advice and do something different. Then come back to it with fresh minds."

Before Zach could say anything, Jasper's mouth crashed into his. He sucked in a tight breath before kissing his partner back. Jasper pulled him closer, the kiss becoming more demanding. Jasper had always been the more aggressive of the two; Zach didn't mind.

Their tongues wrestled and Zach's hands found Jasper's sculpted chest. He ran his fingers down, feeling every peak and valley under Jasper's shirt. His hands found the hemming of his shirt and he tugged. Jasper pulled away to remove the garment when a screeching cry pierced the night air.

"Daddy!" Serenity screamed.

Every desire in Zach came to a halt, and his protective side flipped on. The two barely looked at each other before running to their daughter's room.

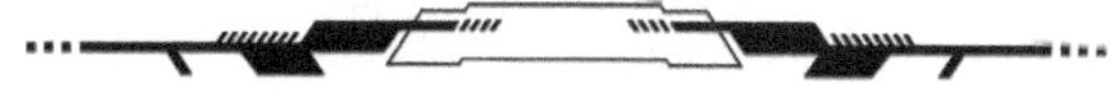

"Snake? Snake? Snake!"

The Game Over screen popped up on the TV. Shira's eyes narrowed and her nose scrunched. She'd played this level a million times, and yet it always tripped her up.

She restarted the level to try again.

"Shira," Orion said. "You've got a message from Jasper. He says it's important and not game-related."

Her brow ticked up. She'd logged off maybe an hour ago. What could they possibly want from her that was actually important and not them trying to get her play again?

She grabbed her phone and looked at her messages.

Are you still up? I need your help out
of game for something important.

She pursed her lips, disliking his vagueness. Why couldn't he just tell her what the issue was right up front? Shira typed back.

Yeah, it's only eight here. What's up?

It's Serenity. She had a nightmare and
Zach and I can't get her to calm down.
She only says she needs you. Will you
please talk to her?

Shira's back straightened. *The poor girl.* What could have spooked her so badly that not even her two dads could help her through?

Of course.

A part of her screamed this was a bad idea. That by

assisting in this moment where only a parent should, she was encouraging the potential for dependence on not only Zach and Jasper, but Serenity, too. One Shira didn't want to cause. She didn't belong in the middle of all that.

But the stronger part of her rationalized this wasn't the time. A little girl was hurting and needed comfort. And if she trusted Shira that much, then so be it.

Her mobile game app pinged, a voice chat notification request popping up on the screen. She accepted. "Hello?"

"Hey," Jasper said. He sounded exhausted.

"How bad?" she asked.

"Wicked bad. She won't tell us what the nightmare was about. And she won't stop crying. She's having nightmares a lot lately, but this one was the worst, topping one she had the othah day. But at least we got her to calm down that time."

The poor thing. "Okay, put her on the line."

His voice quieted as he talked to Serenity. "Sweetheart, someone wants to talk to you."

Shira waited until she heard sniffling. "Serenity?"

The sniffling stopped. "She-ra?"

From the moment the girl could speak, she struggled to say Shira's name. They'd managed to get her to say "She-ra" and Shira was more than okay with that name. Even though Serenity was going to be seven soon, the name still stuck.

"Yeah, it's me. Your dad said you had a nightmare. What's wrong, little Starship?"

Shira loved the nickname. She'd heard the guys use it so much in the past, she started to use it, too. They told her it was related to her name, some old science fiction movie or something like that. She wasn't much for that genre, so she took their word for it.

Serenity sniffed once. "I… I had a dream you went away. You said you didn't want to be around us anymore."

That made her heart ache. "Oh, sweetie, that'd never happen. I'd never do such an awful thing."

"Promise?"

"I cross my heart and hope to—"

Shira's game gave her the *game over* rundown again. "Uh, die?"

Serenity giggled. "You got a Game Over, didn't you?"

Shira put down her PlayStation controller. "Yeah. I was playing an old system game before your dad called. I thought I'd hid well enough, but my cardboard box failed me."

Serenity laughed some more. "You're funny, She-ra."

"Are you feeling better, Starship?"

"A little…" her voice came out quietly.

Shira pursed her lips. "What else is bothering you?"

"Can… can I see you?" Serenity asked. "The othah night I dreamed you didn't exist. No one knew who you were when I asked to talk to you." She sniffed once, as if the memory threatened to bring forth tears again. "I woke up and Daddy promised it was just a bad dream… but…"

Shira chewed her lip, her chest tightening. She wanted to help Serenity, but that request…

"Please, She-ra," Serenity said. "I just want to see you. Cause… cause it will help me be strongah. Since you're so strong."

Everything in Shira's mind stalled. She knew Serenity liked her, and Shira herself cared deeply for the young girl. But, Shira didn't realize Serenity saw her that way.

Shira took a deep breath. "Okay."

She had no idea what she was doing. Jasper and Zach would see her too, and—more panic flooded her mind. She did what she could to fight against it. *They've seen me before on a chat.* A few months ago, when Mercedes was celebrating the memory of her mother, she'd invited Shira and held a video chat with a bunch of friends. That included the two men in question. That'd been the first time they'd seen a live feed of each other; Shira had sent them a photo of her only a few weeks prior, to prove to them she wasn't all that special-looking now that she had all her cybernetics. Of course they'd reacted far differently than she'd expected. It'd thrown her for a loop then. *And even now…*

Shira disconnected the call, making sure Serenity understood she would be right back, and retrieved her tablet. Before she called back, she rushed into the bath-room to make sure she looked okay. Her makeup was on point. Her hair looked nice, the curls she'd done this morning still holding rather well, though taking a closer look, she noted she was going to need a re-dye soon. *One good things about Mercedes coming over earlier.* Hanging out with her friend, even for a short while, forced her to make sure she looked her best so she wasn't bumming it at home all the time. Saved her a lot of trouble now.

Shira leaned on the marble counter, her green eyes and freckled face staring back at her. She touched her false arm with her real one, and then trailed her fingers up to her neck to what looked to be real skin. But as she touched it, the texture wasn't right—an artificial skin that worked specifically for cybernetics.

While some cybernetics on the market had opaque structures, they didn't look right. It was why Narissa chose to go with the clear structures. She understood the stigma her patients dealt with, but she believed trying to hide it so poorly would only make it worse.

That's where this false skin came into play. Another company realized there had to be a better way and developed it. The result was something better than skin-colored opaque casings, but it was still not perfect. Luckily, Shira knew a thing or two about makeup. She covered herself in the skin and used her skills to blend it away until she created the illusion she was more human than she was. There were some places she couldn't hide entirely, like the crook of her neck and parts of her right side, and of course her clearly visible arm and leg, but that had to mostly do with the limitation of the skin.

She took a calming breath. "You can do this, Shira. Worst that could happen is they pull away and not want to associate with a freak." Her eyes lowered. "Not like we're not used to that..."

"Shira," Orion said. "I wish you wouldn't talk about yourself like this. You're not a freak."

Shira's lips quivered, memories of the past surfacing. The loss of her job. The pity. The stares. The comments. *Jeremy's words...* She closed her eyes and blocked it all out. "Yes, I am. No use lying. Can't run from that truth."

She pulled away from the counter, fixing her shirt when she noticed it was out of place. She let out a breath and stopped, leaning over the counter again and opening her mouth. The shiny metal ball of her tongue ring reflected back at her. *I should swap that.*

She wasn't ashamed of it. Shira wouldn't have gotten it if she was. But she knew how Jasper and Zach could get. Getting on this call would be tough enough as it is. The last thing she needed was for them to start up their antics because they saw her piercing.

Shira removed the silver jewelry and decided to replace it with a clear retainer. She could go without, but knowing her, she'd forget to put it back in after the call.

Once that was taken care of, she went back into the living room. She sat down on the couch and found Jasper already trying to call her. She answered, and her breath caught at the sight of the handsome man on the other end—strong jaw, short dark hair, and tan-skinned muscular frame covered in tattoos. He didn't have the typical "father" look, but god forbid you told him he was unfit. You'd end up with a bleeding mouth… and Serenity would get a treat for any reason Jasper could justify.

His striking green eyes stared back at her. It made her heart skip. "Um… hi."

"You okay?" he asked. "I thought you woulda picked up immediately."

Her eyes drifted away. "Yeah, sorry. I couldn't remember where I put my tablet."

He wasn't buying it. But before he could say anything, Serenity tried to grab his device. "Daddy, let me see!"

He chuckled. "Hold your horses, Pumpkin."

"But, Daddy, I don't gots horses."

Zach laughed in the background. Shira also found it difficult to contain her amusement.

Jasper handed over the tablet, and the feed showed Serenity's cute freckled face and bright green eyes. Her long brown hair curled just past her shoulders, where it wasn't messy from her bedhead.

Serenity gasped "She-ra!"

Shira smiled. "See, I do exist."

Snake jumped up on the couch, and Serenity's eyes lit up. "Snake!"

Snake's ears pricked and he barked once, making the girl giggle. He then laid his head down on Shira's lap. Shira placed a hand on his head and felt a wave of calmness washing over her. He was some of the best medicine she had.

The almost-seven-year-old bounced in her excitement. "She-ra, you're wicked pretty."

The compliment sent sudden heat to Shira's cheeks. "Thank you, hon. Now, do you feel better now that you can see me?"

Serenity's eyes fell away, her excitement dying. "A little."

Shira's brow twisted. *What is going on with her?* "What's wrong, Starship?"

"Um…" Her eyes took a minute to fix back to the screen. "How are you not afraid of things, She-ra?"

Shira cocked her head and studied her. She could make up a lie and tell her how easy it is to face your fears, but that felt wrong. At the same time, she didn't really want to confess how broken she was. Not only would it ruin her confidence, but Jasper and Zach would hear, and that wasn't a door she wanted to open with them.

Serenity pulled her blanket tighter to her chest. "You're not afraid of anything, right, She-ra?"

As much as I don't want them to know, I don't want to lie to her even more. "I'm afraid of a lot of things, Starship."

Instead of disappointment, interest flashed across Serenity's face. "Really? What are you afraid of?"

Shira curled into the corner of the couch to get comfortable. Snake repositioned himself to stay with her. "Well, for one, I'm afraid of people, because of how they've treated me."

"Because you have cybahnetics?"

Shira nodded.

Serenity looked down at her lap. "My friend at school is like that. The othah kids are mean to him because half his ahm is like yours."

Shira tilted her head. "And what do you do when that happens?"

"I defend him, 'o course!" Pride radiated off the little girl. It brought a smile to Shira's face. "I'll always defend my friends."

"She got in trouble for hitting a kid last week," Zach said in the background.

Shira pressed her lips together so she wouldn't laugh. As much as the kid probably deserved it, she shouldn't condone the behavior.

Serenity glowered past the tablet. "You weren't supposed to tell her, Zach. Now she's gonna scold me like you did."

Shira snickered. "Well, normally I would, as fighting isn't something I would condone. However"—she adjusted herself—"This time I'll say, good job, Starship."

Her eyes lit up. "Really? Ya mean it?"

Shira smiled. "Sure do."

Zach sighed. "Seriously?"

"*Vati* always taught me to never start a fight. But he sure as hell taught me to finish them. And then there's my personal code—you never turn your back on a friend, no matter what. If fists are needed to defend them, so be it."

"At least someone agrees with me," Jasper said.

Zach groaned. *Interesting.* Sounded like the two butted heads on parenting techniques.

"She-ra," Serenity said. "What does v–va–ti mean?"

Shira smiled. "It's an affectionate way of saying dad in German. Mostly children your age use it, but my dad likes it when I say it, so it's stayed."

Serenity tilted her head. "What do you call your mom?"

"Well, since she's not from Germany, she's happy with anything nice. Sometimes I call her *Mutti*, and sometimes Mama, and other times I just call her Mom."

"Oh. Okay." The little girl pursed her lips. "What else are you afraid of?"

Damn. She'd hoped the derailed conversation would have kept the rest of this one at bay. *Oh well. I can't go back now.* "I'm also afraid of heights. So I get scared around tall buildings, and flying, and anywhere else I'd look down and the ground is far away."

"Have you always been afraid of heights?"

Shira shook her head, her shoulders tightening. Snake pressed himself into her more, licking her hand. "I wasn't afraid of these things until I had my accident."

"Oh…" Serenity's brow furrowed in thought. "Is that why you won't see us?"

She's sharp. Shira shouldn't have expected anything less. As dumb as Jasper and Zach could be, they weren't idiots. They were smart enough to pull off PvP wins in tournaments, at least, so Serenity had to get it from somewhere.

She took a breath. *Here we go.* "It's a large part of it, yes."

Serenity gazed down at her lap. "I thought so. I knew it couldn't have been because you don't *want* to see us."

Shira's chest tightened. There was no conviction behind the young girl's words. She was lying.

"The tournament Daddy and Zach are going to is on my birthday. They said I could go this time. We're also going to see Nana and Pop-Pop. They live nearby." Her eyes lifted back to the screen. "She-ra, I want to see you wicked bad, too."

Oh, shit. Any other moment, Shira would have assumed the boys put her up to this. They knew her weakness to Serenity. But Shira could tell this was all the young girl's doing. *So is it innocent, or was this all a setup on her part?* Shira was her age once. There was an evil genius in her at that age, too. "Serenity, that's a bit of a loaded request…"

The young girl's green eyes lowered. "I know… but that's my birthday wish."

Fuck. Now she was going to be that bitch who'd ruin a girl's seventh birthday because she had issues.

"Well, I have anothah one, but that one is a secret for now."

"Serenity…"

Serenity's eyes widened. "What if… What if I promise to work on my feahs? Would you work on yours?"

Shira wasn't sure how to answer that. Serenity was so innocent. She didn't understand how difficult this would be to do, let alone accomplish in a month.

"She-ra, I promise I'll work wicked hahd on my feahs if you do. You don't want to be afraid of things for-evah, right?"

Those last words made her breath catch. Did she want to live in fear the rest of her life? Ask herself "what if" and "what could have been" all the time?

Shira took a deep breath. "Okay. You win, Starship."

Serenity's eyes lit up. "For real?"

She nodded. "For real. Because if you're willing to face your fears, so can I."

Serenity fell back on her bed into her pillow. "You're the best, She-ra."

"What about me, Pumpkin?" Jasper said. "I thought I was the best."

"Now you're second best."

Shira bit her lip so she wouldn't laugh when he sighed. Zach did chuckle a bit. "And me?"

"You're second best, too."

"But Jasper is second best."

She nodded. "You're both second best."

"Two people can't be second best."

"Yeah-huh."

Orion chuckled from the infrastructure. "I like her."

Serenity perked up. "Who was that?"

"That was my AI assistant, Orion," Shira said.

"Oh! We have one, too," Serenity said. "His name is Alistair. He's funny."

"I do my best to keep you entertained," came a robotic voice from somewhere in their house.

Serenity's mouth opened wide for a big over-tired yawn. Shira smiled. "I think it's time for our starship to go back to port and recharge."

The little girl sighed. "Okay… Will you stay on until I fall asleep?"

Shira couldn't see the harm. "Sure."

"Daddy, will you turn off my nightlight?"

"Are ya sure?" Jasper asked.

Serenity nodded and took a deep breath, as if she were preparing for something. "I'm not going to be afraid of the dark from now on."

"Well, if you want to go cold-turkey, you can." Shira saw his shadow move across the room. "But if it's too much, we can turn it back on and work slowah, okay?"

Serenity shrunk down into her blanket, as if almost regretting the cold-turkey choice, and then nodded. The room darkened, the tablet and a dim light somewhere in the house the only things to illuminate the room. Shira watched Serenity tense up. She needed to help ease her tension. "Starship, would you like it if I sang to you?"

Serenity's head nodded a mile a minute. "Yes."

Jasper came over and held onto the tablet. "I'll hold this so you don't have to worry about dropping it."

He kept it level with her face so the two could still see each other. Shira smiled. "This is a song my mom would sing to me. Now, close your eyes and listen carefully."

Serenity listened and Shira hummed. She wasn't the best singer out there, but it was the thought that counted. And in this moment, from the looks of Serenity's smile, it did count. She added the lyrics in, mixing in the German words, just like her mother had.

Serenity yawned and snuggled into her pillow. "Night, Momma."

Shira's song almost halted. It felt like she'd been kicked

in the gut. This was what she'd been worried about. She didn't want to give Serenity the wrong idea.

Sadness swarmed in her chest. It also brought back the longing. She wanted a family, more than anything. But thanks to that asshole five years ago, that was all taken from her.

Mercedes' words from earlier came back. Could she make this work? Did *they* really want to make this work? If they did, she'd have the family and love she longed for.

She let it slip from her mind and brought reality back. It wasn't going to happen.

When Shira was sure Serenity was asleep, she stopped her song. Not gracefully, but there wasn't a reason to keep going.

"Well shit, I was hoping you'd sing a little longah," Jasper said in a hushed tone. He lifted the tablet and turned it to face him.

She'd almost forgotten he and Zach were in the room. "Yeah, well, that was supposed to be a private performance for Serenity, you freeloader."

His brow rose and a devilishly tempting grin slipped up his face. "And what would it cost for us to get a special private show?"

Shira's face heated. He wasn't talking about that song. "Stop it."

He chuckled and then looked off screen when Zach mumbled something. He nodded and then looked back to Shira. "Can we talk to you?"

Yep, knew this was coming. She took a breath. "Sure."

Jasper stood and moved through Serenity's room, now too dark to get any details. She had to admit, she was a bit disappointed. She wanted to get an idea of what the young girl was obsessed with at the moment.

Shira caught a brief glimpse of Zach's golden hair as Jasper walked past him. The two were nearly identical in height.

Jasper carried her through another room of their small apartment. The way he carried the tablet had her staring right up at him. The angle was a good one. Her eyes dragged over his illuminated, defined, delicious features. *Stop it, Shira.*

Jasper glanced down at her and smirked. "Whatcha looking at?"

"You, ya dolt. Not like I can look at anything else with how you're holding that tablet." She hoped he'd buy it.

He grinned. "That so?"

Damn, he didn't.

Zach came up and draped his arms over Jasper. This stopped Jasper from moving and gave Shira a good look at him. He had a slimmer build than Jasper, but no less defined. And was more fair than she was, down to his hair, that was much longer than the last time she'd videoed with them.

His snaring, ice-blue eyes glinted in the low light. "Did we catch our Shira staring again?"

Jasper glanced at him. "She claims she wasn't."

Shira looked away. "I can end this call."

Jasper sighed. "Lighten up, we're only teasing."

Shira focused back on the screen just as Zach planted a kiss on Jasper's cheek and let him go. It brought a smile to her face. She always enjoyed seeing the affection the two shared. It was so genuine and unapologetic. Relationships like theirs may have been legal and accepted for decades now, but there were still far too many out there who had it out for their kind of love. *Same with Narissa and Ajax's relationship.* It all sickened her.

Jasper and Zach moved into a room with a light on and closed a door. From what little she could see, she figured that it may be their work room. From what she knew, they had a smaller three bedroom apartment in Boston, and instead of using the largest bedroom for sleeping, they opted to use it as their business room.

The two sat down at a table next to each other and rested the tablet on a stand. They stared at her. She swallowed hard. Here it came. "Okay, so what did you want to talk to me about?"

"We wanna help."

# CHAPTER 3

Jasper watched Shira swallow hard for the second time in the last three seconds. Snake climbed up on her, and for a moment he thought they were seeing his training coming into play, until the two of them watched her struggle to push him away.

"Snake, stop. Snake, cut it out. Snake!" The tablet slipped from her hands and crashed to the ground, screen facing the high-vaulted ceiling of her living room.

"Snake, stop being a jealous asshole."

Jasper and Zach exchanged an amused glance. Seemed like no matter how much training a service dog had, they were still a dog.

"*Verschwinde!*" Shira yelled.

The wrestling sounds on her end ceased immediately. Jasper's brow rose. She had a habit of mixing German into her sentences every now and then without even realizing it, but he didn't know that her dog had learned his commands in that language.

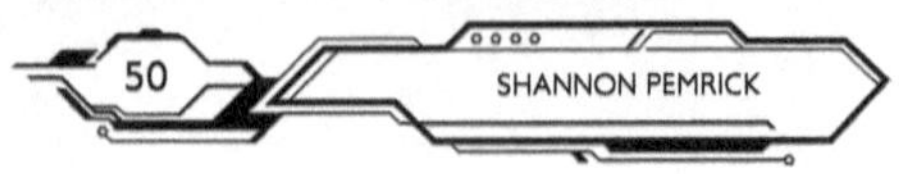

"Holen."

Snake's large head appeared and before they knew it, they were staring into the canine's dark, slobbery mouth. Shira took the tablet from her companion, and then her nose scrunched. The expression was cuter than her game model, just as he'd thought it'd be. "We need to teach you to control that slobber of yours."

She cleaned the screen and then rested the tablet on her knee, her movements deliberately attempting to keep her cybernetics out of view as much as possible. She'd done this while talking to Serenity, too. It bothered him. And from the way Zach leaned closer to him, Jasper suspected Zach thought much the same.

Shira gave Snake an affectionate pat when he hopped back on the couch. Her stalwart companion rolled up onto her, exposing his belly. Shira chuckled and gave him the attention he sought. What she didn't realize was that the action had her angling the camera right at her perfect chest. And the low-cut shirt she wore didn't hurt the view in the least. *Round, perky… no doubt supple and soft to the touch.*

His pants tightened. He wished the shirt was cut lower. Really, he'd rather be able to rip it off her to see—and most definitely feel—the perfection underneath. And by the way Zach tilted his head, he agreed.

When Shira remembered the two of them were still on the line, she snapped her gaze back to the tablet. Her eyes narrowed and she altered the angle of her device. "Really, you two?"

Jasper exchanged glances with Zach. They were not going to apologize for something they weren't sorry for. "What? You were the one showing them off. And

I must say, you should weah that shirt lowah. Or not at all. That'd be preferable."

Her eyes flashed. Even though redness grew over her cheeks, she wasn't pleased. *Great, my mouth made it worse.* She had hot and cold reactions to his and Zach's antics. "Goodnight."

Zach reached for the tablet. "Whoa, wait, wait, wait, Shira. Stop. We'll stop."

He didn't even have to look at Jasper to ensure he'd respond. Jasper could gamble, but he knew when to fold his hand. "Yeah, I'll behave. Promise."

Her eyes remained narrowed. He didn't blame her for not trusting him; he wasn't good at behaving around her. She was just too tempting. Jasper held up his hand, with only three of his fingers extended. "Boy Scout's promise."

She snorted. "You're no Boy Scout."

Jasper shrugged. "I was. But I dropped out just before Eagles. Zach made it, though."

"Now that I can believe."

He was slightly offended by that. Zach ate up the praise, though.

Shira's eyes drifted away from the screen. "Now… you two said you wanted to help."

Jasper's brow ticked up. He was surprised she was bringing it up. He and Zach had no idea Serenity would ask her to talk about her fears tonight. The thought had crossed his mind, once or twice, to ask Serenity to help them convince Shira to meet them, but he'd never actually stoop to that level. Of course, he never imagined she'd do it all on her own.

And now Shira wasn't avoid—

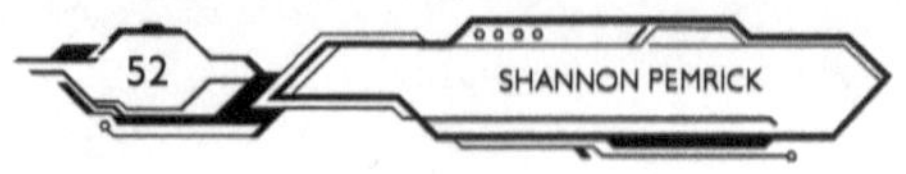

"I don't want your help."

Never mind. "Shira—"

She held up her artificial hand to stop him. The action surprised him. She had been trying so hard not to show her cybernetics. "I don't want your help. I can do this on my own."

Zach and Jasper exchanged looks. Zach's expression showed he wasn't sure what to do about her stubbornness, but Jasper did, for once. It was a big risk, but the only way to get through to her. "Turn the camera, Shira."

Both Shira's and Zach's brows rose. Shira spoke. "What?"

"You've been angling the camera of your tablet to the left, obstructing our view of you. If you're really fine to do this on your own, then stop doing that."

She blinked and then her expression hardened. "I can angle my camera as I please."

"No one is saying you can't," Zach said. "But your unwillingness is showing your fear, not your stubbornness and desire to control your situation."

Her eyes darted away and she chewed her bottom lip. *Fuck.* What Jasper wouldn't give right now to take those tempting lips of hers between his teeth.

"Shira, you've already faced a large part of that fear," Zach said. This brought her gaze back to them. "You're here, on this call with us. You don't show yourself if you can help it."

Not in this way, at least. She didn't have a single image of herself on social media. And any friends or family she hung out with, out of respect for her wishes, didn't upload anything with her in it. Zach gestured to himself and then Jasper. "And yet you sent the two of us a photo of yourself. A sassy image, but sassy is sexy."

Her face reddened and her eyes fell away again.

"And like I said, you're still on this call. No one is making you stay on. Your shoulders are far more relaxed than the last time we did this."

"Let us keep helping you, Shira," Jasper said.

"You don't need to get involved in my mess," she mumbled.

"Maybe not, but we wanna," he said.

She looked at him, fearful but curious. That lovely shade of her green eyes drew him in. "You don't even know what happened."

Jasper nodded. "True, and we're not gonna ask unless you wanna tell us."

He hoped she would. It'd help them so much if they knew exactly what they were dealing with here.

Shira's lower lip quivered a moment, before she pressed them tight together. "I'm not going to give details—"

"We don't expect you to," Zach said. "We don't want you to put yourself under any unneeded stress."

She swallowed and nodded. "Remember… remember that domestic terrorist attack at the convention center in Anaheim, about five and a half years ago?"

Jasper's back straightened, his pulse slowing. Zach's eyes darted to him. *No, she wasn't…*

"I…" Her lip quivered again. "I was there."

Numbness fell over Jasper. The two of them had theorized what Shira may have gone through. Car crash, hiking accident, even a work stunt gone wrong. But that… that event never crossed their minds. The day some deranged religious wacko decided those who enjoyed that type of life didn't deserve to live, so he set off a bomb. *It's too close…*

Buried memories—dark memories—came to the surface. The sounds of medical equipment—the smell of blood and disinfectant—her smile right before—

Zach grabbed his hand, bringing him back to reality. He gazed at Jasper with concerned eyes. Even Shira watched him, her eyes asking an unspoken question. But Jasper couldn't say it.

"That's how we lost Sara," Zach said for him.

We? He'd have to ask Zach about it after.

Shira shrunk down into her couch. "I'm sorry."

"We were at a tournament nearby," Jasper said. He didn't know what he was doing, but he couldn't stop himself from sharing. "She had made plans to meet up with a friend at the convention, and since my parents live there, they offered to watch Serenity."

Shira swallowed. "I'd been there with a friend, too—Tanya. We met a few months before, at a modeling gig in New York. It was her very first gig, and"—she chuckled—"was using a handheld system to keep her nerves down. It's what got me to talk to her. We hit it off and met up at Comic Con a few weeks later. Then I invited her to the convention in Anaheim."

Jasper's lips spread into a line. *That's weird, that's a lot like the events leading up to Sara telling me about her plan to meet her friend.*

Shira swallowed. "We were leaving my hotel room when the bomb went off. We—"

"Shira, you don't need to talk about it," Zach said. "You don't have to force yourself to—"

"Yes, I do." She turned her tablet so they could see

more of her, her cybernetics on display. She tried to smile. "It's the only way I'm going to get better in some way."

Seeing her do this elated Jasper, beyond the fact that they got a much better look at her shapely model-perfect figure. This was one hell of a step for someone who was uncomfortable with the idea of video chatting. He'd caught her lie earlier. It was all too obvious she'd struggled to pick up when he called.

"We were on the sixth floor when everything collapsed." She gestured to her side and side up to her arm. "I was… impaled by a support beam. Took off my arm and half of my torso. Rubble fell on me after that, and that's how I lost my leg and a chunk of my neck."

Shira shook her head. "Tanya's injuries weren't any better. It was a miracle the initial collapse didn't kill us."

Jasper watched her closely as she recounted. He could see how much it hurt her to reflect, but even as the dark memories surfaced, her expression changed—almost as if talking about the pain softened the shell she'd built to keep everything from hurting her again.

Her lips twitched as she fought various emotions. "I don't know how long we'd been trapped, but by some miracle we could hear each other through the rubble."

Her eyes squeezed shut and her breath labored as she struggled. Jasper wanted to tell her to stop, but the words lodged in his throat. She was so determined to tell them. Why, he couldn't understand. She could tell them another time when it was easier, if she really needed to. But it… felt wrong to stop her.

"We talked to each other the whole time. Everything that came to mind to keep us awake until we were found. I found out about her hobbies, and why she wanted to model. She told me a little about her doting husband and his best friend. The two were attached at hip, both to her annoyance and joy. And she told me of their precious daughter." A tear streaked down her cheek again. "And when we were at the hospital, she helped me through…"

She shook her head. Whatever she was about to say wouldn't be shared today. Jasper made note of it in case finding out later would help her. "Within forty-eight hours of being rescued, I lost her. It was devastating. I was in surgery when it happened. I didn't get to say goodbye or speak to her family."

Her lip quivered. "I sent messages to her phone when I was released from the hospital—several times, as if she'd never gone away. I'd hoped I'd get a response either from her, as if the doctors lied and she'd just been moved to a different hospital, or from her family."

Shira curled into herself, longing in her eyes. "Her daughter would be about Serenity's age now. I wanted to meet them. I still wish I could." Her lips twitched again. "Though, I supposed up to this point I didn't really deserve to. She told me to live my life to the fullest, to find new purpose. But I've done nothing but hide away."

She rested her forehead in the palm of her hand. "Look at me. I've gone and rambled on you both. I'm sorry."

Jasper didn't like that she was apologizing. She didn't need to. He went to say something, but Zach beat him to it. "Shira, you don't have to fight this alone. We're here for you."

She looked back at them, a smile forming on her lips, as well as some tinting to her cheeks. "You don't have to be…"

Jasper smiled. "What are friends for, yeah?"

The two of them heard her stop breathing. She stared at them, her eyes wide. A single tear rolled down her cheek.

Shit, what did I say? "Shira?"

She wiped the tear away and then rubbed her face. "Sorry. It's… it's nothing."

Jasper frowned. He went to speak, but she beat him to it. "I'll think about your offer, okay?"

He and Zach exchanged a glance. It was a start, if her long confession wasn't one. Zach spoke, "That's fine. Just promise us you won't back out of this agreement you've made with Serenity."

She shook her head. "I would never do that to her." She let out a breath. "Besides, Narissa already bought me an event pass as a *just in case*, and she would kill me if she found out I was backing out last-minute after making this deal."

The two of them burst with laughter. That described Narissa to a T.

Shira took a deep breath and then pointed to something off-screen. "Snake, *telefon*."

Her dog hopped off the couch and retrieved her cell phone. Jasper and Zach looked at each other. She was asking Snake to do more than they expected she would. Zach chose to ask, "Shira, are you in pain today?"

She let out a half laugh. "I was wondering when that question would come up. Yeah, I am. Meds are keeping it to a manageable level right now, though."

Jasper frowned. "I wish you'd told us. We wouldn't have pushed for those matches had we known."

She shook her head. "It had nothing to do with you. I wanted to play. I hate it when this lingering issue gets in the way of what I love to do, so I tend to push myself too far instead of focusing on my health."

Her eyes dropped and her voice lowered. "After you lose all your dreams, you try to hold onto what little is left."

Jasper's chest tightened. Seeing her reflect on all this made him wish he could just reach through the screen and hold her. Show her she didn't have to go through this alone anymore.

He failed Sara. He watched helplessly as she slipped away. *I won't fail Shira, too.*

"I should let you both get some sleep," Shira said. "I need to make arrangements to work on my issues anyway."

"Don't stay up too late yourself," Zach said. "You need your rest, too."

She nodded and waved, but Jasper stopped her. "One last thing before you go." He grinned. "Would you sing us to sleep, too?"

Heat rushed to Shira's face, her cheeks turning a bright shade of crimson. "Good night, losers."

She then ended the call. Silence permeated the air before the two burst with laugher.

"At least you managed to wait until the end," Zach said.

"I had to, you know that."

Zach calmed himself. "Yeah, yeah."

Jasper leaned on the table. "So, what do you think? More than I expected to get from her."

"It's crazy she was there, too. And to have gone through all that…" Zach shook his head. "I don't know how things will work out with the three of us, but at the very least, I want her to overcome these fears."

Jasper agreed. How they'd be able to help would be up to her, but as long as she leaned on them a bit more, that would be a start.

Zach's comment about Sara resurfaced in his mind. *Now's as good a time as any.* "Hey, what was with the 'we' comment when you told Shira how Sara died? You and Sara nevah got along."

Zach shrugged. "In the beginning, sure, but near the end we were working things out."

Jasper had avoided asking Zach what the issue was between the two of them. Sara never wanted to talk about it, but now seemed like a good time. "What was the issue?"

Zach's gaze fell away. "She didn't like how close we still were, even after I moved away. She knew how much I cared about you, beyond friends, so she was worried I might take you. Even after the two of you married."

That explained some of the passive-aggressive remarks she'd make, especially when Jasper had told her he wanted Zach as his best man. Jasper rubbed the back of his neck. "I'm sorry. I shoulda realized that was going on. I coulda curbed it."

Zach shrugged. "You're wicked dense, but I wasn't going to let her scare me away from being your friend, regardless of how I felt about you. And she started to realize that in the end."

Jasper held his gaze. "I'm glad you're here in my life like this now."

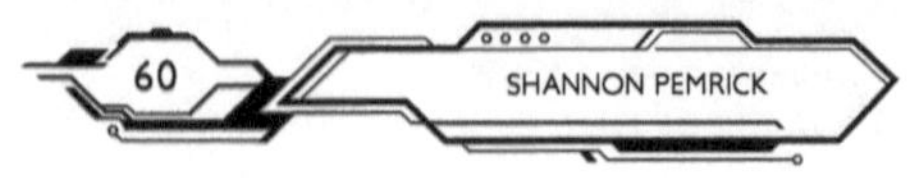

Zach smiled. "Me too."

He then yawned and stretched. Jasper's eyes wandered over his body in appreciation, his blood simmering. They needed sleep, but he wanted to finish what they'd started earlier.

He cupped Zach's chin and leaned closer. Zach had no intention of fighting him off with stupid sleep logic, but just before their lips touched, the floor creaked outside their door.

Jasper sighed and pulled away. "Serenity."

The doorknob twisted and then the door opened a crack. Serenity peered through. "I had anothah bad dream, Daddy."

Great. "How long have you been standing out there?"

"Um… awhile." She didn't come in. He suspected she thought she was in trouble. "I didn't want to interrupt the talk with She-ra. It sounded important."

Zach glanced at him. "How much did you hear?"

She paused. "A lot."

Jasper nodded. "Sweetie, you can come in the room."

She pushed the door open and stood in the doorway, hugging her favorite plushie, an oversized Rathalos. Jasper leaned over and motioned for her to come into the room. She ran over to him and wrapped her arms around his neck, her toy bonking him in the head. He lifted her into his lap and held her close to comfort her.

"Can I sleep with you two tonight?" Serenity mumbled.

Jasper and Zach looked at each other. Zach shrugged, not wanting to say no. He was too soft on these situations. But of course, this forced Jasper to make the tough choice.

Serenity gazed up at him with big eyes. *There is no choice here.* He caved. "Okay, just tonight, though."

She smiled widely. "Thank you."

There went his plans for tonight… and tomorrow morning. Oh well. There was later in the day after she'd gone off to school.

Jasper stood up, cradling Serenity. "Let's get to bed. It's late, and you have school."

"Do I hafta go?" she complained.

"Yes," the two said in unison.

She grumbled and looked away. It didn't last long. She gazed back up at him as they left the room. "Daddy, when is She-ra gonna come live with us?"

Jasper exchanged a glance with Zach. Serenity had grown attached to their friend early on in the friendship. She'd basically grown up hearing Shira's voice on chat. And when Shira allowed herself to have conversations with Serenity, that's when the attachment started.

They both knew Shira tried to keep their contact simple, as it would cause an attachment none of them wanted at the time. But ever since Serenity was five, she'd started asking about Shira's potential to be part of their lives as a permanent fixture.

At the time, it was dismissible because their interest in Shira was minor. But as things continued, it became harder to ignore. And when the two realized what they wanted to do, Serenity figured it out before they could even think to hide it from her, so as not to get her hopes up if they failed.

He couldn't outright lie to her. She'd catch it, she was that sharp. Hell, they'd never gotten her to believe in Santa or the Tooth Fairy. "We're not sure yet."

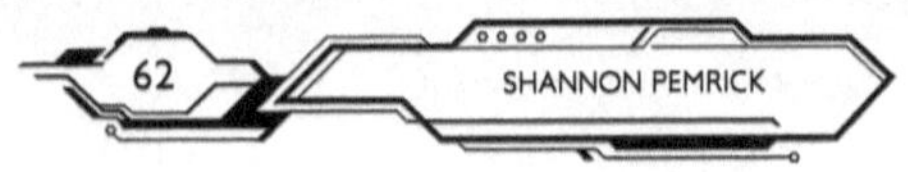

She pursed her lips. "Why not?"

"Because we have to still work on getting Shira to overcome her fears and meet us first," Zach said. "Then we can look into seeing if she's interested."

Serenity looked down at her plush and pouted. "I hope she is…"

Jasper tilted his head. "Serenity, did you have a dream about her not coming to live with us?"

She nodded and then pulled her toy to her face. "She said she didn't want to be my mommy."

Jasper held her close. This was something he'd feared. She may be almost seven, but she was still young enough where she didn't quite understand the complexities of relationships. To her, if you liked someone, you complimented them and gave them gifts until they let you call them your partner. Then you lived happily ever after. *If only it were that easy.*

"Don't worry," Jasper said. "We're gonna talk to her about it."

"Promise?"

He held his pinky out to her. "Pinky swear."

Serenity wrapped her little finger in his. "Can't break it."

Her innocence brought a smile to his face. He wished she'd stay like this forever.

Serenity yawned loudly as the three of them entered his and Zach's room. Zach climbed in first and then Jasper set Serenity between them. He slipped in last and kissed her good night before turning off the light.

But it was a while before sleep found him. Shira's story plagued his mind. Something about it bothered him. Not just the fact she'd gone through it, though. It was like he was missing a piece of the puzzle.

Sleep found him before he could find the answer. But at least the last thing his mind showed him was Shira's smiling face, rather than Sara's as she died.

CHAPTER 4

Shira tapped away on her steering wheel to the pop music playing on the stereo, trying to keep her mind occupied. Mercedes sat next to her, trying not to show how much she enjoyed the music. Mercedes tried to claim she was solely a rock enthusiast, but Shira's tastes were quite good in her opinion, making it hard for Mercedes' claim to ring true.

"I still can't believe the two of them got you to do this," Mercedes said.

"Y—yeah," Shira managed.

The moment she'd gotten off the chat with Jasper and Zach, Shira had texted Mercedes to see if she'd be free during the week to help her out. She wasn't, at least not for the amount of time Shira needed, so they made plans to tackle her first task on Saturday—today. Shira wasn't comfortable doing this on her own, so she made the appropriate calls and plans to work her through the next few weeks leading into November, but today was her first big day. Her emotions were all over the place. She didn't know how this was going to go, but she didn't have high hopes.

Mercedes reached out and grabbed her hand. "Take a deep breath. You can do this. We're starting small."

Downtown San Francisco, a place Shira avoided at all costs, had a number of tall buildings for them to work with. They'd agreed, though, they'd work their way up, so as to make it easier on her to adjust and overcome her fear. And if she couldn't handle these buildings, there'd be no way she could handle going to the convention.

"Cede, how is it that you don't have these issues, too?" Shira asked.

"Well, I don't remember most of what happened," Mercedes said. "I only remember driving in my car and something landing on it. Then I was waking up in the hospital."

That would figure.

Mercedes grinned. "Look, if you need extra help, we can always call your boyfriends."

Shira's eyes narrowed. "Stop. It's not like that."

"Yeah? Then how were they able to convince you to give this a go?"

Shira's eyes darted out the window. "It wasn't them. Not entirely. Serenity is the one who got me to agree to work on this."

Mercedes chuckled. "Of course she did. You can't say no to her." She tapped her lips with a finger. "But, the way you worded that, makes me think your two men did have some pull."

"It's not like that!"

Mercedes brow ticked up and gave a look that told Shira she wasn't convinced.

Shira pressed her lips together. "I… I told them what happened."

Mercedes' eyes widened. "Seriously?"

She nodded. "I meant to just tell them I was there when the event happened, but all the words just kept coming. It wasn't until I almost told them about Jeremy did I realize I was rambling."

Mercedes squeezed Shira's cybernetic hand. "Don't think about him. That asshole doesn't deserve a moment of your time." She nudged Shira. "Instead, think about the two hot guys who are looking forward to seeing you."

Shira's face burned and she swatted her friend. "Stop it!"

Mercedes whipped out her phone, a grin on her face. "I could call them if you wanted."

Shira crossed her arms. "They're at the qualifier."

"That's happening in their city, right?"

Shira nodded. "It's about noon their time. So, right in the middle of everything."

Her friend pursed her lips. "Damn."

"Shira, Mercedes," Orion's voice said through the car dash. "We're arriving at the destination. Do you wish for me to drive past, or park?"

Mercedes left it up for Shira to decide. Shira's mind went a mile a minute. What was the best way to do this? Should she dive right in, or take it slow? Her hands shook. What if she chose wrong? How would that affect her?

Snake pushed his large head up from the back seat and nudged her arm until he was able to worm closer.

Mercedes also placed her hand on Shira's shoulder. "Shira, take a breath. It's okay."

Shira sucked in a hard, shaky breath, and stroked Snake's head. "Just drive by a few times."

"I will do that."

The car rounded a corner, and before them stood tall hotel buildings, all neatly lined up down the long stretch of road. Nothing tall like the skyscrapers beyond them, but viewing the towering structures that reminded her greatly of the convention center from the car already sent her heart racing.

Breathing proved difficult as the car drove down the street. Shira did her best to force the control she needed, and not turn into a panicking mess. Mercedes sat patiently, offering a reassuring touch when things became a bit too difficult for Shira to handle.

The car took a turn and drove away from the area. It took some time for Shira's heart rate to return to normal, though her mind remained on edge. "This fucking sucks."

"You did well," Mercedes said. "It may have been hard, but you were able to keep yourself from going into an attack."

Shira couldn't argue that. She never believed she'd be okay the first time through, and even though she did panic, she didn't become an all-out mess. "Let's try again."

Orion looped the car around and they went through the same process as before. Shira did about as well as the first time, but at least she didn't do any worse.

They repeated this four more times. The last time, she made progress. Mercedes smiled widely. "See, you got this."

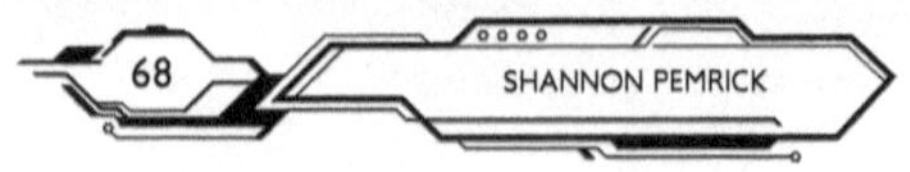

"Orion, please park the car somewhere away from the buildings. I need a quick breather," Shira said.

"Recalculating to the nearest safe parking spot."

Shira and Mercedes chuckled, though Shira's laughter was a bit more forced than she wanted. Orion had picked up his recalculating phrase one day when Mercedes and Shira were making fun of the old GPS systems before AI computer technology. And in this moment, the humor was sorely needed, though that didn't seem to matter to her stressed-out brain.

They parked on a side street and the engine cut. Shira nestled down in her seat with a sigh.

Mercedes pulled out her phone. "Take your time catching your breath. We've got plenty of time."

"I've paid for fifteen minutes for this spot," Orion said. "If you need more time, just let me know."

Shira smiled. "Thanks, both of you."

Mercedes smiled back and texted someone on her phone. Shira took some calming breaths and used her friend's action to refocus. "Takashi?"

Her friend nodded. "He was checking up to see how things were going for you and wanted to plan something for dinner."

"That's so sweet." Takashi was the perfect guy for Mercedes. Sweet, caring, and supportive to a T. Shira envied her friend. Not in a negative, she-hoped-they-didn't-work-out-because-she-was-miserable kind of way, of course.

"Shira, your own boyfriends have also texted you," Orion said. "Would you like for me to read it out loud?"

Mercedes snickered and Shira ground her teeth. "Don't you start with that."

"They also sent a photo."

Shira pulled out her phone and opened her messages.

*We're hoping you're kicking as much
ass as we are!*

The photograph was of the two. They had huge goofy grins on their faces.

Mercedes leaned over to snoop. "Zach's hair looks different. Is he growing it out?"

Shira nodded. "I think so. I don't know how long he plans to grow it, but I'm sure, whatever length it ends up, he can pull it off."

Mercedes smirked. "Someone's got a preference, don't they?"

Shira's cheeks heated. "It's just on some guys, I like it."

"Yeah, and one of those 'some guys' is Zach."

"So?"

Her friend chuckled. "You should send something like that back to them."

The muscles in Shira's neck tightened. Should she? Better yet, could she? Ever since the accident, Shira couldn't stand being near cameras. No one could take her picture if she had a say in it, and if her friends were taking photos, she was sure to stay out of them.

Things got so bad that she didn't even look at old images of herself. Snake was her photo on social media, and really, she mostly used that to show him off to the world. He had quite the following.

What she sent Jasper and Zach a few months ago took her forever to snap. And she told herself that'd be the only one. *But I also said I'd never video chat with them, and here I've gone and done it twice now.*

Shira took a strong breath. "Okay."

Mercedes' eyes widened. "Really?"

She turned the selfie mode on for her camera and held it up. "Yep. Now get in this."

Mercedes, so excited this was happening, overshot and practically fell into Shira's lap. The two burst into laughter. It also gave Shira an idea. "Pretend you're blocking me."

Mercedes laughed more and threw an arm up while still leaning on Shira. Shira ducked a little to hide some, and then gave Snake a command. "Snake, *kopf neigen.*"

When he tilted his head on command, she snapped the image. The result had them roaring. Shira then sent it to the guys.

Yeah, we're doing something at least.

It didn't take long for them to get a response. A photo of the two men with confused looks, captioned with:

WTF????

The two rolled with laugher, tears rimming their eyes. When Shira managed to calm herself, she fixed her hair. "Okay, now we can take the serious one."

"Like, so serious it's stupid funny still, or…" Mercedes' eyes twinkled, making Shira chuckle. She loved her friend so much. If anything good came of her and Mercedes' accidents, it was this friendship. The two would have never met otherwise.

"Basic-smile serious. We'll get Snake in on it, too."

"Well, yeah."

The two leaned into each other and Snake rested his head on Shira's shoulder. Shira rested her artificial arm on his head and snapped the photo. Staring back at it, she had to take a quick breath. *That wasn't so bad.*

Mercedes glanced at her. "Now you need to send it."

She nodded. "Yeah. Give me a second."

Shira typed out a message before attaching the photograph.

Making progress. Promise.

Her thumb hovered over the send button. Her pulse quickened. *Here we go…* She pressed send.

Mercedes squealed and latched onto her. "I'm so proud of you! Now we just need to work on an image for social media one of these days."

"Yeah…"

Her friend let go and tilted her head. "Shira?"

Shira stared at her phone. It didn't seem like much to most, but that'd been a big deal. It took everything in her to do it, and she did. That's why Mercedes was so excited. But she wasn't the only one. The sensation bubbled up deep from inside Shira, sending tingles to her fingertips. This was progress. It came in different forms for her. And she couldn't just focus on one issue at a time if she was going to get better. *I can do this.*

Shira patted her shoulder. "Come here, Snake."

He rested his head on her shoulder and Shira fussed with her hair before lifting the phone again. She gave Snake a good scratch and snapped a picture. "Your fans are about to see your mom for the first time, Snake."

Mercedes' gasped, her hands flying up to her face. "Shira…"

Shira's heart raced as she typed something out. She, like a lot of other dog parents, had a particular voice just for him.

Her hands shook and her pulse pounded in her ears by the time she posted the image. But it didn't stop there. She couldn't. She also uploaded the image as her personal profile image on her own media accounts. She had no idea what would happen next. Anything public had the chance of attracting all kinds of hurtful responses. *Fuck 'em.* She wasn't going to live in fear of judgment the rest of her life.

Shira set her phone down on her lap and took a shaky breath. "What did I just do?"

"The most amazing thing in a long time."

Shira looked to her friend. A tear slipped down her friend's cheek. Before she knew what was going on, Mercedes wrapped her arms around her neck and pulled her in tight. "I'm so proud of you."

Shira hugged her back. "Thank you. I—"

Her phone started going off with a million notifications. The two exchanged a glance and then Shira lifted the phone to figure out what was going on. *So many comments and likes.* Over a hundred and climbing.

Some were good, better than good. Some people called her hot, even with the cybernetics visible. Some were less than stellar, and what she expected, but others jumped to her defense, not something she expected. And even more surprising was the fact some people recognized her and showed their excitement for her to show her face once again. Shira found herself overwhelmed. This wasn't the result she expected.

Her personal profile wasn't bare either. So many of her friends, family, and acquaintances reached out with separate posts to her page. But the one that stuck out to her was her mother's.

> *Look at my beautiful baby. I'm so proud of you. Your father says he's the proudest papa in the world. Kisses from Switzerland.*

That hit her deep. She loved her parents so much. They'd given her more than she could ever thank them for. All she ever wanted to do now was make them proud. *I have to keep doing this.*

She received a reply from Jasper and Zach and opened it.

> *Wow. That stud is lucky to be sur-rounded by two hot ladies.*

She sputtered a laugh. When Mercedes' brow ticked up, she showed it to her. Mercedes also cracked up. "They are something else. That's totally a Jasper line."

Shira rocked her head back and forth. "Zach would say it, too, so it's hard to say who came up with the line."

Mercedes winked. "Well, you do know them best."

Another message came in.

> *We see there's room on your other*

shoulder. Is it up for grabs?

Shira bit her lip. She'd respond a particular way, but Mercedes would read too much into it. Her friend nudged her. "I know that look. Say it like you usually would. I'm going to tease you, either way."

She wasn't wrong.

It might be, but I suspect you both are offering and I don't think that'd work.

I'm sure we could both squeeze.

It'd be tight.

That's how we like it. ;)

Mercedes couldn't hold back her laughter. "You're such a flirt with them."

Shira rolled her eyes. "It's just casual flirting. No different than our trash talk before a match."

"Or during?" Mercedes winked. "I've heard you all go at it. There is no line for you with them when they get you going."

Shira shrugged. "So what? It doesn't mean anything."

"Yeah, sure."

"Cede, seriously. It's not going to happen."

Mercedes threw her hands up. "Why not? They got you to do all this. Why can't they be the right ones for you? They care about you and how much you deserve to heal and be happy."

Shira's eyes fell. "I'm just not convinced it'd work."

Mercedes let out an aggravated sigh. "You're going to be the death of me, you know that."

Her phone went off again.

> *Oh, and we left you a little message on your page. We're happy you finally took that plunge.*

Shira's eyes went wide. *Oh no. What did they do?* She pulled up her image and found their comments—first Jasper's, then Zach's.

> *Look at that sexy lady.*

> *Snake's a lucky stud.*

But that wasn't the worst of it. As she feared, her other friends jumped in to fan the flames.

Ajax was the first.

> *Oh, there we go. Her boyfriends finally showed up.*

And Eli.

> *Signora, watch out. I think they're coming to steal you from your protector.*

Then Kiara.

> *I'm sure if you're real good boys, she'll train you two next ;)*

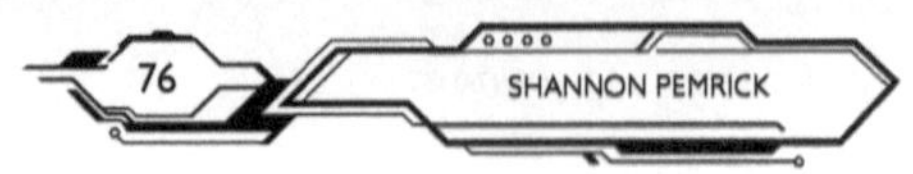

The comments went on and on. And her mother noticed.

Boyfriends?

Mercedes rolled with laughter. It sent heat to Shira's face. "This just got better and better."

Then the inevitable. Her phone rang. It was her mother. Shira took a deep breath. She couldn't ignore this call. She'd be dead if she did. "Hi, *Mutti*."

"What is this talk about boyfriends?" her mother said.

"Can we learn how it went from none to two?" Her father's deep voice asked in the background. His had a light accent that stuck with him, even after all his time living in America.

"Momma, please calm down," Shira said.

"Calm down?" Her mother laughed. "I'm not mad, honey. I just want to understand."

"I could be mad," her father said.

Shira sighed. "It's a joke with my friends."

"No, it's not," Mercedes said.

Shira smacked her. "Stop it."

"Oh!" Her mother laughed. "These are the two men you play that game with all the time. No wonder your friends are teasing you. You're being too slow to snag them."

Shira threw her head back and groaned, while Mercedes roared with laughter. "Really, Momma?"

"Well, why not? They're cute, your age, and they have the most adorable little girl. So if they're interested, what's the matter?"

Mercedes nudged her. "See? I'm not the only one."

"Shira, tell Mercedes we say hello."

Shira cut her eyes to her friend and Mercedes raised her voice. "Hello, Mr. and Mrs. Schneider!"

"Such a great friend you have. Now, back to these boyfriends of yours."

Shira wanted to slam her head on the steering wheel. "Momma, can we talk about this later?"

"Oh, yes, you've been working on your fears. It looks like it's going well. We're so proud of you, honey. I won't hold you up any longer. We'll be home in a few days. Love you!"

"Love you both, too," Shira said, amused by her mother's sudden willingness to bail on the call.

The line died and she sighed. Mercedes nudged her some more, lifting her eyebrows a few times, and then focused on her phone. "Pizza sound good?"

Shira's brow ticked up. "Huh?"

"For dinner tonight," she clarified. "Takashi thinks after a long day like this, pizza would be a good comfort food for you and me."

"Oh, wait, you two were planning dinner for me, too?"

Mercedes chuckled. "Duh."

Shira smiled. "Pizza sounds great. Wings, too, would be nice."

Her friend typed back to her boyfriend. "Done and done. Now, should we try some more fear-fighting today?" She chuckled. "Or am I going to be going on some more teasing sprees?"

Shira rolled her eyes. "Orion, please take us back to the test street."

"Recalculating."

The two women cracked up. She was going to need that humor to get her through the rest of the day.

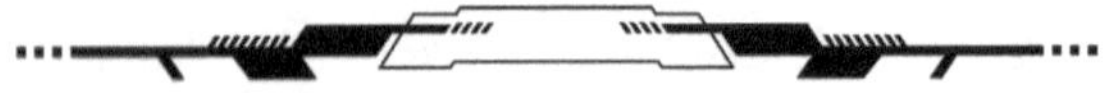

Jasper and Zach's beat-up Subaru pulled up to a quaint ranch-style house with green shutters. The pungent smells of a farm hit their noses even with the windows up. A sheltie barked at them from the porch and then ran over to their car. Jasper climbed out of the vehicle and was more than willing to give him attention. "Hey, Buddy. We're back."

"Buddy, what are you bahking at?" A familiar smiling face peered out from a window inside the house. Her green eyes lit up. "Daddy! Zach! You're back!"

Serenity disappeared from the window. Not long after, the front door swung open and she bolted out, boots barely on and with no coat. A female voice called after her. "Serenity, come back. It's wicked cold out and you're not dressed properly."

A woman in her mid-thirties ran out of the house, a child-size jacket in her hands. She stopped immediately when she spotted Jasper and Zach. "Oh, well that explains it."

Jasper smiled. "S'up, Cheryl."

She shook her head. "You need to teach my niece she needs to weah a jacket when she goes outside. It's cold out now. I've had to fight with her all day while we worked on the fahm."

Serenity crossed her arms. "But, Auntie Chery, I told you, I was getting hot."

"That's no excuse." Her eyes softened. "But even still, you were a great help."

Serenity smiled big and then ran to Jasper's waiting arms. "I had a wicked fun day today, Daddy! We fed the goats and sheep. And I helped make apple cidah. And Auntie Chery taught me how she and Uncle Ray get sap from the trees in the spring to make maple syrup!"

Jasper chuckled. This wasn't the first time she'd done these things with his sister and brother-in-law, but she was always so excited, it might as well be a new experience every time. "That's sick, Starship."

Zach came up and kissed her on the head. "We're glad you had fun while we were at the tournament."

Cheryl leaned against the porch railing. "How'd it go?"

They glanced at each other. "We kicked ass," they exclaimed in unison.

Serenity gasped. "I'm telling She-ra you both said a bad word!"

The three adults laughed. Cheryl was the first to calm. "Is that the girl you've been seeing?"

Jasper's brow cocked. "Huh?"

"Serenity has been going a mile a minute all day, telling us about this She-ra person. At first I thought she was talking about the comic charactah."

"Her name is Shira," Zach said. "She's a friend."

Jasper was surprised his sister didn't know about Shira. He was sure Zach and he had mentioned her at least once or twice around her. *Maybe she just wasn't paying attention.* That wouldn't be too hard to believe.

Cheryl regarded them for a moment. "Then why did Serenity say she was getting a new mom?"

The pair glanced at each other. Jasper spoke. "That's a bit more complicated."

His sister gave a knowing smile. "Ah, that kind of complicated. Well, that's your business, not mine. Though I am curious what she looks like."

"Daddy has a pick-chah of her!" Serenity beamed. "Right?"

"Well, we have a couple." Jasper whipped out his phone and pulled up the one Shira had posted to social media. He'd snagged that one since it was just her and Snake. He walked up the porch steps and showed the image to his sister.

Her eyes widened. "Wow. You really know how to pick 'em. She's gorgeous." Her eyes darted between the two. "And she's interested in the both of you?"

"Like we said, Sis, it's complicated."

She held up her hands. "Fine, fine. I won't pry anymore. And I shouldn't keep you. You both look worn out. I'm looking forwahd to having Serenity next weekend."

Serenity smiled widely some more. "I can't wait to come back! Daddy, can we have a fahm?"

Jasper laughed. "No, Pumpkin. We don't have time for a fahm."

She kicked the ground. "Aw man."

"It just means you can come visit your aunt and uncle instead," Zach said.

This restored Serenity's spirits.

Cheryl handed Zach Serenity's jacket and gave the two a hug good bye. "I'd have Ray come out, but he's doing a run to the packie for his beer."

Jasper waved her off. "We'll catch him next time. Have a good night, Sis."

Cheryl waved and went back into the house, calling Buddy so he wouldn't be in the way. Serenity said her goodbye to Buddy and ran to the car. Jasper and Zach followed. Serenity insisted on getting settled in her booster all on her own.

"I'm a big girl now. I can do it on my own," she'd continue to say. It bothered Jasper a bit how quickly she was growing up.

Serenity cheered in triumph when she managed to get herself buckled. Jasper kissed her on the forehead and praised her, as did Zach. They then hopped in the car and it began to move along the long dirt driveway.

"Daddy, did you tell She-ra about the win?" Serenity asked.

He turned to look at her. "We did. She told us she didn't doubt for a second."

"What did she do today?"

Zach and he passed a look and Zach chose to take over. "Well, she worked on some of her fears."

Serenity cheered. "That makes me wicked happy! When is the co-vention? I want to see her."

Jasper chuckled. "Not for anothah couple weeks, right before your birthday, remember? That's your birthday present."

Serenity let out a deep sigh. "I know. But I really want to see her in person."

"Don't worry, Starship," Zach said. "The time will come before you know it."

She looked out the window. "Daddy, is there anything I can do to help She-ra?"

Jasper scratched his chin, now rough with late-evening stubble. "I'm sure we can think of something."

"Okay. Are we gonna pick out my Halloween costume now?"

Zach laughed. "I knew she wouldn't forget that promise."

Jasper shook his head. "Of course she didn't. Yes, honey, we're gonna see if there are any costumes you like."

Serenity cheered again and then gasped. "Daddy! Break Benji is on the playlist! Turn up! Turn up!"

Jasper chuckled. "Breaking Benjamin."

"Yeah, that."

She still couldn't get the band right, but at least she enjoyed the music. He couldn't bear the thought of her falling in love with terrible music, like pop. He turned up the music and the three of them rocked out in the car.

CHAPTER 5

Cars roared past the sidewalk of the busy road and people pushed their way down the street, all in a hurry to get seemingly nowhere. Shira and Mercedes stood by their favorite sweets shop, *Those Buns Dough*, trying to get Shira's feet to move.

All week, they'd worked on getting her used to driving by the bigger buildings without freaking out. She'd progressed well enough that her therapist, whom Shira had started seeing again, decided she was ready to take the next step. Shira was excited about the progress, and eager to try this new step—until she got here.

She and Mercedes visited this shop all the time, but had never driven beyond. Now she was going to have to take a few more steps and turn the corner to face her fears, and she couldn't do it.

"Shira, you got this," Mercedes said. "You've been doing so well all this week. I know you can do this. Just one foot in front of the other, like everything else in life."

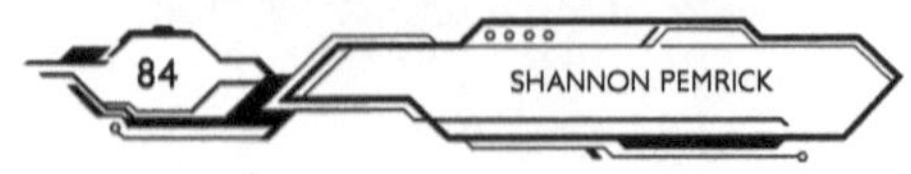

Shira clutched Snake's leash so tightly, her knuckles had turned white. "I know… I just…"

Mercedes smiled. "Take the time you need. I believe in you."

Shira nodded and took a breath to calm herself. It was staggered and shallow, so she sucked in another one, this time forcing more air into her lungs. Her body fought her the whole way. It didn't want to calm.

Mercedes' hand wrapped around Shira's free one. "Would it help to talk to Jasper and Zach?"

Shira's eyes widened. "No!"

The two of them had gotten a late start today. By now, Jasper and Zach would either be done with their second qualifier tournament, or nearly so. And the last thing she needed was for them to see her like this.

Mercedes' eyes softened. "They're not going to judge you."

She knew that. The two of them had been so good to her this past week. She'd been afraid they would start treating her differently, either by finally seeing her as the broken mess she was, or by putting distance between them so they wouldn't have to deal with her shit. But they hadn't done either. It was a too-good-to-be-true situation. And it made for some tense conversations with her therapist.

Mercedes' brow furrowed as she thought. "Can I get at least two steps forward from you? Just an attempt? They don't even have to be big ones."

What does she think I'm trying to do? Shira took a deep breath to calm her emotions. Mercedes was only trying to help. She wasn't even being pushy about it, and it'd be so easy for her friend to fall into that. *Not like I don't deserve some impatient behavior at this point. I'm so pathetic.*

Mercedes took Shira's hand in hers. She didn't say anything, but the contact helped Shira. Her friend's calm aura helped in a similar way to Snake, and he was already doing as much as he could for her as he leaned against her and licked her hand on occasion. She felt bad for putting him through this. His whole job was to help her avoid this kind of state as much as possible.

Shira sucked in a tight breath. *Two steps for him, then.* It may have seemed silly, but Snake was everything to her. The moment her dad picked him out and had him trained just for her, they'd been inseparable. He'd changed her life, and gave her a reason to live, even if she were only living half a life for now. *But I could live a full one, if I face this.*

Shira took one shaky step forward. Nothing bad happened, so she took another. Snake moved with her, keeping close as her source of security.

Mercedes leaned in close. "What got you to move?"

Shira's face heated. "It's going to sound stupid, but thinking of Snake and how much trouble I'm causing my favorite boy."

A sweet smile spread over her friend's face. "That's not stupid at all. Seriously, I love that reason."

"Yeah, too bad it's not helping me move another step, though."

Mercedes pursed her lips. "What if I told you the guys were just around the corner?"

Shira's heels dug into the ground. "I'd run the fuck away."

Mercedes laughed. "Okay, bad idea. Let's see… how about Serenity?"

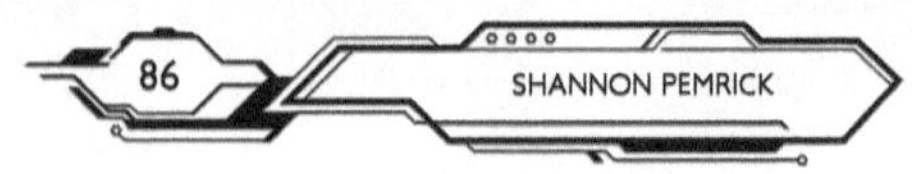

Shira's eyes narrowed and her face scrunched. "Why must you always do that?"

Her friend grinned deviously. "Because as your friend, I'm obligated to irritate you once in a while." Her eyes drifted down to the ground. "And the moment I said her name, you took a step forward."

I... I did? Shira looked down at the ground, though she wasn't able to see the progress she'd made subconsciously, she didn't believe Mercedes would lie to her.

"So," Mercedes said slowly, pulling Shira's gaze again. "What makes you run in fear of the guys and move forward for Serenity?"

Shira chewed her lower lip. That was a good question, and a loaded one at that. Shira almost grunted. No, she knew the answer, she just didn't want to verbalize it.

Mercedes tilted her head. "Are you afraid of them?"

Shira jerked her head back, her brow creased. "Why would I be afraid of them?"

"I'm not sure, that's why I'm inquiring. You always seem to run from the things you fear, so if you're running from them..." Mercedes shrugged and didn't finish the sentence. She didn't need to.

Shira worked her jaw. "I'm not... afraid of them. I just don't... want them to see me like this." Shira swallowed hard, the truth bittersweet on her tongue. "I don't want anyone seeing me in this pathetic state. Honestly, not even you."

"It's not—"

"It is, Cede. It is."

Mercedes was quiet for a moment. "And what about Serenity? What makes her different?"

"She sees me as fearless," Shira barely spoke above a

whisper that time. It pained her to say such words. "She doesn't think anything could break me—could stop me, like I'm some unstoppable force worth idolizing. And I guess… even though I told her I was afraid of things, the idea of breaking that perception in front of her… That hurts worse than my fears themselves."

Mercedes smiled. "She's a lucky little girl to have you."

Shira gave her friend a long look down her nose. "Don't start."

Mercedes shrugged and looked around. "I don't think you have room to talk, since talking about this special family got you to walk."

I what? Shira risked looking around, to find they'd made it to the corner. Her body threatened to lock up, but Shira's numbness prevented her from processing too much of the world around her.

"You may say there's nothing special going on with that family and you"—Mercedes winked—"but results don't lie. And as one of your best friends, I see through you."

Shira was at a loss for words. Was it really because of them she could do this? Or was it just a convenient topic Mercedes used to distract her and use to her advantage?

Mercedes nudged her. "Now, try to do this on your own. Time for the big test."

Shira swallowed hard. She meant Shira would have to actually look at the tall buildings, and walk in front of them. Her breathing became shallower and her heart slammed into her chest. Snake whined and pressed against her, licking her death-gripped hands.

Mercedes squeezed her hand. "It's going to be okay, Shira. I promise."

Was it? Shira's eyes slowly ticked up to the towering

buildings above. Her hands shook and it took everything in her not to bolt.

"Shira, remember, you're outside. You're just going to walk past them. I know you can do that."

Shira swallowed and put every ounce of will she could into taking one step onto the new street sidewalk. *I can do this. I can do this.*

Another step. And then another. Shira's heart hammered in her ears and a suffocating tightness constricted her chest, and yet she kept pushing. Mercedes mumbled encouragement, pushing her farther and father, one step at a time. And then, the backslide.

Panic overwhelmed her, the thought of one of these building collapsing down right on top of her flooding her mind. Shira retreated several steps. "I can't."

Mercedes latched onto her and refused to let her go any further. "Yes, you can. Don't let yourself run from this any more. Think about everything you've missed because you didn't tackle this sooner. Think about what you could be doing once you fight this demon back." Her friend's eyes softened. "I'm sorry if that sounds too close to a guilt trip. I don't want to pull that, really. But I am running low on ways to get you to make progress."

I'm being a bother to her... Every single day, Mercedes had offered to help in whatever way she could. She didn't miss a beat—she didn't complain. And how was she repaying her friend? By failing at the one thing she was supposed to be doing. By not making—*No, that's not right.* Shira was making progress. Mercedes wouldn't be so patient with her if she wasn't at least making some.

Shira took one shaky step forward, and then another. Three more. Four more. And then, no more. She remained planted, unable to force the fear away as one of the taller buildings on the street loomed over her. "I… can't go any further."

"Yes, you can."

I can't… I'm not strong enough right now.

Mercedes worked her jaw and then whipped out her phone. Shira's heart raced in a different way now. "Please don't tell me you're calling the guys."

Shira's phone went off. Her brow twisted and Mercedes smirked. "Nope, they're calling you."

Shira pulled her phone from her back pocket. Jasper's name came up on the screen. Then, the call ended. Mercedes narrowed her eyes, though they didn't remain that way for long when the call came in again, Zach's name now appearing. *Great. They're going to tag team until I pick up for one of them.*

She took a deep breath and answered. "Hey."

"Damn, she did pick up for you," Jasper complained.

Zach snickered. "Told you."

"It's not like I'm playing favorites," Shira muttered.

"Nah, Jasper thought he'd get another chance to call before you decided to finally pick up," Zach said. "Oh, and you need to accept the video feed request."

Her nose scrunched. She really hoped they'd not push it that far. Mercedes, of course, was having none of this reluctance and accepted the request on her behalf. "Cede!"

Jasper smiled. "Bettah. Thanks, Mercedes."

Mercedes winked. "Of course."

Shira looked at the two men and she had to remind herself to breathe. They were far too tempting for her liking. Something everyone was all too good at reminding her about. "Well, here we are. I'm doing my"—she paused when she noticed their gaming station behind them—"Are you guys home?"

Zach nodded. "We've been home for about an hour."

She pursed her lips. "Where's Serenity?"

"At my sistah's," Jasper said. "When you told us your plan for today, we thought we'd prepare to be on standby just in case you needed extra help, so I worked it out with my sistah to have Serenity for a few extra hours."

Mercedes rested her head on Shira's shoulder and wrapped her arm around Shira. "You guys are so sweet to my bestie. Aren't they, Shira?"

Shira's eyes narrowed at her friend. "Don't start."

The boys found amusement in the exchange. Shira also found herself relaxing a bit more.

"So, Shira, tell us what's up," Zach said.

"Okay…" Shira scratched her neck. Not like she could back out of this now. Well, she could, but that wouldn't be good for her. *Just suck it up and tell them…* "I'm on a street with a lot of buildings I don't like, and I just want to run. Mercedes bribed me with chocolate earlier if I do well, and right now I feel like running for the hills is a way better treat."

They exchanged a look. "No."

Mercedes laughed while Shira sighed. "That's real helpful, guys."

"We kicked ass at the second qualifier," Jasper said.

Her brow rose. That was so random. But at this rate, she'd take it. "Easy time like the last one?"

He nodded. "Yeah. I don't know if it's just wicked bad luck we're getting paired up like this, or if the teams are just a bunch of noobs looking to get their foot in the door way before they're ready."

Shira tilted her head. "Sounds like *good* luck to me. Seats you better for the final two rounds."

Jasper rubbed the back of his neck. "Yeah, I guess. I just wanted a challenge."

Zach nudged him and watched Shira. "I told him he should just be thankful, and if it's this easy all the way into the main event, then it just means we have a better shot at the loaded prize pool."

Shira thought about the prize they were after. She knew as a twos team, the pool was much smaller than that of a full fives team. "How much is the prize this year?"

"Well it was only going to be three million for first place, with a nine-hundred thousand for runners-up, and one-hundred thousand for third place, but as of two days ago, they announced they bumped it up to six and a half million for first place," Zach said. "And of course second and third place got a boost, too. It's the biggest pool yet I've seen for twos."

Shira's eyes widened. That was a huge prize pool for their team size. She didn't know a lot about the cost of living in Boston, but it wasn't as expensive to live there as it was in Los Angeles and San Francisco. If they won that kind of money, that could set them up nice for a couple months. "I didn't realize you could make that kind of money with your team setup. I still don't know why you don't get a fives team going. That would set you guys even better."

Jasper rubbed the back of his neck. "That's because of me. We've tried going that route, but I struggled to

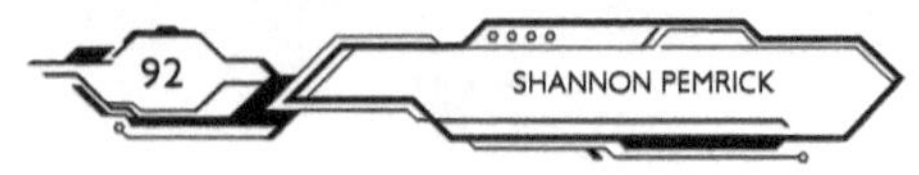

work well with players in that bracket. They're all so pretentious."

"We also tried to make our own team, but we couldn't snag anyone with skill," Zach said. "We wouldn't even get you to agree."

Shira's eyes darted to the side. "It's not because I didn't want to pair up with you or anything. I just don't want to play professionally."

He ran his hand through his hair. "Yeah, we know. But that's the reason. So, we have to go for smaller prize pools, do extra tournaments, and deal with the revolving door of sponsors."

She knew all too well of their hardships. They didn't talk about it a lot, but on occasions it'd come up or she'd catch them talking about money situations while they were waiting for her to join them for matches. Professional gaming had its perks, when the going was good. But there were uncertain times, too, and them being tied to the company they were with didn't help. While they were the biggest out there, their reputation wasn't doing so great, and Shira knew the two would really like to break it off onto their own if they could. But they'd need to somehow snap a permanent sponsor for that. And that wasn't even easy for a full team.

"Oh, how did the costume shopping for Serenity go?" Shira asked. They'd told her other day they'd been to two stores and hadn't found anything and were going to try again last night.

Zach hung his head. "Not good. Serenity is being unusually picky. I think she's trying to avoid having a costume that everyone else will have, and this year, the pickings for girls isn't great."

Shira rubbed her chin. "Do you know anyone who could make her a costume?"

"My mom could," Jasper said. "But Serenity won't tell us what she wants to be. I'm not even sure she knows, even if she's excited for the event."

Mercedes chuckled. "She just wants free candy."

Zach laughed. "What kid doesn't?"

Shira smiled at the two men. "I'm sure you'll figure something out. Maybe third time is the charm?"

"I hope so. I'm gonna get sick of looking at this rate."

Zach laughed. "You got sick of it the first day."

Jasper nudged him. "Like you're much better."

"At least I don't grumble and complain like I'm seven."

"I do not!"

The two went back and forth, prompting Shira to laugh. It helped relieve some tension in her shoulders.

Jasper grinned. "There we go. I'm glad we could keep you calm while you and Mercedes walked down that street."

"We what?" Shira looked around to find they were now halfway down the street and standing in front of a hotel building. Not once did her paranoia snap at her mind and tell her they'd moved. How did they move?

Mercedes grinned. "I took the liberty of guiding you while you were distracted. You're welcome."

Shira stared at her friend, and then at her phone to the two men grinning madly.

"What are friends for, yeah?"

Her gut twisted a bit. Tanya had said that to her, too. The day of the accident, when Shira was struggling with something stupid, her friend was there regardless. And having her friends here with her now, helping her, even

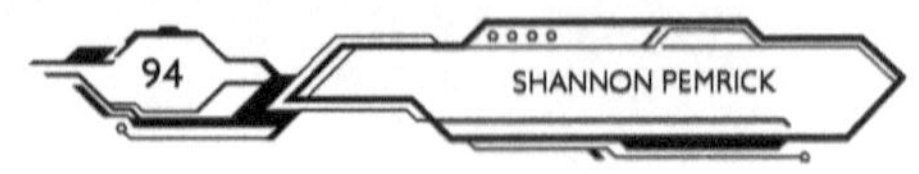

if she was a pathetic mess… it made her miss Tanya again, but also appreciate her friends that much more.

Shira smiled. "Thanks, guys."

"You got this," Zach said. "We know you can."

As she stood there, now aware, her paranoia and fear kicked in, but she was able to fight it back a bit better now. If she could be here while distracted, then she could be here with an aware mind.

"I should let you get going. I'm sure Serenity is excited to go shopping again with you two."

Jasper scratched his head. "I hope we can find her something."

Mercedes chuckled. "Given her age, her indecision isn't surprising. And it's only going to get worse from here."

He groaned. "Don't say that. I don't want this to get any worse."

Shira and Mercedes glanced at each other. He was in for a rude awaking as she got to the pre-teen stage. Jasper didn't miss the exchange and swallowed hard. "I don't like those looks."

Shira smiled widely and waved. "You're going to love the teen years. Bye!"

She ended the call before he could react. As much as she'd enjoy watching him panic a bit, leaving him hanging like that was far more fun.

Mercedes placed a hand on her shoulder. "You did really well. Think you can go the rest of the way without your boyfriends distracting you?"

Shira rolled her eyes. "I don't know, but I'm going to have to give it a shot, because I can't stand here all day."

Mercedes snickered, murmuring about how Shira didn't correct her when she used the term "boyfriends."

Heat rose to Shira's face. She hadn't even noticed her friend had used the word. But before Shira could bite back a retort, Mercedes refocused and helped encourage Shira's feet to move again.

Zach sat back in his seat, watching the amusing conflict flickering over Jasper's face. Shira really knew how to mess with his fatherly instincts. *Not that that tempting body of hers doesn't trigger particular instincts in us both, in another way.* And quite frankly, it confused the hell out him. No woman had tempted him like she could, and this increased video contact with her was only intensifying things.

Jasper shook his head. "She was just trying to psyche me out, right?"

Zach shrugged. "They do say girls are harder to raise in the later years."

The fear returned and Zach couldn't stop himself from laughing. Shira wasn't the only one who enjoyed tugging his chain. Zach loved Serenity like his own daughter. He'd helped Jasper raise her since she was a year old; he'd do anything to keep her happy and safe. But he didn't get as crazy as Jasper. His parenting instinct was a little too much sometimes.

Jasper ran both hands through his hair. "Okay, I need to think of something else, or I'm gonna get wicked mad and ground her for life for no reason."

Zach leaned back as he laughed. This was too great. "Would talking about Shira help?"

Jasper gave him a confused looked. "About what just went down?"

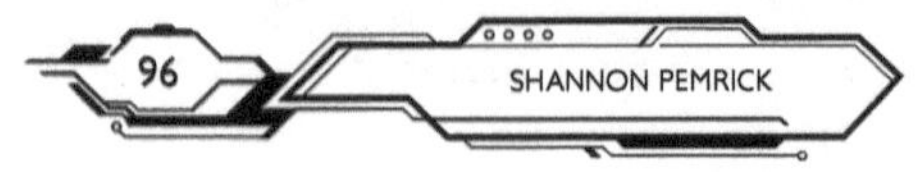

Zach rocked his head. "Sorta. I'm thinking along the lines of getting more involved."

"Shira hasn't given us the okay to help like that."

Zach's brow spiked. "She did, though, by picking up that phone call and staying on. And I'm not saying we should plot something devious or anything. Come up with something to propose to her and let her give us consent."

Jasper opened his mouth and then closed it to think this over. "Fair. So, whatcha have in mind?"

Zach drummed his fingers on the table, not able to meet Jasper's eyes. He'd been thinking about this since the night Shira opened up to them. They needed to get a feel how this was going to work for the three of them. And all subsequent interactions with her had only intensified this realization. "We want to help her, as friends do. But we also can't lie to ourselves that there's an ulterior motive behind our help right now."

Jasper regarded him and then leaned back in his chair. "You want to test the boundaries?"

Zach nodded. "We can't expect to jump right into convincing her at the convention. We need to ease into this."

Jasper's inner thirteen-year-old snickered. "You mean into her."

He shrugged. "And us."

Jasper's eyes flashed, but for now he behaved. "So we come up with ways for us to convince her to drop this 'no guildmates' rule and show her what it's like to be with us. Simple on papah."

Zach nodded. "On paper, yeah. We know she can be sexually adventurous—"

Jasper's eyes cut away and he grumbled to himself. Zach understood. As their interest in Shira had grown, seeing her hook up with others in VR irritated them, though Zach worried it irritated Jasper more. Zach struggled with all this, understanding his own feelings toward Shira, and knowing where he and Jasper still stood as couple, with or without her.

"—but I don't think us going for her at the same time will be a good approach this time," he concluded.

Jasper's brow rose. "Why not?"

He pressed his lips together as he figured out how to word this. "I think going at this full force will push her away. But if we take it slower, pursue her at least once individually, we may be able to curb the reaction and convince her to give us a shot."

Jasper leaned on his knees and scratched his chin. Zach's eyes followed the movement, desire pricking in him. He had a weakness for the shape of Jasper's face. *Come to think of it, Shira's face is hard not to stare at, too.* Well, everyone had something that drove them crazy.

"Are you sure doing this separately is a good idea? I'm concerned she'd be less trusting."

Shit, he has a point. There went that idea…

"But maybe not," Jasper said.

Zach gave his boyfriend a long, exasperated look. "Can you make up your mind? And explain?"

Jasper shrugged. "Shira is an unpredictable woman. Sometimes makes it hard to know the right way to handle her."

Zach shifted in his spot, his focus temporarily leaving Jasper. "I know how you'd like to handle her."

A devilishly tempting smile slipped up Jasper's face. "Don't act like your thoughts are any more innocent."

Were they? Zach had a few thoughts here and there, but Jasper… he'd told Zach a few things he'd like to do with Shira, while Zach watched. And those were far hotter.

"Let's do it your way," Jasper said. "You're usually right about these things."

Zach gave a smug smile. "Of course I am. I'm the brains of the two of us."

Jasper tossed a pen at him. "So, you wanna try first, or should I?"

Zach shook his head. "You first. I think we both know it'd be better if I didn't screw this up immediately."

Jasper's eyes softened. "You wouldn't fuck it up." They glinted, in an alluring way, another smirk slipping up his face. *God, help me through this talk.* "Be open with her and she'll work with you. We know she's the accepting type. That's what'll help us convince her to see we both want her part of this relationship. Whatevah it ends up becoming when she's here."

Whatever it ends up becoming. That sat deep with Zach. He really wasn't sure what their relationship would look like in the end, and that was what unsettled him the most. Would he lose his time with Jasper, and they'd only spend time with all three of them present? Would he lose Jasper altogether? That one thought made him pause for a moment.

It was a fear of his. Jasper hadn't been interested in men his entire life. Really, he wasn't now, except for Zach, and only because of how they bonded after Sara's death. He'd all but given up the hope Jasper that would want him when he met Sara. *It's why I had to move away…*

Jasper tilted his head. "Hey, you okay?"

Zach snapped out of his thought. "Yeah, of course I am."

Jasper wasn't convinced, based on the look he gave. "Zach, if you don't want to do this, we won't. I'm not gonna do anything to jeopardize us."

Zach shook his head. "We've been over this. I'm sure this is what I want, too."

He knew he shouldn't lie. He should be honest with Jasper about his reservations. But because there was a part of him that did want to see where this would go, how it could potentially blossom into something deep and meaningful, he didn't want Jasper to jump the gun and stop things now. Jasper had a habit of overreacting.

"You go after her first. Then I will and then we'll talk about it."

Jasper shrugged. "Okay. We got a plan. Now how to convince her…"

That was a good question. They'd have to get creative.

"You think there are some quests that would help us get her to fight her feah of heights?" Jasper asked.

Zach tapped his finger some more. "I don't doubt it. We'll have to do some searching."

Jasper slapped his hands down on his thighs and then stood up. "Great, we have a plan. Now, for a change of pace because I'm losing focus."

Jasper closed the gap between them and threaded his hand into Zach's hair. Without having a chance to react, Jasper crashed his lips into Zach's. Zach sucked in a deep breath and kissed his partner back. He lifted himself out of his chair, his hands twisting firmly into Jasper's shirt. Jasper angled him to sit on the table, and he was okay with that. He was very okay with these turns of events.

And then Jasper's phone went off. Jasper let out a frustrated hiss. "Every time."

Irritated as he may be, Zach handled it better. Being a parent meant regular interruptions at the worst possible times. "Is that ringtone Stardew Valley?"

Jasper retrieved his phone. "Yeah. I was looking for a new ringtone for Cheryl when I stumbled upon it. Figured it was puhfect for her."

Zach agreed. Even though Cheryl wasn't much for videogames, or anything remotely nerdy, the theme of the game worked well with her line of work.

"I guess Serenity is chomping at the bit to go costume shopping," Jasper said.

"Fingers crossed we find something this time."

Jasper agreed. Zach laced his fingers in with Jasper's as they left the house. Jasper smiled and leaned in for a chaste kiss. It brought a deep smile onto Zach's face. Whatever happened in these next few weeks with Shira, he wasn't going to lose this. He was determined to make sure this stayed strong. *Shira joining and fitting in nicely, like the perfect missing puzzle piece, would make this better, though.* He just hoped their plan would work out like they wanted.

CHAPTER 6

The green BMW M8 Gran Coupe honked when Shira locked it, and she walked up the front walk leading to her house. Today's meeting with Doctor Angelica had gone rather well, though the two of them ended up talking about her relationship with Jasper and Zach more than Shira wanted to. In her opinion, that was the least of her concerns, but her therapist didn't think so. Shira was also certain she might have to watch out for her trying to push any potential relationship with the two men. *No, Shira, stop. Angelica wouldn't do that.* At least, not in the way her paranoid mind thought it would happen.

Angelica was one-hundred percent non-judgmental about a person's preferences. It was part of what made her a great therapist—and would be Shira's undoing if she started to worm her way in and break all of Shira's resolve to keep these two men at arm's length. She just wanted to follow her own rules; they were there to keep her safe. She couldn't risk breaking them.

But that's part of Angelica's job, isn't it? Help me break down walls. Shira blocked the thoughts out. She didn't want to risk calling Angelica up and canceling all her sessions because she was overthinking.

Shira came up to the decorative glass front door and noticed the package lying in front of it. She tilted her head. *That's odd. I didn't order anything recently.* She bent over and lifted it up, finding some difficult-to-read handwriting scribbled all over it. Luckily there was some neater writing beside it to help translate who it had come from.

Jasper and Serenity Quinn
Zach Miller

A smile came to her face. It wasn't a heavy box, nor was it large. When she shook it, very little movement came from inside. "What do you think these knuckleheads sent me, Snake?"

He tilted his head in response.

"Maybe it's empty," Orion suggested from her phone. "Just a box of packing."

Shira's head flew back as she laughed. "I wouldn't put it past them."

She pulled her mail out of the mailbox and then swiped her door key in front of the lock. Shira kicked off her shoes haphazardly upon entering the house and tossed her key deck onto a small table next to the door. She shrugged off her light jacket and dropped it on the floor, deciding she could pick it up later.

Snake waited to be released from his vest, and the

moment he was, he took off into the house. Shira chuckled and carried her package into the living room.

She shook it again once she'd seated herself on the couch, but she heard nothing moving around. Shrugging, she tore into box. Her eyes were met with old crumpled newspaper comics. Her brow ticked up. Those weren't easy to come by these days. Why would they be so rough and careless with something so rare?

Shira reached in and uncrumpled one, to find it wasn't real newspaper. *Ah, well that makes more sense.* She sifted through the unusual packing until she came upon a stuffed creature. Pulling it out, it was an interesting-looking green wyvern of sorts. There was a note attached to the leg, with similar writing as on the box. She was curious which one of the two men had such neat handwriting. It was leagues better than her own.

> *She-ra!*
> *This is Rathian. She's one of my favorite stuffies. She'll help you when you're scared.*
>
> *Love,*
> *Serenity*

Shira's heart swelled. What a sweet little girl Serenity was. *I have to call her.*

Not thinking, she grabbed her tablet and initiated a video chat with Jasper's contact. Her fingers tapped the side of the device as the call rang. *Pick up! I know you two aren't playing games at this time of day.*

On the last ring, the other line answered, Jasper's

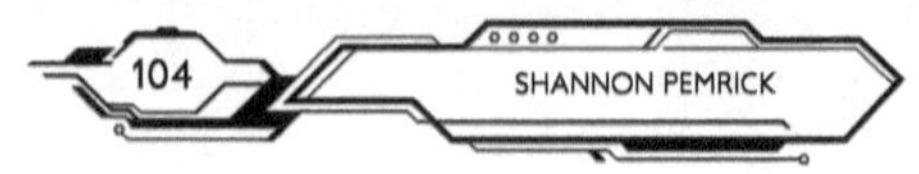

handsome face appearing on the other end. She stalled for a minute. "Uh… I didn't realize I did video chat."

He chuckled. "Well, I'm not complaining, that's for sure. S'up?"

"Serenity is out of school now, right?"

He nodded. "Yeah. We got her from her after school program a little bit ago. Why?"

Shira held up the toy. "Please get her for me."

A wide grin appeared on his face before he looked away from the screen. "Serenity, come out here please."

"Okay, Daddy, one sec," she replied.

While they waited, Zach appeared in the feed. "Oh, hey, Shira."

She waved. "Hey."

A tiny voice gasped. "She-ra is on the horn?"

Serenity's tiny feet scampered across the floor. Sounded like they had old hardwood based on the creaking. Small hands reached into the feed. "She-ra! I'm here!"

The three adults laughed and then Jasper got her to sit on the couch. Her big green eyes peered back at Shira. "Hi!"

Shira's smile practically reached her ears. "Hi, Starship. I wanted to thank you for the package." She held up the toy. "I love it."

Serenity squealed. "You got her!" Then for some reason, she slipped off the couch and ran off. Shira went to ask, but Jasper held up a finger.

Tiny feet stormed through the house until she returned. *It's like a herd of elephants!* Shira tried not to laugh at her slightly disheveled appearance. Serenity held up a red version of the wyvern she'd been given. "This is Rathalos! He's Rathian's mate. They're from a show

I watch called Monstah Huntah. It's awesome. Daddy says it's also a game, but I'm not old enough to play it yet. Rathalos and Rathian help me when I'm scared. So now they can help us both."

Shira hugged Rathian tight with one arm, her chest swelling. This girl was precious beyond words. "You're right. They will help us. Thank you for being so considerate to send her to me. I'll be sure nothing happens to her."

Snake jumped up on the couch and pawed Shira's arm, his eyes on the toy. She pushed him away. "No, not for you."

He whined and pawed her again.

Serenity giggled. "No, Snake, that's for She-ra." The little girl's eyes suddenly went wide. "He won't chew her, right?"

The expression sent a pang of pity through Shira. "Don't worry, Starship, he won't do that. Snake is a hoarder. He'd just steal her when I'm not looking and hoard her in his crate."

Serenity laughed. "He's a doggie dragon! He's silly."

Shira settled deeper into the couch. "So, who helped you write your letter, Serenity?"

She pointed to Jasper. "Daddy did. He's better at writing than me right now."

Shira chuckled. "Well, his handwriting is better than mine, too. I'm jealous."

Jasper leaned into the feed, a smirk on his lips. "I could give you some private lessons."

He would. She did her best not to make Serenity aware of the change to an adult tone. "Thanks, but I think I'm good right now."

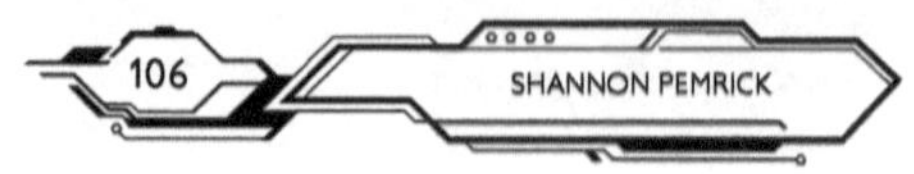

"You sure? It wouldn't be any trouble."

"Yeah, he's wicked good at teaching, She-ra!" Serenity jumped in.

"Starship, how is school going?" She needed to change this topic ASAP, before it got out of hand and she was forced into a corner. Jasper's lips twisted to the side, showing he wasn't pleased, but there wasn't anything he could do about it.

"School is fun," Serenity said. "I still like science. We made a volcano the othah day. And we have a new language class I love."

That was interesting. Shira knew the school system they'd put her into was a good one, they'd started her with Spanish in kindergarten, but she thought they'd wait a few more years before offering more languages. "What language are you learning now?"

"They're teaching us Cant-noise."

"Cantonese," Jasper corrected.

"Oh, yeah, that."

Shira giggled. "That's quite the language to learn, Starship. So you know Spanish, and soon Cantonese—"

"And I know French!" Serenity said.

Shira's eyes widened. That was a lot for someone her age not living in a bilingual home. "That's really impressive, Serenity."

"These classes are fun. I wanna learn more." Her nose scrunched. "But Teach says three is enough."

Shira shrugged. "Maybe for now because you're just starting a new one, but don't let anyone tell you to stop. If that's what you want to learn, then learn it."

This lifted Serenity's sprits. "How many languages do you know?"

"Well, I'm only fluent in English and German. But I know basic conversation in Spanish and American Sign Language."

Serenity's eyes sparkled. "Zach said he'd teach me Sign Language too! Would you teach me German?"

Shira smiled, her chest swelling. "I'd love to, Starship."

Serenity cheered. "You're the best, She-ra."

This made her smile wider. Serenity's happiness meant so much to Shira. "Halloween is coming up. Do you have your costume yet?"

Serenity frowned. "No. I haven't found somethin' I like."

Shira regarded the little girl for a moment. "It's because they don't have what you really want, right?"

Jasper and Zach gave her a confused look that only deepened when Serenity nodded. Apparently she still hadn't explained to them what the issue was, as Shira had speculated. "I want to be a monstah huntah. But they don't gots those types of costumes."

That explained a lot. She'd have to get a custom costume for that. And that made things difficult. Shira rubbed her chin. She wanted to help in some way. It'd also repay them for the thoughtful gift. *Oh, I wonder…*

She stood up and headed for the stairs leading to the second floor. Serenity cocked her head. "She-ra, where we going?"

Shira looked down at the device in her hand. "It's a surprise."

"Oh, okay." She turned her tablet a few times as if trying to re-angle Shira's feed. "Are we going upstairs?"

Shira nodded. "Yep. That's where my room is."

"Your house is wicked big! How many rooms does it got?"

"Five. Not too many, compared to the rest of my neighborhood." Shira tried to make sure this didn't get turned into a bigger deal than it was. Not easy when dealing with children.

"That's huge! Our apahtment is dinky. But Daddy and Zach are looking for a bettah place, right, Daddy?"

"Yeah, we are." His response came out half-hearted.

Shira stole a glance and could see he wasn't one-hundred percent present, as if he were thinking about something. She hoped it had nothing to do with her living situation. For their sake, she wanted to keep that topic off the radar as much as possible.

"Shira, I'm being nosey," Zach said. "Don't you live alone?"

She nodded and entered her bedroom. "Yeah, why do you ask?"

"I dunno, a five bedroom house just seems like a lot for one person to live in."

Fuck, this would come up. Tightness formed in her gut, but she couldn't just run from this. If her therapist found out, she'd be so dead. "I bought it before my accident, with a few things in mind for it. Obviously that was thrown out the window, and I never found it in me to be able to sell and move to something smaller. So, now I use one room for my VR game station and another as a work room. Remaining rooms are guest rooms, for a just-in-case that never happens."

He gave a look that screamed "pity," and she wished he would stop. It wasn't that bad.

Shira slipped into her walk-in closet and Serenity gasped. "She-ra, do you have a mall in your house?"

This took her slightly aback. That was the last thing

she expected out of the young girl's mouth. "Um… no?"

Jasper and Zach laughed at her. Serenity didn't understand. "Then where are we?"

"In my closet."

Her green eyes went wide. "That's your closet? It's the size of my room!"

Shira sucked in a calming breath. *Maybe this was a bad idea.* She didn't expect Serenity to get so excited over all this. She didn't want her version of a comfortable living to become a source of contention for Jasper and Zach. She knew this kind of house wasn't in their reach.

Shira rested the tablet on a shelf. "Hold tight while I try to find the impossible here."

She wandered off deeper into her closet to find the storage bin. She hoped she still had it. Her mother could have taken it, but that was less likely than Shira just deciding to get rid of it during a low point in her life. *Maybe I moved it to my work room? No…*

"She-ra, is that wicked pretty dress really yours?" Serenity asked.

Shira's rummaging halted and she went back to the tablet. "What dress?"

"The red one." Serenity pointed at a red, off-the-shoulder, sweetheart neckline bodycon dress with an asymmetrical hem displaying on a mannequin. *Oh, shit.* She'd been moving things around and hadn't realized she didn't store that away again. "Yep, that's mine."

"You should wear it!"

"Yeah, she's right, you should," Zach said.

Jasper nodded.

Shira noticed how closely he and Zach had leaned

in. Both looked too interested in the prospect. It sent her heart racing, and not in a way she expected. "Um, I need to finish finding this thing."

She made a hasty retreat, busying herself in her search. Shira unfortunately did find herself casting glances over to the dress. She'd never gotten the chance to wear it. It was supposed to be worn to a dinner date the night of her accident. *Jeremy didn't like red, but…* She shook her head free of all the thoughts. He didn't matter and neither did that dress. She needed to get rid of it.

A pile of clothes fell, startling her. She went to pick them up when she noticed the bin that'd fallen off. *There it is!* She pulled it out and opened it. Inside were various folded hand-made garments of clothing. She searched for one outfit in particular, and when she came to the vest with colorful pins and decorative ball cap, she smiled widely.

Shira pulled out the outfit and rushed back to the tablet. "Okay, I found it!"

Serenity cocked her head. "What did you find, She-ra?"

"It's not what you wanted, but it might do." Shira held up the hat, vest, and some fingerless gloves. "How about going as a Pokémon trainer?" She held up a belt with Pokéballs and a Pokédex attached. "I even have extra accessories to make it more authentic."

Serenity's eyes lit up. "She-ra, I love it! Yes!"

That brought a smile to Shira's face. She was so glad this worked. It was a simple outfit, but at least it fit with a similar nerdy theme.

Jasper leaned closer. "Is it gonna fit her?"

Shira looked at the clothes. "I think so. I made it with her age in mind."

Zach now leaned in. "Wait, you made those?"

She nodded and glanced back at the bin. "I used to help my mom make clothes years ago. When I started dabbling in different fandoms, I tried my hand at cosplay designs for different ages and genders. This one I was trying for ten years, but it came out a little smaller than I expected. My mom said it'd fit a seven or eight year old, and Serenity is a bit tall for her age, so that's why I think it'll fit her. You could send over her measurements to be sure, but it's just a vest and gloves. And the hat is adjustable. So, as long as you put her in jeans, a shirt, and some sneakers she already owns, you'll be good for most of the harder-fitting pieces."

The two looked at each other and then her. "Do you have anything we could wear with her? You know, like a family costume theme?"

"Uh…" She looked at the bin again. "Maybe? Let's check here."

She brought the tablet over with her and propped it up before rummaging. Nothing in there would be an exact trainer, as she knew she'd only made one outfit specific for children, but she may be able to do some mixing and matching. At the very least, she may have some more trainer belts and some gym badges.

The guys helped her pick out pieces they thought may work, and she matched them up. The only thing she wasn't sure about was how they'd fit. And she didn't have any more trainer gear.

"Balls," Jasper said. "It'll be hahd to pass anything off as a Pokémon trainah without at least Pokéballs."

"I can make more," Shira said. "That wouldn't be too difficult."

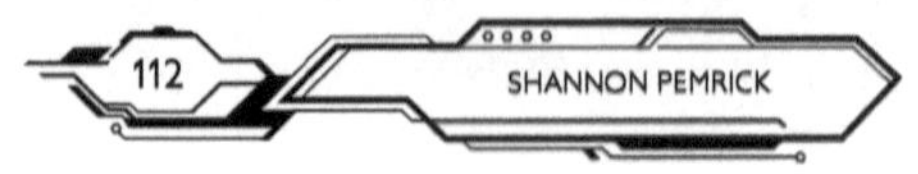

Zach's eyes widened. "Wait, you made the Pokéballs?"

She nodded. "They're made of colored resin from a mold I designed. Everything in this box is handmade. Even the hat."

The two stared at her. The way they did brought heat to her face. "Why are you staring?"

"You're amazing," Zach said.

Her eyes darted away. "It's nothing special. People make clothes all the time. And these aren't anything crazy, like some armor sets I've made."

Jasper tilted his head forward. "You've made cosplay armor?"

Balls. She didn't mean to let that slip. Making armor was a bit of a secret hobby of her. At one point, she'd thought about a LARP and cosplay line within her family's company, but that idea died a long time ago. *With the rest of my dreams…*

"Yeah, but that stuff hasn't been anything special." She shook her head. "Enough about that. I need your measurements to make sure these costume pieces will fit."

"Shira, I've transmitted the measurement instructions to them," Orion said from the house infrastructure.

"Got it," Zach said, looking at his phone. "We'll do this right now."

"In the meantime, you gotta slip on that dress," Jasper said.

The feeling from before returned, bringing a blush to her face. "Why are you so obsessed with that stupid dress?"

He smirked. "Because we wanna see how hot ya look in it. We've never seen you in a dress."

"They're just dresses."

Zach chuckled. "Then it shouldn't be an issue for you to put this one on."

Some of what Angelica told her earlier today came back—about taking chances, even if it'd turn out horribly wrong, so that she could learn how to cope with the bad. Not every bad experience was life-threatening. "Alright, fine. But you to have to give me puppy-dog faces."

The two were all too happy to oblige. The result had her falling over in her laughter. When she'd gotten herself under control, she found them trying to peer through the screen even harder, as if it were some window they could poke their heads through to make sure she was okay.

"Shira?" Zach asked.

"Yeah, I'm fine." She sat up and ran her fingers through her hair, smiling, though unable to meet their gazes. "I needed that, thanks."

Jasper smirked. "Good, now go put on that dress."

She scoffed and then got to her feet, turning the tablet so it'd face the door of the closest where Snake now lay, protecting her from invisible intruders.

"Aww, no show?" Jasper said.

Her face heated. "You have a kid in the room."

"Ah, shit. Serenity, you didn't hear that."

"I'm wicked confused, Daddy," she said.

"How about I get you an ice pop," Zach said.

Serenity cheered and Shira heard her run off. Shira took the dress off the mannequin and she slipped behind the tablet so they couldn't watch her strip down. Jasper's question a moment ago surfaced to her mind as she peeled her pants off. The idea made her pulse quicken, and then she banished it. *No.*

Once she had the dress on—a bit surprised it still fit her, if not better than when she first bought it—she looked herself over in the three-panel full-length mirror tucked in the corner. The dress fit every curve of hers perfectly, and accentuated her chest.

Shira fussed with her hair and double-checked to make sure her real leg didn't look like she'd gotten lazy with her shaving. She then paused. *Why the hell am I fussing?* It wasn't like she was getting dolled up for them. *Though, if I'm honest, the idea isn't unappealing.*

She stepped away from the mirror, only for a pair of strappy black stilettos to catch her eye. *The dress was designed to show off the legs... Oh hell, why not?*

She slipped the heels on and then looked herself over again, smoothing out the dress. *Okay, I look good.* Even with her distracting cybernetics, she could still pull this off. *And I'm able to admit it to myself this time.* That was a nice feeling. But the real test would come when Jasper and Zach reacted.

Technically, it didn't matter what they thought, but a negative response would not help her.

"Hey, Shira, ya done yet?" Jasper asked. It sounded as if he was eating something now. *Probably one of those ice pops they were talking about.* "We've already finished those measurements."

Did I really take that long? It wouldn't surprise her. She didn't dress at light speed anymore, like she'd learned to during her modeling career. "Perfection takes time."

"How do you make something already perfect more so?" Zach asked.

She almost tripped. Did he really mean that? Shira shook it out of her mind. Right now wasn't the time to ponder. She lifted the tablet, still facing away from her, and found a good place to prop it up high so they'd get a better view. She then turned it around and took a step back. "Alright, here it is."

Both men's jaws went slack and their eyes widened as they gazed at her. Zach almost dropped his treat, and Jasper actually did. Serenity picked it up and gave it back to him, waving her hand in front of his face. He didn't blink.

"She-ra, I think you broke him," Serenity said, looking at her.

Shira pressed her lips together to help stifle her laugh. It really did look that way. She did a slow turn to show off the look a bit more. "So, boys, what do you think?"

"You're fucking hot," Jasper blurted out.

That took her aback. It didn't last long when Serenity pointed at him. "Daddy said the f-word."

Shira lightly touched her lips with her fingers, a playful grin spread across them. "Don't worry, Starship. I'll punish him later."

Jasper swallowed, the green in his eyes deepening. *Oh, so predictable.*

Zach leaned in, purposely placing a hand on Jasper's shoulder. The action seemed to bring Jasper back to his senses. "Shira, has anyone ever told you red is definitely your color? You need to wear it more."

Everything in her stopped. *Jeremy hated this color on me.* And he was never shy about sharing that fact. She liked the color, and used to wear it all the time until him. But, he also complained about her hair color, always trying to convince her to dye it to something else, or go natural again.

Shira reached up and twirled a lock of hair, her eyes going to the side and heat rising in her face. She felt hot all over. "Thank you…"

Normally when she got like this, she'd roll and pop up on the balls of her feet, but the heeled shoes stopped her from doing that. She hated the quirks, but it was better than her previous nail-biting habit. And at least these particular quirks could be considered cute.

A buzzer went off on their end. Zach ran off. "Pizza guy is here."

Serenity cheered and ran after him, offering to help carry things. Their family interactions made Shira smile. *They're really lucky.*

Jasper pulled the tablet closer and lowered his voice. "Hey, come here."

Her brow twisted, but she complied. "What?"

"Are you feeling up to playing Lusara aftah we eat?" He smiled. "I came up with an idea to help you fight your feahs in a safe virtual environment."

A way to fight it in game? She hadn't thought of that yet. She'd go out of her way to avoid things even in game, like flying, or taking quests that would risk her getting too close to said fears.

"I know you had therapy today, so if you're not up for it, I undahstand."

They'd found out the other day about her getting professional help again when she wasn't up for PvP. They surprised her with their support of the choice. Then it came out that Jasper had also sought out help when he lost Sara, and Zach grumbled about him benefiting if he were to start going again. She wasn't sure why, and Jasper shut that conversation down pretty quickly. Shira encouraged him to go again if he really did need it. If Sara's loss still affected him, it'd be good for him to fix that. It wasn't good for them to hold all the pain and fear in.

Shira shook her head. "No, today wasn't as hard. Just annoying topics she wouldn't leave alone."

His brow rose. "Wanna talk about it with me?"

She shook her head again, this time harder. "Nope, I'm good."

There was no way she'd let either of them know they came up in these therapy talks in the manner they did. That'd get awkward real fast.

He tilted his head, confused, but didn't push. "Okay, then, if you're sure. So, how about that play offah?"

"What about Serenity?" They didn't usually play the game while she was still up.

"It'll just be you and me," he said. "Zach is spending quality time with the baby."

"I'm not a baby, Daddy!" Serenity yelled out.

"You are to me," he mumbled.

Shira giggled. "It sounds like a great plan."

"Sick." His whole face lit up. "Oh, and that dress? Pack it for the convention."

She pursed her lips. "Why?"

"Because we're going to take you out after, and you should weah something nice. Like that dress."

She didn't like where this was going. "Jasper, don't."

"Consider it a rewahd." He grinned. "Now, gotta go. Suppah. I'll text ya when I'm done."

Before she could protest more, the chat ended, leaving

her standing all dolled up and confused. *They want to take me to dinner, in this?* Her heart beat hard against her chest. She needed to not get excited. This wasn't the right way to act.

Number one rule was no hooking up with guildmates. Number two rule, was not believing someone wanted to actually date her. And number three rule was not getting between people and their happiness. Everything screamed that this situation broke every one of those rules, and she was having a hard time denying rule number two wasn't already broken.

"Shira, are you okay?" Orion asked. "My sensor are picking up unusual wave lengths coming from you."

She took a deep breath and slipped out of her shoes. "I'm just thinking."

"About your two men?"

Her heart thumped a little harder. "They're not mine."

"I sense a chemical change in you. This happens whenever you think of those two. How can they not be with such a reaction?"

She slipped the dress off, letting it pool at her ankles. "I've told you my rules before, Orion."

"Yes, ones that used to make sense because you hadn't been attached to a single person in a romantic sense. But now, that's not the case. Should you not seek out happiness in those you are compatible with, regardless of their guildmate origin affiliation?"

She wrapped her arms around her naked form. "It's more complicated than that, Orion. They haven't seen just how inhuman I am now, only the surface. I have so much baggage I could fill an Egyptian pyramid. They don't… need to deal with that."

Her eyes fell to the floor. "Besides… I can tell they're not both on board with whatever they're trying to do. I can see it in the way Zach looks at me. He has some interest, but not enough for me to believe something could work. And I'm not getting between him and Jasper. They're perfect for each other, and it's going to stay that way."

Shira's eyes widened when her tablet behind her blipped, as if a call hadn't finished going through, and then Jasper's voice projected. "Hey, Shira, I forgot t—"

She slowly turned, to find him staying at her, wide-eyed, his mouth open. Zach appeared on the screen, gazing at Jasper in confusion. "You okay? What has yo—"

He, too, stalled on his words when he laid his eyes on her. A scream tore through Shira's throat and she shrunk back. Snake sprang into action to protect her, but his attempts to get into her lap were making it hard for her to hide herself as she crouched. Unfortunately, they could still see her from this position, thanks to how she'd originally angled the tablet.

She kept her head low, trying to use her hair as a curtain. "Shut it off! Shut the stupid feed off. You stupid piece of shit AI! Why the hell did you answer that?"

Jasper tried to speak, what may have been an apology, but she cut him off. "Turn off the fucking feed!"

The call ended. She shook all over and struggled to breathe. With them now gone, she allowed herself to latch onto Snake. Tears welled up in her eyes. *They saw… they saw…*

Because of the clothes she'd chosen to wear today, she hadn't applied the artificial skin to her side. And with the way she'd been standing, even with her back turned, they wouldn't have missed that. "I hate you, Orion. I fucking hate you."

"They were staring at you."

"No shit, Sherlock."

"You miss my implication, Shira. They were not staring because half of you is cybernetic. They were staring because you're an attractive young woman to them, cybernetics and all."

Her shaking slowed, and she listened to him continue, though her anger toward him didn't change.

"Even Zach showed great interest, according to my sensors. I have downloaded hours of data around human facial expression and body language to better assist you over the years. It was the way he stared that gave him away. He is interested in you, Shira. Whatever you read off him, it does not have anything to do with you."

Shira's breathing started to return to normal. Still, she listened without speaking.

"You have run away for so long, you are struggling to see the very good thing in front of you. It is my job as your assistant, and as your friend, to ensure you're happy. Those men can make you happy, if you allow them. I merely wanted to show you this."

"That doesn't make what you did right. If you were a person, I'd kill you for pulling something so unforgiveable."

"Perhaps. Though, you must remember, I am an AI. As such, I do not have the same capability of emotional response as you humans. My actions are purely based on logic. And my program logic says this would help prove they want you, even if your emotion backlash would be severe."

"But why me?" Her voice shook, unable to keep the lingering fear at bay.

"Besides your outward appearance? Because you make them laugh. Because you are good at listening to their problems, and offer advice as desired." He chuckled. "And because you dote on their daughter almost as much as they do. You're an intelligent woman, Shira. They see this. They see the potential in you. There's a reason you can create such a strong digital persona. You just need to believe in yourself. Like they do—like I do."

Shira sat there, running her fingers through Snake's coat. Was he right? Could she break her rules to find out?

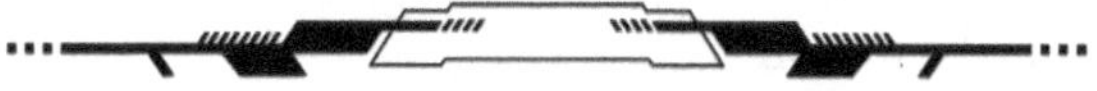

Jasper tapped the side of his phone. Everything inside him twisted. He'd told Shira that once they finished eating he'd text her, but after what happened with that last call, he wasn't sure what to do.

He didn't mean for that to happen. He thought she'd be the one to pick up, and not her AI. Jasper wasn't complaining about the view he'd received. Shapely legs—the curve of her back—those teasing freckles running along that pale skin of hers, reminding him how much he'd give to trail a finger along them, all over her. Her breasts, as they spilled over her arms as she tried to cover them. *And that ass.* God, that tight ass of hers was something to look at. And that thong only made it worse for him. *But the fear…*

He didn't have to see how she hugged herself to

know. Right in her eyes was that unmistakable sight. Jasper knew it wasn't because she was shy. She hooked up with randos in game all the time. It was seeing the real her that was the problem. And now he was afraid she'd push them away.

Zach sat down next to him on the couch. "Text her, Jasper. You're not going to get an answer if you don't."

"I know."

Zach looked over to where Serenity hummed away and colored. She wanted to do something that'd make Shira smile. Their daughter was too precious for words.

"You noticed it, too," Jasper said, his voice low. "She couldn't hide it."

Zach nodded, frowning. "I'm not sure what to make of all the extra cybernetics up her side. I don't remember those ever being there."

"At least I'm not crazy." Jasper's jaw tightened. "In that first photo she sent of herself, she wore a cropped, low-cut shirt. It showed some of that, but nowhere near as much as what we just saw. That shirt couldn't possibly hide all that, eithah."

"I think she wears artificial skin to cover it up." Zach said.

Jasper glanced at his boyfriend. He hadn't thought about that as a possibility. She once explained to them she'd had cosmetic surgeries to fix problem areas. He'd assumed, after seeing that photo of her and getting the explanation of how bad her accident had been, that those surgeries had removed the visible signs of cybernetics in some places. "Why would she do that?"

Zach's brow rose. "This is Shira. The better question is, why wouldn't she? We know she's wicked self-conscious.

She tries to keep up walls so no one sees. No one gets to see her unguarded. That artificial skin would help, as limiting as it is for coverage. And her modeling career would have given her the knowledge on how to make sure nothing looked strange when she wore it. Makeup is a powerful tool."

Jasper looked down at his phone. "That begs the question, how much more is she hiding?"

He didn't care if she had more to hide; he was merely concerned that she was doing it. How long would it take for her to trust them? Would she ever? Would they succeed in helping her build up enough confidence so that she wouldn't feel the need to hide?

Zach rested his hand on Jasper's arm. "Only way to find out is to not look like we're running, yeah?"

He was right, as usual. Zach was always better at keeping his head clear and seeing the bigger picture. God knew he needed Zach because of it. *I need Shira just as much, though.* She had qualities they both lacked. She fit like no one else could.

He typed out a text to her.

If you're still up for that quest, I am.

It took a few moments for a response to come in.

Yes, please.

His pulse quickened. They hadn't lost this just yet.

I'm sorry for earlier. I didn't mean for that to happen.

It wasn't your fault. It was Orion think-
ing he was doing me a favor, in his weird
AI way.

He decided to play dumb.

I don't understand.

Trust me, I don't either.

Jasper chuckled, grabbing Zach's attention. "Sounds like things are okay still?"

He nodded. "Yeah. Hey, Alistair. What would cause an AI to break the rules and do something against what a human wanted?"

"That is a tough question," the AI voice came from the apartment. "It would depend on the rule our human wouldn't want us to break. Our job is to make your lives better. We change in accordance to what you need: a friend or companion, an adviser, a planner, and the list goes on, of course."

Jasper scratched his chin. "What would make you do what Shira's assistant did a bit ago? Answer a phone call at a wicked bad time in her eyes?"

"From what I've gathered from the limited interactions, Shira has come to see her AI as a type of companion. This is no surprise to my programming, given her history. But, in doing so, she overrides many processes, allowing her AI to develop into its own being. It will act much closer to a person than the average AI. And thus, he can do things against her wishes. But of course, our main programming is to help you, and that cannot be overridden by anyone. So this AI of hers would only go to such extremes if it determined the action would aid her."

That was a bit more complex than he'd expected. But at least it gave him insight on the behavior. And it made him feel more relaxed about the situation. Shira may hate her AI's actions, but if it helped her in the end, Jasper wasn't going to complain.

This also helped him understand what he and Zach could still do with Alistair. They'd only gotten him a few months ago, replacing the basic one with only the ability to control the car and transfer data between phones. It worked, but as with many things, they outgrew the limited nature and required the expensive upgrade. The only one who didn't complain in all this was Serenity. She enjoyed talking to the AI. "Thank you for the explanation."

"Of course."

Jasper set his phone on the coffee table. He shouldn't keep Shira waiting. He kissed Serenity on the head. "Have fun coloring."

Serenity gave a toothy smile. "I will, Daddy! You have fun playing with She-ra."

Oh, I will. He bit his tongue and smiled. "I'll make sure we do. And don't worry. I'll be done in time to continue the bedtime story."

She went back to coloring, a smile still on her face. "If you don't, I undastand."

He wasn't planning on skipping out. He enjoyed the nightly readings with her. He wanted her to develop into a bookworm, like him.

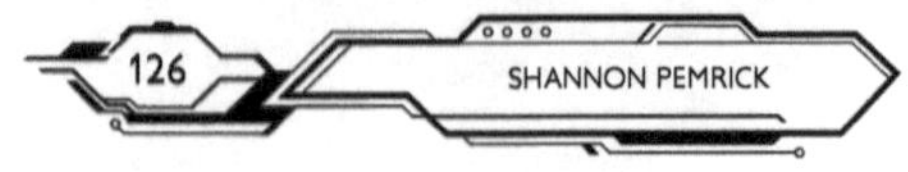

Zach stopped him just as he made it to the game room. He leaned in and kissed Jasper. "Good luck."

"Thanks, I think I'll need it." Jasper leaned in and grazed Zach's ear with his teeth. "And don't worry. I won't forget about you after."

Zach shoved his shoulder. "Tease."

Jasper grinned. "Always."

He then went over to his VR chair and pulled up Lusara Fates on the curved touch-screen monitors. He preselected his rogue class to reduce login loading, and jumped into the seat, hooking up to the neuron sensors. Once ready, he closed his eyes and let the system suck him in.

The buzzing pressure of VR transition finally let up, allowing Jasper to open his eyes. He lay in a large plush bed, in a small room with little decoration. Each member of the guild had their own room, a phased area where only those given permission could enter, much like an inn. They could decorate it as they pleased, but Jasper found no need to.

He opened his friends list, finding Shira not in the guildhall, but at least in town. He invited her to a group.

"Hey, I'm just leaving the appearance wizard," she said. "Wanted to change things up with this model."

"No worries." He climbed off the bed. "Meet me outside of town, East side."

"You sure? It's no trouble going to the guild hall."

"Yeah, saves time." He didn't want her to know his plan just yet. She'd freak, and make it harder to get this objective accomplished. It would really push her boundaries, but Jasper believed in never doing thing by halves.

Jasper walked through the guild hall and out the enormous double entrance doors. He pulled out a large orb from an inventory pouch and squeezed it. The orb flashed and a basic horse mount appeared. Jasper mounted the creature and took off into the city of Balgara, zipping past NPCs—non-player characters—and players alike until he reached the outer gates of the human city. Jasper glanced around, but didn't see his favorite elementalist.

"Behind you," a familiar voice said.

He spun around in the saddle of his mount. Shira rode atop a glowing blue stag, pulsating gems protruding out of its body and lightning sparking about it. It was a rare PvP mount acquired through tough achievements, and changed depending on the race and class using it. He and Zach had looked into trying it to complete it themselves, but ultimately didn't have the patience for it.

Of course, that's not what threw him. Shira looked… like herself. From the red hair and freckles, down to the body proportions. *This is why she went to the alteration shop? He expected a hairstyle change, or even some tattoos—God what I wouldn't give to see that on her—*since it wasn't uncommon for players to make changes to their avatars every now and then, but this was a bit more than usual.

Her face scrunched and he found it just as adorable as ever. "Everything okay?"

He shook himself out of his thoughts. "Yeah. You just surprised me with the avatah change."

She looked down at herself. "With the recent patch update for character model customization, I decided to take a chapter from Narissa's book to help me appease my therapist. If I look like myself here as much as possible, I can't pretend I'm someone I'm not."

Jasper turned his mount around and strode up beside her. "I think that's an excellent idea. If it'd help, I could run over there and change this avatah."

Shira's brow spiked. "I don't know how that'd help me."

He chuckled. "Because then you can't pretend I'm someone else."

She snorted and rolled her eyes. "Yeah, trust me, you'd make sure that couldn't happen. Besides, you'd have to change race, and that costs real money to do. That's an expense I don't want you to be burdened with."

Jasper rested his hand on her thigh, making sure to hold eye contact. "You'd be worth that cost."

A flush spread across her cheeks. She glanced away. "So what quest are you taking me on that's supposed to help me with my issues?"

He couldn't deny he was a bit disappointed. *Baby steps, Jasper, baby steps.* If he paced this right, that flush would be a different kind by the end of their excursion. "I found a quest in the Mi'jah Mountains."

Her gaze snapped to him, her eyes wide. "You what?"

He smiled. "I know you can handle it. And there's a nice rewahd for completing the objective."

"Jasper, that's halfway across the map," she argued. "That'll take us a while to get there by ground mount."

Jasper hopped off his horse and dismissed it. "And that's why we're not getting there that way. Hop off your giant deah."

"W—what?" Her quiver sent a pang in his chest. "We're not flying there."

Jasper summoned a red dragon mount decked out in spiked armor. A two-seater mount reward for participating in a special PvP charity tournament last year. "C'mon, hop off that mount of yours."

Shira backed up instead, her eyes tight. "Jasper, I—"

He grabbed her hand. "No running from this, Shira. You're getting on the back of this dragon with me."

Shira's eyes narrowed and the two had a silent battle of wills. In the end, he prevailed somehow. Shira sighed and dismissed her stag. Jasper mounted his dragon, and offered his hand to her. She hesitated and then extended a shaky hand. Her breath came shallow as they held eye contact, but the moment their hands met, calmness visibly overrode her fears.

Jasper did all he could to be patient and confident for her. For him, this part should be easy, but he could see how knowing this mount could lift off the ground would make this one of the most difficult challenges she'd faced yet.

Shira took a quick breath and then scampered up into the saddle. She wrapped her arms around him so tightly that he found it hard to breath. Jasper rested his hand on hers. "Take a deep breath. I'm not going anywhere until you're able to let up on this death grip. I know this is difficult, and I'm going to be patient, but it'd be wicked nice to be able to breathe soon."

"Sorry…" she mumbled into his jerkin. After several moments, her hair spilled over his shoulder as she rested her head on the base of his neck. A fruity smell wafted off of her, invading his senses. He'd caught it before many times, always wondering if it came from a particular shampoo or body wash, or even a perfume she favored.

Jasper hoped it was a shower product. He'd love to scrub her head to toe. Zach could help. They'd focus on different sides, eventually abandoning the wash for a bit more fun.

His cock hardened, making his already tight pants uncomfortable to wear. As the fantasy lingered, as well as her intoxicating scent, desire pulsed through him. "You smell nice." *Why did I just say that to her?*

Her grip adjusted. It was no longer as tight, almost soft, like a loving hug. "Thank you. It's probably my body spray. It's my favorite."

Damn, not shower product. Well, the fantasy was still nice. And possible. "I think it's my favorite, too."

Shira pressed her face into the back of his neck again and took a deep, controlled breath. Several more moments passed before her breathing would return to normal. Her death grip loosening wasn't far behind.

Jasper patted her hand. "That's better. Ready to take off?"

"N–no."

"Shira, you can't fall off this dragon," he reminded her. "I can't even crash it. The game makes sure it's not possible."

She nodded. "I know."

He reached down and squeezed her thigh, glancing back at her. "You're safe with me, Shira. Nothing is going to happen to you as long as I have a say in it."

Her green eyes stared up at him. Such a brilliant shade they were. And those plump lips, slightly quivering—if one kiss could make this go away for her, he'd gladly do it.

Shira swallowed hard. "Okay."

Jasper smiled and they took to the sky. Shira's eyes clamped shut and she screamed, deafening him for a moment. *Man, she's got a set of pipes.* It was a good thing the game couldn't make him go deaf.

When she continued to panic, he squeezed her thigh again. "Shira, babe, it's okay."

Her screaming ceased immediately and her nails dug into his armor. "You did not just call me babe. Again."

She hated that pet name for some reason. They could never get from her why, but the wrong PvP opponent to call her it always received a mark of death from her. Like that sorcerer last week.

Jasper grinned. "It got you to stop freaking out, didn't it?"

She blinked. "I guess so."

He gazed out beyond his dragon. "Take a look without looking down."

He'd chosen to stay low enough to see the tree line, but this height was a good test for her before he really pushed her boundaries.

"D–do I have to?" Shira managed. "Me being up here is stressful enough."

"Do you want to be able to walk into that convention center without passing out?" He glanced back at her. "Bettah yet, don'tcha want to be able to go on vacation again with your folks, instead of staying cooped up at home hiding from your own shadow?"

Her eyes constricted, but she nodded. "I do, but…"

"But what?" Jasper was doing his best to not push

too hard. He didn't know a lot about this kind of trauma, but he'd been smart enough to do a bit of research and find out what he shouldn't do. Most likely he would do something wrong, probably a few things wrong, by the end of the night, but he'd try his best to do right by her. He wanted to understand. He wanted her to get better.

Shira closed her eyes and buried her face into his armor. She didn't answer the question.

"It's okay to be afraid," he said. "Everyone is afraid of something. There's no shame in it."

"I need… I need to be strong," she whispered. "No one can see me…"

Jasper let go of his reins with one hand and rested it over hers. "Let me. Let Zach. Let us both see the real you. Let me help you to be truly strong."

Shira peeked up at him, her eyes fearful. Her lower lip quivered and for a moment Jasper feared he might cause her to cry. That was one thing he couldn't handle.

However, to his delight, that didn't happen. She let her eyes drift out beyond them. They darted back before they went out too far, but she tried again almost immediately. Jasper let her do this at her pace, gauging her strength of will with each attempt. When she managed to finally gaze out for about three seconds, he chose to speak up.

Jasper reached back and threaded his fingers through her hair, cursing his character's gloves from stealing away his sensation of touch. Shira gasped and pulled away. "What are you doing?"

He frowned. Not the response he wanted. "I was going to tell you I was proud of you."

She gazed at him warily. "But why touch me like that?"

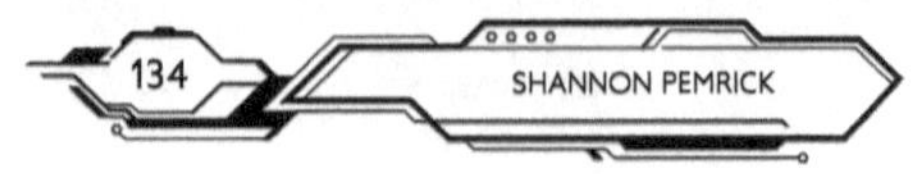

"I didn't think it'd be an issue. You do like your hair played with, after all."

Pink tinted her cheeks. "How did you know about that?"

He grinned. "I heard you tell Mercedes once."

Shira's eyes darted away. "Well, don't do that. It's weird. And completely out of context."

"Is it now?" He chuckled. "So, tell me, do you like your hair pulled, too?"

The pink on her face developed into a deep crimson. "I'm not telling you that."

"Oh, c'mon. No need to be shy." He glanced back at her again. "Zach does."

Her eyes flicked to him. "Is that why he's growing it out?"

Jasper laughed and focused on flying again. "Possibly. You'd have to ask him. Now, tell me your ansah."

She remained quiet for a moment and then muttered, "Maybe."

Perfect. It was one thing he enjoyed. "See, not so difficult to say. Now, look around some more. I'm gonna have to increase our altitude soon, and I don't want you deafening me again."

Shira sighed and continued her task until the time came to fly higher. She held onto him with another death grip and buried her face once more. "Shira, you need to stop hiding."

"I know."

"No, don't tell me 'I know' and then not do it."

"Jasper, you have no idea how hard it is for me to be on this mount right now. I'm trying not to have a damned panic attack. Trust me, it's not pretty."

He sighed. He'd pushed too hard, like he feared he

would. *Think, what else can I do?* "Thanks for offering to teach Serenity."

She peeked up. "You don't have to thank me. I should thank you for not stopping me."

Jasper shook his head. "I'd never do that to her. I want to encourage whatevah passion she has, as long as it's a healthy one. To my delight, she's becoming quite the little book worm like me."

Shira's brow ticked up. "You? I never pegged you the type."

He glanced back at her. "I go through at least three books a week. And I'm old-school enough to read physical copies when I can."

"Those aren't easy to come by." She regarded him for a moment. "All our public libraries have gone to digital, and there's only one store in all of California that sells hardcopies, and that's in L.A. Where do you find them over where you are?"

He shrugged. "Internet searches and yahd sales. You find all kind of crazy things in yahd sales."

Shira rested her chin on his neck, trying to avoid his spiked leather spaulders. "Are you happy Serenity is into languages?"

He nodded. "Even with translation technology readily available and in use all the time, knowing the language firsthand will always be more useful."

"Well, I will do my best," Shira promised. "I'm not great at teaching, and since it's a second language to me, it won't be perfect, but it'll be better than her trying to learn from the internet."

Jasper's brow furrowed and he glanced back at her. "I thought German was a primary language for you."

"No. I didn't start learning until I was almost fourteen."

"Isn't your dad from Germany? Why would he wait so long to teach you?"

Shira was quiet for a moment, staring at him as if he'd sprouted a second head. *Well, a second head with a brain… Half a brain, she'd say.* "I thought I told you about that."

His brow spiked. "Tell me what?"

"Jasper, I'm adopted."

The brakes slammed in his head. Adopted? That… that explained a lot, all of a sudden. "Oh."

She tilted her head. "Is that a problem?"

His nose scrunched. "Why would that be a problem?"

Shira shrugged. "I dunno. Your response was weird, so I wanted to make sure."

"Sorry. That was just unexpected."

She chuckled. "Sorry. I thought you and Zach knew. I could have sworn it came up before. But that could have been Mercedes and Narissa and a few others. They've met my parents, which would clear up a lot of the misconception."

"Ya sure?"

"Oh yeah, they're like night and day, and I don't look anything like them."

Jasper rested his hand on hers. "Well, I'm glad they adopted you."

Shira leaned in and smiled into his neck. It sent an unexpected jolt through him. "Can this mount fly any faster?"

He didn't hide his surprise. "No, but are ya sure you'd want it to?"

She nodded and looked out beyond them. "I'm getting used to this."

"How do you feel?"

She smiled, the sun sparkling off her eyes. "Free."

Jasper watched her take in the cloudy sky spanning for miles. Her hair blew about, wild and untamed, like her. It was the perfect color for her. He could see why she dyed it that way. Serenity still didn't understand that hair couldn't be that color red naturally, but hopefully one of these days she'd get it.

He reached out and tangled a lock around his finger. Shira's eyes fixated on him. She reached up and grasped his hand, but didn't make him let her go this time, much to his delight. He could stare at her like this for an eternity, running his hands through—

Shira gasped and pointed in front of them. "Look out!"

Jasper whirled around just in time to see the mountain they were heading straight for. He released her and pulled on his dragon. Shira wrapped him in another death grip as the dragon veered away. The large creature's feet hit the mountain's surface and pushed off.

Jasper let out a breath when he righted his mount and circled around the mountain. "That was fun."

Shira pulled on his pointed elven ear. "No, it wasn't."

He leaned with the pull and looked up at her. "I told you nothing bad would happen on this flight."

Her eyes narrowed. "We almost crashed into a mountain!"

"Had I kept going, the dragon woulda run up the mountain, flapping its wings since it couldn't get ground traction."

Her face scrunched in such a cute way. "Really?"

"Really, really." He sat back up. "And, I don't see you freaking out."

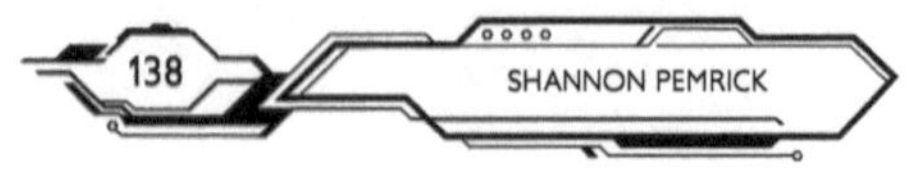

She remained quiet and he stole a glance back. She gazed around, her eyes wide with her reality. "You're right…"

Shira looked at him and then buried her face into his back again, hugging him tight. But he could tell this wasn't a fearful response. "Thank you…"

He smiled and banked around the mountain. "I know you're not exactly *cured* of your feah. But you've made a wicked huge stride. And now that you have, we can staht the real quest."

Shira peeked over his shoulder and looked down below them. Her death grip returned, but she didn't freak out. Below them sprawled an arctic forest. Nestled not too far from them was a small home and a larger building behind it, smoke billowing up from the house's chimney. They'd made it.

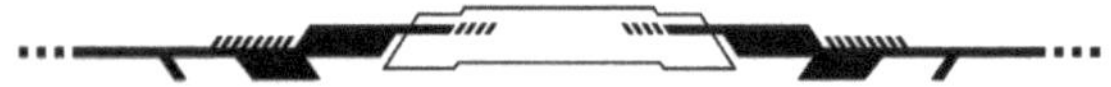

Shira did her best not to panic as she and Jasper descended. No easy feat, but Jasper's calm demeanor gave her something to cling to. She still couldn't believe he'd gotten her on the back of this thing, let alone flown them this far. The landing was smooth, and Jasper had the dragon walk toward a snow-covered stone house with a large building behind it.

A cold wind blew, making her shiver and press into him some more. The one thing she hated about this game's real feel was the temperature simulations. It was never enough to harm anyone, but that didn't mean you couldn't be miserable in some of the more extreme climates. "I hope you brought something to handle this cold."

He glanced back at her. "Don't tell me you're cold."

"You might not be, arctic boy, but this California girl needs a jacket for anything sixty-five and lower."

Jasper snorted and focused ahead. "Don't worry, I packed something."

She held out her hand for a trade. "Well, give it."

"Not yet. It's got a time limit, so I don't want you wasting it."

Shira narrowed her eyes. "Is it a hot potion?"

"Duh."

She should have figured. While cold-resistant accessories like cloaks and rings were ideal, they were expensive, so hot potions were a cheaper investment for short-term needs.

The two of them arrived at the home and dismounted. Shira hugged herself tight. She was glad the sexier armor she favored didn't add to her susceptibility to the cold. She liked that the impractical looks were treated practically in the game. Made game play more fun.

Jasper led her to the backside of the home, where the quest marker showed up on their map. The large building behind the home turned out to be a stable—and not just any stable. Shira gazed around at the pure white gryphons nestled deep within straw- and fur-lined nests. A dwarf NPC puttered about, doing various chores.

Shira gave Jasper a questionable glance. He grinned. "Read the quest he offers and you'll get it."

She pursed her lips, but did as he said. The dwarf greeted her when she engaged and opened the quest prompts. Shira's heart sank as she read about a recent avalanche due to some unusual quake activity. It'd caused problems with the snow gryphon nests, and some were in need of rescuing. The dwarf requested seven eggs to be returned to the stable.

Shira didn't accept the quest right away. "Jasper, what kind of terrain is this quest for?"

"Mountainous, of course."

She licked her lips, narrowing her eyes at him. "That's not what I meant, and you know it."

"It's going to test your feah limits. That's all I can tell you." He placed a hand on her shoulder. "Now accept the quest."

She chewed her bottom lip and then accepted the quest without looking at the reward. She could back out at any point if this got too difficult, but she had to try to tackle it. She wouldn't get any better if she ran away. *Besides, it's a game. Nothing can go wrong in a game.*

The dwarf thanked her and then resumed his duties. Jasper grabbed her hand and pulled her out of the stable; Shira stared at their entwined fingers. He'd been doing a lot of touching today. The actions were starting to send off warning signals, but she struggled to stop him. It wasn't like the lust-driven attention she'd grown accustomed to with her choice of a sex life. Each touch had a purpose—a meaning—and always felt like there was an incredible amount of adoration behind it. She'd honestly been enjoying the attention, even though she knew it was wrong to. Even now, she knew she should pull away, but couldn't.

The cold wind of the forest slammed into her once they exited the building. Her face scrunched. "Can I have that potion now?"

Jasper chuckled and opened his inventory. A bottle with orange liquid appeared in his hands. She held out hers and initiated a trade window. Jasper placed the potion in her hand but didn't finish the transfer.

Shira's brow spiked. "Why are you stalling?"

"I have one condition."

Her eyes narrowed. "You're the one who dragged me out here. Why do you get to make conditions when you could have picked a better location than your native home land?"

Jasper's head flew back as he laughed. "Mass ain't a tundra."

"Might as well be," Shira muttered. She wasn't a fan of the cold.

Jasper drew closer, his hot breath beating down on her. The strength of the cologne he always wore enticed her. He and Zach always smelled good; it infuriated her most days. "Cold weathah is nice, though. Gives a good excuse to cozy up to those your close with."

Shira placed a hand on his chest to stop him from coming any closer. "I'm sure Zach makes for a great cuddle buddy. You can go ask him if you'd rather do that."

He pouted. "You won't sub in for him?"

She sighed. "You know that answer. Now, can I please just have my potion? My nipples are going to be able to cut diamonds at this rate."

An interested smile spread across his face. "I wouldn't mind seeing that."

She punched his chest. "Potion."

"Alright, alright, but I did say I had a condition."

She sighed. "Then tell me what it is already."

Shira gasped when he reached out and pulled her close, pinning her against him. "A kiss."

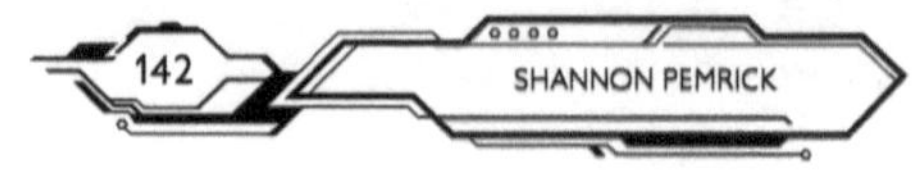

Heat surged through her, her heart's pace quickening. "W–what?"

He leaned in closer. "You heard me. My condition is a kiss."

"J–Jasper, you can't ask for that." Shira tried to push away, but he had a strong grip on her. "Zach—"

"Already knows I was going to ask this condition of you." He grinned. "He was just disappointed he'd have to miss watching."

Shira's heart pounded in her ears. He was bluffing. Jasper held her gaze. *He's not bluffing.* "I–I have rules."

"Not to hook up with guildmates." He nodded. "I know. But I'm wicked sure that doesn't mean you can't kiss one."

Fuck. He was right.

"It's just one kiss, Shira."

She chewed her lower lip, but then stopped when his gaze on her changed. That was too tempting of an action for someone like him. *It's just one kiss. What could go wrong?* A lot. So many things. But Angelica told her also to take risks. Sometimes she needed to do something stupid and learn to deal with the consequences. *Fuck it.*

Shira popped up on her toes and crashed her lips into his. They both sucked in a tight breath, his taste tantalizing. Her heart leapt as long-forgotten sensations coursed through her. Kissing was always a means to an end for her, never anything more. But this… these sensations… feelings of desired intimacy—true-connection intimacy… was that the right description for this? She didn't know. Whatever this kiss did to her, it certainly caused something different to stir within her.

She pulled away first and tried to disguise her short-ness of breath. "That good enough?"

A tempting grin slipped up the side of his face. "More than enough."

Jasper closed the trade and the potion ended up in her inventory. Shira took a step back from him—this time he didn't stop her—and consumed the potion. The biting air disappeared as warmth filled her and a buff appeared in her stats. She let out a sigh of welcomed relief. She'd get to be like this for an hour.

Shira realized Jasper was watching her intently. She immediately looked for where the quest pointed for them to start. A path up the mountain looked like an obvious spot to start, based on the direction they needed to go. She pointed as she turned. "Shall we start?"

"Sure." He came up beside her and she let out a sharp gasp when his hand slapped her in the ass. Her pulse quickened again and she did her best to hide all the other reactions that contact caused. But he caught on and chuckled. "Good to know."

Heat surged through her. "Good to know what?"

He glanced down at her as he walked past, a sly smirk painted on his lips. His eyes danced, as if his revelation excited him or something, and then he continued on without saying another word to her. *I think I'm in trouble.*

"C'mon, slowpoke, the potion timer is ticking."

Shira shook herself and ran to catch up. The two of them trudged through the snow drifts, up the mountain pass. Jasper cast quick glances back to her, probably to ensure she wasn't thinking of running, but otherwise continued.

When they made it over the ridge, she froze. Below

them, where more forest or even a mountain should have been, there fell a rocky chasm. Snow gryphons flew about, distressed. Shira swallowed hard. "Jasper?"

"This is a miscellaneous quest added to help excite players for the *Old Kingdom* expansion release. Since they had to push the release day back a few weeks, they added in a bunch of teaser quests," he said, staring down into the broken-away land. "Some old god of earth did this."

Shira's hands shook and she took a step back. "I… I can't—"

Jasper grabbed her hand and pulled her close. "Yes, you can."

The intensity of his eyes snared her. Could she? That chasm went straight down. If she fell—

Jasper rested his forehead on hers. "This is a game. This isn't going to harm you. It's a broken mountain, not a building."

"B—but I could lose my balance…" She hated how her voice shook. She hated feeling so pathetic.

"I won't letcha fall." He grasped her chin so she couldn't look away. "You have my word."

Shira's lip quivered and she swallowed hard. "Okay."

Jasper grasped her hand and guided her down a path she'd missed in her panic. *Duh, Shira.* Lion Rage boasted about their ability to create a greater immersion experience than other companies, but even they put in the basic linear options if players wanted to go that route. This reduced a risk for her. She wasn't scaling sheer cliffs. *I can do this.*

She glanced down at her and Jasper's locked hands. She shouldn't allow this, but the confidence he exhibited traveled to her through their connection, giving her more courage than she could muster on her own. *I can do this.*

Jasper led Shira down the steep incline. Loose rocks around them clattered down into the chasm, keeping her heart racing. She squeezed Jasper's hand and he gave her a reassuring squeeze, not looking back. His determination to watch ahead helped keep her nerves from frazzling any further.

Shira gasped when she slipped and fell back. Jasper dug his feet into the ground and turned, grabbing her legs and pinning them so she wouldn't slide down the incline. "You okay?"

She nodded and then got back on her feet, rubbing her ass. "Yeah, just hurting a bit."

Jasper smirked. "I could help with that."

Shira rolled her eyes. "Thanks, but no thanks."

He shrugged and continued on. Shira followed, though the lack of contact with him this time allowed her to overthink this. What if another quake happened? What if she slipped on a ledge and Jasper couldn't react in time. What if—*Calm down, Shira. It's okay. Remember what Angelica said.*

She took a deep breath, and then another. It took five to get her brain to shut off. She hoped this fear would go away soon, because she wasn't looking forward to doing this forever. Jasper glanced back at her, but didn't say anything.

The two of them made it to the first ledge on the path. Shira leaned against Jasper, taking controlled breaths as she tried to look out beyond them. She couldn't depend on him to encourage her if she wanted to get better.

Jasper reached behind him and wrapped an arm around

her, glancing about. "Tell me when you're ready and we'll start looking for nests."

Shira nodded and took the time to adjust. She took a deep breath after a few moments and then spoke, "Okay, let's go."

Jasper took several careful steps onto the thin path, and she followed. He set a slow pace, only taking a few steps at a time to let her adjust to this terrifying experience. The wind buffeted them, though it was nothing too risky to deal with at the moment.

When she couldn't fight her overwhelming fear, Shira took a step back. Jasper reached out and pulled her closer. "No, none of that."

"Jasper…"

He chuckled. "I'll pin you to this wall if I have to."

Heat threatened to rush to her face, the mental image of him throwing her against a flat surface, pinning her with his body while he ravaged her flooding her mind. She shut out the tantalizing image and surfacing desires.

Jasper gave her a strange, unreadable look, then forced her to keep moving with him. Her hands shook, each step small and difficult. She refused to look down, knowing she'd be unable to continue.

"Help me look for these nests," Jasper said. "It'll keep your eyes off the open side of this path."

"O—okay, I'll t—try." Shira cursed herself for sounding so pathetic. *It's a good thing I'm not trying to impress him or Zach to be my boyfriend.*

She forced her eyes to scan the sheer cliff. A broken and caved-in spot caught her attention, as well as a pile of sticks jutting out of a flat area within the cave-in. She pointed to it. "Let's check up there."

Jasper turned so his back faced the open ravine, and gestured for her to lead up the rocky surface. "Ladies first."

Shira pulled into herself. "Jasper…"

He touched her elbow with a light hand. "I'll be right behind you. I promise I won't let anything happen. You gotta do this."

She took a deep, shaky breath and then nodded. Shira stepped in front of Jasper, and he nudged her to keep going. She gave him a sidelong glance that didn't last long, as it required her to look out beyond the ledge. Shira searched for places to climb up to the possible nest, finding several nooks to jam her hands and feet into. *Definitely a nest.*

Shira's whole body trembled, making it difficult for her to climb. Jasper reached out a hand, resting it on her ass. She narrowed her eyes down at him. "What do you think you're doing?"

He shrugged, his eyes far too innocent. "Giving you a hand, as promised."

"More like copping a quick feel."

He smirked. "You'd know if that's what I was doing."

Shira didn't believe him one bit, but refused to argue. It'd only waste time. She pulled herself up farther and Jasper did just as he claimed, lifting and steadying her. Her head peeked over the ledge, and just as she'd hoped, a broken nest made of twigs and pelts lay before her. Inside rested several large white-and-gray-speckled eggs. "Jackpot."

"How many?" Jasper asked.

"Three."

"Sick!"

Shira collected them into her inventory and her quest updated. "Did this count for you, too?"

He helped steady her as she climbed down. "Yes."

"Oh, thank god." She didn't care how desperate that sounded. She didn't want to have to do this for each of them individually. She doubted Jasper would make her, but he was going through all this trouble for her, so she'd refuse to end this excursion until they both had completed quests.

Once Shira's feet were firm on the ledge again, Jasper took position in front of her, though not before squeezing her rear. She squeaked, her heart skipping a beat, and then gave him a hard stare.

He grinned as he passed her. The look screamed, "told you so."

The wind picked up, and before the two knew it, it turned into something much stronger than they expected. Shira tried to shield herself by turning in, but the strength of the gale off-balanced her. She screamed when she lost her footing.

Jasper grabbed her and pushed her against the wall, pinning her body with his. The wind howled and raged. Shira trembled, her mind going into a reactive frenzy of awful images—her losing balance and falling into the ravine below—the small ledge crumbling beneath them—on and on, her brain continued to bombard her with all manner of negative situations.

He leaned in and whispered in her ear. "It's okay, Shira. I've got you. Nothing will happen as long as I'm here."

Her fear-stricken eyes peered up at him. She studied every little feature on the face looking back at her, from his sincere eyes to his determined, locked jaw. Shira didn't see an elf avatar. She saw past that to the man behind the screen. The one she'd become accustomed to seeing every few days. The one of two faces determined to help her; patient and understanding of her circumstance. All more than she deserved.

Jasper grinned when the wind died down. "Guess I got to pin you after all."

The comment made her acutely aware of their proximity—his frame against hers—his strong, tempting scent. Her heart thumped against her ribcage. She knew she should come up with something witty, laugh it off, and move on, but words lodged in her throat. Her eyes cut away to the ground. "We should get back to questing before the wind picks up again. I'd really like to not repeat that experience."

Jasper pulled away, his face unreadable. "Okay."

Minutes passed and the search for the last four needed eggs was a slog as Shira fought her crippling issues. So much so, they had to use another hot potion when hers ran out. Jasper remained patient, for what reason Shira couldn't figure out at this point. He could be spending time with his family, or practicing matches for the next qualifier. Both were far more important than dealing with her bullshit problems.

Jasper found the last required egg, and excitement rushed through her. Now they could leave this mountain. She'd done well, considering, but it proved she still had a long way to go. *I'm not sure I'm going to be ready in time for the convention.*

Jasper grasped her hand. "Before heading back, we have one last thing to do here."

Shira's brow twisted. She'd gotten a bad feeling from the way he looked at her. "And what is that?"

He tugged her to come closer. Her feet dug into the ground. He stood too close to the ledge for her liking. Jasper tugged again. "You need to come closer."

Shira shook her head. "Not until you tell me what you want."

Jasper pulled harder, winning out in the battle of strength, holding her against him. "You need to stand at the ledge and look down."

"Nope. Fuck that." She tried to struggle away. "Nope, nope, nope."

His grip held fast. "Shira, take a breath. It's gonna be fine. You need to try to do this. Just once."

"No!" She struggled harder, this time succeeding in getting her back to hit the rocky wall behind them. Jasper still held onto her. "I'm not ready for that."

"Are you sure?" He lifted her chin. "I know you know yourself bettah than I do, but when your feah kicks in, you struggle to think straight. Are you sure you're not ready to give it one try?"

Of course she was. Wasn't she?

Her eyes wandered away from his gaze to the far mountain side, a mirror image of the side they stood on. *Can I do this one last thing?*

Jasper slipped behind her, his chest pressing into her back and his hands resting on her hips. He bent close to her ear. "I'm right here with you."

Shira's heart slammed against her chest, every fiber of her being screaming at her to run. Jasper pulled her into him more, resting his face into the crook of her neck. His warmth seeped into her, calmness crashing against her fear. Shira's eyes ticked down an inch, the broken cliffs of the far side now all she could see. She swallowed hard and repeated until she looked straight down.

Her vision distorted and her head spun as she stared. Her breathing labored, and she dug her nails into Jasper's gloves. Jasper turned his head and pressed his lips against her neck. The kiss, soft and tender, brought everything in her to a screeching halt.

"Back up," he murmured as he tugged her to follow.

She complied, taking a step back every time he did until he'd pulled her into an alcove. Jasper continued to hold her close, allowing her nerves to calm. He kissed her neck again, this time a little farther back. "I'm proud of you."

Shira gasped, a wave of unwanted emotions rushing through her, and pulled away, her hand covering the spot. "What was that for?"

He chuckled, his eyes dancing. "To see how you'd react. It helped you change focus the first time."

Her eyes darted away. "Well… don't do it again. It's weird."

Jasper regarded her for a moment and then shrugged. "Okay." He stepped closer and took her hand. "But really, I'm wicked proud of you. This hasn't been easy."

Shira continued to stare at the ground. "I don't want you getting your hopes up. These types of issues take years to get over—sometimes it's not possible for it for it to go away completely. And even with today's progress, I'll be lucky to be well enough for the convention."

He reached out and lifted her chin, stroking her cheek with his thumb. "Rome wasn't built in a day. Any positive progress is a win, and you had a lot of it today. I pushed you fahthah than maybe I should have, but you proved just how resilient you are. You will win this fight. No matter how long it takes."

A demure smile crossed her lips. "Thank you."

Jasper smiled back, holding her gaze before opening a game menu. "Now, we can either walk back, or fly back. Your choice."

Both options sucked, but one would be easier at this rate. "Summon that dragon of yours and get me out of here."

Jasper chuckled. "One princess-saving dragon, coming up."

She punched him in the arm. "I'm no damsel."

"Oh, you misundahstand." He grinned. "I was referring to myself."

The two laughed, Shira nearly losing her balance. It helped relieve some of the lingering tension in her. Once calmed, he summoned his mount and hovered over the small ledge. The creature's large bat-like wings flapped strong as Jasper held out his hand to her. "Let's go collect our rewahd."

CHAPTER 8

Jasper landed his dragon easily, Shira only flinching a slight bit this time. She slid off the giant creature and stretched. He used the moment of dismissing the mount to look her over. The quest had put her through a lot, but seeing her now, and noting how relaxed she appeared, he didn't regret choosing to do this. He only wished there was more he could do.

Watching her fight against herself, either her fear or her mental belittlement battles she couldn't hide from him, gripped him tight. He did his best to help by distracting her enough to refocus, but there was only so much she was receptive to. He wanted her to let him and Zach in. He wanted her to understand it was okay to lean on them—that they were there for her, no matter what.

Shira set a pace to the stable and Jasper lagged behind, taking in the sights. The sway of her hips, the confidence of her walk. Everything about her made it hard to focus on much else. *Just like it is with Zach.* Shira may not have been receptive to his minor advances, but she wasn't immune. She fought hard, but not enough for him not to see.

She tossed a glance back at him. "You coming, or what?"

Not yet, but soon if you work with me. He ran to catch up. "Yeah, sorry, lost in thought."

She passed him a suspicious glance and then continued on. They entered the stable and engaged with the dwarf, handing in their quest and watched the barn phase. The stalls were now fuller, and gryphons flew in to land in the nests with eggs.

When a follow-up quest popped up, Shira cocked her head. "What's this?"

Jasper grinned. Now was the time to see her really get excited. The first quest offered a monetary reward, but the follow-up was where the real reward lay, for Shira and for him. "Read it and find out."

She opened the prompt and her eyes widened. She glanced at him and then took off for the dwarf's house. Jasper accepted the quest and followed at a slower pace. Jasper's boots crunched in the soft snow—a sound he loved; he couldn't wait for the snow to start falling. Fall was nice, but winter was even more fun. Of course, Miss California needed to build up a tolerance for winter.

He watched her continue on, tossing glances back at him now and then. The action stirred something within him. Between the constant touching, the kisses, the need to save her, and now this, he was beyond done behaving.

Jasper's pace quickened. He ducked through the small door just as Shira squealed. On the far end of the home, lit up by a roaring fireplace, sat a now-cracked-open egg on a well-crafted table, and a gryphon cub peering up at Shira with big eyes. Shira reach out and lifted the small creature into her arms, snuggling it. Jasper's quest *pinged* and he auto-completed it, choosing to skip the animation of the creature hatching from its egg.

He didn't care to relish the experience of obtaining his own non-combative pet. Watching Shira do it for him was far more rewarding. He smiled. She'd told him a long time ago, gryphons were one of her favorite mythological creatures. So when he found out this quest rewarded one, he had to bring her on it. The fact it worked on her fears was only a bonus.

Jasper drew up close to her and she looked up at him, her eyes sparkling. "Thank you, Jasper. Thank you, thank you, thank you!"

He reached out and rested his finger under her chin. "I'm glad you're happy with your rewahd. I thought it'd be suitable for the stress I put you undah." A grin slipped up half his face. "Now, I'd like to take my rewahd."

Her eyes widened, but before she could say anything, he claimed her lips. The two of them inhaled, Shira letting out a surprised whimper. She placed a hand on his chest and pushed away. Irritation flared inside him. This wasn't what he wanted.

Shira still held her gryphon, but this time much tighter to her chest. "What do you think you're doing?"

His shoulders moved in a semi-shrugging motion and took a step forward. "Breaking rules."

She struggled for words and took another step back. "No, you can't."

He mirrored her. "Why not?"

"It's wrong. You and Zach—"

Jasper shook his head. "I already told ya, Zach and I talked this ovah." He grinned when her expression twisted in her confusion. "It wasn't the kiss he was disappointed he'd miss."

She visibly swallowed as her breathing changed. Jasper smirked. That excited her. He took a step closer and this time, she didn't retreat. That was good. Though her eyes darted away; he needed to fix that.

Jasper reached out and lifted her chin with his index finger. "Break a rule, Shira. I promise this one time you do, you won't regret it."

She leveled her eyes with him. "No awkwardness after? Just sex."

"No awkwahdness," he promised. He would not be so foolish as to agree this was merely sex—a means to an end. She was more than that. He wanted more than that from her. For the three of them.

He'd struggled accepting love after Sara. He fell into the trap of feeling as though he'd betrayed her. But he'd learned, with help, it wasn't wrong to love more than once. Of course, nothing had prepared him to love more than one person at a time.

And while he couldn't quite say he loved Shira, he was dangerously close, and that meant he had to accept that it was something possible for him. As long as Zach remained on board—he would never let him go after everything they'd gone through.

Shira's tongue dragged over her lower lips, her eyes full of thought. Jasper had to fight the groan on the tip of his own tongue, desire simmering. She was one hell of a tease.

The gryphon hatchling disappeared from Shira's arms

and she popped up on her toes, pressing herself against him. Her lips brushed his as she spoke. "Don't make me regret this."

Jasper's heart leapt into his throat when she pressed her warm, inviting lips against his. Her taste and smell teased him, just as before, when he convinced her to kiss him earlier. He needed this—needed her.

His lips pulled into a half-smile. "I'm looking forwahd to optimizing your utility, if you know what I mean."

She chuckled against his lips. "Dork."

"In this moment, I'm your dork." Jasper framed her face with his hands and kissed her harder, allowing this need that'd built over the years to spill out. Shira whimpered and pressed into him more, digging her nails into his armor. That all needed to go.

Fumbling with his menu, Jasper tossed away whatever armor he could without looking. Shira hummed when his jerkin disappeared, and dragged her nails over his sculpted chest. Every muscle of his responded in turn, hunger building in him.

There was still too much between them, though.

Jasper lifted Shira up by the thighs, receiving a surprised squeak, and set her down on the table. Even though he hadn't removed all of his gear, he went to fussing with hers, hoping to find something that would release her.

Their kiss broke, and Shira chuckled, her tongue darting out and licking his bottom lip. "Let me help you with that."

In one click, all her armor disappeared, putting her on display for him. Jasper's eyes raked across her soft form, every curve, peak, and valley perfect and in place. "Gorgeous."

A pink flush of arousal formed on her cheeks and collarbone, and her perky breasts heaved the longer he drank her in. "Yeah, avatars are great."

Jasper dragged a finger over her collarbone, between her breasts, and down her stomach. Shira caught her bottom lip between her teeth. It made him harder. "No, I'm talking about you. And I won't stand for any arguments."

He knew her well enough to know she'd rationalize the avatar's "superior" appearance. Truth was, it didn't compare to her, and he'd give anything for this to not be virtual.

Shira's eyes turned playful. "Fine. But we still have an issue. This is when you need to finish undressing yourself."

Jasper glanced down. He hadn't done a half-bad job in his blind attempt. He still had bracers, epaulets, and pants, and the pants were really all that needed to go.

Off they went. His throbbing dick sprang free, Shira's eyes falling to it. Jasper grinned when he heard the quiet gasp. But she wasn't going to get this yet. No, he was going to savor this moment with her, no matter how tempting it was to dive right into her.

Jasper wrapped his hand around the back of her neck and captured her lips again, nipping at the soft flesh. His other hand slid along her waist, down to her hip, his fingers biting into her soft skin. Shira groaned and pressed herself against him, dragging her nails down his chest again, this time unrestricted from sliding lower.

Anticipation gripped him. Jasper released her mouth, trailing fevered kisses down her neck, occasionally nipping her skin, enticing quick gasps from her. Shira's touch reached the base of his shaft, her fingers lazily circling it. Jasper pressed his teeth a little harder into her shoulder. Shira moaned and then trailed a soft touch up his hard cock before wrapping her hand around him.

Jasper sucked in a tight breath and groaned as she stroked him, each pump sensational. Shira threaded her free hand into his hair and held him close, nipping at his avatar's pointed ears.

He wasn't ready to give her what she craved yet, as tempting as it was. Jasper needed to drink in everything, memorize it all. He forced Shira to release him and pinned her back on the table. Her chest heaved with heavy, anticipating breaths and her eyes danced with desire.

Jasper grinned. He liked this view. But there were a few more he'd like to have. Jasper dipped his head and kissed between her breasts. Shira responded with a hitch in her breathing and a slight arching of her back.

"Jasper…" she said in such a quiet tone it sounded similar to a moan, sending a wave of heat and electricity through him. "No more teasing, please. Give me something."

Jasper chuckled against her skin. "As you wish."

He kissed the inside of her breast and then again, closer to her rosy nipple. His tongue darted out, flicking the taut bud and she gasped, her hands threading into his hair again. Jasper teased her nipple again before wrapping his lips around the hardened peak. He sucked and nipped the sensitive bud, playing and teasing her other breast. Shira moaned and begged for more, pressing against him. Jasper was more than happy to oblige.

His hands slid over her belly and along her outer thighs,

before gliding up her inner thighs where he stopped, caressing her skin. Shira groaned in frustration. Jasper chuckled, sucking her nipple harder until she whimpered. He let go with a *pop* and glanced up at her. She stared back, her eyes pleading.

Jasper licked her other nipple and then slid his thumbs between her thighs into her wetness. The uninhibited gasp she let out simmered his blood. Desire crawled along his skin as he stroked her.

"Jasper…" she moaned.

That broke most of his resolve. He needed to see her writhing in pleasure. Jasper sucked her rosy bud a moment longer before letting go. His eyes met hers again, and he slipped a finger inside her. Her mouth parted, accepting him, but it wasn't enough. Jasper inserted another and then another before he was satisfied with her reaction.

Eyes and mouth wide, Shira moaned as he thrust his fingers, her nails scraping the wood table. Jasper leaned in and kissed between her breasts, trailing down. He kept his eyes locked on her as he did. The desire in hers only served to build his.

His mouth dipped lower and lower, until he settled between her legs. Jasper's tongue darted out, flicking on her sensitive flesh. Shira's hips bucked when she gasped. He grinned, pinning her hips down and diving in with his mouth. Her taste seared into his mind.

Shira grabbed a fist full of hair and moaned. He continued to assault her with pleasure until he felt her tightening around his fingers. He pulled away. Shira let out a frustrated hiss and sat up, her eyes burning into him. "Jasper—"

He kissed her, and pulled her by the hips to the edge of the table. His hard dick pressed against her, throbbing and begging to be used. Shira's frustration melted away. She reached down and stroked him again. Need crawled over Jasper skin. He couldn't wait any longer.

Their kiss broke and he held her hips captive as he nudged her legs wider. "Ready?"

She nipped his lower lip. "Is that really a—"

He slid inside her, her mouth falling open and her back arching. His groan mingled with hers. Fuck, she felt good—almost too good. *No such thing as too good.* Not with Zach. Not with her.

Jasper rocked his hips, finding rhythm in his thrusts. Shira met his motions. She also leaned in and grazed his skin with her teeth, burning his desire and driving him crazy. Jasper pushed her onto her back, pinning her down with one hand at her stomach.

The two of them held intense eye contact as he took her. Her chest heaved with heavy breaths, matching the pounding of his pulse in his ears.

Jasper reached between her thighs and stroked her. Shira's eyes hooded and her head rolled back. "More."

His rhythm never faltered. She could beg for more if she wanted. And she did. She begged and begged—the sound so pleasing to him—until she reached her peak.

Shira's back arched, and her nails dug into the table. Her hips bucked against him, teetering him on the edge of release. A pleasure-filled scream tore out of her throat, ecstasy consuming her. Jasper continued to thrust until he plunged over the crest, groaning and spending himself inside her.

His motion slowed to a stop, both of them breathing

heavily. Shira brushed a wayward curl out of her eyes, a quiet hum coming from her. She was pleased, but not enough. Jasper wasn't done with her.

He dipped his head and captured her rose bud between his lips. It hardened and she gasped. "Jasper?"

Jasper's hands tightened on her hips, keeping himself buried in her. One thing VR had over real life, virtually no "down time" to keep you from enjoying yourself. Only the mind would put a damper on things if you went too long at it. And Jasper was going to take advantage of every moment.

He let go of her nipple with a *pop* and gazed at her. "Need another moment?"

Shira's fantastic eyes glowed, her desire sparking. "No. But I wouldn't mind changing up the positioning."

A grin spread across Jasper's face. "Would be my pleasure."

As quickly as he could, he flipped her over. Shira gasped and then groaned alongside him when he reentered her. The sensation of being inside her, and hearing her pleasure coming with such ease, was almost enough to send him over the edge again. Seeing her backside again didn't hurt. Every curve of her was perfect. It didn't matter that it was an avatar skin. He could see past it—see her, cybernetics and all. And at this rate, he wouldn't be able to get enough.

Shira turned her head to look at him, bracing herself on the table with her forearms. "You would pick this position."

He smirked. "There's more than one reason I pick rogue for a class."

Her eyes danced. "I have expectations for this position. I hope you understand."

Jasper's tongue flicked against his teeth and he reached out, grabbing a fistful of her gorgeous hair, and gave a firm tug. She gasped and then again when his other hand smacked her tight ass. "Don't worry. I'm more than happy to oblige."

Her mouth opened to say something, but only a moan sounded when he thrust into her. Jasper rhythmically dove in, skin hitting skin. His and her breathing labored and her moans intermittently changed to begs and pleas for more. He could listen to such music all day.

Shira pushed against the table to meet his thrusts, increasing the pleasure for them both. She was so responsive and unafraid to take what she wanted. Jasper loved it.

He knew she was close when her breathing labored and she only begged for more. Then, she screamed an uninhibited cry of satisfaction, convulsing around him, milking his own release. Jasper abandoned himself to the pleasure, grunting alongside her dying cries.

When they stilled, he barely held himself steady over her. After taking a moment to come down from his high, Jasper extracted himself and rolled onto the table. With a quiet, satisfied hum, Shira rolled to sit up. Jasper reached out to keep her close, but she pushed his hand away, confusing him.

"No offense," she said, barely glancing his away. "I'm not into cuddling."

That was disappointing, as was this feeling of a rift forming between them. Jasper sat up. "I didn't peg you as the type to reject that."

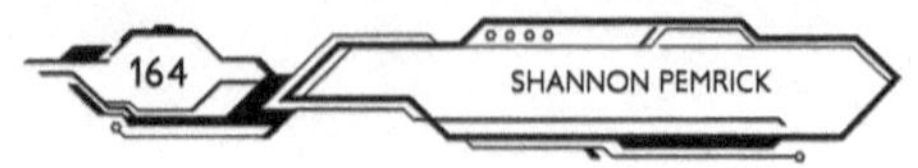

She shrugged, kicking her legs. "Never got into it."

Why does it feel like she's lying? He couldn't shake something was off. "Was all that not satisfying enough?"

Shira slipped off the table and positioned herself between his legs, her hands on his thighs. "Other than teasing me a little longer than I would have liked; that was more than fantastic."

Jasper should find her words reassuring, but something nagged at him. What happened to the connection they just had? His gut twisted with realization. *She's treating this as just sex.* Just because he didn't promise it as such, didn't mean she wouldn't. *What do I have to do to change that?*

Shira reached out and brushed his cheek with the back of her hand. "Don't give me that look."

His brow spiked. "What look?"

"Disappointment." She trailed her fingers down his neck, rousing him again. "I can fix that."

Her promised fix, while enticing, wasn't the one he'd have liked. Jasper probably shouldn't have gotten his hopes up that she'd see it more than just sex, but he didn't want her to think this was a one-time deal. He wanted her to understand this was a long-haul desire. *But without Zach's side of this yet, I can't even broach the subject with her.*

Shira dropped to her knees and didn't hesitate to wrap her lips around his cock. Jasper's head rolled back and he groaned. Without Zach's side of the approach, all he could do was enjoy this moment he had with her. For all he knew, it'd be the last.

The metallic clicking of a grandfather clock echoed through the small room decorated in plush cloth furniture, potted plants, and a small wooden desk. A young woman with russet-brown skin, wearing a blue button-down blouse and black slacks, sat in a loveseat while Shira lounged on an adjacent couch. The scent of lavender filled the air, an attempt to keep patients relaxed. In her years of coming here, Shira didn't know a time when it didn't smell this way.

The woman's soft brown eyes watched her as Shira avoided eye contact. Her painted red lips spread into a warm smile. "Shira, I would prefer you not avoid this topic this time."

Shira toyed with the strands of a fully pillow. "I know, Angelica, I know."

"These two men are important to you, that much you've allowed me to know." Angelica leaned her head to the side. "You talk freely about your friendship with them, and their adorable daughter, but you're so resistant to open up about how you feel in this relationship with them."

Shira refused to look at her therapist. She just didn't want to talk about it. Not with what happened last night. She never meant for it to go that far. It was amazing and fun, but she shouldn't have said yes to it. It was only going to cause her problems.

"Your face is red," Angelica observed. "And I can see you're stuck inside your mind again. Talk to me, Shira. How does your relationship with these two men make you feel?"

Shira's lip twisted, her eyes drifting to a basket filled with various fidget objects. She'd never used them in her visits, but she wondered if it'd be a good way to calm her rigid nerves as she mulled over Angelica's soft-spoken question. "I… don't know."

Her therapist crossed her legs. "What happened?"

Shira pulled her legs to her chest and rested her forehead in the palm of her hand. "I fucked one of them in the VR game last night."

Angelica was quiet for a moment. "That's quite the jump from not knowing your feelings to having a sexual encounter with one of them."

Shira's shoulders lifted in a half-hearted shrug. "Sex is sex. You don't have to have some deep connection with a person to have it. I should know, I hook up and leave all the time in VR."

"We're circling back to the 'why' I ask you a lot with this choice." Her therapist adjusted herself in her seat. "As well as heading back toward my original question, how do these two men make you feel? You made rules to keep them from being a choice, and yet you have broken one of those rules for at least one of them. Why?"

Shira's fingers tapped on her knee. "I don't know."

Angelica tilted her head. "Do you not know, or do you not wish to share?"

Shira wasn't sure how to answer that question. *Both, maybe?*

"Do you love them?"

"No." She'd said that a little too quickly.

Angelica waited a moment for an explanation, but when Shira didn't continue, she responded, "How do you feel about them then? Be honest and open with me, Shira. You know I'm not here to judge, only help. Polyamory works for many people."

Shira's lip quivered. "Because... I don't... know what it means to be loved that deeply."

How pathetic did that sound?

Her therapist waited for more. Shira shook her head, her chest tight as conflicting emotions raged through her. "Flynn and Anita have been great adoptive parents. But they were the first to show me what love was. I don't know my birth father. My mother was an unloving drug addict who tried to use me as currency more than once for her next fix."

She paused for a moment, words all jumbled in her mind. "Those on the street I thought were loyal to me... turned their backs when they found out I was willingly moving in with Flynn and Anita." Her eyes darted to her cybernetic hand, which clenched as the hatred seeped in. "I thought I'd found someone who loved me, but the moment I became a robotic freak, he tossed me aside."

Her eyes darted to Angelica. "Why would I be stupid enough to believe two men, who are happily together and have a family, actually want me now?"

Shira looked down at her knees, tears brimming her eyes. "I don't even know if they do, or if this is just some random fun thing they want. Jasper, maybe. He's weird enough to be into it. But Zach? I don't care what Orion says. He's not on board. I can see it. And this stupid decision I made last night is going to cause problems. I don't want to be *that* woman."

Angelica didn't speak. Her eyes said, "Thank you for sharing this emotional piece" but her posture said, "You know why I'm not verbalizing it." This was a typical response when Shira rambled during an emotionally charged verbal dump. It forced her to figure out what part of the rambling needed to be focused on. Shira hated it, but also understood why she did it.

"Orion told you what happened in the closet, didn't he?"

Angelica looked down at her tablet. "He gave me quite the detailed report, including his own assessment of the situation."

"You think I'm overreacting, then." Shira couldn't hide the bitter accusation. She knew she shouldn't be nasty about it, Angelica was there to help, but Shira hated this part of their sessions.

Angelica shook her head. "Not at all. Not only would that be unacceptable for a human to do, it's also unacceptable for an AI. No amount of self-reprogramming should have ever made it okay for him to decide to do that." Angelica tapped her fingers. "However… something he noted does have my attention. According to his assessment, you were less upset with them seeing you naked, and more with seeing your cybernetics. Is this true?"

Shira chewed her lower lip. "It's… not entirely inaccurate."

Sure, she was uncomfortable they saw her naked without her consent, but that hadn't been why she'd freaked out.

"But?" Angelica pressed.

Shira's fingers tapped on her knee, her mind bouncing all over the place. She didn't know how to answer.

"Fear is a natural reaction to the unknown." Angelica smiled. "But do you think it's wise to live in fear?"

Shira frowned. "No. That's why I'm here."

Angelica nodded. "Exactly. So, I need you to make that leap. What are you withholding from me, and yourself?"

Shira slumped into the couch. "This whole situation confuses me."

Angelica adjusted her sitting position. "Good, now we're getting somewhere. Open up to me about what confuses you. Don't hold back."

"Is *everything* a good answer?"

Angelica laughed. "I don't think I have to answer that question for you."

Shira sighed. "I don't know. How I feel is a fantastic place to start, I guess. It's where you'd want me to start, since it's the root of most of my problems—and what you've been asking this whole time."

Angelica gave a closed-mouth, now-you-got-it smile.

"I think… I know… they're attractive. I'm attracted to them. I wouldn't have broken a rule and fucked Jasper if that wasn't the case. They're great friends. But do I want more than friends? I don't know." Shira ran her fingers through her hair. "A part of it sounds nice. Having even just one person love me for real sounds nice, if a fairytale. But two? That feels like a stretch to me. Why me?"

"Why not you?" Angelica asked.

Shira sighed. "Please don't repeat what Orion said to me."

"I don't have to, since you've already heard it." She smiled at Shira. "I helped with his re-programming when you had your accident. While I don't agree with his method in the slightest, I do agree with what he said. Just look at your friends, Mercedes and Narissa. They have relationships, despite their cybernetics, and they're happy. So why can't that be you as well?"

Shira's eyes drifted away. "Well, that's where my feelings lie right now—in limbo. Because I don't understand why they'd possibly want me." She shook her head. "Jasper said what we did was okay, that he and Zach talked about it before he brought it up with me. But a part of me isn't sure how on-board Zach really is. He's such an unknown to me, I can't even begin to think I'll find myself in the same situation again any time soon. I don't see what Orion claims to have sensed."

"Why not talk to him about it?"

Shira's back straightened and her eyes went wide. "Are you crazy?"

Angelica gave an amused expression. "Perhaps. But you won't know the answer unless you talk to him. I can't give you all the answers, not when it comes to others. I'm not them. For all we know, there's something else at play, and speculating isn't going to help you."

Shira leaned against the couch, chewing her lower lip. This was such an asinine idea.

The grandfather clock chimed. Angelica frowned. "Our hour is up. If I didn't have another appointment, I'd ask you to stay for us to work on this more."

Shira pushed herself off the couch. "It's okay. I need to process this."

Angelica rose. "Please consider what I'm saying, Shira. Opening up to more than me will help you."

Shira nodded, though her mind didn't latch onto the agreement. Angelica could tell, too. They embraced, and double-checked Shira's next appointment before she headed out.

The drive home passed quickly. Shira climbed out of her car, Snake barking like mad in his excitement at her return. She didn't like leaving him home, but after Shira found herself relying on Snake too often as a distraction from uncomfortable topics, she and Angelica agreed it would be good for Shira to handle therapy sessions without him.

As she headed for the door, a text came in. It was Zach.

Are you busy?

Just got home from therapy.

How'd it go?

Okay, I guess.

Angelica's suggestion to talk to Zach about her

concerns tugged at the back of her mind. He was reaching out to her, so maybe he really was okay with things?

> *Are you up for doing something in-game,*
> *or would you prefer some time alone?*

Shira paused just inside the front door, Snake whining and rubbing against her, trying to get some attention. *Jeez, it's like I've been gone for months.*

> *Just you and me? Or you, me, and Jasper for*
> *threes?*

> *You and me. Jasper took Serenity out.*
> *I thought we'd work on a fear.*

Shira tapped her phone. This was a good sign, right? Should she use the opportunity to talk to him about the event between her and Jasper? Angelica would say she needed to, but could she muster the ability?

> *Yeah, I'd like that. I just need to check on*
> *something and then I'll jump on.*

> *Great. Meet me at Steadfast Inn. I'll*
> *have the quest and share it with you.*

Shira headed upstairs.

> *Can I know anything about the quest?*

> *You'll be dealing with heights.*

Shira rolled her eyes.

Real helpful.

;) I try. Now, hurry up.

He was a bit impatient. It made her pulse skip.

Shira entered her studio and made her way over to a desk with round silicone molds. She jiggled one of the molds, finding the resin inside stiff. *Good.* They still need a number of hours to finish curing before she could take them out, but soon she'd be able to finish Jasper and Zach's accessories and ship them off in time for Halloween.

Shira checked on a piece of leather she'd dyed earlier that day. She snatched up the piece and went over to the working set she'd started, sizing up the new piece that would need to be riveted on.

Playing Lusara Fates tickled her creative mind all the time. She wondered about the practicalities of armor and weapons, and what would need to be altered to make them wearable and still keep their fantastical appearance.

This piece of armor had come about because of Jasper's latest gear upgrades for the tournaments Lion Rage provided to reduce the impact of the late expansion release. As a leather-wearing class, he was the perfect muse for this creative outlet. Shira wished she had some sort of metalsmithing skill to try out her or Zach's gear, but she doubted that would happen anytime soon. *This is just a hobby no one will see anyway.*

The idea of making a functional LARP and cosplay

line surfaced in her mind, but she dismissed it. That was a long-forgotten pipe dream.

Shira turned to leave the room, making a mental checklist of what she'd need to tackle next on the projects, when a black foam horn on the floor caught her attention. She picked it up and turned it in her hands. It'd been a piece she'd made too short for a cosplay piece. *I thought I'd stored this in my scrap bucket.*

She shrugged and went to toss it in the general direction of the scraps, but stopped. She glanced at the leather armor and then at the foam piece, and then at the curing trainer gadgets. *I wonder…*

"Orion, can you please send a full measurement request to the guys for Serenity? I want to try something."

"Are you going to make her a cosplay armor set for Halloween?" Orion asked.

"No, that's too little time. But I might be able to cobble something decent together by the time the convention comes around."

"May I suggest you also finish something for yourself?"

Shira's brow furrowed. "Why would I do that?"

"Well, so you and Serenity can cosplay together at the convention. I believe this would be a good stepping stone for you."

He did have a point. Cosplay, especially good ones, brought on a lot of attention. *But, that also means—* Shira shook her head. "I'm not ready to have strangers take my picture yet. I need more time."

"Very well. The request has been made."

She thanked him and placed the horn on a workbench. She whipped out her phone to research Monster Hunter armor while heading for her game stations.

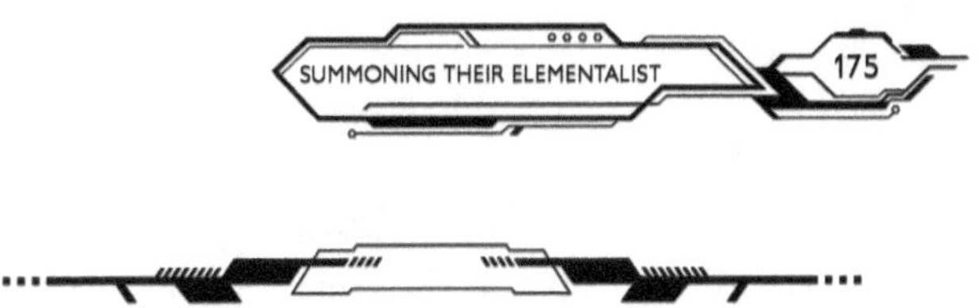

Zach peered around the corner of a building, looking for Shira while also praying Stacey wasn't still around. She'd been hounding Jasper and him all day today when they were between matches, and then when she found him online alone, her attitude switched to a creepy friendly one. He had to switch his online status to invisible and leave the spot he told Shira to meet him at, just to get away from her. He'd tell Shira to meet in a different location, but he thought he'd have fun surprising her.

Thinking of her sent his heart racing. He'd picked an easy quest for her, figuring it best not to stress her as much as Jasper had. He had a habit of pushing a little too much too fast, whereas Zach preferred to take it slower. And it wasn't just the quest. His pulse thumped harder in his veins while his stomach knotted. That was, if he could muster the courage to approach her about it.

Zach was always excited to see her. Any mention of a possibility to be around her elated him to the same degree as spending time with Jasper. *But at the same time… after what happened with Amy…*

He just wanted to scream. The constant raging conflict made him dizzy at best, and made him second-guess every interaction with Shira on a regular basis. And now he had this one shot. He wasn't as much of an idiot as Shira sometimes thought he and Jasper were. If he messed this up today, that was it. *I'm surprised this separate approach didn't run her off from the start.*

Zach had no doubts, though, based on what Jasper

had divulged about Shira's initial resistance, that she was overthinking what happened. She'd jumped to the wrong conclusions, and if he didn't curb that today, there would be no "them." And as happy as he was with Jasper, as they were talking about this daily, it was chipping away at his doubts and reservations about making it happen.

Something moving by the inn caught Zach's attention. A grin spread across his face when he spotted Shira standing outside the building, looking around. Zach slipped out from behind the building when she turned away from him, and he did his best to come up on her quietly, which was no easy feat with his armor.

Shira gasped when he covered her eyes with one hand and pulled her close with the other.

"Boogie, is that you?"

The light tone she used had him cracking up and he let her go. "You know, you're supposed to be afraid of the boogieman."

She winked. "The boogie man is a cuddly bunny, compared to the German stories my dad told me."

A cold sensation ran up Zach's spine. Those were stories he'd make sure Jasper didn't tell Serenity just yet.

"Zachariah, there you are!" Stacey's grating voice cut in. "Why did you run off on me like that?"

He cringed and turned to see her heading straight for them. "I told you to never call me that, Stacey. It's just Zach."

Stacey pouted. "Why did you run away? I wasn't scolding you."

Shira slipped her arm around his, lacing their fingers together. Her warmth teased him. "He didn't. He just needed to find me since we have plans, and you harassing him for no reason wasn't helping. C'mon, Zach. This quest won't get done itself."

Stacey scowled at Shira. Zach shrugged at his menace of a manager and allowed Shira to drag him off in a random direction. He glanced back to make sure Stacey didn't decide to follow, and then took the lead, keeping his hand still entwined with Shira's. "This way."

He led her to an open area and summoned his double-rider dragon mount. Shira hesitated to join him on the creature's back. He held out his hand. "You did this with Jasper yesterday. It's just as safe. Well, more so, because I'm a better driver."

Shira chuckled. "As long as you don't nearly crash us into a mountain, I'll agree with you."

Zach's brow ticked up. Jasper had left that detail out. Must have scared Shira half to death, even if there was no possible way to crash a flying mount. "Don't worry, we're not going anywhere near mountains."

This brought a smile to her face, and his. Her smile could brighten a room. He wanted to be the source of that smile all the time. *Well, Jasper, too.* A bitter taste hit his tongue and he tried his best to banish it. Jealousy was not something he would put up with. He didn't need to be, and it'd just ruin things.

Shira finally climbed up onto the dragon and wrapped her arms around him. It was then he wished he didn't always go with such practical armor styles. For her benefit, Zach gave her a countdown from three, and his mount soared into the air. She whimpered, but luckily didn't shriek into his ear as she'd done to Jasper.

He patted her hand. "You did good."

She took a shaky breath. "You'd think after the torture Jasper put me through last night, I'd be able to handle this."

Zach shook his head. "We both know it takes time for the fear to go away. But you didn't shriek like a banshee, so I'm going to say that's major progress."

She slapped the back of his head. "I don't shriek like a banshee!"

"That's not what Jasper says." He gave her a grin that alluded to a double meaning.

Shira's face reddened and she looked away. The reaction would have assured him, if it weren't the flash of guilt he saw cross her eyes. *Fuck.* He really couldn't mess this up today.

"So, what are we doing today?" Shira asked to change the subject.

Zach opened his quest log and shared the quest with her. "A haunted tower needs some searching. Someone is missing a family heirloom, and they think it's in there."

"Haunted?" She laughed, a light, whimsical sound that kicked up his pulse. "Like *evil, soul-sucking ghosts* haunted, or *someone spreading rumors to keep others out* kind of haunted?"

He shrugged. "Dunno. It'll be wicked fun finding out, though."

Shira rested her chin on the back of his neck, sending a warm sensation down to his groin. There was no doubt this woman was different from any other he'd had the pleasure of meeting. It was alarming, but he wouldn't allow himself to blunder this chance.

"How tall is the tower?" she asked.

"Several stories."

She let out a breath. "And here I thought you'd be nicer than Jasper."

Zach chuckled and patted her hand. "I thought something more practical would be better for you."

Shira grumbled about him being too smart, getting him to laugh. This eased some tension in him. He needed to focus on this part of his task first. It was the most important part, because if he and Jasper couldn't help her get to the convention, nothing could come of their relationship.

Well, we could visit her in San Francisco. His brow scrunched. Why hadn't they thought of that? That would have gotten them in-person with her sooner, and a family vacation was in order. His and Jasper's busy schedules, and sometimes limited funds, made it hard to take Serenity places. But if they played their cards right with this tournament, they could pick up a permanent sponsor that would allow them to drop Tri-com and not have to fuss with all the fees associated with winnings, and publicity pitfalls when the company did something stupid.

Unfortunately, the two of them had been stupid enough to sign their most restrictive contracts. It would be hard to escape, but not impossible.

A fair hand waved in front of his face, snapping him out of his head. "Hello! Lusara to Zach. Lusara to Zach, come in."

His eyes fluttered and then he shook his head. "Sorry, lost in thought."

Shira leaned against him and tilted her head. "Care to share?"

He glanced back, a smile on his lips. "Just thinking

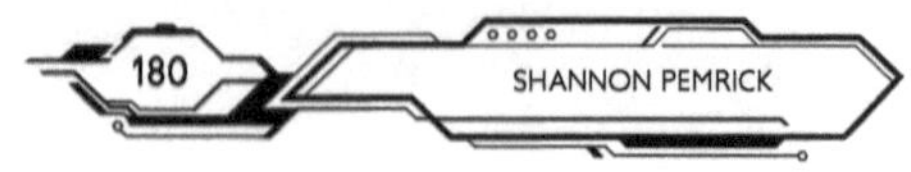

about how excited Serenity will be to finally go on a vacation trip. We don't get to take her away from home often."

"Well, she'll have fun in L.A." She smiled at him. "So much for a little girl to do with her dads."

Dad. Did Serenity see him that way? She knew Sara was her mom, and they'd never discouraged her from calling him "dad," but they'd never forced it, either. She'd never uttered the word to him, always calling him Zach, or *Bat* when she was just learning to speak.

He could ask her, of course, but a part of him felt a bit silly for getting hung up on the semantics.

Shira poked his cheek. "You're doing it again."

Zach shook his head. "Sorry."

She rested her chin in the crook of his neck, quickening his pulse. "Do you want to talk about it?"

He waved it off. "Nah. It's just something I do. Jasper hates it."

She pulled away, sending a pang of disappointment through him. "Well, I can't say I hate it, because that'd make me a hypocrite. Just don't stay too long in there. That's a rabbit hole that's not good to crawl into."

Zach patted her thigh. "Don't worry. I won't."

The short flight to the tower breezed by. Shira handled it and the landing well. It pleased Zach. Maybe soon she'd be able to handle planes and travel again.

Now they stood at the base of an old rundown tower with decorative eaves and roofs inspired by Japanese architecture. Shira swallowed and popped on the toes of her feet, rolling back onto her heels, and then repeating. He'd noticed her do this once before. He assumed it was a nervous habit of hers.

Zach laced his fingers with hers. "Ready?"

Her eyes didn't leave the tall building. "N–no."

He squeezed her hand. "Tell me when you are. There's no rush."

She gave a curt nod and focused on breathing. He suspected this was about to be the first time she'd step foot in a tall building since the accident. He knew she and Mercedes were working on getting her used to being closer to them, but he was sure they had yet to enter one together.

Shira closed her eyes and murmured out loud. "If I just pretend it's Cybro Industries, I can go inside. I can do this."

Zach tilted his head. "You can go into Narissa's building?"

Shira nodded. "Yeah. It's the only building like it that I can step foot into, and it took a lot of time to get to that point."

Zach had seen the building in pictures before. She was farther along than he thought. If Shira could go into a building like that, then she could handle anything, if she could only stop her fear from tricking her.

He tugged at her arm, prompting her to take a step forward. "You're ready."

She dug her heels into the ground. "No, wait."

Zach tugged her again. "You said you can go into Cybro. Then you can walk into this building here." He held her gaze. "I know you can."

She didn't blink, and then nodded slowly. "O–okay."

One step after another, he led her through the broken-down doors and into the abandoned tower. Her eyes

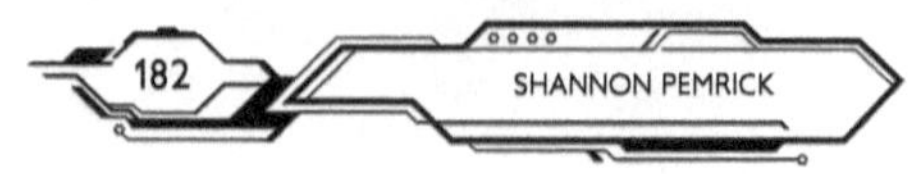

darted around the run-down interior, but she didn't try to run.

Zach's grip remained strong as he tugged her to follow. "The quest says the heirloom is located on the top floor."

"That's it?" Shira's eyes remained wide. "Just go up the stairs and get the item?"

"Based on the quest, yeah." He shrugged. "We might run into an enemy, or a trap or two, but I picked an easy quest so the objective didn't get in the way of the more important goal of facing your fear."

Shira swallowed and nodded. "Okay... sounds like something you'd do."

Zach regarded her a moment and then stepped closer. "Is that a good thing?"

Her brow twisted. "Of course. You and Jasper have different ways of handling a situation. I'd have preferred this first, but what's done is done."

A twinge of regret hit Zach. He'd given Jasper the okay to go first, based on personal factors: because he was so gun-ho about Shira, while Zach was still sorting out his head. But he hadn't considered how differently they would each approach the fear aspect with Shira—

"Though, maybe not." Shira looked for the stairs. "The mountain cliff was terrifying, but..."

She didn't need to finish that sentence for him to understand. Zach squeezed her hand. "The building isn't going to fall, Shira. I made sure of it in my research. This is a safe quest for you to overcome your fear."

Her lips twisted, and her eyes were unable to meet his. Zach watched her shoulders tense and he fought her attempt to slip from his grasp. She won out in the end. "I'm sorry you have to do this for me. There are so many more important things you could be doing."

She held her arm close to her body with her other hand and took several steps toward the far-off wall where the stairs leading up were housed. Zach reached out and touched her chin; this got her to look at him. "This is the most important thing I could be doing. That's why I'm here."

A shade of pink rose into her cheeks. He enjoyed the sight—a more vulnerable look she didn't let just anyone see. Not even he or Jasper had gotten the privilege to see it very often. She was always trying to be strong, even when she didn't feel it herself. He admired that, to a degree, but he admired her courage more.

Shira gave him a wan smile and took a few steps closer to the stairs. "Let's see if I can get to the next floor without panicking."

Zach followed her. "Well, you do have stairs in your house, right?"

She glanced back at him. "Yeah. I can do a two-story house just fine. Anything more, things get weird for me."

He nodded, getting the perfect idea. "Then, see each floor like that of a house. Once you get to the next one, pretend it's the first floor and you have to get to the second."

Her tempting lips twitched. "Already a step ahead of you."

Of course she is. Shira was an intelligent woman. And she lived with her fear, unlike him. But he didn't take her words as reprimanding. No, instead he found them relieving. It showed him that she really did want to do this. And he'd be there to help.

Zach followed her up. The steps creaked with each bit of movement, making her nervous, but that didn't stop her. *Note to self, don't let her come visit us in Boston until this issue is resolved.* Not only were they in a third-floor apartment, but they lived in a historic building. While safe, the floors creaked all the time.

They made it to the next floor and looked around. There wasn't much here, besides a couple of holes in the floor and turned-over chests and bookshelves. Zach wasn't sure what this building had been used for—the quest hadn't given any information—and so far the interior wasn't screaming out the answers, either.

The two of them cautiously made it to the next set of stairs, Shira doing much better than he'd expected. Her only trouble spots were the holes in the floor, which didn't surprise him. Up the next flight, they stopped halfway. Something rummaging around on the third floor caught their attention.

Zach and Shira exchanged glances and he decided to take a peek first. No doubt it was an enemy. It would be too easy of a quest without any.

Shira pressed herself against the wall, and he did his best to slip past her. His gear snagged hers, pulling her into him. Zach caught her, and she let out a quiet *oof*. He murmured an apology and tried to extract himself, but whatever he tried, it wouldn't work. Shira rolled her eyes and made him sit down on the stairs. The rustling on the floor above hadn't changed any, so he figured it wouldn't be an issue to just go along with her. What he didn't anticipate was his own reaction to her.

Zach's hands rested on her hips as she sat in his lap. Her sweet, tempting scent surrounded him; his pulse quickened. Shira, on the other hand, appeared unfazed and fussed with the interlocked armor, eventually freeing them.

She smirked at him, keeping her voice low. "That's how you do it."

Zach found no words could form on his tongue, so he nodded. Her eyes lingered on him for a moment, curiosity flashing over them. He probably looked like a complete idiot right now. A deer in the headlights at best, an inexperienced teenager at worst.

Shira slipped off him. "Now, you or me first?"

He jumped to his feet. "I got it."

Zach crept up the stairs and peered into the room. A bird flapping around caught his eye. He relaxed and let out a sigh before waving her up. "It's just a bird."

"Zach, look out!" Shira screamed.

He whirled around to find an orc swinging a large hammer at him. The weapon slammed into him, sending Zach flying. He crashed into the floor a few feet from the stairs, the orc lumbering forward. Gray-skinned, single-minded humanoid creatures with sloping foreheads and large tusks, they weren't anyone you wanted to meet in a dark alley—especially not a whole pack of them. Lucky for him and Shira, it looked like this one was alone, although there was no doubt they could take on a few of them if they had to.

Zach drew his broadsword and lunged at the enemy, his sword clashing with the hammer. He swung again, landing a hit on the creature, only to be hit himself and pushed back several feet. *Damn, a knock-back effect.* He'd have to be extra careful with that.

The orc rushed him, a rage overcoming the creature.

Zach blocked and dodged, looking for an opening in the orc's frenzied swings. An arc of lightning crashed into the orc, the humanoid screaming in pain. Zach's eyes darted to the stairs, where Shira crouched near the top—not ready to come up, but not backing down from the fight, either.

Zach took advantage of the opening Shira gave him and sliced into the orc, killing it. He let out a breath and sheathed his weapon, taking a look at the loot. He only found one thing of value, an emerald necklace. It appeared to have spellcaster enchantments on it. He pocketed it. It'd be handy for later.

Shira continued to peer over the top step as he made it back to her. He smiled. "Need help?"

"No… no… I think—" She stared at his hand when he extended it, hesitating with her words.

"Take my hand," Zach said. "I'll help you."

She took a deep breath and accepted his help. Her legs shaky and eyes darting about, she now stood with him on the third floor. *Only four more to go.* "When you're ready, we'll make it to the next floor."

Shira nodded. It took her ten minutes to move, each step painstaking for Zach. The idea of thinking this was just a bottom floor didn't seem to work so well, thanks to that orc. He wished there was something he could do to help her handle this better.

They made it to the next set of stairs, and this time he had her go up first. She didn't want to, but he didn't give her a whole lot of choice. When they reached the fourth floor, it took him joking about carrying her the rest of the way to get her to step off the stairs. The defiance in her eyes sparked desire in him. It was that will of hers that first drew him in and kept him coming back, as confusing as it all was.

Floor five went more smoothly, but for some reason she struggled to step onto floor six. Not even light nudging helped. Zach leaned in close, keeping his voice low for her sake. "What's wrong?"

Her lip quivered and her voice cracked. "This floor… this floor is the same…"

Shit. He should have known. "It's okay, Shira. This isn't the same place. It's just a tower that happens to have a sixth floor."

"I know… but…"

She clamped up, her eyes tight and her knees trembling. Zach needed to think of something, or else she'd go into a panic attack, and he wasn't the greatest at helping someone out of that.

He slipped his arm around her waist and held her close. "I'm here. I may be a thousand miles away in another building, but I'm also here. With you—for you. Nothing will happen to you as long as I'm here. You have my word, Shira. You're safe."

Her breathing slowed and he watched her take controlled breaths to calm herself. When her wits came back, he nudged one leg with his knee. This time, she complied and took a step onto the floor. Zach didn't let her go without him, encouraging her to take many more steps until he was comfortable giving her the space she needed to find her own strength in this situation.

Her fingers dug into his gauntlets. "Wait."

"I'm not going anywhere," he said, trying to pull away a bit. "I'm still here. Just not suffocating you."

"You weren't." Her grip tightened and she turned to look at him. "You're comforting."

Zach's heart beat hard in his chest. *Those green eyes of hers.* Even though an avatar replica, they were close enough. There was something about them, different from Jasper and Serenity, drawing him in. He couldn't get her out of his mind since the moment he saw her eyes in that photo. And he didn't want to.

Zach's hand touched her waist again. She found him a source of comfort. It wouldn't be right to take that away. Jasper always said he was a bit too soft sometimes, but he didn't care at this moment. Zach wanted to keep her close, to feel the curve of her back and the softness of her form against him. Take in the texture of her hair. Wrap himself up in her scent and drown in—

The floor beneath Shira creaked and then splintered. Shira screamed when it broke underneath her, pulling him out of his trance. Zach sprung into action, grabbing her tight and pulling her into him, away from the crumbling floor.

Shira shook in his arms, and he did his best to calm her with a soothing tone of hushes. He stroked her head until her shaking slowed and she was taking deep breaths in his chest. Zach looked down at her. "Better?"

"I think… I think I'll be okay."

Zach lifted her chin. "No, you *are* okay. I promised nothing would happen to you. And I've kept that promise."

Shira stared at him and then looked around the room. "Yeah…"

Zach didn't push her to move this time. After that

unexpected experience, he wasn't going to rush this. He much preferred to keep her against him anyway.

Shira looked up at him again, gazing at… something. It made him hyper-aware of himself. Was there something wrong with his avatar? Was he making a weird face at her without realizing it? Was he—

Shira's lips pressed against his. A fleeting kiss, but one that sent his mind into shutdown mode. A sensation only Jasper had ever managed to give him, and his approach was far different from this tender one of Shira's.

She pulled away, taking a step back and averting her gaze. "Thank you."

Why wouldn't she look at him? Did she feel ashamed? Zach hoped not.

"We… we should continue," she managed. "Last floor is above us, right?"

"Uh, yeah." Zach took a step toward her. "Why don't I go first this time? I don't want you to experience another one of those traps."

She nodded, her eyes still not meeting his. "Thanks."

He slipped ahead of her and set a slow pace to the stairs. They found a similar trap as before, and this time Shira pulled him back. He gazed down at her as he held her tight. "Thanks."

She gave an awkward smile and shrugged. "Payback."

This was such a fascinating side to her. In his years of knowing Shira, he'd only ever seen her as a confident woman, if a little too mouthy. For the longest time, he didn't think there was a vulnerable side to her. And if there was, he'd never be at liberty to see it. And yet, here he was, viewing just how present it really was in these last few weeks.

He honestly liked it, realizing that she was more… real. Now if only he could make sense of whether his own wants were real or not… and shake the lingering feeling of betrayal.

"Zach, you can let go now," Shira said.

He pulled himself from out of his head. "Oh, right, sorry."

Zach pulled away and Shira took a step for the stairs. The moment he did, he mentally kicked himself. He'd missed a prime opportunity with her. He could have given her "payback" as well. Maybe it would have squashed the doubts in her about her actions with Jasper—as well as the doubts he was having.

He now needed to find another moment, and hoped it wasn't too late.

Shira placed one foot on the bottom stair before peering over to him. "You coming?"

Zach shook himself. "Uh, yeah—sorry."

His response got her to giggle for a second before she got the nerve to make a slow attempt at getting to the last floor. Zach followed her up, murmuring words of encouragement to keep her going. Then, her feet touched the seventh floor.

The two of them stood in the middle of the near-empty room. There was only a single armoire in the room. No enemies, so that was good. Shira twitched as she tried to convince her feet to move toward the dresser, to no avail. Zach reached out and grasped her hand with his. She looked to him and smiled. They'd go together.

One step, then two, they eventually made it to the armoire. They each took a handle and opened it. Inside lay a single wrapped item. It was small, no larger than a hand mirror. Zach guessed that might be what it was.

Shira lifted the item, their quests marking as complete, and then looked around frantically. Zach chuckled. "What, thinking this is one of Mercedes' and Takashi's treasure hunts?"

Shira snorted. "Can't ever be too careful."

He took her hand. "I'd never do that to you. I would, however, make you do this."

Zach tugged her to follow him to a window. She sighed. "You're really going to make me look down, too?"

He chuckled. "Yes."

Shira sucked in a tight breath. "Okay. Let's see how bad I freak."

Zach led her to the window and slipped out onto the roof. Shira took a moment to breathe before making her way out with him. Her legs wobbled as she stood there on the roof, staring out at the expansive landscape beyond the tower. Zach let her come to the edge with him at her own pace. Besides the sixth floor, this would be the hardest thing for her to face in the task.

Inch by inch, Shira shuffled closer. She'd backstepped a few times as well, but always rebounded and progressed. Zach took a keen interest in every change in her. If at any moment he thought this would trigger something, he'd end it. He wanted to challenge her, not traumatize her.

Shira snatched his hand when she came within reach of him again, her gaze silently gauging their distance from the ground below. Her feet remained planted in place there, and in the end, she didn't make it to the edge. Zach wasn't going to push it. She'd made it this far, so he'd count it a success.

Zach took several steps away from the edge of the roof and let her follow in her own time. Shira let out a breath of relief when her back hit the wall. Zach placed a hand on her shoulder. "You did fantastic."

"Yeah, well, at least one of us thinks that."

He reached out and took her chin, turning her gaze to him. "You should. The fact that you got as far as you did is progress."

Her gaze lowered. "But not enough. At this rate, I won't do well at the convention center."

Zach's brow furrowed. "I don't understand. It's not like we're going to make you go out on a roof and look down."

Shira looked up at him. "No, but Gamer Nine is held in a multi-story building, and the first three to four floors are always sectioned off for the event. If I go to any of those floors and look down, I'll have to deal with this same sensation. If we go to relax in a hotel room, I will have to fight so much to do so." Her eyes fell away. "There's more to it all than facing my fear of heights once or twice with moderate success."

"Shira, look at me," he commanded. She didn't, so he lifted her chin with his fingers. "Look at me."

She hesitated and then listened.

"This wasn't just a moderate success. You've flown on the backs of VR dragons. Stood at the highest point of a mountain chasm. Climbed a tower nearly as tall as where everything happened. Faced the one floor that should have left you crippled in a ball of fear right now. Don't you dare downplay your achievement, you hear?"

Her wide eyes stared back at him. Zach caressed her cheek with his thumb. "Do you understand?"

Shira gave a slow nod. "Y—yeah."

He smiled and looked inside the tower. "Good. Now, I have something for you."

Zach pulled out the necklace he'd looted earlier and offered it up. "I took this off the orc; I thought you should have it. A reward for doing so well."

Shira reached out and took it, accepting the trade prompt. "Wow, it's beautiful. Thank you. It's even an upgrade."

That delighted him more than he expected it would. He watched her swap out the jewelry, the necklace now visible around her neck. It went nicely with her gear. As he gazed at her, he started to wonder what she'd look like with only the piece of jewelry on.

He shook himself of the thought. He needed to get her out of the tower before focusing on that task. "Let's get you down from here."

"Sure."

The two climbed in through the window and made their way below. Zach triggered a floor trap on the sixth floor, but Shira had his back for that one. When they made it to the fifth floor, Shira's mood improved drastically. It gave him an idea. "Hey, why don't we race to the bottom?"

Her brow cocked. "You want to race down this old thing?"

He gave a light shrug. "Why not?"

Shira regarded him for a moment and then slowly walked behind him. *What is she up to?* "You're not afraid your armor will slow you down?"

Zach chuckled. "Lusara Fates doesn't have a weight restrictions with armor, remember, babe?"

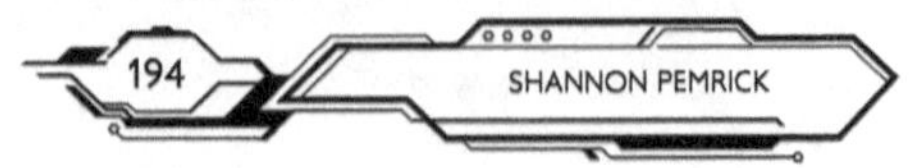

She reached up and tugged his long hair. It sent a pleasant rush of sensations through him. "Don't call me 'babe.'"

He calmed himself. She was right. Shira had expressed her displeasure for the word often enough that he shouldn't have jested with it. Though, she'd never told them what made her twitchy about it.

Zach studied her as she stood next to him. "So what is it—did an ex you hate call you that?"

She didn't look at him. "Why I don't like it, isn't your business. Now, are we going to race or not? I'd like to get out of here."

Ouch. Okay, so ex-issue was right. That was good to know. "Get ready. Get set. G—"

"Go!" Shira took off.

"Cheat!" Zach ran after her.

She made it to the stairs far faster than he did, and started to descend. Zach pushed himself as fast as he could down the stairs and through the fourth floor, but couldn't gain a lead. When they made it near the bottom of the stairs, he jumped over the railing and took off running. Shira sprinted past him. *The fuck?*

She glanced back with a grin and disappeared onto the next floor. Again he tried to cut her off, but she pulled the same maneuver. *How is she so fast?*

As he raced after her down the last flight of stairs, something dawned on him. *Why did she walk behind me before we started?* It didn't put her any closer to the stairs. *Oh, no she didn't…*

Shira bolted out the entrance to her freedom before he could make it off the steps. By the time he made it out, she jumped and cheered for her "win." If he hadn't caught onto her little secret, he may have been a bit more excited for her.

"Good job, you little cheat."

She stopped her joyful dance. "I only left a few seconds before you. Hardly cheating."

Zach advanced. "No, but you did change your boots out for a pair with a speed enchantment, didn't you?"

Shira bit her lower lip, sending need right down to his groin. "You didn't say I couldn't." She then took off down the road.

"Get back here!" Zach gave chase, but her boots gave her a distinct advantage. He didn't have anything like that on him, so he needed to get creative. He summoned a ground mount and lessened her lead. Shira glanced back, her eyes going wide, and pushed faster. At this rate, she wouldn't be able to summon a mount of her own.

When Zach came in range, he jumped off his mount and grabbed for her. Shira threw him a curve ball when she pivoted and changed directions, forcing him to give chase on foot again. He lost a great deal of his ground on her, but he wasn't easy to lose. Jasper may keep going forward, but Zach could use his head now and then.

Spotting a tree near a far-off alcove, he adjusted his angle to force her in that direction. It worked. So preoccupied losing him, and looking back too many times to gauge the distance between them, she didn't notice the dead-end he'd sent her toward until it was too late.

She tried to circle around the tree and lose him, but he expected that and grabbed her. Her back hit the tree trunk, his arms pinning her in place.

Her alluring green eyes gazed up at him, and a sheepish smile spread across her lips. "You win."

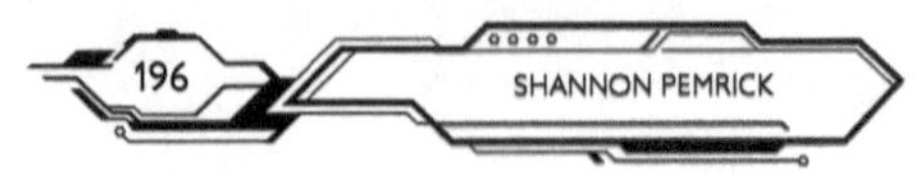

Zach leaned closer. "You going to apologize for cheating?"

Shira stuck her bottom lip out into a pout. Regret gripped him. *God, she's good.* And he thought Serenity knew how to get him. "But I didn't cheat, Zach. You never said I couldn't change out my gear."

"If that were the case, you wouldn't have tried to hide it."

Her big eyes gazed up at him. *Fuck.* "I just wanted the surprise to be more fun is all."

"That may be, but you still tried to deceive me. Now apologize."

Shira stared up at him for a moment before suddenly popping up on her toes and pressing her lips against his. Not expecting such an action, he locked up. *Wrong thing to do, idiot!*

She ended the kiss and pulled away from him, her eyes going elsewhere. "Sorry. I shouldn't have done that."

He went to say something when she took a few more steps away, still not looking at him. "I didn't mean to step on any toes. I believed Jasper when he said it was okay last night."

Zach's chest tightened. "Shira, I—"

She looked at him. "It's okay. It's not my intention to get between you two. You don't have to force yourself to be on board with this." Her eyes dropped again. "I didn't really expect anything different, if I'm completely honest here."

It felt like someone had punched him in the gut. He was screwing this up. He needed to say something. "It's not you, Shira. It's me."

Her eyes snapped up to him, her brow cocked. "Did

you just give me the corniest break-up line in the books?"

This gave him pause. "I… didn't mean for it to sound that way."

She placed the side of her finger against her mouth, muffling a tiny giggle. Zach ran his fingers through his hair. "But, as stupid as it sounds, that is the issue. You've done nothing wrong. I—"

He sighed, not sure how to word himself.

Shira took a step closer, gazing up at him. "What?"

He licked his lips. "This is something I'd like to talk to you about in a better setting. Let's… go back to the guild."

She gave him a curious glance but pulled out her teleportation stone. He did as well and activated it. A bright light surrounded him and then he was in his room.

CHAPTER 10

Shira glanced around her room before sticking her head out into the hall. Zach had already stepped out of his room a few doors down, looking around to see if any guildmates were around to see them. The last thing she needed were more rumors to spread, and she suspected he was in the same boat.

She waved him over and he slipped into her room, looking around at the wall-to-wall clutter of various trophies, art, tapestries, and in-game knick-knacks. "I see you like to decorate."

She shrugged. "It's fun seeing how much customization I can do before it creates a mess. Do you not do this?"

He rocked his head back and forth. "I've got a few PvP trophies and tapestries. Jasper doesn't decorate at all."

Her baby gryphon resting on her bed caught his eye. "When did you get that?"

Shira smiled wide, unable to hide her excitement.

"Last night with Jasper. It was the reward from the quest he picked."

He snapped his fingers. "Should have thought of that myself. You're a sucker for cute animals."

Heat rushed to her face. The claim wasn't wrong.

Zach tapped his lips. "Though, are you sure that was your reward for the quest? I'm pretty sure Jasper was."

Her cheeks burned hotter while regret gripped her chest, and she looked at the floor. Zach lifted her chin. "That was supposed to be a kind crack at you. I told you, I'm not upset with what happened last night."

Shira moved her gryphon cub and sat down on her bed. She patted the open spot next to her. "Well, then I think that promised explanation is in order, because I'm confused."

That didn't come close to describe the buzzing emotions in her head, but it was a start.

Zach sat down and took a moment before speaking, struggling to hold eye contact with her. "Like I said before, this is all on me, not you. It's… I've only ever been attracted to two women."

Tension released from Shira's shoulders. He never talked about any women he'd been with, so she assumed it wasn't a preference of his. It was why she couldn't believe he may want to be with her like Jasper did.

"The first one, Amy, was a good friend of mine," Zach said. "Neither she nor I had ever been with the opposite sex before. And because we had… less than accepting parents, we thought we'd fake it to get them off our backs for a while."

Shira rested her hand on his. Zach never talked about his parents. Never mentioned them visiting him, Jasper, and Serenity, or they them. Now she knew why.

Zach glanced down at her hand. "During that time, we tried to see what we might be missing. We did our best to act as a real couple, not just for show, and I did start to feel something real with her. Enough where I consented to adding the sexual aspect to our bizarre relationship."

He rested his face into the palm of his hand. "It didn't work out so well. We decided it was better for us to stop trying to fit a USB into an HDMI port and just be friends. I knew at that point women weren't for me." He paused a moment. "Until I met the second woman to tempt me."

Shira waited for him to reveal about this special second woman. When his eyes snapped up to her, realization dawned on her. *Oh…* Zach leaned in, cupping her cheek, and kissed her. The touch of his lips, feather-light and warm, sent butterflies fluttering about in her stomach.

"You," he murmured when he pulled away. "You came crashing in like an out-of-control berserker and turned everything off-kilter. You've thrown me into enough loops I don't know which way is up anymore. Only Jasper has ever done that to me. And that's why this limbo we're in now is my fault. I don't know how to react to all of this with you. I'm wicked confused on how to feel."

He wasn't the only one. Shira didn't expect this kind of confession from him. His actions were hot and cold so often, she thought she might be imagining the hot. But now it made sense, in a way. Where they stood was a little muddy, but that was easily fixed. *I'm not the only one who has to work on their fears.*

This wasn't going to be a permanent thing. It was one time for him, just as it had been for Jasper. A way for all of them to get out some pent-up sexual tension that'd built up over the years. That's all Zach felt now—what she felt and tried to deny.

And because Zach mentioned that he and Amy had stayed friends, Shira felt a little more okay with what she was doing. While not exactly the end of the world, losing these two would hurt a lot, and it'd be difficult to adjust to a life without them in it in any way.

Her tongue darted out and teased his lips. "I've got an idea that may help."

Zach, to her delight, didn't move away. His lips brushed hers as he spoke. "Oh yeah? I'm interested in hearing it."

Shira rose to her feet, leaving him confused. "I can't make any promises, but with my experience, I may be able to make this second try more enjoyable. If you're up for it."

Zach swallowed, his eyes widening a bit, and then he nodded. Shira positioned herself in front of him, their knees almost touching. "If you want to stop at any time, tell me. I'm not going to do anything you don't want."

He gave another slow nod in response.

"First, take off what armor you're comfortable with at this very moment."

Zach hesitated, but piece by piece, his armor disappeared into his inventory until he sat on her bed with only a tabard covering him. This amused her, but she wasn't going to pick on him. Instead, her eyes raked over him. Even with the material covering him, she enjoyed how the fabric clung just right to his form. She'd enjoy

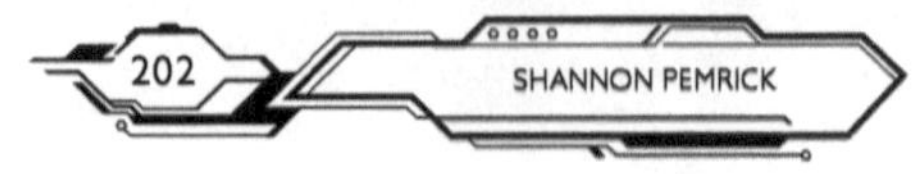

it more if it were on the bed next to him… after being ripped right off by her. *Whoa, girl, easy. Stick to the plan.*

Shira licked her lower lip before gesturing to herself. "Now, tell me what to take off."

His brow furrowed. "I'm not sure I understand. All of it needs to be off if we're to do anything."

Shira chuckled. "So you want me to remove everything at once? Or would you rather I go piece by piece?"

His eyes glinted, lust mixing with realization. "Oh."

She grinned, her pulse quickening. His interest even before seeing what lay beneath the armor excited her. "Oh, indeed. So, what would you like?"

Zach leaned back on his hands. "I wouldn't mind a little striptease. Or what this game will allow for one."

Shira pulled up her armor window. "Then tell me was to remove. That makes it more fun."

"Gloves," he blurted out.

An interesting, but safe start. She complied, though for added effect, she let the gear drop to the ground. Zach's eyes followed the armor. She waited for his next request.

"Um… those annoying boots of yours."

Shira chuckled. She half expected him to want those to stay on. Most of the men she hooked up with did. But given she'd cheated him out of a race with them, it only made sense.

The boots came off and she flung them across the room, the armor clanking as they went.

"Pauldrons and bracers next."

Those clattered to the ground as well. This left her breastplate and pants, though the breastplate didn't leave much for the imagination. Shira placed her hands on her hips as Zach's eyes trailed over her.

"The rest, now." His voice had grown deeper, almost throaty. The sound sent a shiver down her spine.

Shira's fingers hovered over her armor panel. "You sure you're ready?"

His eyes met hers. A slight flush tinted his cheeks, but his eyes gave away the desire building in him. *No doubting that look. He wasn't lying about his possible feelings toward me.* She almost grunted out loud. Attraction, yes, but feelings? She wasn't convinced—with either man.

"Shira, take the armor off, now." The firm command sent a fiery spark straight to her core. Between the two, Jasper had always been the more dominant type, but it appeared Zach also had it in him when he wanted.

Shira removed the breastplate first, her supple breasts bouncing from the sudden release. Zach's eyes glinted as he following their hypnotic motion. The necklace he'd given her earlier remained on, a nice little accent in her opinion.

The pants came off next. Now bare and on display, save for the jewelry she wore, she watched Zach take a moment to pry his eyes away and run them over the rest of her. An appreciative smile spread across his lips. It made her heart thump.

His gaze returned to her face, their eyes locking. *Those eyes...* They weren't the eyes of some avatar. She saw right past them to the real him—just as she had with Jasper.

The heat in her core intensified. Shira enjoyed this. It wasn't every day this type of appreciation was given to her... even if it was just a game avatar he liked.

Deciding she'd given him ample time to appreciate from afar, she moved closer and slipped onto his lap.

Zach's hands found purchase on her ass, and he swallowed, his jaw going slack and his eyes wandering over her. His erection pressed against her femininity, his tabard the only thing protecting her.

Shira rested her hands on his and encouraged them to move. He gave little resistance as she slid them over her thighs and up her sides to roam her body. Her lips parted, the sensation of his firm hands touching her skin simmering desire in her blood.

She missed this for her real body—the pleasant sensations of intimacy she'd never have again. The artificial nerves were great simulators, but it'd never be a substitute for what she could feel on the side of her that was still human.

Zach's hands slid over her breasts and pebbling nipples. Her eyes hooded, her breath hitching. A dangerous grin spread across Zach's face as he teased and played, sometimes gentle, other times a bit rough. This was Shira's favorite part of foreplay. She didn't care how long he took with this.

One of his hands migrated down her flat stomach to her inner thigh. Shira swallowed, anticipation gripping her. Zach's eyes ticked up to hers and he slipped a finger between, into her slick heat. She gasped, her heart skipping and slamming against her chest. He flicked his finger against her sensitive heat, pleasure coursing through her. A quiet moan escaped.

Zach smirked, removing his finger. A mere tease, both frustrating and desirable. His hand returned to her chest, both now pinching and rolling her sensitive buds between his fingers.

Shira rocked her hips, his hardness pressing into her.

Desire crawled through her, her hands clutching his tabard where they rested on his chest. She needed more.

Zach reached up and touched her chin, his thumb sliding over her lower lip. She caught his quiet groan before he gave her chin a light tug. "Come here."

He pulled her in before she could think to comply, his lips crashing into hers. Warm and demanding, he stole her breath. She whimpered under his touch, her body aching and begging for more. Shira threaded her fingers through his hair, pulling him closer. She needed to feel him against her.

Their kiss broke and he dipped his head, trailing kisses and nips down her neck and over her collarbone. Shira groaned and then gasped when his tongue flicked over one of her taut nipples.

"Did you like that?" His voice hummed over her skin.

She swallowed hard. "Yes. Do it again."

He did. And then again and again. His tongue circled and flicked and teased, his hand teasing and massaging the other. Zach pressed his lips over her aching bud and captured it, sucking and then tugging hard. Shira moaned, pleasure pulsing in her veins. "Keep doing that."

Zach hummed against her skin and switched sides. Shira tightened her grip on his hair and pulled him even closer. But it wasn't enough for her. She needed more.

Shira slipped a hand between her thighs, stoking her needy desire. Her mouth fell open, but before she could fall into the pleasure, Zach pulled away. This pulled her out of her bubble of fun and into a state of confusion. "Wha—"

Zach placed a finger over her lips. "I'm enjoying the show."

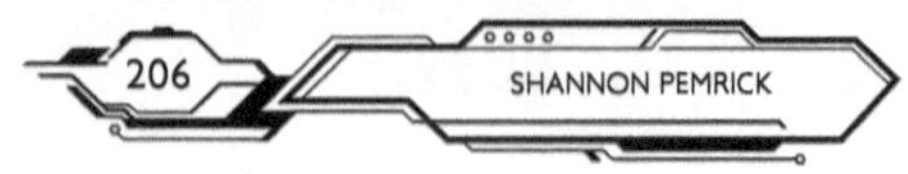

Shira chuckled. "This is all one interactive show."

He ran his hands up her thighs and cupped her ass. "Is it, now? This isn't a *create our own adventure*-type situation?"

Shira continued to stroke herself. "That requires a different setting."

Zach's hands squeezed her and he leaned in with a teasing lick against her rosy buds. "Is that so? Well, then we may need to discuss that at some point. But right now"—his teeth grazed her aching peaks—"Tell me what you want in this stage of the interactive show."

Shira walked her fingers up his chest. "Are you sure you're ready for that request?"

His menu opened and his tabard disappeared, his erect manhood springing forth. *Impressive size.* One of the odd new features of this game, players could alter *every* feature of their choosing. She wondered how close to real life it was, then shook it from her mind. *This is a one-time thing, Shira. Don't do that to yourself.*

A grin spread across Zach's face. "I'm sure."

He kissed her, deep and hard enough to steal her breath again. She ended her self-pleasuring and circled the base of his shaft with a feather-light touch before gripping his hardened appendage. Zach's breathing hitched as she stroked him and his grip on her ass tightened, pulling her high on her knees. Her pulse hammered and desire thrummed through her body as she rubbed his hardness against her sensitivity, teasing them both.

Their kiss broke when she hovered over him. Zach's breathing slowed, his lust-filled eyes snaring her. Shira eased herself over his shaft, her lips parting and a quiet moan escaping them as she accepted him inch by inch.

Zach's grip on her tightened, pulling her against his hard form.

When fully seated on him, Shira didn't give Zach much time to process the new sensation before she rocked her hips. He groaned, the muscles in his arms and neck twitching, but he didn't stop her. Shira found a rhythm that suited her, leaning against him for the best angle she could obtain at the moment.

"Shira," he groaned. She grinned and nipped his neck, gaining a hiss in response.

Zach leaned back, meeting her movement with his own thrusts. She gasped and moaned; the new sensation he added—powerful. Her heart pounded in her chest, her breasts bouncing against him, their sensitivity sending sparks down to her hot core. "Zach…"

But he wasn't done. Zach trailed his fingers down her back, over her ass, and gripped her thighs, spreading them further. His thrusts penetrated her deeper and she let out a deeper groan. Shira threaded one of her hands back into his hair while dipping the other between them and into her dripping femininity, stroking herself.

The pounding, the stroking, it all set her body on fire. Then, before she could utter it, ecstasy burst through her. A pleasure-laced scream filled the room.

Zach's grip on her thighs tightened and he thrust harder, his breathing laboring. He pressed his forehead on her chest, his hot breath beating against her sensitive skin. Then he grunted and abandoned himself in his own release. It lasted a moment before his movement slowed, then he stilled, their heavy breathing now the only sounds to fill the room.

Shira's heart pounded in her ears. *These two men…*

She'd hooked up with her fair share over the years, and sex was just that. A means to an end. She didn't lie to Angelica when she said that earlier. But sex with Jasper and Zach, even if the actions were the same as with others, wasn't like her past experiences. These two were something else—she couldn't place it. And that frustrated her on multiple levels.

She spoke once her heart returned to a more manageable pace. "That better than your first time?"

Zach hummed, pulling her closer. "Much."

He pressed his face into her chest and mumbled something. Shira giggled. "What? I don't speak boob muffle."

He tilted his head up. "I said it would have been even better had this been the real you I was spending time with."

A frown slipped across Shira's lips and she looked away. "This body is far better."

Zach's eyes narrowed. Before she knew what was happening, her back hit the mattress. Shira stared up at Zach while he hovered over her, his hands pinning her wrists to the mattress. "Don't you dare say that."

She wanted to voice an argument, but the words died in her throat under the intensity of his gaze. She'd never seen him like this before. Her heart pounded hard in her chest.

Shira eventually managed to find her voice, though it came out quieter than she wished it had, and she didn't say what she intended to. "Are you going to punish me?"

Why did I ask that?

"No, that'd be Jasper. I'd have fun watching, though."

She swallowed hard. That was an appealing image. "Is that why you're growing out your hair?"

Zach shook his head. "I'm doing that for me. It's only a bonus for him."

Interesting. Shira tried to wiggle her hand free, but he held firm. "I'm not letting you go until you take back what you said."

Shira's eyes narrowed. Apparently she couldn't distract him from topics like that. "I know what I'm talking about, Zach."

"I will not allow you to say those things about yourself." His eyes became intense again. "It's not true."

Wiggling some more, and finally resorting to some tickling between his fingers, Shira managed to slip her right hand free. She reached out and cupped Zach's cheek. "Feel that? Warm. Real."

She placed her hand on his chest and pushed against him, forcing him to sit beside her. She grabbed his hand and ran it along her right side. "And here—Soft. Warm. Real."

She did the same with her leg. "And here, too. That's what this body offers. Like anyone's body should. But I'm not like that anymore. Everything here"—she gestured to her entire right side—"Cold and hard. Nothing about it is human. Nothing about that is appealing—or wanted."

Shira turned and hung her feet over the edge of the bed. That was her reality. It was nice finding someone you connected with deeper than most. It was a wonderful thing to be consumed by love. But it was an entirely different matter falling for someone you've never truly touched, only to find out they were nothing like you imagined.

This was her. The woman on the other side of the

screen who looked appealing, but didn't feel so great in your arms.

She sighed. *I should go.*

Before she could stand, Zach reached out and wrapped his arm around her. "Come here."

Shira pried his arm off. "If you're looking to cuddle, it's not going to happen."

Zach didn't pull his arm back. "So did I—"

"It's nothing against you," she said, knowing what he was thinking. "I told the same to Jasper. I'm not a cuddling person."

"Never?"

"No." The lie tasted just as horrible now as when she'd spoken it to Jasper. But she had to keep it this way. Shira twirled a lock of hair. *I have to…*

Zach sat up and rested his chin on her shoulder. "Well, I'm not ready to let you leave yet."

Was he looking for more? She wouldn't say no to another round. Even if he wasn't, she couldn't see any harm in staying. It could help prevent any awkwardness that might spring up between them. Shira rolled her head back to look at him. "Okay. Tell me your and Jasper's story."

She was a sucker for those.

Zach wrapped his arms around her again and pulled her into his lap. She couldn't prevent the tiny squeak in response. "We met in grade school, second grade. My family had moved from Vermont because of my father's job. Didn't have any friends and I was too shy to make any. One day during recess, a kid I always had trouble with started to get too physical, and out of nowhere Jasper clocked the kid in the face. He shouted at the kid to never be mean to me again and sent him running. He helped me up and then didn't lie his way out when a teacher came over to find out what happened when the bully tried to get us into trouble."

Shira laughed. "Sounds like him."

Zach nodded. "He was a scrappy kid back then. But a good heart, like now."

"And you two were inseparable ever since?"

He nodded again. "For a long time after that, at least."

Shira frowned. She didn't like the sound of that. "What happened?"

Zach sighed. "Jasper and I had a strong bond. We did everything together and supported each other through everything." He frowned. "Then high school came along. I struggled through these years. I started to realize I wasn't attracted to girls the way Jasper or the other guys around us were. It was confusing at first. And when Jasper poked and prodded when I didn't act in ways he expected me to, I was nervous about telling him, so I always blew it off or avoided the topic."

He grunted. "I had nothing to worry about, of course. Jasper cornered me and made me tell him what was up. When I finally spilled, he laughed at me for being so stupid about it. His acceptance threw me for a loop, but what got to me the most was his insistence on finding me a nice boyfriend, finally."

Zach hid his face in the palm of his hand. "That guy had no sense of shame."

Shira laughed. "Can you really say he does now?"

Zach laughed along with her. "That's true."

His laughter died and the frown returned. "Jasper became my rock at that time. My parents found out about my orientation and tried to send me to therapy. When that didn't work, and they couldn't force me to abandon a part of who I was, they kicked me out."

Shira's eyes widened. She figured they may not be good people, but that was horrible!

"Jasper and his family took me in. I was grateful, but at the same time, conflicted. Around that time, I also started to see my relationship with Jasper differently. He was everything to me, and on more than one occasion back then, I admitted to finding him attractive. But I knew he wasn't into me like that. It took some adjusting, living with him and dealing with the growing feelings, but I managed. I refused to ruin our friendship because his smile made my heart skip."

Zach rubbed the back of his neck. "Then, just after graduation, he met Sara, and I knew the first moment I saw them together, that was it. It hurt wicked bad, but still I wasn't going to be anything but supportive."

Shira grasped his hand. She could only imagine what kind of pain that caused him.

Zach's head dipped. "I moved out of Boston around that time. I needed to get away and allow myself to move on, but not cut ties with Jasper, because I'd never do that. I just needed to figure things out in my life, and a part of me still wanted my parents' approval. Even though I lived with the Quinns for over two years, I hadn't cut ties with my parents completely by that point."

Zach's lips twisted. "The pain never went away, and it stayed a dull ache when the two of us decided to jump on the VR madness and play professionally. Then there was Sara. She didn't make any it easier on me; she always thought I was going to swoop in and steal him."

He grunted. "I really wanted to, but Jasper loved her more than life itself. It made me so angry she didn't see that." He shook his head. "Even when I stood by him at his wedding, she thought I'd call for an objection."

Shira's brow furrowed. She didn't know much about this Sara, but she'd assumed she was a sweet woman. *Sounds like she had a bit of an unhealthy, possessive side.* "Did she ever chill out?"

Zach nodded. "Yeah, but it wasn't until she and Jasper were expecting Serenity, and even then, things were still a bit tense and being worked on up until the end."

Shira circled into him. "And then the rest is what I know."

Zach reached up and threaded his fingers through her hair. She liked to have her hair played with; the sensation it brought on soothed her. *I shouldn't let him, though.* But she didn't stop him. She instead sat there listening to the beating of his heart.

"When everything went down with Sara, I rushed back to Boston to help in any way I could," he said. "I had no intention of doing anything more than assisting him through that difficult time, to help him transition over to being a single father..."

Shira glanced up at him when he went quiet. "But?"

Zach chuckled. "Sorry. Just remembering that day things changed. Jasper was having a rough day and snapping over everything little thing. He wouldn't listen to reason at all, and I'd had enough. I kissed him to make him shut up."

Shira's brow rose and then she laughed. "You really went with such a cliché move?"

His shoulders lifted into a half-hearted shrug. "I wasn't

thinking about my feelings for him at the time. They were building up again because of how close we were living, but he made me so mad. I dropped everything to come back and help him, believing that he'd only see me as that best friend who still had his back. I was completely unapologetic for my actions to shut him up, and then I tore into him. I figured that'd be the end of things for us, that the stress was too much for us to handle and that would be what broke us." He shook his head. "I was wicked wrong."

Shira giggled. "Cliché."

Zach tugged a strand of hair, and she involuntarily gasped when pleasant sensations zapped her. A devious grin spread across his face. "Jasper must have loved finding that out."

Shira caught her bottom lip between her teeth. "He wasn't complaining, that's for sure. But we're off-topic."

Zach shrugged again. "There isn't much to tell past that. The first time was just us letting out pent-up stress. But then we kept coming back for more until we realized this was just how we were now. Jasper didn't back away from it like I thought he would."

Shira smiled. "He doesn't have to like all men to see something in you."

He gazed down at her, curiosity in his eyes. This puzzled Shira. Why did it feel like... *Oh, no...* "Zach, do you question his feelings?" *Please say no, please say no.*

His eyes fell away. "On occasion."

Something invisible punched Shira in the gut. She really hoped that wasn't going to be his answer.

"I try not to. I believe every word when he says he

loves me. But there's always this nagging bit that tells me he's not…"

Shira pulled away. She needed to stop this. "Zach, he does."

She reached out and framed his face with both her hands. His warmth seeped into her skin. "I see it. Every time I'm around and he looks at you, there's nothing but unyielding devotion. The way he talks about you when you're not around, his words carry so much unapologetic love. It doesn't matter that you're the only man to ever come into his life like this." Her thumb caressed his cheek. "He's not going anywhere on you, Zach."

Zach's face relaxed and he smiled. "Thank you."

Shira smiled back and pulled her hands away. She didn't want to risk pushing anything further. Whatever stupid thing she was doing with them right now, it needed to stay a one-time deal. She would never break her third rule. And if Zach already struggled with doubt, her entering the relationship with them would only make it worse. *This was fun and all, but I'd rather not break something else so precious.*

Shira went to stand. "I should get going."

Zach wrapped his arms around her again, his hands cupping her breasts. "Not yet. I'm not done."

She tilted her head, her brows pressed together. "What else did you want to talk about?"

His hands massaged her breasts and he leaned closer, his hot breath on her neck. "No, not talking. I'm not done with you."

Zach pressed his lips against the back of her neck, his teeth nipping her skin. Shira let out a tiny hiss, her nipples hardening under his touch, throbbing need pulsing between her thighs. "I want to hear you scream louder this time."

She shouldn't encourage anything, but another round couldn't hurt, right? As long as she made sure he was in a position that lacked extra intimacy, she should be okay. She'd log off after, and tomorrow they'd go back to the way they were before, the long-standing sexual tension between them gone.

At least, that's what she told herself.

She rolled her head back, embracing the building sensations in her body. "Alright, once more. That's it."

His eyes flashed with something unreadable.

"There's only one position that will achieve what we both want."

Zach grinned in her ear and then flipped them both over in one strong move. Shira let out a gasp when she hit the bed face-first. "I'm partial to this one, too."

Kisses and nips trailed down her back. It arched in response, and her ass wiggled against him. She was eager to let him take control this time and see what other pleasures he offered. It was the only time she'd get to, after all.

CHAPTER 11

The game system released Zach, but he wasn't up for moving just yet. His whole body pulsed with both euphoric sensations and physical need, having not been satisfied beyond VR. It was one experience he wasn't quite used to, even though he and Jasper took full advantage of VR when they could. *And doing that all with Shira, instead—*

"I was wondering if you'd ever come out."

Zach's eyes snapped to the table, where Jasper lounged in a chair, a bottle of Guinness pressed to his lips. A small desk lamp near him remained the only light in the room, and the rest of the house appeared dark.

"How long have you been sitting there?" Zach asked, pulling out of the gaming pod.

"Long enough to watch how much fun you were having." Jasper took another sip. "I enjoyed watching your expressions, and the occasional sound."

Zach made his way over to the table. "Serenity in bed?"

Jasper nodded. "She was disappointed you missed story time, but undahstood since you were *helping* Shira." He offered the bottle to Zach. "I know you'd rather have an IPA, but we're still out."

Zach sat down on the table and took a sip, then handed the bottle back. "I'll live."

Jasper drank some more before setting the bottle down. "So, what's your verdict?"

Various emotions flashed through Zach. The last few hours with Shira had been fantastic. She'd handled his unsurety well, and being intimate with her had been far better than with Amy—no contest.

And while different from what he was used to with Jasper, it had been just as amazing. Beyond the intimacy, spending time getting to know Shira in a different way, gave him a greater appreciation for her. Something about her made her irresistible, and the very thought of her not being around unsettled him.

But something negative also nagged at him.

Maybe it was the way Jasper looked at him right now. He was so eager to bring her in, more so than Zach felt himself, even if he told himself he was. Why, though? As much as the idea appealed to him, why wasn't he as excited as Jasper?

Was it because he was so new to this? That Jasper had more experience with women, one he missed and craved? *Would he be happier with her than me?*

"Every time I'm around and he looks at you, there's nothing but unyielding devotion." Shira's words seeped into his mind. She believed their relationship was strong. So why didn't he?

Jasper waved his hand in front of his face. "Hello? Earth to Zach. Earth to Zach."

Zach blinked, pulling himself out of his head. "Sorry. I'm processing, since I didn't get the chance when I hopped out of game. Yes."

"Yes, you're on board?" Jasper sounded skeptical.

Zach nodded. "That's what I want. There's something about her that won't let me say no and be happy."

Jasper stood and positioned himself in front of Zach, placing his hands on either side of him. "You have no resahvations at all?"

"None." Zach said it with a straight face, but the lie left a bitter taste on his tongue. He should be honest about this—tell Jasper that he was nervous about it but still wanted to try.

Fear held him back.

If he said anything about his reservations, Jasper might see that as a "no, but you want this so I'll make myself be okay with it." And right now, even with how confused Zach was, he knew that wasn't the right conclusion. He was sure about one feeling—the idea of seeing Shira standing beside them, and not with them, created an ache in his chest. Thinking about it made him miss her, miss something he wasn't sure he had.

Zach leaned in and gave Jasper a chaste kiss. "If I recall correctly, you wanted to swap *notes*."

Those hadn't been Jasper's exact words when he'd held back details about his tryst with Shira, but Zach knew his boyfriend well.

Jasper chuckled and leaned in, kissing him back, harder than Zach had. "Yes, that'll be fun."

Zach gave another chaste kiss, just to tease him. "Kissing her?"

"Amazing."

A chuckle escaped Zach's throat. "Holding her?"

Jasper grabbed Zach by the hips and pulled him a little closer. "Amazing."

"Sex?"

His boyfriend's teeth sunk into Zach's lower lips. "Wicked amazing."

Even though his response had been expected, based on the other two responses, Zach couldn't contain his laughter. "So, were these real notes you wanted to swap, or cliff notes?"

Jasper kissed Zach's jaw and then nipped his ear. "I was thinking more along the lines of reenactment. Like right now. I took her on a table in a quest-givah's house."

That was a tantalizing image. And definitely an angle Jasper would take right away. "Missionary or doggie?"

Jasper hummed and kissed Zach's neck, who rolled his head back to give him better access. "Both."

Zach's pulse quickened. "I wish I were there to see that."

"And you?"

"Her bed in the guild hall."

Jasper kissed Zach's jaw again. "Safe, but effective. Decorations in her room? They say that shows a window into someone's personality. And I know you'd take in that kind of detail."

Zach laughed, pulling him out of this sensual game a bit. "You'd have a heart attack. She purposely tries to push the game's limit for junk decorating."

Jasper groaned in dismay. "Fantastic."

He couldn't lie, Zach wanted to see the two of them in the same room for a few days. Jasper was such a damn neat freak, if Shira wasn't in any way, that could get interesting. "She did add that pet you got her."

Jasper grinned. "That makes me feel a bit bettah. Now, how did you take her?"

"I'd rather show you." Zach whipped his shirt up over his head and tossed it haphazardly—mostly to get a reaction from Jasper, which he did—a narrowing of his eyes, but still a reaction.

Jasper leaned in, but Zach pushed him back. "Not yet."

His brow spiked in response. "She stood here while you removed your armor?"

"Just down to my tabard." Zach fussed with his pants. "But I don't have one of those on hand, so this will have to do." They hit the floor and Zach situated himself on the table again, his hard shaft at the ready for some sort of attention and relief. Between VR and now this, he'd gone and riled himself up. "Now you. Nice and slow."

Jasper's eyes glowed. "You got a strip tease, did ya?"

His partner's growing excitement, and the memory of his time with Shira, simmered his blood, his member hardening. "What the game would allow. She even let me pick what she removed."

Jasper took a strong breath. "Lucky you."

Zach chuckled. "You could have too, had you not gone in for the kill so quick."

Jasper pulled his shirt over his head, nice and slow as Zach instructed. His muscles stretched and tightened just right, showing off his fantastic physique. One thing the two of them made sure they didn't neglect, despite having sedentary jobs. "I didn't go in for the kill right off. Just couldn't stop myself from convincing her to show off that sexy body of her. I made sure to appreciate it all, nice and slow."

Zach leaned back on his hand, his eyes trailing Jasper's form as he fussed with his belt. "Which is exactly what I did."

Jasper chuckled and released himself from his pants, his clothes pooling at his feet, and his eager and ready erection springing forth. Jasper took a step forward, his legs bumping Zach's knees. "Now what?"

Zach beckoned him closer, and Jasper bent over. Zach reached up and cupped his boyfriend's face before claiming his lips. They both inhaled deeply. "Then she climbed on my lap and let me do what I wanted to her." His hands ran along Jasper's strong body, speaking between kissing. "Feel her up. Kiss her. Fuck her. She encouraged it all."

Jasper continued to kiss Zach back, wrapping his hand around the back of Zach's neck. "Sounds as fun as my experience."

"Let me guess, you made sure she put that mouth of hers to good use." Jasper never turned down a good blowjob. He enjoyed them way too much to say no, no matter the mood he was in.

Jasper chuckled. "Actually, no. At least, not right away. She offered that at the end."

Zach's brow spiked. "That's wicked backwards for you."

"Maybe, but getting her to beg before that was worth it." Jasper grasped Zach's golden hair and tugged enough to for him to expose his neck. "As were the screams she made."

Zach's heart pounded in his chest. If this is how he'd

handled Shira, he was sorry he missed it. "Her sounds are fantastic. Just like yours."

Jasper looked him in the eye and Zach's mouth dried. "Yours, too. And I want to heah that now."

He crashed his mouth into Zach's and stole his breath. Their tongues wrestled and hands roamed each other's bodies, needy and hungry, just as Zach felt with desire burning in his veins.

Jasper's hard length pressed against him. Zach raked his fingers down his partner's chiseled chest until he came in contact with Jasper's erect member. He wrapped a firm hand around it and stroked. Jasper groaned against his mouth and reached down to return the favor. Zach's head rolled back, breaking their fevered kiss, desire burning through his veins.

Taking advantage of Zach's exposed neck, Jasper trailed firm kisses and stinging bites down. Zach groaned and stroked him harder. Jasper groaned and pushed away, going for a nearby drawer. Zach sat up and fisted his throbbing flesh, his eyes raking over Jasper's backside.

Jasper pulled out a tube of lube and returned. He kissed Zach hard again, desperate and hungry, as if their lives depended on it. He nudged Zach's knees, who eagerly opened and exposed himself. Zach hissed when Jasper applied the cool lubricant over his tight hole, working his fingers inside. A strangled, anticipating groan twisted in Zach's throat.

Jasper chuckled low beside Zach's ear. "I hope you're ready."

God, was he ever. It felt like he'd waited hours for this.

Jasper nudged Zach's entrance with his hardness and then pushed inside. Their groans mingled, Jasper pushing

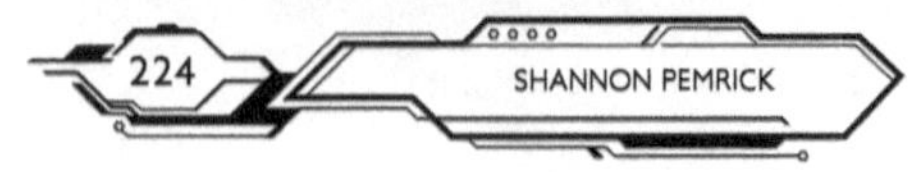

farther until he was fully seated. Jasper moved his arms to brace beside Zach's head, and the two stared into each other's eyes, desire between them palpable.

"Would you say she feels as good, or better?" Zach wasn't sure why he asked, especially right now, but he couldn't take it back now. And a part of him was curious—almost fearful of the answer.

"I'm not comparing." Jasper reached out and grabbed a fistful of Zach's hair, tugging hard. "Can't compare. It's not bettah or worse, and it's also not the same. You're both right—perfect. And you'd bettah not start comparing, eithah."

To Zach's surprise, the thought hadn't crossed his mind. Why was he afraid Jasper would have compared, when he wasn't? *Because Sara.*

As Zach stared up at Jasper, he caught the harrowing shadow lingering in his boyfriend's eyes. "I just know you."

Jasper leaned down, their noses nearly touching. The intensity of his eyes seared Zach's soul. His pulse quickened. "I won't lie; I did compare Shira to Sara. And it hurt, knowing I enjoyed Shira's time more than I evah remembah with Sara. Because I know what Sara and I had was wicked real, even with our share of problems. But I will not compare the two of you. If I'm allowed to have two favorite ice creams, then I can have two favorite people."

Jasper thrust hard and fast into Zach, canceling out any more conversation they may have had. He could try to think on Jasper's words, but he'd rather lose himself in them at the moment.

The impact of Jasper's hips and balls slapping against

the pale flesh of his ass sent wild, out-of-control sensations blazing through Zach's skin. Jasper pulled him in for a rough kiss before holding him firm to stare into Zach's eyes.

Reaching between them, Jasper wrapped his rough, calloused hands around Zach's throbbing shaft and set a strong stroking pace in sync with his thrusting. The added sensation heightened Zach's pleasure. His head rolled back, groaning. He was so close. Painfully close.

Their breathing labored and synced as one. The table creaked under them, for a moment worrying Zach it may break under their weight. Jasper's increased thrusting brought his mind back to the proper focus.

As climax built in Jasper, it swelled inside Zach as well. Then ecstasy roared through his boyfriend. Jasper abandoned himself to the pleasure, groaning loud and spilling inside him, his stroking never letting up until Zach's turn arrived.

Zach came hard, coating Jasper's hand with a sticky mess. His pulse raced in his ears, unsure if his cry of pleasure left the room and threatened to wake their daughter.

They slowed to a stop and collapsed in a breathless pile. Jasper held him close, kissing Zach's skin just right to get his sensitive muscles to react. It frustrated him, but Jasper enjoyed the light teases.

Once they both found feeling in their bodies again, Jasper pulled away and got a t-shirt to clean themselves with. He then sat on the table next to Zach. Zach leaned against his boyfriend, a hum of euphoria still coursing through him. Jasper wrapped his arm around Zach's shoulder and pulled him closer, pressing his lips against his temple, sweet and tender.

"Did Shira really tell you she doesn't do this?" Zach asked.

"Yep." Jasper rested his forehead against his head. "But she's full of shit. It's just her way to keep distant."

Zach chuckled. "At least I'm not the only one who saw through that." He worked his jaw. "With her usual stubbornness, and her propensity to keep us at arm's length, do you think what we're trying to do is possible?"

Jasper nodded. "Now that we've both agreed to pursue, it'll be easiah to convince her we're serious. Of course, we now have to figure out how quick to push this."

Zach agreed. "Not too fast, or she'll run. We've got a month before the convention. We've agreed, even if we somehow don't make it through the qualifiers, as unlikely as it is, we'll still go."

Jasper grunted. "I'm not great at slow. And if you expect me to wait a whole month to do anything, I might lose it."

A grin spread across Zach's face. "I never said we couldn't do small things. We just can't expect her to take us seriously if we tried to jump her tomorrow or even by next week in a tag-team style match and then asked her to date us."

Jasper let out a breath. "Why can't it be that easy?"

"Because life isn't as perfect as Serenity's interpretation of it. As much as we both wish it were."

"Truth."

Zach kissed Jasper's forehead. "Let's get to bed. We've got an early morning tomorrow."

Jasper grunted and reluctantly got to his feet, retrieving his clothes to toss in the hamper. With a sly grin plastered on his face, Zach reached out and slapped Jasper in the ass.

Jasper stopped and took a moment before turning to look at him, his brow raised high, his stunning green eyes pinning to Zach. "You sure you want to play that game?"

He advanced faster than Zach anticipated he would, and grabbed a fistful of hair, pulling his head back. A groan escaped Zach's lips when Jasper's other hand trailed across his sensitive member. "Because we can play that game, if you really want."

Zach swallowed. As much as he would like to, he wouldn't be able to handle that right now. "I'll behave… for now."

Smirking, Jasper leaned in and kissed Zach hard before pulling away and letting go. "We'll see how long it takes Shira to get into more trouble than you."

Zach snickered. "I'm already prepared to watch quite the show with that mouth of hers."

Jasper's eyes glowed. "I'm looking forwahd to it."

Cars roared and honked while people pushed their way down the sidewalks. Shira leaned against a building taking deep breaths, her heart slamming in her chest. Mercedes stood next to Shira, holding her hand. Snake sat between them, pressed against Shira's leg, licking both of their intertwined hands.

The two of them had traveled to Los Angeles a few days ago to meet up with Narissa and work on Shira's last hurdle—standing in front of the convention center. And she'd been doing decently until now, when two cars had collided. The sounds of the screeching of tires and clashing of steel had sent her into an immediate panic, as well as Mercedes.

They looked up when Narissa, a curvaceous woman with umber skin and dark curly hair, came around the corner. She carried two bottles of water in her hands. "They're almost cleaned up out there, nothing serious. I also got you two some water."

"Thanks, Narissa," Mercedes said, taking the offered refreshment.

"How are you both doing?" Narissa asked, her dark eyes soft.

"I'm doing better," Mercedes said. "It doesn't usually take me long to recover after seeing that. Shira…"

Shira nodded, taking more deep breaths. "I just need a bit longer."

Narissa came up to her and wrapped her arms around Shira for a comforting hug. "Take all the time you need."

Shira appreciated both her friends' patience with her. She wouldn't have gotten this far without them. *Or Jasper and Zach.* Thinking of them made her heart skip.

The two of them had worked with her between matches these last few weeks. No awkwardness had reared up after what she'd experienced with them, something she was thankful for. But the tension hadn't gone away like it was supposed to. In fact, she was sure it'd gotten worse, as well as Jasper's and Zach's antics. *Of course, I haven't exactly been keeping myself in check, either…*

Narissa dipped her head, looking Shira over. "You okay? You're looking a little flush."

Shit. She hadn't exactly been open to her best friends about what had gone down with Jasper and Zach. They'd freak out and see it as more than it was. Shira nodded and took a swig of water to play it cool. "Heat is getting to me a bit."

Neither looked convinced, but they also didn't press. Narissa instead changed the subject. "Why don't we take a break from all this and get some lunch, then and head to Cybro? It'll give you some more time to calm down, and I have something I want to tell you both."

Shira and Mercedes exchanged a glance. Why not tell them here? "Sure, sounds like a good plan. Sushi?"

"I was thinking more along the lines of sandwiches."

Mercedes' brow twisted and she pursed her lips. "You're saying no to your favorite lunch?"

Narissa shrugged and walked off. "Not feeling it today. Picard, please call the car."

"Of course, Doctor," a smooth voice said from her phone.

Shira and Mercedes looked at each other again. They weren't buying it. Something was up and they both wanted to know what.

While waiting for the car, they agreed on a sandwich shop and made a delivery order. Narissa's white Passat pulled up soon after.

Mercedes chuckled as they all climbed in. "I'm surprised Ajax hasn't gotten you a new car already. We all know he's got expensive tastes."

Narissa let out a breath. "He's trying, but so far I've thwarted that. I don't need a new car. This one is new enough and there's nothing wrong with it." Her phone stared to ring with an old Star Trek theme song. "Speak of the devil."

She answered. "Hey." Ajax spoke, but was too soft for Shira to hear. "Yeah, I'm still with the girls. We're going back to Cybro to eat, and then help Shira some more."

Shira tried to lean in close to eavesdrop, but Narissa swatted her away. "No, I haven't told them yet… Yes I do plan to… I know you're excited, but you have to wait…" She sighed, a light playful one. "I love you, too. Bye."

She hung up and Mercedes giggled. "You two are adorable."

"And total teases," Shira said.

Narissa held up a hand. "I didn't plan that. He's just excited."

Mercedes leaned on the console, her eyes bright. "And now I am. So spill!"

Narissa laughed. "When we get to Cybro. You can wait another five or so minutes; it won't kill you."

Shira smirked. "No, but it might kill your boyfriend."

The car filled with laughter. It died down when Shira's phone buzzed. She pulled it out to find a text from Jasper.

*Serenity wants you to see her before we
go trick-or-treating tonight.*

Shira smiled and typed back.

I'd love to see her.

Jasper and Zach had confirmed everything worked out when the package arrived, but Serenity didn't want Shira to see her in the costume. Shira suspected it was for this very reason.

Narissa leaned on the back of her seat. "Which boy-friend made you smile this time?"

Shira's head tipped back and her phone hit her knee. "Stop, would you?"

Mercedes also leaned on her seat. "We do it because we love you, and because you wouldn't stop with us."

Something gripped Shira tight in the gut. She looked out the window. "I don't want to talk about this."

"Shira, what's the matter?" Narissa asked.

She should tell them—tell them what she did with

the guys. Tell them the number of times these last few months she pictured herself with Zach and Jasper, included in their family. How happy that made her, only for reality to crash back in and remind her that her place was outside of that circle, looking in, because if she edged closer, she'd ruin something good. "I just don't like to talk about this, okay?"

Her friends remained quiet, though Shira felt their pity rolling off in waves. She wanted that to end. She wasn't a charity case. She didn't want some silly pity party. She made this decision on her own. *Even if they are the rare few who can look past my freakish nature, I'm not that horrible person who would break up a happy relationship and family for my own selfish wants.*

"So, what did they want?" Mercedes asked.

Shira looked at her friends again. "Serenity wants me to see her in the costume I helped make her."

The two melted. They knew about the costume; Mercedes had come over when she'd been packing it for the postal service.

Narissa peered at the time. "They'll be heading out in two hours, right?"

Shira nodded. "About that, yeah. I'm thinking, even if our lunch goes over, we'll still have some time to go back to the convention center before they call."

Her friends smiled, happy she was taking this fear issue so seriously.

"We have arrived," Picard said from the car dash.

Shira peered out the window as the car pulled up to a large building towering over the others around it. A sign reading *Cybro Industries* had been affixed halfway up the structure.

The three climbed out of the car, the midday Los Angeles sun bearing down on them, and made their ways up the front steps. Their feet echoed through the lobby after pushing through the rotating entrance doors.

A mousey young woman with thick-rimmed glasses sat at the reception desk. She looked up from her computer and smiled. "Welcome back, ladies."

"Thank you, Amy," Narissa said. "I ordered food, so if you could let me know when it arrives, I'd appreciate it."

Amy continued to smile. "Of course, Narissa."

Narissa thanked her and led the way to the elevator. When it reached their designated floor, the doors opened and all three exited, making their way down the long hall of glass-enclosed offices and laboratories until they came to an office with a plaque reading *Dr. Narissa Okafor, EVP*. Narissa pushed open the door and ushered Shira and Mercedes in. She glanced around before entering.

This re-engaged Shira's and Mercedes' interest. Shira crossed her arms. "Okay, spill."

Narissa's lips pressed together and her shoulders tensed as she took in a deep breath. "I'm pregnant."

Neither Shira or Mercedes reacted. Shock blanketed Shira's mind—it didn't take long to wear off. Excitement burst through her the same time as Mercedes. They both squealed in unison and jumped their friend. Even Snake picked up on the excited buzz and spun in circles. Narissa laughed, moisture rimming her eyes.

By the time they'd all calmed down, someone new stood outside the door. A tan-skinned man with strong features, large muscular build, and a cybernetic right arm entered the room, a big smile on his face and food bags in his hand. "I could hear the news being broken from the elevator."

Shira and the girls laughed. Mercedes went over to him to give him a hug. "We're happy for you too, Ajax, don't worry."

"Too crass to ask if it was planned?" Shira asked.

Ajax chuckled. "It was."

"Sort of," Narissa countered. "Should have taken longer."

"You gave me a challenge, I met it." He came into the room, kissed her, and set the bag of food on the table. "This is also yours. Delivery guy had just dropped it off when I came in."

"That challenge should have been impossible to meet," Narissa said, not letting go of this for some reason. "Especially not that fast. Statistically, it's impossible."

Shira and Mercedes looked at each other and then back at Narissa and Ajax. "Uh, I think we need some filling in here."

Narissa smiled. "Yeah, I never went into those details with you two. We can talk about it over lunch." She winked at Shira. "I'll try to keep it short so we don't keep your *not*-boyfriends waiting."

Shira's eyes narrowed and she crossed her arms and looked away. She really needed to figure out how to get them off her back without doing something stupid and relationship-damaging.

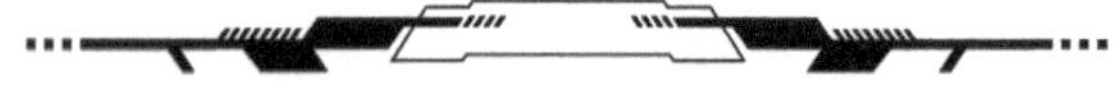

Jasper tapped his tablet, trying to get it to work. *Piece of shit, work!* Of all the times this could act up, it was right before they went out. And Serenity would not accept doing this call after trick-or-treating.

He looked up to watch Zach fuss with a part of Serenity's costume. That was another issue in itself, she'd gone through another growth spurt, and they had to alter some of what Shira made for her, with Shira's help over video chats. Jasper sucked at things like that, but Zach, while not great, had a better grasp. Cheryl also helped, thankfully.

They also had to modify it to be a bit warmer, as a nice cold front came in early and didn't want to leave. That'd bummed Serenity right out, but Shira knew just how to fix that issue. It wasn't the trainer costume Serenity wanted, but with everyone encouraging her, it just made her costume that much more unique, she came to love it as the days grew closer to Halloween.

"There, all set," Zach said.

Serenity jumped around cheering; they had to calm her down so as to not anger the neighbors below. He hated having to do that, but until they could find a house within their budget, they had to be courteous.

"Now, where did I put my camera?" Zach mumbled.

Jasper went back to fussing with the tablet. "On the table."

"Got it, thanks!"

Jasper looked up from his task to watch Serenity and Zach have fun and be goofy for the camera. He smiled. Photography may just be a hobby for Zach these days, but for the amount of joy it still brought him, a part of Jasper wished he'd stuck it out as a career.

The tablet's screen flashed, and then all sorts of prompt attempts Jasper had overloaded the device with all activities at once. His face contorted, which is what Shira, Mercedes, and Narissa saw when the device auto-accepted Shira's call. The three of them laughed at him.

"Do I want to know what caused that face?" Shira asked. "Because it better not be us."

"Tablet is on the fritz, and it picked up your call without my prompting," Jasper said.

"Apologies, Jasper," Alistair said. "That was my doing. I thought you wouldn't want to miss the call."

"Oh, thanks." He really needed to get used to using the AI.

"Daddy, tell She-ra I say hi," Serenity called out.

"Hi, Starship," Shira said. "Are you ready for me to see your costume?"

"In a minute. Zach and I are taking pick-chahs."

Shira smiled. "Okay."

A car roared by on Shira's end, and Jasper realized the three women weren't inside a building. It looked like they sat on some steps. "Shira, where are you?"

She tipped her device up, showing him a large building. "The convention center."

His eyes widened. "You're already able to sit there?"

Mercedes latched onto Shira. "That's because we know what our girl needs to fight this battle."

"Hey, we've been helping, too," Zach called out. "Don't you try and take that credit."

She stuck her tongue out. "Well, who's here helping her now?"

Jasper narrowed his eyes. "Serenity has school. And Shira would kill us both if we pulled her out."

Shira held her head high. "Damn straight."

Serenity gasped. "Daddy, can we go see She-ra

tomorrow? I don't hafta go to school." She ran over to him with big eyes. "Please? Please, please, please?"

Jasper almost sighed. *Thanks guys.* "No, Starship. You have to go to school. And hotels are expensive."

Narissa waggled her finger. "Hotel costs are covered, since you two made it into the tournament." She winked. "And the company wouldn't mind extending the days the three of you stay."

"Not helping." As much as he liked the idea of using their connections with Ajax and his company to flying over there tomorrow, Serenity needed to go to school. She was already going to miss a week during the convention, since he and Zach had already decided they'd stay a few extra days for a full family vacation. And it'd give them more time with Shira.

"Please, Daddy?" Serenity begged. "I promise I'll be wicked good!"

Zach climbed onto the couch next to him. "Yeah, Daddy, please?"

This got Shira and the girls laughing. Jasper, on the other hand gave him an unamused look.

Serenity placed her hands on the tablet. "Daddy, I want to see She-ra. Please!"

Jasper pressed his lips together. "You want to see her?"

She nodded.

"Okay, you can see her."

Serenity's eyes lit up, but then died when he flipped the tablet around. All the adults laughed when she pouted. "That's not what I meant."

"Oh, but, Starship, I really want to see you in your costume before you go out and have fun," Shira said.

Serenity perked up. "Oh yeah!" She then realized

there was a larger audience on the other end. "Who are they, She-ra?"

"This is Mercedes and this is Narissa," she said. "They're friends of mine and your dads."

She played with her fingers and acted shy. "Hi."

"Hi, Serenity," Narissa said. "It's nice to meet you. Your dads and Shira talk about you all the time."

"I like your costume," Mercedes said.

Serenity smiled wide and spun around. "She-ra made it for me! I'm a Pokémon trainah! Oh, and look"—she climbed on the couch between Jasper and Zach and removed one of the mini plush keychains from her belt—"Daddy and Zach got me these Monstah Huntah keychains to add to it!"

"That's awesome, Starship," Shira said. "You look amazing. You've got the best costume today."

Serenity cocked her head. "Where is yours, She-ra?"

"There's a big time difference between us, remember? Trick-or-treating won't happen for a few more hours here."

"Oh, okay. Can I see you in your costume when that time is?"

Shira smiled. "Of course. Now, I shouldn't keep you from your fun. And it's looking like your daddy and Zach still need to put their costumes on."

Serenity looked up at Jasper and then to Zach. "Yeah, I distracted them. You need your costumes."

Jasper reached for the tablet. "We will in a minute. Just need to ask Shira something."

"What's up?" Shira asked.

"We'll be coming in a day earliah than the convention." Jasper smirked. "We were hoping you'd considah meeting up with us and maybe showing us around. Since it'll be our first time in L.A."

Shira shrugged. "Yeah, sure. I'd love to."

Mercedes and Narissa grinned behind her. They knew what was up.

Zach and Jasper exchanged glances and then he smiled at her. "Sick. We'll figure out the details as things draw closah."

CHAPTER 13

Shira let out a deep breath as her car pulled up in front of the convention center. Her knuckles turned white as she gripped the steering wheel, unable to look at the building yet. The last week and a half had been full of difficulties. She'd make progress and then lose ground just as fast. But as of yesterday, she'd stood inside the lobby without losing her mind.

Of course, Mercedes and Narissa had been with her each step of the way, unlike today. And she had the added stress of meeting Jasper and Zach in person. Shira didn't know how this would go. Sure, she was excited to meet them. But she was more nervous over-all. Gameplay with the two of them still hadn't gotten any easier. The sexual tension had continued to build, and Shira struggled to not get lost in the fun of it all. She knew if she did, she'd do something she'd regret.

Snake nudged Shira's arm, forcing his way under it. She gladly wrapped him in for a comforting hug. Her tongue piercing scraped across the roof of her mouth and she worked her jaw. In her nervous state, she'd forgotten to swap it out for the retainer. Shira knew she didn't need to hide it, she just wasn't sure she was ready for the guys' antics once they found out about it. *I'll just have to be careful how much I open my mouth.*

"Shira," Orion said from the dash, his voice now smoother and less robotic, thanks to a voice pack Narissa had helped her upgrade him to. "I've informed Jasper and Zach of your arrival, per your earlier request. I've also acquired a parking space once you've exited."

"Thanks." She took a deep breath and looked herself over in her rearview mirror, fussing with her hair and double-checking her makeup. She also made sure her artificial skin was properly blended so she looked a bit more human. "Okay, Snake, time to see if all this practice will pay off."

She opened the door and slipped out, Snake jumping out after her. Shira double-checked his vest was secure, since he had somehow managed on many occasions to slip free of a strap or two while in the car. Then, she collected her courage and started to move toward the first set of steps leading up to the convention center.

The muscles in her neck and all along her back tensed as she took each step, her eyes pinned on the looming building. Snake nudged the hand gripping his leash.

"It's okay, Snake. I've got this."

She repeated the words in her head. She'd done this all week. She could do it now. *Just think of who you're meeting.* Her heart skipped. *No, not that.* Friends. Two friends and their adorable daughter. It'd be nice to meet these friends she'd known for so many years, truly face-to-face.

But at the same time, a part of her couldn't settle down. Meeting someone over the game and chatting over voice chat was one thing. This… meeting them in person? Even taking the step to video chat with them didn't compare.

And meeting these two in particular—She shut the thought out. She was just meeting friends. Close friends… each of whom she'd slept with once in VR… and maybe—definitely—continued to fantasize about—when she knew she shouldn't.

Shira's feet made it to the first landing and she took a deep breath. Only one set of stairs to go, and then her bigger test. *No, I can't think that way.* Everyone had constantly repeated that tip to her. If she didn't change her perspective, then she wouldn't be able to fight these challenges properly. *A few more paces and I've conquered the fear.* That was better.

"Well, well, well, what do we have here?" a familiar masculine voice called out from behind her.

Something clicked a few times and another man spoke, also just as familiar. "I think our elementalist finally came out to play."

Shira whirled around to find Jasper and Zach grinning at her, though Zach's face was half obscured by a camera. "Guys…"

They both looked comfortable, enjoying the warm weather with tight-fitting t-shirts and shorts. She could only imagine how nice it felt, compared to the cold days they'd described having as of late. *That's not what you're truly focused on, though, Shira.*

As much as she shouldn't admit it, she couldn't get over viewing them in person. They were two handsome men in images and video, but in person… real and tangible, they were dangerously sexier than she'd noticed.

Jasper's grin deepened. "I think we've left her speechless."

"She's not the only one. Videos and photos don't capture her beauty." Zach chuckled. "She should be a model."

Jasper's eyes flashed, the hue almost changing. "I could think of a few modeling opportunities she'd be wicked perfect for."

Heat rushed to Shira's face and she looked away, tucking a strand of hair behind her ear to distract her. It wasn't hard to guess what he was thinking. "Guys…"

She didn't understand what was wrong with her all of a sudden. She should be spitting off some sort of sassy comeback, or at the very least, brushing the attention off like it was nothing. It would be so easy in game. But now, here with them right in front of her… Something was different. Something she didn't want to put into words.

Jasper came up to her and flicked some of her hair out of her face. "Oh, I think we're embarrassing her."

She sucked in a tight breath and stepped back, her cheeks flushing hotter. Her teeth caught her bottom lip and she punched him in the shoulder. "Jerk!"

Jasper clutched his shoulder and mouthed a silent "ow" and then chuckled as if the impact hadn't actually hurt him, which she suspected was the case. She hadn't put a whole lot of force behind the punch.

Zach's finger pressed down on the shutter button of his camera. "There's that famous spirit we know and love."

Shira's eyes went wide and her back rigid. She snapped her gaze to Zach. "No pictures!"

Before he could react, she reached out for the camera. "Please don't. Please."

Her hand rested on the camera lens as he lowered it from his face. "Please."

Zach placed his hand on hers, his eyes soft. "Easy, Shira. I'll stop. I'm sorry. You've posted a few pictures online, so I thought you'd be okay with it."

She took a breath, trying to will herself to relax. "I'm still working on that part." She swallowed hard and forced herself to breathe. "But I'm not ready for people other than me to take my picture."

He nodded and let the camera hang at his hip by the strap. "Okay, then I promise no more unless you tell me it's okay."

The tension in her shoulders loosened. Shira nodded. "Thank you."

She looked at their hands. He still held hers, the warmth of his inviting and comfortable. His hand fit around hers so well—*No.*

Shira pulled her hand away and looked at them both, taking a deep breath, and doing her best to release her death grip on Snake's leash. "Well, you're both here. I'm here. It's great to see you both in the flesh, finally."

The two shared a strange glance and then Jasper spoke. "It's wicked good to see you too. How are you holding up?"

"Great! I'm just great." She forced a smiled. "Couldn't be better."

Zach gave Jasper a sidelong glance. "The sarcasm is strong with this one."

This got Shira to chuckle. "Coping mechanism. And I'm not going to apologize for it." She looked around. "Now, where is our little starship? I didn't expect she'd stay hidden this long, with how excited she was to see me."

Jasper tossed his head toward the convention center. "Inside with my parents. We wanted to come out and see you first to make sure you were composed enough to see her."

That was thoughtful of them. "Your parents are here?"

He nodded. "Our flight actually came in late yestah-day. We stayed with them last night and they drove us up here."

That was kind of them. And it explained why neither of these two looked at all worn out from flying. *I wonder why they told me they were flying in today.* It didn't really matter in the end, but she was curious. "That's great. I'd love to meet them."

"They're eagah to meet you too, but first." Jasper opened his arms. "A proper hello this time, instead of a wicked awkward jumble of forced words?"

A half-smile slipped up the side of her face and she accepted. Jasper wrapped his massive arms around her, pulling her into a tight embrace. She wasn't expecting such a difference in their height, her face squishing into his hard chest. She could feel the definition of his abs through his t-shirt, and his all-too-familiar musky and faint hickory cologne scent enveloped her.

And his hug... better than his game model. It was stronger, almost protective. And the way she fit against him—*Nope!* Shira was the first to pull away. She thought she caught a glimpse of disappointment crossing his

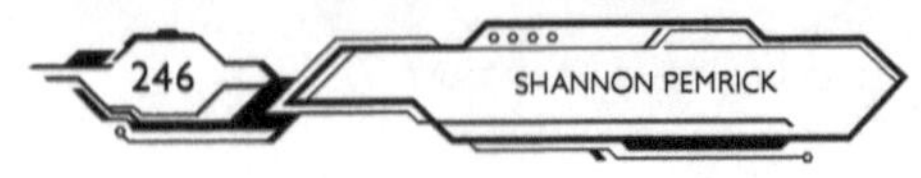

face, but it didn't last long enough for her to be quite sure.

At this point, she'd insist on getting inside to see Serenity, if it weren't for the fact it'd be unfair to Zach. And as much as she didn't trust herself with him, either, she wouldn't treat them differently just because of her own stupid internal conflict.

Zach offered a hug in much the same manner as Jasper, and when she embraced him, she experienced a similar situation as with Jasper, but also different. His cedar wood smell was just as powerful, and he, too, had a strong grip, but it had a different comforting effect on her. The sensation it brought enticed her to relax against him, as if everything was right in the world and there wasn't any need to be anywhere else.

She pulled away before she lost her senses. "There, proper greeting."

The two of them chuckled. Shira caught Jasper's eyes going down to Snake, who sat at her feet, ever faithful and patient. "You can pet him."

He worked his jaw and then shook his head. "I'll wait."

Zach leaned closer to Shira and whispered, "I give it ten minutes. He can't resist petting dogs. It's fun watching him go up to strangers to ask. Doesn't matter if it's a mastiff or a Pomeranian."

Jasper pointed at Zach. "Don't make fun of the fluff puffs."

Zach rolled his eyes. "They're not real dogs."

"They are. And if carrying them around in a bag is a requirement to ownership, give me the gayest-looking bag out there."

Zach gave him an incredulous look. "What the hell is that even supposed to mean?"

Shira sputtered out a laugh as the two went at it. So Jasper was a dog person, through and through. That was good to know. And quite the image in her head, watching all sexy and tattooed-up Jasper making cute kissy sounds to a Pomeranian. *Shira, stop with the sexy descriptions.* "Well you're in for a treat when Snake is off-duty. He will not say no to another playmate."

Jasper rubbed his hands together. "Excellent. Now let's get you inside."

Shira nodded, though she did take a deep breath. This interaction with them had been so fun and natural, she'd forgotten all about the convention center. But now she couldn't, and her lingering fear threatened to take hold again. *I can do this.*

Just as before, she took the steps as they came, and was thankful she didn't have any backslide in front of these two. On the contrary, she felt like she could conquer this far better than before. *It's like I'm facing my fear with them in game. Just… in real life, finally.* She shouldn't get used to such dependence, but she'd be lying if it wasn't nice to have a security blanket.

Shira stopped short in front of one of the many sets of doors leading into the building. The glass allowed her to see inside, and just as she'd fought with herself the last few times she'd come this far, she again battled with her rising fear of entering.

Jasper and Zach both placed a hand on her back, not saying anything and being patient with her. It was more than she deserved from them.

She took one more breath and grabbed the handle,

yanking the door open, and walked in. Shira's breath came short as she now stood in the expansive lobby. Furniture and potted plants were strategically placed throughout the area, with a single permanent shop nestled in a far nook. Decorative columns rose several stories past each floor's mezzanines, up to the glass ceiling. An information booth stood at a short distance in front of her, and in another corner of the lobby, a receptionist for the hotel that shared the building space spoke with customers.

I did it. She continued to look around, making sure she listened to her therapist's advice about handling this situation. She pictured it crowded with people, with deafening chatter. To her relief, while making her tense, none of this set her off. Snake stood beside her, alert, but not engaged in extreme training behavior. So far, this had been her best attempt yet.

"You're doing great," Zach murmured.

"We're wicked proud of you," Jasper said.

Their praise helped. She wished she didn't need it, and hoped that one of these days this would be a mere distant memory, but for now, she'd take her victories as they came.

A little girl telling some story caught Shira's ear. *I know that voice.* She looked around, finding Serenity sitting at a table, speaking to a man with tan skin and deep brown eyes, and a woman with short brown hair, light skin, and bright green eyes. Both appeared in their late fifties. Shira's feet moved without her telling them to.

The man and woman noticed her approach and turned their gaze. This caused Serenity's story to end and her stunning green eyes turned to Shira. They widened and the brightest smile spread across her face. "She-ra!"

Serenity scrambled off her chair and ran for Shira, her lanky legs covering more ground than Shira anticipated. She quickly opened her arms, dropping Snake's leash, and wrapped Serenity up tight, lifting her off the ground and spinning her around. The little girl was a bit heavier than Shira expected her to be, and taller, too. *This growth spurt the guys said she went through was no joke.* At least she had her cybernetics to lean on for help. One good thing about them, they could carry heavier loads than biological parts of the body. It unfortunately caused those with cybernetics to be unable to play professional sports, and there was no league specifically for those with them.

"I'm so happy to see you, Starship," Shira said.

Serenity hugged her tight around the neck. "You made it! I'm wicked happy!"

Shira ceased her spinning and kissed the little girl on the cheek. "I promised I would. And you know I don't break my promises."

Serenity giggled and looked down at Snake. "Hi, Snake!"

The German shepherd wagged his tail and panted. Shira could tell he liked this excited atmosphere over Shira's nervous one earlier.

"I'd pet you, but you're working. So later, I promise." Her words touched Shira. She was glad she took what she'd learned to heart. Shira knew how hard it would be for a girl her age who loved dogs to control the urge to want to pet one, even with a vest.

Serenity turned to look at her grandparents. "Nana, Pop-pop, this is She-ra."

Shira set Serenity down so she could greet the two properly. She held out a hand. "Pleasure to meet you."

Her grandmother opened her arms. "I'd prefer something less formal, if you don't mind."

While Shira wasn't used to such contact with those she wasn't familiar with, she didn't refuse the woman. It didn't seem right in this moment, and Shira knew it'd be good for her to get used to physical contact with people.

"It's nice to finally meetcha," her grandmother said as she pulled away from the hug. "I'm Christine, and this is my husband Scott."

Scott offered a hand to shake. "Good to meet you, Shira."

Shira didn't hesitate to return the gesture. Just like Serenity and Jasper, the two of them had a thick Boston accent. It was heavier than Shira expected, given Zach didn't have it as bad. *Though, to be fair, he did say he moved to Boston as a kid, and he did leave after high school, so that might be why.* It made her realize she'd never inquired as to why Jasper's parents lived here in California.

"Serenity chats our ears off about you all the time," Christine said, a half-smile spreading across her face. "And I can see why."

Scott chuckled. "Not sure who talks about her more, though, Serenity or the boys."

Heat threatened to rise up in Shira's face. Jasper and Zach couldn't possibly talk about her *that* much, right?

"Five to one, Serenity talks about Shira more," came a computer voice from one of the guy's phones. Shira guess that to be their AI, Alistair. "Though, not for a better lack of trying. She merely speaks more than them on average."

"Yeah I do!" Serenity said, quite proud of that fact.

The adults laughed.

The young girl picked up Snake's leash. "She-ra, you dropped this."

"Why don't you hold onto him for now?" Shira offered.

Serenity's face lit up. "Can I really? That won't mess up Snake's job?"

Shira rested her cybernetic hand on her head. "Not at all. In fact, it may help him do his job better."

"Yay!" She held the leash close to her chest, as if protecting it from anyone who would try to steal it.

Christine gave Jasper an odd look Shira wasn't able to read well, before speaking. "Did you manage to figure out the resahvation trouble while you were gone?"

Shira cocked her head. "Reservation trouble?" *Narissa booked their rooms herself, because she didn't trust Ajax to remember. They shouldn't be having any issues.*

Jasper shook his head, seemingly knowing what she was thinking. "Their computer system is on the fritz. They're having trouble finding a lot of resahvations."

"You should probably check on yours," Zach said. "Just in case."

"I don't have one," she said. "I'm staying at our family vacation home in Manhattan Beach."

Scott whistled. "Manhattan Beach? Must cost you a pretty penny to live there."

Shira gave an awkward shrug. She didn't want to bring attention to that in front of the guys. "It's not as bad as other places around here."

"How long is the commute?" Zach asked. "Seems silly not to just stay here."

Shira scratched her good arm. "I'm not ready to tackle staying here yet. And the commute isn't *that* bad."

His brow rose. "Isn't traffic here in L.A. wicked bad?

Boston can get ridiculous at prime hours, but there's always way less people than here."

Shira rocked her head back and forth. "If I time it wrong, yeah. I'd be looking at a two- to three-hour commute. But I'm generally an early riser, so getting places on time isn't that hard. Without traffic I'm only looking at thirty minutes. And Narissa is allowing me to use Cybro's parking, so I'm not fighting for spots here. That's a ten-minute walk from here if I'm slow."

Jasper shoved his hands in his pockets. "That's not as bad as I thought."

"You wouldn't happen to have an extra room in case our reservation doesn't work out, would you?" Zach boldly asked.

Shira winked. "I might have an extra closet or two."

Serenity gasped and ran to Jasper. "Daddy, can we stay with She-ra? We don't need to stay at no stupid hotel."

Shira and everyone laughed. Jasper rubbed his daughter's head. "We'll consider it, but if the resahvation gets fixed, we need to use it. Hotels are expensive."

Serenity's face scrunched as she pursed her lips. Her face relaxed, as if an idea struck her, and then she looked to Shira. "She-ra, can I stay with you? Daddy and Zach can have the hotel and we can have fun." She rushed over to Shira and latched onto her pants. "We could have a wicked fun time! We could watch movies, stay up late, do nails."

Shira struggled to keep a straight face as Serenity continued to list off the fun things they could do together, as a plea for Shira to agree to let her stay with her.

Zach crossed his arms. "Serenity, all this sounds fun. You can't have all that fun without us."

She looked up at her other dad. "Then tell Daddy we hafta stay with She-ra!"

Zach looked to Jasper, his eyes far too innocent. "Yeah, Daddy, we have to stay with her so we can have all that fun."

Jasper held up his hands, shooting Zach an irritated but slightly amused look. "What is with you three ganging up on me all the time? It's wicked unfair."

"Excuse you." Shira crossed her arms, her eyes narrowing. "I haven't said anything, thank you. So don't be pinning any blame on me."

Christine's and Scott's laughter pulled their attention. At least these two were getting a kick out of this.

When they calmed down, Christine spoke, "Well, while you three figure out your arrangements, the two of us should be going. It'll also allow Shira to show you around, like you mentioned last night as a game plan for today. Isn't that right, Jasper?"

"Uh, yeah, that's the plan," he said. "Though we didn't have any timeframe about it."

The way Christine spoke, it intrigued Shira. Something was off about her words. "You two are more than welcome to join us. I don't want to take away the precious time you don't normally get to spend with them."

Christine came up, smiling at Shira, her eyes squinting as she did, and patted her on the cheek. "You're so sweet. But don't you worry. We had our time with them yestahday and this morning, and we'll have more after the convention."

Something still felt off about this, but Shira decided it wasn't her place to push. "Alright, if you say so. I'll do my best to make sure they don't get themselves into too much trouble."

Christine winked. "If they end up in jail, leave them there. It'll teach them a lesson."

Serenity cocked her head. "Daddy, you're going to jail?"

Everyone but Jasper laughed. He threw his hand up in defeat, shaking his head and muttering to himself. Zach assured Serenity no one was going to jail, and the adults were just joking. The little girl didn't get it, but luckily dropped the subject, going to a new one. "If Nana and Pop-pop aren't going with us, what cah are we taking?"

Shira smiled. "Mine, of course."

"We'll just have to do a switch-a-roo with her cah seat," Scott said.

"That's no problem," Shira assured. "Should probably also put their luggage in my trunk."

"Aww, I don't wanna use my cah seat," Serenity complained. "I'm a big girl now. I don't need it."

"You're still not big enough," Zach said. "It's the law."

Serenity crossed her arms and huffed.

"Shira, I've pulled the car up," Orion said through her phone.

Christine fanned herself, raising her eyebrows at Shira. "Wow, listen to that voice pack."

"Lady Christine, I've done the same," a male voice said from her own device.

It was Shira's turn to return the expression, minus the hand motion. "Lady?"

Christine winked. "A woman can dream."

Shira caught Scott rolling his eyes and glancing at the boys; they were doing their best to keep their amusement hidden. This was one interesting family.

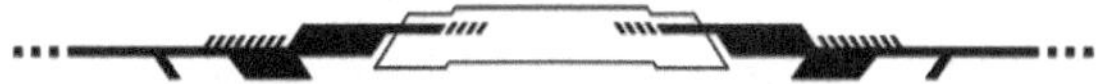

Christine clapped her hands together. "Now, let's get you kids off having fun."

Serenity ran a few paces ahead in her excitement, but was forced to stop or slow down when Snake refused to leave Shira's side. Zach found it amusing, and liked that it kept his daughter from going crazy, since she refused to give up her leash-holding job. The fact that Shira allowed Serenity to hold the leash surprised him. He would have thought she'd need to have contact with Snake at all times, especially while they were in this building.

But Shira was proving just how resilient she was. He and Jasper kept a close eye on her as she interacted with Jasper's parents. They'd worried about her state when she struggled to walk through the doors. But after she had the needed time to prepare herself, and took a moment to take in the building from the inside, it was as if her struggles had become a distant memory. Even now, as they headed for the doors, she showed no signs of the stress from before.

Zach felt an immense rush of pride. She'd come so far in such a short amount of time. *There's nothing this woman can't do if she puts her mind to it, is there?*

Jasper squeezed their entwined hands. His eyes didn't leave Shira and Serenity as they gabbed on about something with his parents, but he didn't have to for Zach to understand. He had the same thoughts as Zach.

Zach's camera bounced against his hip. He hoped she'd continue to make progress by the end of the week.

Zach would jump at the chance to capture her beauty himself. Seeing her standing outside that first time had stolen his breath. But he hadn't expected her beg and plead for him to not take her photo.

And knowing Serenity wouldn't want to wander too far from Shira, it put Zach into a predicament. He'd planned to capture the moment of Serenity's first family vacation as much as he could. But if she was going to attach herself to Shira's hip…

Serenity gasped and ran ahead—as far as she could, at least, still refusing to let go of Snake's leash. "She-ra, is that really your cah?"

Zach squinted against the harsh late morning sun to see a green BMW M8 sitting at the curb in front of Jasper's parent's minivan.

"Yep, that's it," Shira said.

Damn… She acted like it wasn't a big deal, either. *Probably isn't for her.* They didn't quite know what kind of life she lived. Sure, they knew she had great modeling career in the past, and her family was well-known in the business—*and there's the matter of the large house she has*—but Shira never talked about her financial status. Not even when she'd find out he and Jasper were struggling financially during bad tournament months and she would offer to help to ease their burden with Serenity's needs. She never flinched or hesitated, as if money wasn't an obstacle for her, but would purposely avoid any questioning when either of them would show concern about how much she'd help out. Now, the reality of how wealthy she may be was starting to be driven home for Zach.

"The color is pretty," Serenity said, her eyes wide with awe. "Does it have two colors in it?"

"That's right. It's called iridescent. Mercedes did it for me as a birthday gift."

"That's wicked cool." She looked to Zach and Jasper. "We need to do that to our cah."

Jasper chuckled. "I think the subie needs more than a coat of paint."

"Yeah, like a full replacement," Zach muttered.

Jasper swiped at him, and Zach jumped away. Jasper hated it when he made comments about his beloved car.

Serenity tugged on Snake's leash. "C'mon, Snake. Let's go check it out!"

Shira lightly grabbed her chin and mouth so as not to laugh, and followed so Serenity wouldn't be running off alone, even if it was only a short distance. Scott split off to get Serenity's booster seat. Christine passed Zach and Jasper a long look.

Jasper shrugged and shook his head with furrowed brow to indicate he didn't know what the look was for. Zach wasn't much better on the uptake.

"Don't let this one get away," she mouthed before catching up with the girls.

Christine and Scott had found out about their plan because of Cheryl. She liked to gossip with her mother, so, while annoyed that the information hadn't come from their mouths, it was to be expected.

While Zach had grown up with this family, even to this day, their level of acceptance still astounded him. Christine had nothing but advice for them, none of which they were sure how to utilize, with Shira's known stubborn nature, but they were willing to give it a shot. She even had a few tips how to help Shira through her problems, that may also work to break through these annoying rules of hers.

Jasper and Zach made it to the car by the time Scott had reached it with the booster seat. Shira folded the passenger seat down and went to work securing it, though she did need some help. Jasper was all too inclined to provide that assistance and Zach let him. He knew, when it came to their daughter's safety, it was best to let Jasper handle things.

Instead, he handled the suitcase switch. Zach was glad there was a hotel issue. Sure, it sucked because Ajax's company was paying for it if it sorted out, but because Shira openly offered to let them stay with her, it'd make it easier to push for her to give them a chance. Zach still fought with his own personal concerns, but this hiccup felt like a sign this was going in the direction it should.

Jasper had the booster seat secured by the time Zach finished his task, and Serenity was eager to climb in. So much so, she nearly forgot to say goodbye to her grandparents. Of course, she insisted on buckling herself in, so while she did that, Shira had Snake jump into the back. Christine and Scott said their goodbyes, both expressing their hope that they'd be able to see Shira again.

This left them to figure out seating arrangements.

"Fair warning, the back is pretty cramped with her and Snake in there," Shira said. "I didn't really factor that when I agreed to show you around."

That was fair. They didn't think about the implication, either. Zach and Jasper looked at each other to figure out who would be the lucky one to sit up front with her, when Serenity decided for them. "I want Zach to sit with me!"

Jasper chuckled and tapped Zach on the back of the shoulder before lifting his seat back up so he could sit down. Zach couldn't deny he was a bit disappointed. Ultimately it wouldn't hamper anything, but Jasper seemed to luck out better with Shira. He struggled to not see his own bad luck as some sort of sign.

Zach climbed into the car on Shira's side, and once she was seated, the vehicle started up. Loud pop music blasted from the stereo. Shira was quick to turn it down, though not off.

Jasper stared at her. "What is this garbage playing?"

Shira's face scrunched. Even when offended, the expression was cute. "It's not garbage."

"I thought you had bettah taste in music than this." He reached for the stereo. "We're not listening to this."

Shira held up her cybernetic hand. "Touch my stereo and this comes slamming down on your skin. And I can assure you, it doesn't feel half as kind as a real hand."

Jasper's face turned a shade of red as he sucked in a tight breath. Zach chuckled, finding this all amusing. Jasper, of course, did not appreciate the lack of support. "Traitor."

Zach leaned forward, stage-whispering in Jasper's ear. "Remember, shotgun shuts his cakehole. Or does that not apply to you when you're in that seat?"

His eyes darted to Serenity as she danced in her seat. "Besides, looks like Shira isn't the only fan."

Jasper's head whipped around and watched their daughter enjoy the music. "Daddy, I love this music. It makes me want to dance."

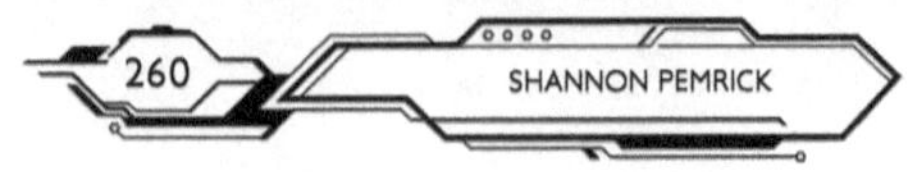

"Shira," her AI said from the car. "I've rearranged your playlist to be child-friendly."

Shira smiled. "Thanks, Orion. Make sure Jasper can't change anything."

"Noted."

Jasper threw his head back as he groaned, mumbling, "Why me?"

Zach and Shira roared with laughter. Zach noticed, as Shira enjoyed herself at Jasper's expense, she covered her mouth. *She never does that.* He'd also noticed earlier, the way she spoke and looked at them was a bit different, but he wasn't sure if it was due to them meeting her in person for the first time, or something else was up with her. He made a mental note to keep a close eye on her.

Jasper scrubbed his face. "Okay, I need a distraction before I go insane. Where are we going?"

Shira shrugged and looked out the window at the moving traffic. "I didn't set a destination. We're pretty much cruising until we decide on something."

"She-ra, what is there to do here?" Serenity asked.

She turned her attention back into the car, adjusting herself to face the back. "All kinds of things. There are museums, galleries, aquariums, and the zoo. There's even the beach, but it's not really warm enough now to go swimming."

"But it's wicked wahm!" Serenity said. "It's puhfect for swimming."

She wasn't entirely wrong. Last Zach checked, it was just over seventy degrees. A stark contrast to their thirty-five when they left Boston.

"It may feel warm, Starship, but trust me, the water won't be fun to swim in."

Serenity pursed her lips. "I wanted to go to the beach."

"I'm sure we still can," Zach said. "We have all week."

Shira leaned on the arm console. "Even if you can't go swimming, you can play on the beach." She smiled sweetly at her. The expression made Zach's pulse jump. It wasn't an expression he saw on her face often, but he liked it. "And if you really want to swim, I've got a pool. It's heated and everything."

Serenity's eyes widened. "You has a pool?"

"Yeah. It's common for people with houses here to have pools because of how hot it gets during the summer."

"Daddy, can we get a pool?"

Jasper chuckled. "No, we live in an apahtment."

"And no, a small one in your room isn't possible," Zach added, knowing her ways of trying to rationalize.

Serenity kicked her feet, pouting. "Not fair…"

"Why don't we talk about food?" Shira said. "It's close to noon, and I'm sure you three are getting hungry, with the time difference. And we've got all kinds of choices to choose from."

Zach hadn't thought about the time. "I'm not actually hungry."

"I am, a little," Jasper said. "But not enough to make a stop."

"Because you're always hungry," Zach murmured. Jasper reached back and swiped at him, missing, and then getting pawed at by Snake. The car filled with laughter.

Shira gasped and clapped her hands together. Her eyes lit up so much, whatever was on her mind had to be good. "I just figured out where we can go. Orion, bring us to The Last Bookstore."

Jasper's eyes widened, his jaw going slack. "Did I hear you right? Bookstore?"

Shira smirked. "Yep. Only store in California where you can still buy paper copies. I told you about it."

Zach smiled. This woman was something else. Of all the activities she could suggest, it was on Jasper's top-five list.

"Are you sure you wish to go there?" Orion asked. "It's in the opposite direction."

"Yes!" Jasper shouted. He pointed to the GPS. "Bang a u-ey up here."

Shira jerked her head back, her face twisting. "Bang a what?"

Zach doubled over with uncontained laughter. She reacted just as he'd expected. While she'd been exposed to quite a few *unique* ways Bostonians spoke, that hadn't been one yet.

"Boston to California translation: Make a U-turn," Orion said.

Jasper's laughter joined Zach's. Serenity held her hands up to her face as she giggled away, though Zach doubted it was more than just her joining in the lively situation.

Shira rolled her eyes and shook her head, mumbled to herself for a moment. "Yes, Orion, I'm sure that's the new destination. And please *make a U-turn* at the next legal location."

Zach managed to quiet himself down until that little jest. A quick snicker escaped him.

"Recalculating."

This time, it was Shira's turn to laugh while Zach and Jasper sat confused. Her AI's personality was a unique one, and it seemed Shira liked it that way.

"Yay, books!" Serenity cheered. She then started singing a made up song about books, amusing everyone. This would be a good experience for her, too.

CHAPTER 14

Dim lights flashed past the train car as it zipped through the tunnel. Zach sat next to Jasper in a pair of seats behind Shira and Serenity. Snake lay at Shira's feet, silent and still. Serenity looked around, eyes wide, trying to take in the ride as much as possible, as if she'd never been on a subway before.

The original plan was to park downtown, but Shira's usual garage was closed, and due to the time, street parking wasn't going to be an option. So Shira decided they'd take the subway, working it out with Narissa to head back to near where they started so they could use Cybro Industries' parking. At the same time, the two of them worked up a late lunch date.

Jasper and Zach were on board with the idea. It'd help them to work with Ajax on any last-minute discussions about tomorrow, and anything that needed to be addressed for the convention as a whole. And this just got the lot of them together as friends.

Serenity's head whipped back so fast to follow a passing light, Zach though she'd give herself whiplash. Jasper chuckled. "Serenity, you're acting like you've nevah been on a subway before. It's no different than the T back home."

Serenity peeked over her chair to look at them both with big eyes. "Nu-uh, that's not true, Daddy."

"How so?"

"Because this isn't home, duh."

Shira choked on a laugh and Zach had to use all his willpower not to react. Even Jasper was left speechless for a moment. He worked his mouth and blinked before nodding. "Yeah, you're right. This isn't home. My mistake."

Serenity's face scrunched as she gave a smug smile before whipping around in her seat and jumping right into asking Shira a million and one questions about the train station, the bookstore they were going to, and even completely unrelated topics. Shira was patient with her, and proved to be great at staying calm when Serenity got too excited and interrupted her.

Jasper squeezed Zach's hand and he squeezed back. The scene was perfect. *Almost... too perfect.* He did his best to banish the negative thought. Zach had to get a hold of this negativity and figure out how to be rid of it.

He wanted this. He wanted her, just as much as he wanted Jasper. These past few weeks with their casual flirting and her pushback when they'd started to get too close again had been torture. He didn't understand what happened. They both thought they'd made progress.

But they agreed not to broach the subject with her until they got the chance to see her face-to-face. And now that she was here, they had to figure things out, and fast. They had five days, maybe a few more if they could convince her not to bail on them after the convention, to get this right. That meant Zach had little time to get his priorities and wants on board with his growing interest.

The train came to a halt at Pershing Square, their stop. They followed Shira out onto the platform and up the escalators to the downtown street above. But not before Serenity insisted on reading the platform sign, with some help. Outside, buildings reached high into the sky, cars roared about, and crowds of people pushed through the streets to get to their destinations.

Shira's shoulders tensed, her eyes tight as she looked about. Snake sat beside her, leaning in to offer his security. Serenity clung to her leg, curious about the new area. Zach glanced at Jasper. He, too, had noticed it. It amazed Zach what Shira was willing to fight through.

Zach came up behind her and wrapped his arms around her chest, speaking low in her ear. "Take the time you need. We can be patient for you."

Her skin felt hot against his, and Zach thought he caught a slight redness to her cheeks. "O—okay, thanks."

She took a deep breath and then pulled away. "I'm good now. The store is only two blocks southeast of here."

Jasper grabbed Serenity and lifted her up onto his shoulders. "Okay, then I'll put our starship in port so she gets a good view and doesn't get lost."

"And who is going to keep you from getting lost when we get there?" Shira asked.

Zach shook his head. "We should say our goodbyes now."

"I'm not *that* bad," Jasper muttered, making Zach and Shira laugh.

Serenity pointed in a random direction. "Daddy, I can see so far from up here! Let's esplore."

"*Ex*-plore, Starship," Jasper corrected. "And what about the books?"

"Oh yeah! Books time!" She started singing her books song again.

Shira lead the way to the store, Serenity asking all kinds of questions about it. Jasper, surprisingly, knew a great deal about the store, from its origins as a converted bank to its unique interior layout. Apparently after Shira told him about it in game one day, he'd done all kinds of research, and had planned to stop in during their trip at some point. Shira suggesting this today became an even bigger deal to Zach. She really cared about their interests.

Then something dawned on him. What did she know about them besides that they PvP'd for a living, had a daughter, and one of them an obsession with books. *And that we can satisfy her in bed through the game.* Zach realized there was a lot she didn't know about them. She didn't even know about his love for photography, and his previous career path around it.

And the same went for them knowing her. They knew parts of her past, but somehow they'd never really gotten to know the current her. How big of a nerd was she? What did she do when she wasn't playing Lusara Fates? What were her strangest quirks?

How could they know she'd make a good fit in their lives if they didn't know these things? There was so much to cover with her this week.

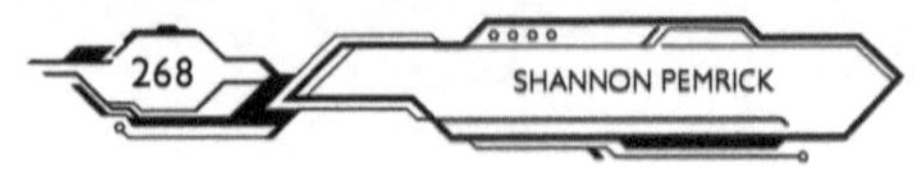

They came to a corner where Shira stopped and faced the high-rise building with tall pillars and stone architecture. The outside screamed early-1900's bank architecture. It was nothing like what you'd see built today. A neon sign hung in the window, *The Last Book-store*. No one had neon signs anymore. *Well, except Vegas.*

"We're here," Shira said. While stating the obvious, it was probably for the best, based on how Jasper stared at the building, his mouth agape.

A few moments passed, Zach and Shira allowing Jasper to take in the marvel, before Shira asked Zach's help to get Serenity down, who was getting antsy and not being heard by Jasper. Zach had no issues getting his daughter down, Jasper offering no resistance, though he still hadn't snapped out of his awed state.

Shira moved behind him and pushed him toward the propped-open doors. "C'mon. You have to go inside before you faint."

This helped snap Jasper out of his state and he nearly ran the rest of the way. Zach held Serenity's hand and they followed in a far calmer fashion. Upon entering, they were met with a large, open floor, with tall pillars reaching a neo-classical ceiling and hanging lights. Art-work was strewn about the walls, and couches sprawled through the middle of the room, several taken by patrons wishing to rest or read. Shelves upon shelves lined the room, books filling them to capacity.

"I've died and gone to heaven," Jasper murmured as he gazed around. "Quick, Shira, what can I find down here?"

She giggled, watching as his brain shut down from the overload. With the research he'd already done, he'd know this answer. "Downstairs there's a comic and graphic novel section, a rare book annex inside one of the former vaults, vinyl records, and a few other miscellaneous things."

Zach's brow ticked up, excitement building. "Vinyl?"

She nodded. "Yeah, they've got a pretty good selection. Something you're interested in?"

"Very much."

"Clearly, since he missed the part about books being in a vault," Jasper shot.

Shira laughed. "In a few of the vaults, they have book displays. They're cool, so make sure you check them out." She tossed her head to the right of the building. "When you're done checking things out downstairs, make sure you head upstairs to the labyrinth. It's a sight to behold. And that's where I'll be before hitting up the graphic novels."

Serenity let go of Zach's hand and gabbed Shira's. "What's the lab-inth, She-ra?"

The name certainly caught Zach's attention, too, as well as Jasper's. Before Shira could explain, Jasper jumped in. "It's the area this place is most known for. They set it up as a type of maze, the walls all made up of bookshelves." He started to get antsy. "Where are the stairs? I need to see it."

Shira pointed with the hand she held Snake's leash with. "This way."

In an instant, Jasper took off, Serenity calling after him. "Daddy, we walk inside, 'membah?"

Zach laughed as Jasper came to a screeching halt. "She told you."

Jasper rubbed the back of his neck. "Yes, you're right, Serenity. I just got ovah excited."

Shira walked past Jasper, Serenity still holding her hand, and left the briefest of touches on his shoulder. It was a simple touch, but Zach sensed a tinge of intimacy from it. Whether that was her intention or just him imagining things, he wasn't sure. "Take it easy, Jasper. This place isn't going anywhere. We've got all day. My reservation for lunch can turn into dinner. I know the owner, so it wouldn't be an issue."

Shira had chosen the place to eat. She didn't name it, wanting it to be a surprise, but she'd revealed it was one of the most authentic German restaurants in the area. For some reason, it didn't surprise Zach that she knew the owner of the place. Maybe it was because he sort of expected her to know a lot of people, given her modeling history and her family's line of work.

"What about Narissa?" Zach asked. "If we stay too long, we'd have to let her and Ajax know."

Shira chuckled. "I'm sure she probably expects us to change the time. But if we want to do so preemptively, I could let her know."

Zach gazed around. "Might be for the best. I didn't realize this place was so huge."

Jasper nodded. "I don't want to rush out of here."

"I want to look at books!" Serenity cheered.

Shira chuckled. "Well, okay then. I'll make arrangements."

She whipped out her phone and sent off a text, presumably to Narissa, before making a phone call. It didn't take long for someone to pick up on the other end, and she went to speaking with them in German. The rate she spoke at showed her fluency in the language.

Shira laughed, spoke a few more words, and then hung

up. She sent off another text before addressing them. "Okay, we're all set."

"Great! Let's go upstairs," Jasper said, impatient as ever.

Shira snickered alongside Zach and beckoned them to follow. Serenity once again insisted on holding her hand. Zach loved the sight and wished he could capture the moment.

He and Jasper followed their two favorite people to the back of the store and up some stairs in a dankly lit stairwell. Book categories were painted on the steps with arrows pointing right, and two arrows pointing left with labels in regards to some art studios and galleries. *A neat little detail.*

At the top of the stairs, an interesting art display greeted them. Some sort of surrealist creation of books flying out of a dresser.

Jasper smiled. "Fitting."

Shira let them admire the art piece before banking right away from the art studios and into what was no doubt the labyrinth. Wooden bookshelves stood tall and had been placed at strategic angles. Signs with arrows hung from the ceiling, giving some direction as to where to find a particular subject, but they weren't clustered together, forcing one to explore on their own.

One particular shelf stood out to Zach. It looked like all the others, except the books were stacked in a way that created a hole for you to peer through. The "no touch" sign called it the book loop. Jasper wandered over to the backside and peered back at them. His eyes were so wide with wonder and excitement, Zach was elated. It'd been some time since he'd seen his boyfriend so in awe at something.

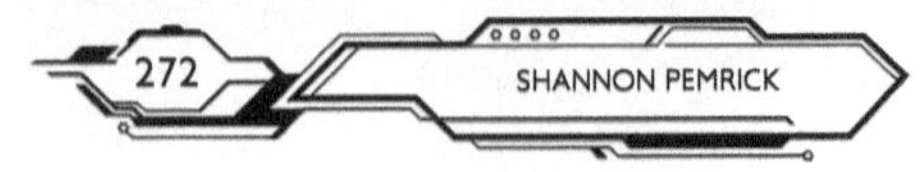

Serenity left Shira's side and matched up with her father's face on this side of the book loop. *What a perfect shot...*

Shira leaned closer to him and kept her voice low. "You can take pictures here."

His eyes snapped to her. "We're allowed?"

She nodded, smiling. Zach didn't hesitate to lift his camera and alter his settings before snapping some shots. Near the end, Zach noticed something peculiar behind the loop. "What's that?"

Jasper turned to look where Zach pointed. "It does exist..."

He took off toward an arch of books, Serenity hot on his heels. Zach looked to Shira for an explanation.

She smiled. "That's the infamous book arch wall. It's a ramp that leads into the horror vault."

Vault? She'd mentioned something of the sort downstairs. Zach walked around the book loop case and sure enough, tucked against the wall was an old vault door, a sign reading *Horror* set above the doorframe.

Serenity's giggling drew his gaze, and he watched her and Jasper play in this book tunnel. Zach snapped a few pictures before Shira rested her hands on his and lowered the camera.

"Go join them," she said. "Pictures are great, but memories are better."

She had a point. He wanted to capture the moments so much, he forgot about being part of them.

Shira removed the strap from his person and took the camera. "I'll hold onto it."

He thanked her and walked to the back side of this tunnel to interact with his family. Serenity ran up and down the ramp, her eyes wide and sparkling. Zach grabbed her, causing her to squeal a bit, and lifted her up so she could touch the books.

"They're real!" she exclaimed.

They are? Both he and Jasper touched the books. Sure as hell, they were.

A camera shutter clicked and all three turned to see Shira leaning on the short, curved bookshelf used to guide customers into the vault. Zach's camera was poised in front of her face. Snake rested his head on the shelf watching them. Shira pressed the shutter button again, capturing whatever faces they had in the moment. They had to be good, because she laughed after.

"Oh, so you can take pictchas of us, but we can't of you?" Jasper said.

The camera lens tipped down as she gazed back at them, her chin dipped and her eyes looking up. "How many in-the-moment photos do you all have as a family, compared to just one of you and Serenity? And further, how many of just you and Zach do you have that aren't selfies?"

Zach and Jasper looked at each other. Besides staged ones, and maybe the occasional photo Cheryl or Christine took, one of them was always behind the camera.

"I'm no photographer," she continued. "But my experience modeling has allowed me to be able to take more than a few acceptable shots. And they'll be better than not having any at all."

It all sounded legit, but Zach wasn't sold, for one reason: Jasper had a point. She still had a ways to go with her fears, and Zach was all about helping her face them. "I'll let you use my camera—on one condition."

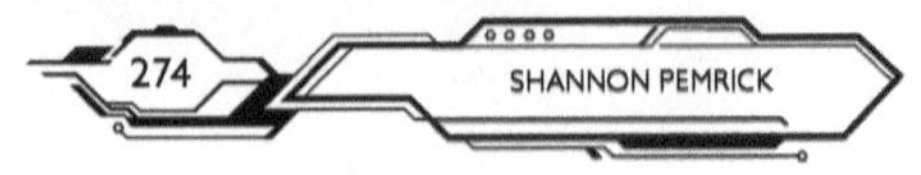

Her brow ticked up. "Which is?"

"I'm allowed to take one photo of you today."

Shira pursed her lips and her nose scrunched. He loved her expressions. She then let out a tight breath. "Okay. But only one, so you'd best be careful and make it count."

Zach blinked, shock rippling through him. He didn't expect that response. "R—really?"

Shira lifted the camera and snapped a picture. "Yep. You also can't delete that priceless snap. Those are my terms."

Zach didn't care what kind of face he and Jasper were making. It was worth getting her agreement. And it meant there could be more later if they played their hand right. "Deal."

A half-smile slipped up the side of her face and she stood up straight, through rather slowly—painstaking, if he were honest, with the way her whole form moved in one fluid, tempting motion. "Now, go check out that vault, you'll think it's pretty cool."

"Not going to join us?" Jasper asked.

She shrugged. "Not into horror."

He strolled over to her and leaned on the bookshelf. "Easily scared?"

Shira leaned closer, prompting Zach to approach slowly, to get a better view of this. "You jump-scare me, and you're going to get a bloody lip. Out of pure reflex."

Jasper's head dipped as he laughed. Zach also found it amusing.

Serenity tried peeking over the bookshelf. "It's okay, She-ra, I don't like being scareded eithah. We can watch or read something less scary. Like supaheroes!"

Shira's eyes squinted as she smiled at Serenity. "That's a wonderful idea, Starship. I love superhero movies."

The two got to chatting about which ones they would watch, allowing Jasper and Zach to slip into the vault to check it out. But Zach kept his ear open on their conversation. Shira included Power Rangers in her lineup for some reason, Serenity adding Teenage Mutant Ninja Turtles in response. Shira was more than excited to praise Zach and Jasper for parenting her right in that regard.

The books didn't interest Zach as much as the unique nature of the room did. Wall-to-wall books of horror and what appeared to be some crime and paranormal took up the space. It wasn't as big as he had expected a vault to be, but wasn't any less interesting. It was as if the concept for this room was to keep the dark themes contained within.

Once they were satisfied, they moved on, Shira allowing them to set their course from here. Aimless wandering became their quest, and Zach soon learned how easy it was to get lost in this place if you weren't careful. *It's like they want you to get lost… just like in IKEA.*

Jasper wouldn't complain, that's for sure. Zach was confident they'd need a room *just* for him and his collection of books once they found a home to buy. As it stood, they didn't have sufficient room at the apartment for his current selection, making this trip slightly dangerous. Zach knew Jasper would go overboard if not kept in check.

A wall of color caught Zach's eye. He broke away to find out what it was, and it wasn't long before the others followed. The colors turned out to be books, all organized based on a visual gradient. His inner artist

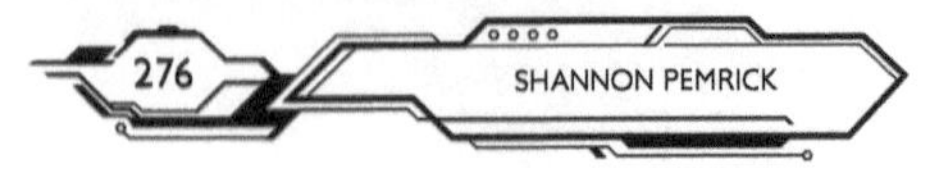

leapt with joy, and he knew it'd resonate with Jasper's obsession for organization.

"I'm looking for a book with a blue cover," Shira said.

Jasper laughed, and it took Zach a moment to realize what she meant, thanks to his distracted state. When he did, he also couldn't contain himself.

"What is this wall?" Zach asked.

"This is their dollar section. All the books here are priced a dollar and under," Shira said.

Jasper immediately started checking out the books. Zach rolled his eyes. "Remember, we only have so much space in the suitcases."

"Or you could ship them home."

Zach's eyes snapped to Shira. Hers twinkled with so much mischief it both infuriated him and amused. "Don't give him ideas."

"Too late," Jasper said, taking a book from the shelf.

Zach let out a long, drawn-out sigh. *Here we go.*

Serenity tugged on Shira's pants. "She-ra, are there books for me here?"

Shira pursed her lips as she gazed at the wall before looking down at Serenity. "I don't think they have any in this section. But there is a kids' section."

Serenity's eyes sparkled. "I wanna go there!"

Shira took her hand. "Then let's go. Jasper can catch up when he's done."

Everyone looked at him to not find him listening, and instead pulling another book off the shelf. He had four already in his arms.

"Remember, Jasper, you only have so much space in your arms," Shira said as she turned and walked off.

"Huh?" Jasper looked at her and his brow furrowed. "Wait, where is she going?"

Zach chuckled and stepped her way to follow. "Finding books for Serenity."

"Oh, wait, don't leave without me, then." He immediately abandoned the wall of books. *My wonderful, one-track-mind boyfriend at his finest.* Zach had to admit though, it was a trait he loved to hate.

They navigated the maze of books and art pieces until they came to an area labeled *Kids Books* on what looked like a green chalkboard and colored chalk.

Serenity squealed at the sight of all the colorful books, and left Shira's side to paw her way through the shelves she could reach. Jasper was quick to remind her to be careful, as she was known to get a little too excited with her books back home.

Zach lifted his camera and snapped a quick picture. The area here had different lighting. He didn't want to take a handful only to find out later they didn't come out right and needed extensive post editing. After a few adjustments, he was set and took more photos, some of Serenity and some of her and Jasper.

As he did this, he turned his lens toward Shira, who perused the options as well. He could take a shot now, but it didn't feel like the right moment yet. Zach had to be extra careful to make it count. He wouldn't take more than what he agreed on, except maybe in a rapid-click style to ensure he got *just* the right image and then delete all the extras. He'd be true to his word and not do anything to break her trust.

Shira gasped and picked up a paperback book. "They *do* have them!"

Zach came closer. "Have what?"

She held up a book with two children on the cover, wearing white tunics and running from an exploding volcano. "Magic Tree House. I loved these books as a kid."

He took it from her to look over. He'd heard of them, but had never read any himself.

"I only ever owned one book, *Sunset of the Sabertooth*. I still have it. It's in rough shape, from how much I read it when I couldn't get my hands on another one in the series from the library."

"How come your parents didn't buy you more?"

The light and excitement in her eyes died. "My mom didn't have the money. I only had that one book because someone had a garage sale and was selling it for a quarter."

Oh, right… He'd forgotten Jasper had told him about her being adopted. He wondered what happen to her mom to put her in the system.

Serenity came up to her. "She-ra, whatcha gots?"

Shira's melancholy demeanor had disappeared and she smiled at his daughter. "A book you might like. It's a historical fantasy series."

Serenity pursed her lips and her brow furrowed. Zach noticed the expression was similar to one Shira made sometimes. *Is she picking it up from Shira, or is it mere coincidence?* "I dunno what that means."

"And I'm not familiar with it," Jasper said. He took the book from Zach to inspect.

"It's a books series that has a magic tree house that two kids can go back in time with, to experience a historical event or time," Shira said. "That gives it both qualities of fantasy, science fiction, and historical fiction."

"That sounds like a fun tree house!" Serenity exclaimed. "I want one. Daddy, can I have a tree house like that?" She tugged on his arm. "Can I, Daddy? Please, please!"

He chuckled. "No, Pumpkin, you can't. We don't have a tree for a tree house."

She pouted, but Zach came to the rescue to avoid any possible tears. "You can have the next best thing, though, Starship. We can get you one of these books so you can go on an adventure."

Serenity gasped and clapped. "Yay! She-ra, can you read one to me? There's a chair right there. We could both fit."

Would that be allowed? Zach had noticed all the seating scattered about in this maze of books, but he wasn't sure if they were just for people to rest in, or if customers were allowed to just sit and read.

"I could read to you for a little bit, but only long enough for us to figure out if you like the book," Shira said. "They don't like people reading for free. They are a store."

Serenity nodded. "I undahstand."

"Alright, then take a look at these books and pick one out."

Serenity clapped and pawed through the selection. Zach watched, enjoying the eagerness that came from her. Even if he wasn't as big a bookworm as Jasper, he hoped she never lost this enthusiasm for reading.

Jasper searched the other shelves for books, pulling out a few books to read the back and either place back on the shelf or tuck in his arms.

Zach's gaze pulled back when Serenity told Shira she found one. It had a tiger on it. *Sounds right.* They were her favorite animal… right now. Her favorite animal switched every two months, it seemed.

Shira guided Serenity to one of the plush chairs and they sat together. Snake settled by Shira's feet, quiet as a shadow like always. Zach poised his camera. If he was going to find the perfect shot today, this would be the moment. Jasper ceased his search and joined Zach, watching Shira read out the first chapter. Serenity also tried to read on her own, Shira being patient as ever, using a soft approach to her corrections.

Zach snapped photos, angling the framing to get mostly Serenity, and anything that was Shira wasn't fully identifiable. It wasn't against the rule—technically.

"I told you one photo, Zach," Shira said, not looking up from the book.

"And I'm sticking to that," he said, taking another snap of Serenity looking up at Shira, confused. "I'm only photographing Serenity."

"Uh-huh. We'll see about that when I take that from you."

Zach chuckled and kept at it. And then came the shot he was hoping for. The two looked at each other, smiling, and a tip of the book came into the shot. The camera shutter snapped at lightning speed several times.

Shira gave him an exasperated look and he couldn't resist snapping one photo more than what he'd agreed. "Really?"

"I snapped a bunch to get *just* the right image, with plans to delete all but one." Zach lowered the camera. "Then I broke my promise and snapped that one because it was too good to pass up."

Her lips pressed into a thin line, her eyes hardening.

Zach had hoped she'd be amused, but now he was starting to regret being cheeky. He shouldn't make light of the broken promise, or her feelings. He could have very well damaged her trust there.

"Starship, what do you think of the book?" Jasper asked, trying to diffuse the situation.

"I love it, Daddy!" She smiled wide. "I want more."

He gestured to the bookshelf. "Okay, then pick out four more."

Their daughter's eyes went wide as planets. "*Four*? I can really pick that many, Daddy?"

Jasper smiled. "Early birthday present."

She gasped. "You're dah best!"

She scrambled off the chair and scampered over to the bookshelf to pick out her books. Shira leaned back, her expression a bit dismayed. "I didn't realize how much it'd hurt to no longer be the best in her eyes."

"Don't worry, She-ra, you'll be the best again wicked soon," Serenity assured.

Zach chuckled and went to looking over his rapid-fire snaps of the two of them to pick out his favorite. "Ain't that the truth."

Jasper also laughed, and then helped Serenity understand what each book's contents were so she could make the best choice. While Zach went through the photos, Shira came up to him and lightly grabbed his hands.

He looked up at her. "I'm deleting them as promised. I wasn't lying."

She looked at him with level eyes. "You still broke your promise."

He frowned. "I know. And I'll delete it. But I'd like you to see them both first."

Shira worked her jaw, conflict raging in her eyes. She then let out a breath and moved to his side, removing any personal space as she leaned against him. Her artificial hand rested on his back. "Okay, let me see."

Her warmth seeped into him. He couldn't focus on the images when she was this close—with her breast pressed against him and her hand teasing his senses from behind. It didn't matter that it was artificial. It was still her.

Shira reached around with her other hand and clicked the display button to filter through the shots he'd taken. This brought him back to his senses enough to watch her go through the series of ten photos left of that one moment. Her brow furrowed. "In all my years of modeling, I do not understand this. They're all the same image. Why take so many, and why take so much time picking one?"

Zach shook his head. "There are differences, or potential ones. Getting a series of snaps ensures a greater possibility of getting the right image. The one that screams *perfect*."

"I don't get it, but I'll watch your process for the sake of sick curiosity."

Zach smiled and scanned through the images, going through a process of elimination to reduce the numbers. Shira muttered to herself about not understanding, keeping him amused. In the end, he eliminated all but one, the perfect shot. "So, what do you think of this photo?"

"Beyond it looking exactly like the other *thousand* you deleted, I like it." She smiled as she expressed this. "This was a great photo to take." She looked at him. "You really know what you're doing."

He smiled at her. "Thank you." He then angled the display toward her more. "Ready to see my *illegal* picture?"

Shira grunted and waited. Zach paused for dramatic effect and then switched over to her annoyed reaction. She immediately sputtered out a laugh, pulling away from him, waving the thing away. "That... that is the most ridiculous face ever captured of me in a long time."

"Ridiculous?" Zach looked at her miffed expression in the photo. "I think it captures you perfectly."

She smacked him in the shoulder with her real hand. "It does not."

Zach smirked. "Sure it does. Just like right now."

She flicked him in the nose and then looked down at the image again. Her lip twitched. "You can keep that."

His brow rose. "You sure? I'm more than willing to delete it. I did promise only one, and I'd prefer to have the other one."

Shira nodded. "Yeah, I'm sure."

Zach regarded her a moment. "You're doing better with this than you expected, aren't you?"

She licked her lower lip, making his pulse skip, and not just because of the action. Zach realized why she was acting oddly when talking or otherwise opening her mouth. The unmistakable shine of a round metal ball in her mouth glinted through her briefly parted lips. She had a damn piercing.

In their video chats, she never had them, but Zach had a good guess she'd removed it before getting on with them. She knew them well enough to be cautious if she wasn't up to dealing with any *antics*. Zach knew if Jasper figured this out, he'd have a field day. *I'm not going to tell him.* It'd be fun for Jasper, the least observant in this room, to find out on his own.

Though why didn't she take it out before meeting with us? Given the way she was trying to hide it, she didn't want them to know yet. Maybe she forgot. Stress did funny things to the brain.

"I thought this would be harder," she said, bringing him out of his head. "My brain certainly convinced me it would be. But seeing these two images…" She shrugged. "Maybe it's the quality of them. Maybe it's just another example of me overreacting. We all know I'm great at that."

Zach chuckled. He reached down for her artificial hand and pulled it up to his lips, kissing her lightly. The false nerves in this prototype registered right before him, as her eyes dilated for a moment, and a flush crossed her cheeks. "That's just something we love about you."

The color in her face darkened and she turned her gaze, pulling her hand away. He liked seeing her like this. Her vulnerable side, something she didn't let out often enough, was alluring. "So, uh, guys, did you find the books—"

She halted and scanned the area for Jasper and Serenity, as did Zach. They were nowhere in sight.

"Um…"

"They went to do some more exploring," Orion said from her phone. "And I also did some searching in the store's catalogue. They have that book you've been searching for."

Shira threw her fist into the air. "Yes! I'll have to go find it." She looked to Zach. "Why don't you find the others and explore with them? Be good for you three to have a bit of family time here."

"Uh, yeah, sure…" That wasn't what he wanted to say. In truth, he wanted to stick with her. Jasper would have left to give him a chance to work his way in with Shira some more, and he didn't want to risk losing the ground he'd clearly made this whole time. But what was done was done. *There's still more time.*

Shira took a few steps back. "And what we agreed on still stands, you hear? I may be more okay than I thought, but that doesn't mean you can start taking more pictures of me."

Zach winked as he lifted the camera. "I'll change your mind. Just you wait."

She turned, her cheeks changing a shade again, and her voice lowered, as if she were talking more to herself than to him. "He just might."

Zach grinned and went searching for Jasper and Serenity, using Alistair's guidance to track them down. The three of them did all kinds of exploring for—Zach wasn't sure how long really. But he didn't quite care. Seeing how much fun Jasper and Serenity were having in this place, he didn't regret a minute of it.

About the time they were finally winding down from their excitement, they went looking for Shira. They found her and Snake in the military section, a few mangas and short books that looked a lot like the tree house books she'd gotten Serenity excited about tucked under her arm, and a large hardback tome with ornate bindings in her hands. She paged through it.

"Find what you were looking for? Zach called out.

She looked up and smiled. "Yep. Adding to my collection, and making sure this is the book I've been searching for."

Jasper came up to her to peek over her shoulder. "What is it?"

"A history of military strategies over the ages," she explained, closing the book up. "It's one my dad doesn't have. I've been searching all over for it."

Zach's brow ticked up. "He a military buff?"

She nodded. "Yeah, he served in the German military for a number of years before getting out and settling down with my mom. His passion for the subject never waned, though."

Zach found that interesting. He wasn't sure how someone went from a military career to fashion design, but apparently it happened. Shira also once said she enjoyed war games, which was one reason she was drawn to PvP in Lusara Fates. Zach now wondered if her father's interests influenced hers.

"Wow, he must be really buff and strong, right, Shera?" Serenity said.

She laughed. "Well, he used to be. Now he likes my mom's cooking too much, and I don't think he's gone out for a run in a number of years. He could stand a few tips from your dads."

Zach and Jasper laughed. At least she noticed the hard work they put in.

Shira pulled her books closer to her body. "Now, is everyone set, or are we staying longer?"

Everyone's eyes fell on Jasper's overencumbered arms. Shira snickered. "I think I created a monster."

"No, you just let him out of his cage unsupervised," Zach said.

They all laughed some more before agreeing to check out and get dinner plans underway. To torture Jasper a bit, Zach insisted Shira check out first at the small counter made of books. It didn't take long for the cashier to get through her small stack, which did, in fact, contain a few more of those tree house books. Zach wondered if she'd gotten them for Serenity as a gift for later, or for herself.

When the total came up, Shira lifted her cybernetic arm and swiped it over the card scanner. It beeped and her books were paid for. Zach's brow ticked up. "Shira, question."

She glanced back at him. "Yeah?"

"I thought you had artificial nerves. Didn't those fail to work with the payment chip add-ons for cybernetics?"

"The first round didn't, but Narissa fixed that issue recently."

Serenity cocked her head. "What does art-fish-al nerves mean?"

"*Artificial* means fake. The prototype technology in my cybernetics allows me to feel."

Serenity gasped and poked Shira's arm. "You can feel that, She-ra?"

She smiled. "Sure can."

"That's wicked cool!"

The woman behind the counter, who had been focused on putting Shira's books in a cloth bag she purchased, now heard part of their conversation. "Wait, did you just mention artificial nerves?" The woman's eyes widened. "Are you really a prototype tester for the one Cybro Industries announced?"

"Um, yes," Shira said.

The woman's hands slammed down on the counter, her eyes wild with excitement. "You must tell me what it feels like."

Shira jumped back, though more out of surprise than fright. Jasper and Zach exchanged looks and Snake became more alert.

The woman shrunk back, her cheeks tinting red. "I'm… I'm sorry. I got a little carried away. You see, my son was in an accident a few years ago, and he unfortunately lost his leg because of it. He's lost so much drive, I thought I might lose the bright boy who loved to play sports and get into all manner of trouble until my hair was gray." Tears welled up in her eyes. "Then I heard the tech announcement, and I knew I had to get him on the waiting list. I just… just need…"

Zach's chest tightened. The amount of distress in her voice, Zach couldn't even begin to imagine the pain she'd endured.

Shira reached across the counter and took the woman's hand. To Zach's surprise, she used the cybernetic one. "It's hard to explain the feeling I get from having these. But something I think your son will relate to is these nerves—while not yet perfect—even for the most recent style that was installed a few days ago—it makes me feel more alive than I have felt in almost six years."

A tear streaked down the woman's cheek and she squeezed Shira's hand. "Thank you."

Zach found himself choking up. He did his best to swallow it and stay composed. Shira was something else. She'd just given hope to this woman with only a vague but still powerful explanation of this tech's impact. He wished she'd see how amazing she was.

Snake popped up, placing his front paws on the counter. The woman let out a startled gasp. Shira pet him on the head. "I think it'd be a good idea if you touched him. It's Snake's job to calm others down."

The woman hesitated, but then reached out for the shepherd. Snake licked her hand and nudged her until she rested her head on his. Zach watched the visible change in the woman as she calmed down, feeding off Snake's loving, calm nature. *Amazing.*

Once the woman calmed, she thanked Shira again. "Do you mind if I ask something personal?"

"How many cybernetics I have?" Shira guessed.

The woman nodded. "I know it's usually rude to ask, but based on how you've talked, I feel as though that arm of yours isn't the only one. And if someone with more than my son can be happy again, then I'm sure I can get my happy boy back."

Shira smiled and stepped back, pulling up her pant leg to reveal a part of her cybernetic leg. "Let's just say, I've got a lot. Without them, I wouldn't be alive."

"Thank you. That will help me show him there's still hope." The woman got to ringing Jasper out, Zach slipping the one vinyl he picked out into the stack. "Okay, who is the bookworm?"

Jasper raised his hand, as did Serenity.

The woman smiled. "That's what I like to see. Raising her right."

Jasper glanced down at their daughter. "We try."

The checkout process continued, the total nearly giving Zach a heart attack. *There goes a ton of our spending money.* He was going to have to make sure they were more careful going forward. At least, though, these books would be well-used, so it wasn't a total waste.

The real fun came when Jasper had to carry them out.

Two canvas bags were barely enough, and Jasper insisted on carrying them himself. Even after Shira let them know the walk to the restaurant would be a few blocks.

Shira shrugged. "Okay, suit yourself. Don't complain when you get tired."

CHAPTER 15

A deep sigh escaped Shira's lips as Jasper carried on and on about how "tired" he was and why couldn't they get a ride share to the restaurant instead. He also threw in a few "are we there yet" lines. "Jasper, if you don't stop, so help me, I'm turning this walking caravan right around."

"Nice going, Jasper," Zach said. "Got Mom angry and dragged me down with you."

"Hey, we agreed we'd do everything together, didn't we?" Jasper said.

The three of them laughed. Serenity looked down at them from her perch on Jasper's shoulders, confused. A sports car roared by, grabbing her attention. Shira loved watching her easily distracted mind try to take in this city. She wondered how the little girl would handle a convention center.

"You think that was Ajax and Narissa?" Jasper asked, watching the car disappear down the road.

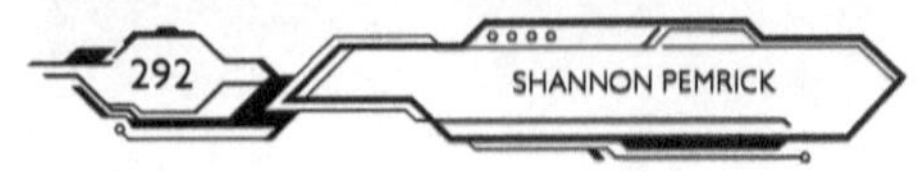

"No, that wasn't one of his fancy cars," Shira said. "Plus, I'm pretty sure they're still stuck in traffic."

Ajax had the bright idea to take a "shortcut" to avoid the early evening traffic. Turns out, he brought them down a construction zone, getting them stuck worse than they would have been on the main road. Shira could only imagine Narissa's annoyance with him.

"Speaking of destinations, can we know where we're going yet?" Zach asked.

Shira's face scrunched as she thought. She supposed it couldn't hurt to tell them the name. "Zwergstraße Küche."

The two faltered in their steps, Jasper stuttering out, "Z–uh–what now?"

Shira laughed and repeated herself, continuing to walk. "Zwergstraße Küche."

Serenity tried to say it, but it was more gibberish than anything. "That's wicked hahd."

"It's going to be a hard language to learn, Serenity. But I know you'll master it." Shira smiled. "I believe in you."

Serenity pulled her arms vertically against her chest, her fists balled up, and a serious, but still adorable expression creased her face. "I will learn it!"

"What does it mean?" Zach asked.

Shira turned to face them. "Dwarf Street Kitchen."

His brow ticked up. "Is that to be funny, or is there a meaning behind the name?"

Shira continued on. "You'll see."

Jasper let out an exasperated sigh. "How much long-er?"

She pointed to a parking lot full of cars. "Almost there."

Zach looked around. "That's just a parking lot. Where's the actual place?"

"It's not on the main road. Customers park there and then walk."

Jasper let out another playful sigh. "But my feet hurt."

"Daddy, you're doing a lot of complaining," Serenity said.

Shira bit her lip so she wouldn't laugh. Here it came.

"That's because I'm playing, Pumpkin," Jasper said. "I'm just doing it to get on Shira's nerves."

"Well, it's annoying me."

"You do it, too."

"Yeah, and you tell me it's annoying, too."

Shira hid her face in her hand. *Oh, this family.*

Another sports car roared by. This time, the model and color caught her attention. A red Corvette. *Is that them?* The combo wasn't exactly unique, especially in Los Angeles. She focused on a sticker in its back window. She couldn't see the exact details from this far away, but it looked similar to ones people had for Lusara Fates. Then it stopped short and went in reverse. *Gotta be them. Only Ajax would be stupid enough to do that on a main road.* Luckily there weren't any cars driving through at the moment.

The sports car came to a halt and the tinted passenger side window rolled down. Narissa's beautiful face greeted her.

"Hey, stranger," Shira said, leaning on the door. "Need something?"

Narissa grinned. "I might. Depends on what you're offering."

The two laughed.

Narissa shook her head as she looked behind Shira. "You boys have no sense of shame."

Shira turned to see them staring at her backside. She stood up and crossed her arms. "Really?"

Jasper shrugged. "Narissa said it. No shame."

Ajax leaned over so he could see everyone. "So I don't get a citation and don't see the blood bath Shira might unleash, I'm going to go park now."

Shira laughed and stepped away from the car. When they regrouped in the parking lot, Shira and Narissa embraced in a hug and Ajax greeted Jasper and Zach before allowing Narissa to greet them with a hug as well.

"It's so good to see you both in person finally," she said.

"You too, Narissa," Zach said as he pulled away.

She bent down to greet Serenity. "And it's so good to meet you, Serenity. Do you remember me?"

Serenity played with her fingers and wiggled her shoulders and she avoided eye contact. "Uh-huh... You're friends with Daddy, Zach, and She-ra."

"That's right."

Jasper placed his hand on her head. "You don't have to be shy, Seren."

"I know..."

Narissa stood up, still smiling, yet accepting Serenity's need for more time to warm up to her. "Why don't you all put your spoils from the bookstore in the car where they'll be safe, and we can all head to the restaurant? Get food ordered, so you two and Ajax can get to talking work while we ladies do the smart thing and relax."

It didn't take long to get to the restaurant. The small stucco-and-brick building with a clay shingled roof was tucked away in an offshoot road. Jasper and Zach marveled at the building.

"This is a restaurant?" Jasper said.

"Name is fitting, based on location and size," Zach said.

A loud chatter of patrons was unleashed when Shira swung open the wooden door. While not deafening, it was a bit noisier than Shira expected. Thursdays, even for dinner, were usually one of their slower nights. She hoped it wouldn't pose a problem.

They entered a small entryway, with bench seats and various German sports memorabilia, from events to history, to even political movements of importance. Old papers and digital screens written in the language were tacked up alongside signs and clothes.

A woman Shira didn't recognize stood at the host podium. *She must be new.* And beyond her was a quaint, tavern-like setup, from the wooden bar to the tables.

Shira greeted the hostess. "Hi, I have a reservation for the Schneider party."

The waitress nodded and looked at her list. She frowned. "Give me one moment. There's a note here I have to check on."

Shira's brow rose, but she didn't put up a fuss as the hostess left. Instead, she focused on Jasper, Zach, and Serenity, who gazed at the memorabilia around them.

Serenity pointed to a screen article in her reach, depicting a small old building squeezed between two large modern ones. "She-ra, what does that one talk about?"

Shira went over and bent down to look at it. "It talks about the first Zwergstraße Küche established in Germany."

"Can you read it to me?"

Shira smirked and then read it in German.

Serenity giggled when Shira finished. "Now in English!"

Shira chuckled and translated. "Zwergstraße Küche, established 1965 after Leon Meier won the old tavern in a game of Blackjack, quickly became popular because of its menu choice of traditional German meals of various time periods. The business was left to his son upon his retirement, who passed it to his daughter. The tavern has continued to keep its notoriety and stay a family business to this day, eventually passing into the hands of brothers Luis and Felix Meier, though only Felix currently runs it today."

Zach scratched his chin, Shira's eyes following the motion and making her too far aware how much she liked the shape of his face. "I wonder what happened to Luis to give up such a long-standing tradition of running the business. Sounded like it was a good business to run."

Before Shira could answer, a deep voice chuckled, and spoke with a light accent. "I opened a branch here in America."

Everyone turned to see a tall, clean-shaven, muscular man in his late fifties with tan skin, and short chestnut-and-gray hair. His dark brown eyes were light and cheerful.

"Uncle Luis!" Shira went over to him and wrapped her arms around his neck for a quick hug.

Luis chuckled and hugged her back. "It's so good to see you, Shira."

"Uncle?" Zach questioned.

"Well, he's not technically my uncle. He and *Vati* served in the military together. Momma's the reason he came over to establish this place, though." She nudged Luis in the side. "Hooked him up with a pretty American girl. He thought establishing a family restaurant branch here would impress her."

Luis shrugged. "It worked."

Everyone laughed.

"Now, Uncle Luis, is there a reason your hostess needed to check on our reservation?"

Luis rocked his head back and forth. "Ja… sort of. I left the note so I could come and see you when you first arrived. But… Ben accidentally gave your table way when we became overwhelmed by customers. We're cleaning a table now for you all."

Shira tilted her head. "Why is it so busy here tonight?"

Luis shrugged. "Hell if I know. Whatever's been causing it, I don't want it to happen again. We've had a higher number of unsavory types come through the doors. I stopped counting how many I threw out after ten."

Shira grimaced. "Sorry to hear that."

Luis looked to Jasper and Zach and nodded to their entwined hands. "Anyone gives you two trouble, let me know immediately."

Jasper grunted. "Oh, so we're dealing with that kind of unsavory."

Shira's shoulders tensed. Why did it have to be that kind of trouble? She just wanted people to leave them alone and be happy.

Narissa placed her hands on Shira's shoulders. "Don't worry. We have our attack dog to deal with an unsavory types, don't we?"

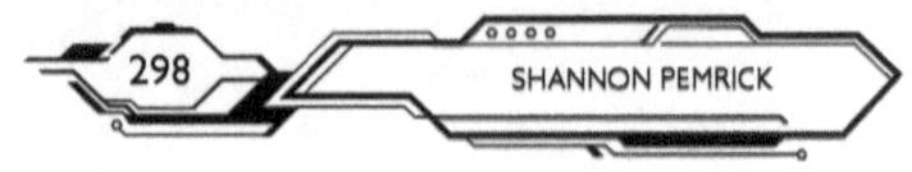

Shira pounded her fists together. "You bet."

Luis belted out a hearty laugh. "Zat I have no doubt. But I'd rather deal with zem myself. It is my establishment."

Shira shrugged. "No promises, you know that."

The hostess from before returned and looked to Luis. "The table is all set for them."

Luis clapped his hands together. "Good. Let's get you all seated. I'm sure you're hungry."

They all followed him into the establishment, to a pair of wooden tables pulled together. Menus were set between laid-out utensils. Jasper and Zach sat across from Ajax to make it easy to converse about the tournament. Narissa sat next to him, and Shira would have slipped into the chair beside her, had Serenity not insisted she sit next to her, while also insisting she had to sit next to Zach. Shira opted for an end seat to keep that side from being too crowded while still appeasing the little girl.

Before she could sit, a pale, older woman with bouncy red hair and curvy figure came rushing from somewhere in the back of the building. "Wait, don't you dare sit down before you give me a hug, young lady."

Shira laughed and embraced the woman. "It's so good to see you, Aunt Tiffany."

They pulled away and Tiffany continued to smile. "I just wanted to be sure I saw you. Ben insisted on serving you today. He'll be right over after he fills a drink order. Since I'm here, can we get you anything, or do you need some time to think? Recommendations? I see three new faces here."

"Wow, I feel like we're getting the royal treatment here," Zach joked.

Narissa laughed. "Come with Shira, and you'll get this treatment every time."

Shira rolled her eyes and sat down. Snake slipped under the table and lay at her feet. "You know what I'll have, Aunt Tiffany."

Tiffany chuckled. "You could stand to try a different brew every once in a while, you know?"

"I do. After I have at least two of my favorite."

The woman shook her head and looked to Shira's friends. Narissa ordered a water, as did Ajax. Luis was not impressed. "One of you has to at least try one of our fine pilsners or lagers."

Ajax shook his head. "I've been eight years sober, I'm not looking to mess up my life again."

Shira's brow cocked. *I didn't know Ajax was an alcoholic.*

Narissa held up her hands. "And it's not good for a pregnant woman to drink."

Jasper's and Zach's mouths dropped. "You're what?"

Narissa laughed. "Surprise!"

Serenity's eyes lit up. "You're having a baby?"

Narissa placed her hand on her stomach. "Yes, I am."

Serenity's hands shot up into the air and she cheered. "Yay!"

Jasper looked to Shira. "Did you know?"

She let out a snort. "Duh. She's my best friend."

He scratched his head. "Wow. Well, congrats, you two."

Zach nodded in agreement.

"And if you get bad morning sickness, let me know. When Sara was pregnant with Serenity, we found one heck of a cure for her."

Narissa's shoulders relaxed and she sighed deeply.

"That would be amazing. I can barely keep anything down. I don't even know how well dinner will go."

"Try ordering something with protein for your meal," Tiffany suggested. "Should make it easier on you."

Narissa smiled. "If I can stand the smell. I'm not liking how sensitive I am to smells already."

Tiffany nodded, understanding the less-than-great sides to pregnancy, and looked to Jasper and Zach. "And what will you two have?"

"While I'd normally ask about IPAs available, I think trying a pilsner from here would be a better idea," Zach said. "I'll take whatever you recommend, for the surprise factor."

The mention of IPA made Shira's neck muscle twitch. Not the best preference, but it could have been worse.

"Going against the grain, considering where we are, I prefer a stout," Jasper said. "Guinness, if you have it, but I'll take any you have."

And now it had just gotten worse. Shira worked her jaw and kept quiet. *At least he didn't ask for some skunk-piss drink.*

Luis shook his head and shot Shira a look, as if she were responsible for their lack of taste. Zach noticed their exchange. "What's with the looks?"

Narissa giggled. "Shira is a bit of a beer snob."

Shira scoffed. "Am not."

"Oh, yes you are," Tiffany said. "You and Luis both are terrible. Even Ben has his moments because of Luis. It's ridiculous."

"Zey were both raised knowing good brews," Luis said. "Me as well. We only drink ze best."

Tiffany shook her head and looked to Jasper and

Zach. "Ignore them. You have fine preferences. But if you want to try one of the German brews over a stout at some point tonight, I recommend trying the Doppel Bock." She then looked at Serenity, who had watched the adults with curious eyes. "And what would you like, honey?"

"Juice!"

Tiffany smiled. "What kind? We have many flavors."

"You gots apple?"

"Yes, of course."

Serenity smacked her lips together. "Please and thank you."

Tiffany praised her politeness and rattled off the order before slipping away, making sure Luis went with her so as to not cause any trouble.

That didn't stop Jasper from starting some with Shira. "You're really hating on my choice? What gives?"

Shira let out a long sigh. "I'm not hating. I didn't say a word."

"But you think it's bad."

She worked her jaw. *Oh, fuck it.* "I think you could have better taste."

Narissa snickered. "See?"

"But isn't that bock brew Tiffany suggested similar to a stout?" Zach asked.

Shira pointed at him. "Don't you compare the two like that. Bock is superior."

Jasper narrowed his eyes. "We'll see about that."

He left the table to talk to Tiffany at the bar. He returned empty-handed, but Shira knew Tiffany would bring out whatever he ordered.

"Okay, now that we have that settled, sort of, we

should look at these menus to get our meal choices figured out so we can let you boys talk about the business side of the convention tomorrow," Narissa said.

Everyone looked at their menus while holding light casual conversation.

"I'm surprised by these low-tech menus," Zach said, looking at the simple two-sided posterboard-material menu.

"Luis wanted to give this an older, timely feel. So he opts for paper menus, and physical waitstaff instead of ordering via tech."

"The dual language is an interesting touch," Jasper said.

The menus were written in both German and English, to add to the authenticity of the place. Shira noticed they'd added a few more options to the menu, but she decided on her tried and true favorite.

Since she finished first, she offered to help Serenity pick so Zach could have more time looking. "What is your favorite thing to eat?"

"Potatoes!" Serenity said without hesitating.

Jasper chuckled. "That's an undahstatement. She could have potatoes any way, every meal of the day for the rest of her life."

Serenity nodded. "They're nummy."

Shira smiled and pointed to an item on the menu. "Then you'll like *kartoffelpuffer*. They're potato pancakes."

Serenity gasped. "Nummy! I want that."

That was easier than Shira expected.

"She-ra, what are you having?" Serenity asked. "You didn't take long."

"I'm having my favorite dish here, *hasenpfeffer*," Shira said. "That's a rabbit stew."

The little girl's eyes went wide and she gasped. "You eat bunnies? How could you eat a cute bunny?"

Jasper, the ever-so-protective parent, whipped around in his seat. All the others' eyes fell on Shira, thinking Shira was about to send Serenity into a fit of tears. But Shira wasn't worried.

She rested her cheek on the palm of her hand. "You eat steak, right, Starship? And chicken, too?"

Serenity sat back in her seat, her face scrunching as she thought. "Yeah, both are yummy."

"Do you think cows and chickens are cute?"

Serenity nodded.

"Me eating rabbit isn't much different from you eating steak or chicken, then, now is it?"

She worked her lips back and forth. "I guess so…" Serenity then shook her head. "But I don't want to eat bunny."

Shira and the others chuckled. She reached out and tapped Serenity on the nose. "And you don't have to."

Serenity happily kicked her legs. Shira glanced up to see Narissa and Ajax looking down at their menus again, but Jasper and Zach watched her. They didn't look annoyed or anything, on the contrary, rather happy. But Shira got this uneasy feeling it was more than that and she didn't like it. "What? Why are you two staring?"

"A gorgeous woman mothering a child is hard for a lot us to ignore," a man said from behind Shira.

She turned to see a lean young man, around his early thirties, with tan skin, chestnut hair, and brown eyes. He carried a tray of drinks with him. "I don't know what you're talking about, Ben. I'm not mothering her. Just explaining."

He chuckled and set the drinks down on the table. "Say what you want, doesn't change anything."

Shira's lips pressed into a tight line. She wasn't mothering Serenity.

Ben greeted everyone, introducing himself, and handed out the drinks, offering Shira her two Hafeweizens first.

Zach's brow rose. "You're having two beers?"

Ben laughed. "You kidding? She'll have a good five or six before the meal is over."

Shira shook her head. "Not today. But, yes, that's the usual amount."

Zach's brow rose for a moment and he grasped his pilsner close to his lips. "Good to know."

Jasper got his Guinness, as well as another dark brew. Shira figured it was the bock Tiffany suggested. Appeared Jasper was aiming to prove her wrong. She was up for that challenge.

Narissa and Ajax got their drinks, and Serenity was last with her glass of juice. Ben smiled at her. "Do you like to color?"

Serenity gasped and nodded so much Shira feared her head might pop off.

Ben whipped out a long piece of paper with all kinds of fun designs on them, and some crayons. Serenity didn't hesitate to start, though Zach reminded her to use her manners. She thanked Ben and resumed.

"Now, do you all know what you'd like to order, or do you need more time? Suggestions?" Ben asked.

"What's your stew of the day?" Ajax asked.

"*Sauerbraten*—beef stew."

Ajax nodded. "I'll have that, along with some currywurst. Wait." He glanced at Narissa. "Make that bratwurst."

His consideration for Narissa's sensitive nose made Shira smile. He was so good to her.

Ben took the order down and looked to Narissa. "I'll have egg noodles."

Ben wrote it down, while speaking. "An order of *spätzle*, got it. With or without wurst?"

Narissa thought for a moment. "Going to play it safe and say without."

"Okay. And you three?"

Zach opted for *kartoffelkloesse*—potato dumplings—trying his damnedest to say the word correctly but failing. He also ordered schnitzel. Jasper tried the same with the *scheeinshaxe*—pork knuckle—and succeeded about just as well.

Serenity ordered her potato pancakes, mimicking her fathers' tries. With everyone's order in, Ben tucked his order pad away. Serenity stopped him. "You forgot She-ra."

Ben smiled at her and patted Shira on the shoulder. "Shira never orders anything different when she comes here."

Shira grunted. "Never know, I might surprise you one day."

"That'll be the same day that *Vati* doesn't get on my case about not hitting the gym enough."

Everyone laughed and Ben excused himself, allowing the men to get down to business.

"You'll need to arrive tomorrow earlier than normal," Ajax informed them. "The media is making a big deal over the fact I've chosen to sponsor a team this year."

"Well, duh," Shira said. "GameTech hasn't ever sponsored a team before. And seeing as you're the reason

Lusara Fates is even on the map the way it is now, it's a big deal. Especially since you've decided to sponsor a two's team instead of a full five."

Narissa took a sip of her water. "Told you so."

Ajax sighed. "Regardless of that fact, it means I need you two an hour early for a special conference. And expect all kinds of media harassment during it. And maybe a little after."

Jasper's eyes glanced to Serenity for a split second. "Bettah not be aftah. Serenity is to stay out of their attention."

"We'll do our best to keep her out of it," Narissa said. "The con has a very specific policy regarding children, so we'll make sure they abide by them."

Shira lifted her glass to her lips. "And if they don't, they'll be put through the wringer with my lawyers."

Zach's brow lifted. "Yours?"

Shira chuckled. "You don't work in the modeling industry without getting some of the best out there. Everyone thinks they can infringe on your rights because you put your face in front of a camera for money."

Ajax clasped his hands together on the table. "GameTech has its own lawyers, too. You'll be covered."

Jasper didn't look convinced. "Even still. I don't want her neah that room. Shira, would you—"

He stopped and stared as she guzzled down her first beer. "Uh, watch her?"

Shira let out a breath as she set the empty glass down on the table. "You don't have to ask me. You know I will. I'm not keen on being anywhere near that conference hall with camera sharks, either."

Narissa smiled. "I'm sure the two of them can find

something to do in the hotel room until the convention officially starts."

"Hotel room." Zach pulled out his phone. "Yeah, about that."

She gasped. "Don't tell me your rooms were affected."

He nodded. "Doesn't look like I have any update, either."

Ajax looked between them. "I wish you'd told us sooner. We have to come up with a game plan for where you'll stay. You can't get a hotel for miles because of the convention."

Jasper jerked his thumb toward Shira. "Shira offa'd to let us crash at her place."

Narissa gave a closed-lip smile before taking a sip of water. "Of course she did."

Shira's brow rose. "What's that supposed to mean?"

"Just that it makes sense. Always coming to their rescue." Narissa chuckled. "It's cute, and fitting."

She made it sound so simple, but Shira knew Narissa, and knew her reasoning was anything but.

"I'll work with the hotel to ensure the room situation is fixed up," Narissa said. "Just in case the commute becomes too much and you'd rather stay on site."

Ajax rubbed his hands together. "Good. With that settled, we can talk about the tournament."

The three went on while Shira and Narissa had casual conversation and praised Serenity every time she showed her coloring work.

Their food eventually came out, and more than a few eyes fell on Shira's meal, as a plate full of stringy pale mass was included. Serenity cocked her head. "She-ra, what's that?"

"It's sauerkraut." She took a big helping onto her fork and shoved it into her mouth.

Serenity scrunched her nose. "Daddy eats that. It smells funny."

Shira's eyes darted to Jasper, who was also already eating some of his that had come with his meal. *At least he has some proper taste in the food department.* Though, Shira tried not to be critical of this particular preference. It was a rather acquired taste. "Have you tried it before, Starship?"

She shook her head, her nose still scrunched. "Don't wanna."

"Okay, you don't have to." Shira then dipped into her stew, which didn't look like the kind of stew an American would expect. There was always far more meat than liquid in German stews. This difference was made apparent by the way Ajax looked at his meal and then shrugged and dug in.

Shira shoved some in her mouth; the delicious mix of spices and meat melted on her tongue in one glorious symphony. She didn't eat like this often, unless her mother invited her over for dinner. Shira didn't see a reason to go this far out of her way to cook such meals for only herself, and maybe a little bit for Snake as a treat, like what he ate now.

No surprise to her, Luis and Tiffany had made him a special plate. They always did. Serenity giggled away as she watched him eat his meal under the table, while she happily munched her potato pancake.

The only one not eating at this point was Narissa. She stared down at her food, her face tight. Ajax stopped mid-bite and looked at her. "Something wrong?"

Narissa swallowed. "All the food around me is making me nauseous. Trying to keep it down so I can eat a little."

Shira frowned. She really did have it bad. She suddenly realized that whenever they'd had lunch together these past two weeks, she'd hardly eaten anything. And not for a lack of trying, either.

Narissa took a deep breath and tried to eat some of her noodles. They appeared more plain than they usually made them here, but Shira suspected Tiffany had done that for Narissa's benefit.

Three bites in, Narissa dropped her fork and shook her head, her eyes wide with regret. "Nope, shouldn't have done that."

She flew out of her seat and ran for the bathroom. Ajax watched her retreating form helplessly. Shira was sure she caught traces of regret.

"It's going to be okay, Ajax," she said. "The sickness will pass."

"I know." He frowned. "Just hard to stay excited when she's going through this. We agreed to this without me thinking about what would be asked of her."

"It gets easier," Jasper assured. "You learn what sets it off and what's safe. And even with Sara unfortunately having to deal with it through her whole pregnancy, she admitted it wasn't as bad after the first trimester."

Ajax rubbed the back of his neck. "Yeah, but that doesn't make me feel any less guilty and responsible."

Shira chuckled and stood up. "Well, she didn't get impregnated by Santa Claus."

Jasper and Zach laughed, and to Shira's pleasure, so did Ajax. Serenity just looked confused, like always.

"I'll go check on her. You three keep eating and chatting."

Shira slipped through the restaurant and into the ladies' room, where Narissa was unmistakably losing her stomach. "Need someone to hold your hair up?"

A larger stall door unlocked and then Narissa went back to retching. Shira didn't hesitate to go in and give her friend a hand, holding her lovely curly hair out of the way and rubbing her back to help relax her.

Several minutes passed before Narissa finally found her body calming down. "Thank you."

"You don't have to. I'm your friend, and here for you even when your body is rebelling against your baby-making decisions."

Narissa chuckled before washing out her mouth. "Would be nice to keep some sort of food down. Especially something like those noodles. They were good."

"I'm sure things will calm down soon enough." Shira rubbed her friend's back some more. "Now, feeling well enough to at least sit back at the table?"

"Not yet," she said. "I have one thing I want to ask you now that I've got you alone."

Shira sighed. She already knew what was going to be asked. "I've not changed my mind, Rissa. I'm not going to sign that contract."

"Please reconsider." She grabbed Shira's cybernetic hand. Her warmth seeped into Shira. As much as she liked being able to feel again on that side, it was still requiring a lot of getting used to in certain situations, even after all this time of testing. "You've made so many strides, just to come here and do all kinds of normal things. You went to the convention center alone to meet the guys. You drove around town until you decided to go to the bookstore. You *walked* downtown to do so."

Shira pulled away, holding her hand close to her body. "That may be, but I'm not ready. Not quite yet."

Narissa's brow rose. "Quite yet? Interesting way to word that." She studied Shira for a moment. Shira tried not to react to the scrutiny, but her friend was sharp, and caught the minor slip up. "What happened while you were out with them?"

Shira avoided her friend's gaze and chewed her bottom lip. "Zach… he… he's a photographer."

Narissa took a step closer. "And?"

"And at first, I told him not to take any pictures, after he took some when I showed up at the convention center." She worked her jaw. "But after my first freak out… at some point, I… I willingly agreed to one photo."

Narissa gasped. "You agreed to that? You didn't feel coerced?"

She shook her head. "No. And when I looked at the photo… I didn't panic that time." She looked at Narissa. "I didn't feel the need to beg him to delete it, Rissa. I don't know how to describe what happened. It's so foreign, and—"

Narissa grabbed her shoulders. "Easy, Shira. Take it easy."

Shira took a breath, realizing just how fast her heart rate had gotten. Was she talking fast too? Did she start to panic without knowing? *No…* "I'm fine, Narissa, really."

Her friend cocked her head, staring at her with keen brown eyes. "You really weren't panicking. I'm sorry. I didn't mean to misread the signs."

Shira smiled and placed a hand on hers. "It's okay. I know you meant well. And it did help bring my focus back. I might have gone into a full-on babble, trying to understand what happened with me if you hadn't stepped in."

Narissa cocked her head. "It is an interesting situation. When you hear me propose the idea of modeling, you still get nervous and feel the need to be defensive, yes?"

Shira nodded.

"And when the topic of taking your photo is discussed with those two, you feel the same? Even after you agreed to the one?"

Shira nodded again. "At first it was as bad as your request. But then when I agreed, it felt more like I was preparing to take a photo of myself to post of social media. Then when Zach tried to ask again while we walked here, I was quick to shut him down. I didn't feel panicked, but I wasn't comfortable again discussing the topic."

Narissa rubbed her chin. "Interesting. Sounds like we're making progress, but situationally. I think you should try to say yes again the next time he asks. What do you think?"

"If you think it means I'll say yes to you, you're wrong."

Narissa chuckled. "I'd be lying if a part of me did want that eventually, but this goes beyond this want. Maybe they hold a key to getting past what's holding you back. Your fear of cameras is a state of mind. They're obviously doing something to make you not think about that block. So why not try to capitalize on it? So you can move on from your past." Narissa grinned. "Even if you don't model for the company eventually."

Shira leaned against the wall holding her arms tight to her body. Could she do that? The muscles in her shoulders tightened the moment the thought came through. *Better yet, do I want to?*

Angelica had hinted the camera issue may be less fear of the past, and more her fearing the unknown. After five years of suffering, she'd come to find it as an unfortunate source of comfort. It was her new known, and anything beyond it, even if it could help her, was treated with fear because it was too unknown.

"Of course, it may mean getting nice and close to them to achieve this." Narissa winked. "Not that they'd mind, with how they've been looking at you while you've handled Serenity all night."

Shira refused to make eye contact with her. She didn't want to get on this topic—didn't want to think about how naturally she fell into place around them. *How much I don't feel like an outsider looking in, when I should...*

Narissa tapped her arm. "Lighten up, I'm teasing. You know I have to."

Shira swatted her away. "Sure you do."

"Let's get back to the table. I'm sure the boys are wondering what happened to us, and no doubt Ajax is worrying himself sick and blaming himself for the condition I agreed to put myself in."

Shira chuckled. "You've got no idea."

They slipped out of the bathroom and rejoined the men and Serenity. Ajax fussed so much as Narissa sat down that she fell into a laughing fit. Shira could hardly contain her amusement, either, as she found her seat. Part of her amusement came from her noticing Jasper had put a nice dent into both his beers.

"So, I was right, wasn't I?"

He rolled his eyes. "Yes, they taste different, but the stout is better."

She narrowed her eyes. "Take that back."

He lifted his Guinness to his lips and winked. Shira's lip curled. *Uncultured loser.* She lifted her second glass to her lips, but halted when her ears picked up two people making remarks behind her. Something about Narissa and Ajax's relationship was said. Shira's grip tightened around her drink. Then the inevitable came from their lips, the moment they described Serenity and their disgust at her being subjected to such an environment with the—

Shira spun around and tossed her drink at them, standing in the process. The glass smashed against the wall between the two low-lifes, who jumped. Her shoulders tense and teeth nearly bared in her building rage, she stared them down. "Don't you dare finish that sentence!"

Her focus was so strong on these two who were recovering, she barely heard Ben calling out to his parents about the altercation, and a chair scratching against the floor as someone stood up.

One of the men wiped some of the beer splatter from his jacket, his eyes livid. "What do you think you're doing, you robotic freak?"

"The likes of you aren't welcome here." Shira's eyes narrowed. "Get the hell out."

"Up yours, homo lover," the other subhuman said.

That's it! She went to take a step forward to swing at him when strong arms wrapped around and restrained her. "Shira, don't!"

"Let me go!" she roared, struggling against him. "He deserves to have his face beat in."

He held strong. "No, you won't solve this with vio-lence."

The first ingrate stood, chuckling. "Look, a pacifist fag and a woman who thinks she's more than a decent lay. Cute."

The muscles in Zach's arms twitched and he muttered, "Fine, have it your way, asshole."

He freed Shira and she lunged for her target. Not expecting this, he didn't have time to react, and her cybernetic fist collided with his face. The man hit the ground with a *thud* and didn't get up.

Signals flooded Shira's artificial nerves and her brain's neuro-mod, but her rage blocked out what would have been an overwhelming situation. She turned her atten-tion to his companion, who was on his feet and taking fearful steps back. *Typical. Cowardly piece of—*

A log of an arm wrapped around Shira's waist and lifted her up effortlessly. An unfortunate squeak escaped her lips as she was pulled out of her state and hung with limp limbs. She looked up at Luis, his face red and twisted with rage, but still in control—unlike how she had been.

"Ben, get him out of here and wait for ze police," Luis said through tense teeth.

Ben grabbed the unruly man and dragged him out, one of the other workers assisting to ensure he didn't get away before the cops arrived. Two others dragged the unconscious man out while Luis turned and carried Shira back to her seat. *I forgot how ridiculously strong he was.*

He set her down and forced her to sit. He walked away. "Stay zere."

His voice was authoritative, a reminder of whom she'd

crossed by not listening to his request before. She was in a lot of trouble.

Snake rested his head on her lap and she pet him to stay calm. What kind of punishment would he come up with for her? He could be rather creative, though, nothing could be as bad as him making her and Ben run five miles down the beach, wearing cold-weather gear in ninety-degree heat. She was sick for days after that. The silver lining there, her mother punished him for it, and he never went that far again with his punishments.

Her friends sat in silence watching her. Even Serenity was quiet, though she appeared rather awestruck. Shira looked down at Snake. That really had been a stupid thing to do. She shouldn't have let her anger get the better of her like that. Even if it felt good to put them in their place, she'd caused a scene, made a fool of her friends, and caused trouble for Luis, Tiffany, and Ben when they didn't need it.

A glass landed on the table in front of her, pulling her out of her head. A beer sat in front of her. She looked at Luis, confused, only to see he had three other glasses with him. "Uncle Luis?"

He stared down unblinking at her. "Drink."

"Just the one, or…"

"Drink."

Okay… She was about to find out what horror was in store for her. She lifted the glass to her lips and gulped some of it down.

"All of it."

She kept going until it was finished. Shira set the glass down on the table and let out a breath. Luis gave her another beer. "Drink."

She downed this one as well. Luis gave her a darker brew and expected her to drink this immediately as well. Her stomach hurt from the first two, but this was her punishment, which she rightfully deserved. And it wasn't *that* bad.

Shira didn't hesitate to take her first gulp, but she sure did regret it as the creamy but bitter and granular taste hit her tongue. Her face scrunched as she pulled it away. "What—"

"Drink it."

Shira frowned. "You gave me a stout."

Jasper's head flew back, a roar of laughter tearing through him. He slapped the table several times.

Shira's nose scrunched and she muttered into her glass before she drank it, "Not funny."

Getting the stout down was a chore, but she managed, thanks to Ajax getting pumped up from this and banging on the table, chanting her name. Serenity joined in and soon the entire restaurant was egging her on. Shira finished the glass and slammed it down on the table. The chanting didn't stop.

She took steady breaths, her stomach recoiling from how quickly she'd just downed the three beers. Shira's eyes ticked to Luis' hand, where he still held one last glass, a smaller one that was pale yellow in color. She got an uneasy feeling from this, but she couldn't back down. Before Luis could hand it to her, she reached out and snatched it.

She could already smell the off scent of it. She knew exactly what he was doing to her. *Well, down the hatch.* Shira choked the moment the skunky brew touched her lips, but she pushed through that, gulping down the liquid one painful swallow at a time.

The glass slammed down on the table and Shira buried her face into her arm, breathing deep and feeling her stomach churn and fight against the torture she'd just put it through. The whole establishment exploded in one excited uproar.

By the time it died down, she'd caught her breath, but her stomach still threatened to bail on her. She looked up at Luis. "Skunk piss, really?"

Zach and Jasper collapsed on the table in a fit of laughter. *At least they're getting a kick out of my misery.*

Luis patted her on the shoulder. "Punishment. Next time, don't attack someone. Let me handle it."

Narissa let out a slow sigh and sipped her water. "That's never going to happen. There's a reason she's called the *attack dog*. She even knows what type of trouble that kind of behavior brings to my neuro-mods. We struggled with the calibration to handle such impacts." Her eyes cut to Shira. "And the nervous system prototypes are even more finicky, which she knows. Yet, here we are."

Luis' head flew back as he howled in laughed. "Ja, zat does sound like her."

Ajax leaned back in his chair. "Yes, but what kind of dog is she? We've never established that."

"She's like Snake!" Serenity exclaimed. She turned her head and bent lower in her seat to look under the table. "Right, Snake?"

He slipped out from under the table, licked her in the face, and then retreated back. Serenity squealed, wiping her hands all over her face while smiling. This got the adults laughing.

Luis placed his hand on the young girl's head. "Zis adorable little one is right."

"I'm gonna be just like She-ra when I'm big!" Serenity announced. "I'm gonna be wicked pretty, and smart, and loyal to my friend. And if anyone tries to hurt them"—she punched the air—"POW! I'll hurt them first. I'll be bad-ass like She-ra!"

Jasper immediately tried to correct her for using "bad-ass," and asked her to use a different word from now on. Serenity didn't understand why she couldn't use the word, cause she didn't see it as a bad word.

Luis laughed. "Yep, she'll be just like her." His eyes darted to Jasper and Zach. "Good luck with zat."

He walked away while Jasper and Zach gave each other concerned looks.

"What's that supposed to mean?" Zach finally asked.

"It means, you obviously don't know Shira well enough," Ben said as he passed. It appeared he'd been relieved of his restraining duty. "She's got enough crazy stories to make you think twice about her being a role model."

Shira swiped at him. "Don't go telling them my truths, now. You're ruining all my fun."

Ben laughed and headed off. Jasper leaned on the table. "Well, now I gotta know. Best to know what kind of corruption you're planting on my daughtah."

Shira winked and sipped on some water to settle her stomach. "Maybe another time. For now, we should finish our meals and probably call it a night."

Narissa nodded. "I agree. With the hotel issues, you three still need to get settled in at Shira's, and you have an early day tomorrow."

Shira called Luis over for their check, once he'd finished talking with a police officer. Ajax took the whole bill, much to Shira's protests. He tried to claim it was a business expense, given them talking work most of the dinner, but Narissa also pointed out he would do this even if it wasn't.

As they got ready to leave, Shira saying goodbye to Luis, Tiffany, and Ben, Jasper ducked low in front of her and lifted her over his shoulder, carrying her to the door, his hand dangerously close to her ass.

Shira struggled. "You caveman! Put me down this instant."

"Nope, don't need you running off and getting into any fights now."

Zach wagged his finger at her. "Consider it our punishment for not behaving and setting a wicked bad example for our daughter."

Shira's arms straightened, and her hands balled into tight fists. "I'm not a bad example!"

"Yeah, you keep thinking that."

Shira sighed and resigned herself to her fate—for now.

CHAPTER 16

The BMW slowed on the downward-sloping hill and pulled up to a multi-level stucco-and-stone house with a two-car port garage, clay shingled roofing, and small manicured front lawn. Two large arched doors with a connecting balcony sat above the garage, decorative lights spaced between and next to them. To the right side of the house, past the front door, was another room of sorts with a large bay window.

Jasper stared out, his mouth agape. It'd been some time since they'd been to such a large home. When he and Zach had done some house shopping in the past, they'd looked at a few this size, but found them to be well outside of their budget. He doubted this house was any cheaper. *It's California. It's definitely more expensive.*

"Wow, She-ra, is this really your house?" Serenity asked, her eyes wide and sparkling. "This is so much bigger than our apahtment!"

Shira opened her door. "Yep. My parents and I both own it as a vacation home. One of many."

They had more homes? Jasper glanced around some more, noting the styles of the neighboring homes. *How much money does this family have?* Her family name had been thrown around a few times, like they were a big deal, but Jasper had never gotten around to investigating just how much. Now he was regretting it.

"That's wicked cool." Serenity glanced about another time before fussing with her car seat buckle, refusing Zach's help. Zach tried to reason with her, but she was stubborn. It brought a smile to Jasper's face.

Jasper climbed out of the car and helped Shira with the suitcases, though she was being just as inflexible as Serenity with accepting help. Serenity got her stubbornness from him, however, and his determination had won him two of the three suitcases, and one of the bags of books.

By the time the two came to this "agreement," Zach and Serenity were out of the car, hanging out by the half-wall separating the driveway from the yard. Jasper glanced about for Snake, hoping they hadn't left the dog in the car.

Shira pointed to her side. "He's right here."

He looked down to see the black dog sitting at her feet, patient as always. "How… when…"

She laughed and shut the trunk. "He slipped out with me while Zach and Serenity were trying to compromise."

"I've never come across such a quiet dog."

"Why do you think we named him after my dad's favorite videogame character?" She lifted the extendable handle of serenity's suitcase and walked over to Zach and Serenity, Snake following. "C'mon, let's get inside."

Serenity cheered and ran up the stone step walkway leading up to the front door. Shira's car pulled into the garage, leaving Jasper last to catch up.

The three of them made it to the wooden door long after Serenity. Shira swiped her keycard and pushed the door open, leading them into the foyer.

The walls of the entryway were painted white and had wooden moldings running across the bottoms of all walls. They all stood on high-quality stone flooring. Above them hung a crystal chandelier.

Jasper looked to their left, finding a small wooden-floored gathering room furnished with quality couches and chairs, various paintings and mirrors on the wall, a throw rug, and a well-crafted coffee table. A small chandelier hung from the high ceilings, and long curtains decorated the arched doors behind the couches.

To their right was a dining room, decorated with a fine wooden and glass table and matching wooden and leather chairs. A throw rug covered the wooden floor, and more art hung on the walls. Much like the other room, the bay window worked as the main light source, though a small chandelier also hung from the ceiling.

Zach's eyes fell on the lighting of the house. "You left some lights on."

"No, I think Camila is still here," Shira said.

Jasper's brow rose. "Camila?"

"Our housekeeper." Shira gazed up the curling staircase leading to the second floor. "Camila, are you up there?"

Jasper and Zach glanced at each other. Shira had a housekeeper.

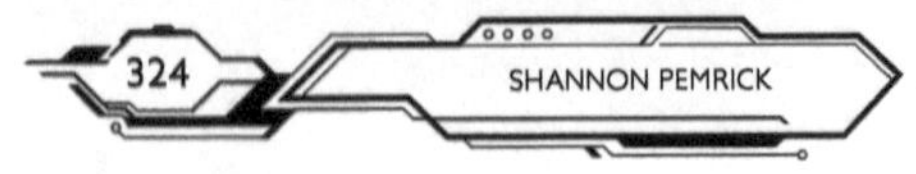

"Yes, Shira, I'll be right down," came a feminine voice.

"Don't rush. Just wanted to let you know I'm back with my guests."

"Their rooms are almost ready. They can bring their things up."

Shira gestured to the staircase. "You heard the lady. You're also welcome to leave your suitcases down here and explore first. I don't mind either way."

She knelt down and removed Snake's service vest. He took off running into the back end of the house. Serenity looked to Shira with wide hopeful eyes and Shira nodded once.

Serenity squealed, kicked off her shoes, and ran after the dog. "Snake, come back! I need to pet you now."

The three of them chuckled. Jasper was proud of her. She'd done well doing exactly what he and Zach had taught her with service dogs. He understood just how hard it was to ignore the temptation to treat Snake like any other pet, especially for someone her age. Shira's giving permission to pet him once or twice while they'd been out hadn't helped that. Serenity deserved this reward.

Shira kicked off her shoes haphazardly, just as Serenity did, without moving them to somewhere he thought was more appropriate, like some sort of shoe rack. Jasper resisted a twitch to mention it or move the shoes for her. It wasn't his home.

His hand clenched when she tossed her keys on a nearby table, instead of hanging them up on the hooks on the walls above it. "Shouldn't you hang your keys up?"

He knew he should have kept his mouth shut, but it bothered him.

Shira waved him off. "I'll take care of it later."

A muscle twitched in his neck. That wasn't the response he'd hoped for.

"Why don't you give us a tour?" Zach suggested. Jasper knew it was a way to distract him, and he appreciated it. This was going to be hard for him to get used to. But if she didn't live the same way as them, they'd have to figure it out, because he didn't want that to be the deal breaker for them. It would be too petty of a reason.

Shira shrugged and gestured to the two rooms. "You've already seen our dining room and living room. We mostly use them for parties."

The two following her to the back. "Stairs lead to the top floor. Those are just bedrooms, an extra bathroom, and the design studio."

"How many bedrooms?" Jasper asked.

"Only four. There were more, but we renovated it down so three of them could be converted to master suites."

Jasper and Zach exchanged glances. Three master bedrooms? Was that really necessary?

Shira continued, gesturing to a door in the hallway wall under the stairs, and then another on the opposite side after the dining room. "Behind door number one are stairs leading down to our entertainment room. It's a good mix of sports memorabilia and nerd shit. It also has a bar and home gym. And door number two is a half-bath."

She led them into the back of the house. "And here we have our family room and kitchen."

Just as Jasper expected, down to the open-concept style. The kitchen was to their right. It had modern appliances, wooden cabinets, granite counter tops with tiled backsplash, a granite-topped island counter, and a modern box chandelier hanging above. A large window opened the room up to the backyard. Tucked in the back of the kitchen was a small hallway. It appeared to lead to the dining room.

"We've got beer and wine stocked in the back of the kitchen, with more counter space and another half-bathroom," Shira said.

No doubt all brews I won't like. He never pegged her to be a beer snob. At least she didn't throw it in his face, only making the comment when he pushed.

"Per your request, Shira, I've ordered a case of Guinness to be delivered tomorrow for Jasper," Orion said from the house infrastructure. "I've also ordered an IPA for Zach based on Alistair's list."

Jasper looked at Shira. "You didn't have to do that."

She shrugged. "Look, just because I don't drink it, doesn't mean I'm not going to be a hospitable host."

He smiled, appreciating the thought, then continued to look around.

The family room looked even cozier than the living room, with plush furniture, a fireplace, and a large TV. A throw rug covered the tile floor. Large nano doors led to the backyard.

Zach wandered over to the door and peer outside. He whistled. "Come take a look."

Curious, Jasper followed, gazing out at the covered patio and backyard. Under the patio ceiling sat elegant furniture. To the left was a fireplace and TV built into a stone wall display, with a built-in BBQ setup jutting out of the patio covering. A ceiling fan spun above the patio table. Stone tiling covered much of the backyard, all the way over to the pool and what looked like built-in spa. The rest of the lawn was well manicured, and dressed with various bushes and trees along the stone walls separating them from the neighbors.

They'd only seen the first floor of her home and Jasper was already overwhelmed. He figured Shira lived in style, but this was even more than he pictured.

"So…" Jasper's eyes darted around. "You don't have to ansah this, but I'm curious. How much is this house worth?"

Shira thought for a moment. "A couple million."

His brain stopped. Zach didn't take the news any better. "A—a couple million?"

She nodded, her eyes neutral. Jasper knew that look. She didn't want to tell the full value because she knew they may not react well to it, but also didn't want to draw any attention to the withheld information. Shira was no stranger to pride and boasting, but she never went overboard and knew when to keep quiet. That's why he and Zach never knew about all this.

Zach licked his lower lip. It sent a jolt through Jasper. "So, say I had a million dollars. What house could I buy here?"

Shira pulled her hands behind her back, looking away and popping up on her toes once. "Um, you couldn't buy one in Manhattan Beach."

Jasper and Zach glanced at each other and then back at her. Jasper spoke first. "What is the cheapest we could get here?"

Shira's lips pressed into a line and her eyes flickered. They were making her nervous. They'd have to be careful if they pressed. "You could get a burned-down house for three and a half million."

Their jaws dropped. "Seriously?"

She nodded, her eyes going to the kitchen when Serenity chased Snake in there. "Happened a few months ago."

If that was the case, her vague assessment of this home was not close to its real value.

"I should go check on Camila."

She turned away, taking several steps before Jasper and Zach both reached out with a hand and claimed each of hers. They glanced at each other, sharing a knowing look. They were both on the same page with this.

"Shira, you don't have to be ashamed you have money," Zach said.

She didn't turn to look at them. Her head remained tipped down as if she were looking at the floor. "I'm not ashamed."

"What is the issue, then?" Jasper asked.

"I know how hard you two work to put food on the table. Sometimes, the money doesn't come in because of bad months at tournaments and you have to pick up odd jobs. And then when you have good months, you ration it because you know the bad times will come back." She took a breath. "I don't have to work that hard. Between my past career and my parents' business, I don't have to do anything more than sit on my butt if I don't want to. The game-to-life currency transactions I make, and occasional work I do for my parents are just so I don't feel useless, not because I need money."

He didn't expect that explanation. Jasper and Zach exchanged a look. Zach reached out and grasped Jasper's free hand. Jasper squeezed and then the two of them rested their foreheads on her shoulders. Shira tensed, but didn't pull away.

"Please don't see it that way," Zach said. "You worked long before we did."

Jasper chuckled. "Wicked long. I was sitting on my ass playing videogames trying to avoid going to school, while you were getting up at the ass-crack of dawn for a shoot or traveling to some event."

He lifted his head and squeezed her hand, an interesting experience since it was her artificial one and didn't have the same give as a natural hand. He didn't care. "You worked wicked hahd for what you have now. Don't hide that just because we made different choices or circumstances beyond anyone's control were at play."

Shira took a moment and then squeezed their hands back. "The house is worth about twenty-eight million."

If he weren't so excited by the fact she'd opened up, he would have needed to sit after that reveal.

Serenity ran through the living room, but the moment her socks hit the tile flooring, she slipped and fell on her face. Shira let go of the men's hands, hers flying up to her mouth as she gasped. Jasper's muscles tensed and Zach took a step forward. Snake skidded to a halt and rushed to the young girl's side, sniffing her.

But Serenity giggled and lifted her head. "Oops."

The three of them let out a sigh. Jasper figured it was a good time to put a stop to any more possible injuries. "Seren, I think it's time to calm down now."

Serenity sighed. "But, Daddy, I'm having fun."

"Maybe, but you shouldn't be running in the house anyway."

His daughter picked herself up off the floor, grumbling.

Jasper's shoulders tightened. "What was that?"

"Nothing."

"Don't give me lip."

She cut her eyes to him. "I'm not."

Shira jumped in before any arguing could transpire. "Starship, if you behave, I'll let Snake sleep in your bed tonight."

Serenity's eyes sparkled. "Really?"

Shira nodded.

A big smile spread across her face. "I'm gonna go upstairs and check out my room now. C'mon, Snake."

She ran for the stairs.

"No running," Zach called.

So she started hopping.

Shira chuckled. "Well, we didn't say she couldn't do that."

Jasper glanced to her. "And we didn't say you could make those kinds of bribes with our daughtah."

He wasn't all that upset over it, just would have preferred she allowed him to handle it.

She held up her hands. "Oh, don't be mad. Telling her she can have Snake sleep in her bed isn't that big of a bribe. My parents used to make small bribes like it with me all the time."

"You were a teenagah."

She shrugged. "And she's almost a pre-teen."

Jasper's eyes narrowed and his muscles tightened. "She's only almost seven."

Shira crossed her arms. "Down, papa-bear. Whether you like it or not, she's getting older. Two years, she'll be a pre-teen."

Zach snickered next to him and Jasper glared. "Don't

encourage her. You should be taking my side. She's your daughtah, too."

He smirked. "I can't help it. You're wicked overprotective with her."

"I am not."

Shira gave a closed-mouth chuckle. "Course not." She turned and took a few steps and then stopped, tossing her head back to them. "Don't worry. I was only teasing you. I understand you feel I overstepped, and I respect that. I won't step on your toes again, and will let you both handle her. You are her fathers, after all." While Jasper appreciated her words, the way she worded it… didn't sit right with him. "But if it's okay, I'm going to spoil Serenity while she's here."

Jasper and Zach exchanged looks. "Just don't go overboard."

A devious grin spread across her face and she walked off. "Overboard it is, then."

Jasper smirked at Zach. She was making this all too easy for them. At this rate, they'd get her where they wanted in no time.

As they watched her walk away, her hips swaying in a hypnotizing rhythm, need pulsed deep in him. That moment couldn't come soon enough.

CHAPTER 17

Shira's car pulled into a parking spot in the garage under Cybro Industries. Her seatbelt flew off and she jumped out, doing her best to not ding the car next to her. Jasper was already out before her and trying to fuss with Serenity's buckle, though she wasn't making it easy on him. Even in her tired state, she wanted to get herself out.

Shira pushed Zach toward the stairs. "Both of you go. I'll get her and meet you there. I can be late; you can't."

They agreed and rushed off, though Jasper had to double back for a moment to grab his forgotten badge. Shira went to working with Serenity, the little girl's eyes barely open as she fussed with her buckle. Snake sat patiently at Shira's side.

"You know, if you hadn't stayed up all night, you wouldn't be this tired," Shira said.

Serenity rubbed her eyes. "But I was wicked excited."

Shira wasn't even sure if Serenity had slept until getting

in the car. The undesirable heavy traffic became a blessing for her, at least. Not so much for Jasper and Zach. Not only did the traffic mess them up this morning, they'd already gotten out of the house late, thanks to them all oversleeping their alarms.

Normally Shira wouldn't have, since she typically rose early, but because she wanted to make sure Jasper and Zach got enough sleep for their first big day in the tournament, she offered to stay up with Serenity, since all attempts to calm her to sleep hadn't worked. Had she known the guys weren't so great at getting up, she would have planned that out better.

"When can I have nom-food?" Serenity asked.

"Once you let me help you get out of this car seat, we'll get some food at the convention. We might even be able to eat with your dads if we hurry."

Serenity reluctantly gave up on her failed attempts to free herself, allowing Shira to get the buckle with ease. With her now out of the car, Shira locked it up and they headed for the stairs. She didn't set a particularly fast pace. Between Jasper and Zach getting a good head start on them, and her and Serenity still having to get through security, Shira doubted Serenity would get the chance to have breakfast with them. *She can just have it with me.* That would give Shira time to figure out what to do with Serenity, activity-wise, when her dads were in matches. She doubted Serenity would be interested in sitting still and watching them for several hours.

Walking to the center helped Serenity wake up a bit, her curious nature wanting to take in the sights again, even though she'd seen it all yesterday. And when they finally arrived at the center, her eyes bugged out seeing the line of people.

"She-ra, are all these people here for the co-vention?"

Shira nodded, gazing at the building and crowd. "That's right. We'll have to stand in line because of a security check. Can you do that?"

Serenity took a deep breath. "Course! I'll be wicked good."

Shira rubbed her head. "That's what I like to hear."

The two of them slipped into one of the lines. Everything seemed to close in around Shira and her mind threatened to run off on her. It nudged at her fears and she took several calming breaths to fight it off. She'd worked hard for this moment. Narissa, Mercedes, Jasper and Zach all helped her to get this far. Shira knew how far she'd come. It'd taken her a lot to allow herself to reach out to the hands that had been offered for so long. They'd been patient and unwavering. It was more than she deserved, but she appreciated it nonetheless.

She could do this.

The line didn't move fast, making each moment feel like an eternity. A few texts back and forth with Jasper and Zach told her they were still in line, too. *It's crazy how many people are trying to get in this early.* Sure, there were some things happening before the opening ceremony, but not enough to rush the doors this early, in Shira's opinion.

True to her word, Serenity did her best to be patient. She got a little antsy near the end, but having her hold onto Snake's vest helped curbed some of it.

Just as they reached the front of the line, Shira received another text, this one from Jasper.

This coffee line is just as stupid long.
Even Narissa and Ajax are in line.

She typed something back quickly before approaching the security guard.

Damn, that is bad. Serenity and I are now just getting to the security point. When we're inside I'll let you know.

The security guard scanned her and Serenity's badges, and once those checked out, he had Serenity go through the scanning machine first. When she was clear and standing next to someone in security on the other side, Shira and Snake were summoned through. Shira didn't remember the last time he'd gone through a security check point. He did well, and did a great job at keeping her calm as the machine scanned them.

I can do this. I can do this. Each breath was a struggle, but Shira gripped every fiber of courage she could muster within her. She even allowed herself to lean on thoughts of Jasper and Zach. She shouldn't, knowing how dangerous it was to lean too hard, but they'd been too instrumental to her healing for her to not rely on them now. She wouldn't be here if it weren't for them. She wouldn't have confronted a single fear that kept her in the same isolating safety pattern. And Shira was glad she finally let them in a little.

Yesterday had been fun, and she wouldn't have experienced any of it had it not been for them. She wanted more days like it. Even if... even if it risked too much, it was hard to not keep wanting more than she should probably take.

The security guard cleared her to leave the machine and rejoin Serenity, who smiled wide. "See, I behaved!"

Shira bent down and kissed her on the forehead. "Yes, you did. Now, here's your badge. You're to keep it on you at all times. Put it on and we can go find your dads."

"Nom time!" Serenity cheered, throwing her badge around her neck.

Shira checked her phone, spotting the text Jasper had sent after she'd put it away.

Great. I'll order for you two.

We're through. Let me know where you're at so we can meet you. Serenity is chomping at the bit for nom-food.

Ha! Course she is. She's ravenous when she fully wakes up. Just stand by the event map kiosk on the first floor. We'll come to you.

That wasn't a horrible plan. Beat having to stand in another line. "Okay, Starship, we're going to stand somewhere so your dads can find us after they get the food."

"Okay." The little girl looked around. "Where we going?"

Shira led her to the map. Curious, Serenity gazed up at it, trying to make sense of where things were. Shira used this time to look up what was going on today to make a plan. There'd be a lot to entertain her, and even

Jasper and Zach when their matches were done, but she also had to think of Serenity too. *I should have planned before coming here.* There were several days of this event, and while spontaneity was fun, it was smart to have a basic plan to lean on.

Her musing was cut short when someone spoke. "Shira?"

Her body went rigid. She knew that voice… *It can't be him…*

She turned to see a man around her age with a god-awful spray-on tan, blue eyes, and short bleached hair approaching her. Shira's breath came short, her eyes tightening. Of all the people her past could have thrown at her, why torment her with him? "Jeremy?"

Shannon Pemrick is a full-time USA Today best-selling author of slow-burn romantic fantasy, fuller-time geek, and dragon obsessed. She also has too many novelty mugs, not enough chocolate, and a forbidden love-affair with all things shiny. When she's not burning her fingers across a keyboard handing out adventures and HEAs, she's rolling dice and getting lost in RPGs or searching for brides for her dragon overlords.

You can learn more about Shannon by visiting her website at:
Shannonpemrick.com